UNBROKEN

UNBROKEN

Danielle Leneah

Donnelly Bootcamp Series

Book Four

Boettcher-Tuufuli Publishing LLC

Editing by: Krystlynne Muscutt

Copyedited by: Rebekkah Wilde

ISBN: 978-1-7325461-7-2

Printed in the United States of America

First Edition: July 2020

10 9 8 7 6 5 4 3 2 1

Dedication

To those who pushed me to continue writing this series, and to publish it, this book is for you.

Acknowledgments

Wow, it is amazing that this adventure that started five years ago has ended up here. For something that started out just keeping me busy while on vacation, it has turned into something really special. It started a new chapter in my life and has been the constant that kept me sane through all my trails over the last few years.

There have been several people that have helped me along the way and deserve a little recognition. At the top of my list is my editor Krystlynne. I'm not even sure how to express how much you have meant to me. You have stuck by my side for the last five years when I wasn't even sure I could write one full novel. You have pushed me and helped make this series what it is. It's so hard to believe this is the end of the series. It isn't enough, but thank you from the bottom of my heart to the top, for everything you have done for me. You are AMAZING!!!

I also want to thank Rebekkah for taking on the tedious job of copyediting. I always appreciate your words of wisdom along the way, and while my story writing abilities might be good (or so I think), my grammar isn't always on point, so thank you.

Then there is my family. Kids, I know momma works and then "works again" late into the night, but I promise you I love you more than anything. Thanks you guys for putting up with your "crazy momma" and always understanding why I'm always so busy. You guys are my life and I live for you. To my sister Mandy, who has been there for me so much over the years and help me out with the kids when I overwhelm myself with work. I couldn't have survived all this without you, I love you. To my Mom and Dad, I couldn't have asked for two better parents. You guys are the best and have always been there to support me any way you can – I love you guys! And I can't forget Kelly. Girl you are a knight in shining armor. It is funny how cousins can grow apart, and then come back together in such a crazy way. Thank you for always helping me out when you have absolutely no obligation to do so. I love you and appreciate everything.

Last but certainly not least is my fans. From my family and friends to the people I've never met, it has been nothing but support. I've always said, all it would take for me to feel this was all worth it was one happy reader. Well I got that and more. Being a newer author is always hard and I'm so grateful that I found you. You guy's are amazing!

UNBROKEN

PROLOGUE

SOMETIMES HAPPINESS JUST isn't written in the stars for everyone. While a blessed few get nothing but an overabundance of it, others skate through life with periods of good and periods of bad. The unlucky ones only get a glimpse of happiness before it is tragically ripped away. It creates a small speck of hope, only to be torn from the very soul that prayed for it so desperately – like a sick joke.

I'm now convinced that my life is only destined for the latter of the three. After being sent to a bootcamp and finding the love of my life, we battled for each other, losing our way here and there, but ultimately fought our way back. Dealing with the horrors of my past, getting through the pains of his, there were just so many obstacles to overcome. It seemed never ending, one roadblock after another, and just when we finally thought we were going to be able to get past it all and live a life of happiness, it all came crashing down like a ton of bricks.

There is only so much a person can endure, only so much you can expect someone else to endure because of you, and when it seems as if the devil himself is out to break not only your heart but your soul into pieces, it's all too easy to give in – to stop fighting, to stop trying to reach that better place and let the darkness take you. If living like this brings so much pain, why not give in and give up? In a life filled with so much pain, getting by is not always the same as living.

CHAPTER ONE

(Friday, December 25th)

WALKING THE DESERTED downtown street, there isn't a soul in sight. Something doesn't seem right, though I can't quite put my finger on what. The sun is shining brightly and as I stand at one end of Main Street, I can see the other end of town off in the distance. A mix of one and two-story buildings, mostly brick, line both sides of the street of this one-stoplight town like it's straight out of an old movie. This town is so small, it's impossible to fathom how people actually enjoy living here. However, at the moment the point seems moot since there isn't a person in sight.

My feet begin moving aimlessly toward the other end of town, not sure of where and why I'm going. Inside the shops, the lights are on and the signs hanging on the doors show 'open' but again, there's no one. An eerie tingle slides down my back, making me shiver despite the heat of the shining sun.

Making it another block down the road, I decide to go into the pharmacy that's on the corner. There are always people in there and right now the lack of connection with anyone is starting to creep me out. I push open the door, but I'm only met by silence as it's as abandoned inside as it is outside. The low aisles allow me to see everything. The space is open all the way to the back where the pharmacist is usually standing talking to customers – but there's nothing, completely abandoned.

"Hello?"

The echo bounces around the room for a fraction of a second and then there is silence once again. I'm officially confused and freaked out as I turn myself in slow circles, trying to hash this current situation out in my head. Granted, this town is small, but I've never seen it like this. If something was going on, then why would all the stores look as if they're open still – nothing out of place? It's almost as if everyone has disappeared into thin air.

A flash of light from somewhere outside catches my eye. I quickly head back outside, looking for the source of the only movement I've seen in what feels like forever. As I turn around taking in everything, another shiver runs through me as my eyes notice the sky has become dark with a thick cover of cloud. Before I can question the sudden change, a figure off in the distance draws my attention.

"Finally!" Walking as fast as seems appropriate to not make me look like a lunatic, I make my way toward the person. As I get closer, a smile spreads across my face as recognition hits me.

Instantly relief fills my body from head to toe.

"Jeff!" I shout at his faraway form.

His head snaps up and his eyes don't quite meet mine as he looks right past me – no happiness or interest in his eyes, just pure anger. His face contorts into a smug look and instead of walking to meet me, he turns and heads toward the side-street he is facing.

"Jeff?" I shout again, but this time he doesn't acknowledge me.

Panic rises in me and I can't help but begin to run toward him. It no longer matters to me if I look crazy, I don't want to be alone and bad vibes are screaming throughout my entire body. "Jeff!" I yell as he disappears behind the building. My run turns into an all-out sprint as I chase after him.

No matter how hard I push my legs, it feels like it is taking me much longer than it should to reach the edge of the building and the longer it takes, the more the panic rises. After what seems like a lifetime, I finally make it around the corner and come to a sliding stop. In the middle of the road about two blocks down, Jeff stands facing away from me. His hand is resting on a much larger man's slouched shoulder.

What the hell is going on?

"Jeff?" my voice carries once more as I cautiously stand waiting for him to acknowledge me.

He doesn't respond, he merely stands there talking to the other familiar man. It doesn't take long to realize that the man he's talking to is Aerick. There's no way to mistake his almost overbearing and perfectly shaped outline. Only there's something wrong, his posture is small and weak instead of tall and confident.

"Aerick?" I almost whine, craving some sort of acknowledgment.

Aerick falls to his knees and hunches forward, burying his face in his hands as his body begins to shake violently. Jeff follows him, kneeling at his side and moving to place both his hands on Aerick's shoulders. My chest is suddenly heavy with sadness and fear. *What would possibly hurt Aerick so bad that he would act this way?* I've never seen him like this, and what's even stranger is the fact that Jeff is the one consoling him.

An overwhelming need to comfort Aerick moves my feet forward in a rush, but as I begin shuffling toward him, everything else around me seems to stand still. Pushing myself faster, I try to reach them, but it becomes clear the faster I go, the further away they're getting, even though they are stationary, kneeling in the middle of the road.

"Aerick, Jeff, please!" My begging cries call out so loudly that they echo off the empty buildings, but it does no good, they just get further and further away. *What is going on? What is happening?* A cold chill runs over my body as they fade into the distance.

"Please, please don't leave me alone!" I say in defeat as my legs slow down and my lungs gasp for breaths that no longer fill them completely.

"Please..." My whisper fills the cold, empty air around me. I'm alone again. Coming to a stop, my legs give out and I fall to my knees – I'm at a loss. This isn't fair. *Why is it that I always end up alone in the end?*

The air turns ice cold as I sit there mad, sad and confused. Then I feel it. A dark creepy feeling crawls up my back as I sense a presence behind me. Not the comforting, happy presence of those I love and care about, that I was praying for.

My body becomes rigid as the ground stirs directly behind me. "Hello again," the deep rancid voice breathes behind me. "You will never get your happily ever after!"

CHAPTER TWO

(Friday, December 25th)

SHOOTING UP IN bed, I try to hide my heaving chest from Terrie, who's making her bed.

"Merry Christmas!"

Geez, pipe down with the cheerfulness, I'm not in the mood after that dream! I drag myself out of bed and start to get on my workout clothes. I'm clueless as to why I subject myself to this cruel and unusual punishment now that I'm not even a cadet here.

"Hurry up or we'll be late. There's nothing worse than getting your man's glare for showing up to P.T. late."

Giving her a glare of my own, I show my own protest to her words, but she's right. It's funny how he can make you feel so much like an errant, disobedient child with only a look. At least it isn't only me that feels that way.

"You know, I wish you two would go back to your happy-go-lucky attitudes. He was so much more tolerable then." She gives me a pointed look.

"What? I've tried but he's still acting weird around me."

It's true. Saturday night everything seemed to be mostly back to normal, but I've come to believe that was strictly because of the alcohol. The next morning, it was as if Saturday night never happened and he went right back to the way he had been acting. Things have lightened up a little since then but not much. Other than the hugs he gives me before we part ways at night, he's very reserved when touching me. I know there are still questions in his head and I'm pretty sure he's still harboring some blame for what happened.

While I appreciate his respect in trying to ease back into our physical contact, I'm really tired of him blaming himself for not saving me from Liz and Sean. I was kidnapped, bad things happened and no matter what he did, there's no way he could have saved me. The blame falls on me, not him. After everything that happened with Liz, I should have been more alert. My dumbass should have known better than to go off so close to dark by myself. Everything that happened was from my stupidity, not the inability to protect me on his part.

I quickly braid my hair to the side, then throw on my coat, beanie, and gloves while Terrie waits for me not-so-patiently by the door. We head out into the freezing cold toward the stage. It's been snowing almost non-stop since Monday. The nearby freeway has been closing on and off over the last few days for avalanche control down at Snoqualmie Pass.

I wonder if we'll even have P.T or if it will be a repeat of the last few days. After so many days of repetitive work, I don't know which is worse. At least the snow has stopped for the moment and the morning is still and quiet. Terrie and I stomp through the new snow that has fallen over night, making our way over to the stage. The sky is still dark; but, with all the lights reflecting on the snow, it's as bright as the evening at sunset right after the sun disappears over the horizon. Everyone has already formed into lines on the path in front of the stage because the snow is too high everywhere else. As expected, Aerick gives us a look of disappointment for our tardiness as we join the other staff members in the back of the group.

Although Luther has not ordered it, the entire staff, including himself, have been out here every morning this week to help out. Things around here seem to work like that, it's just implied we're expected to pull our own weight and help out with everything. Gavin has also caught on to the unsaid atmosphere of the camp and has joined us.

Aerick's attention quickly moves away from our late entrance and back to the group. "As I was saying, we will be shoveling snow for P.T. again today. We will stay in our same groups. My group will take the west side, Brand's group will take the east, Trent's will take the south side and Paulo's will take the north. I expect all walkways and entrances to the buildings to be clear in time for breakfast. Shovels are in front of me so let's get to work.

You're dismissed."

Well so much for a 'Merry Christmas'. We all move to grab the snow shovels from the stage and break into our groups. Aerick split up all the staff on Monday when we first started shoveling snow for P.T. Naturally, he put me with himself, but you wouldn't notice there was anything between us by the way he keeps me at a distance most of the time.

I make my way to our assigned area for today, trailing at the back of Aerick's group with Tia and Andi. They'll only be staying to help out for a short time before they go to the mess hall to prepare breakfast. Tia has been told not to work too hard, but she insists on helping, just like everyone else. In so many ways, I see myself in her. She's so strong, loyal, and sometimes even defiant. I suppose several of us girls here at camp fall under that same category.

I was initially upset at Andi when I overheard her talking about me the other day, but I don't hold it against her. She's similar to the rest of us. We all say things and I'm sure she was just reacting to the situation. Her animosity wasn't really against me, it was merely about me getting all the attention. She enjoys the attention and, quite frankly, I don't mind if she has it. I figure holding it against her won't do anyone any good.

As we get to work, Skyler starts mumbling out his complaints about having to do work. Listening to this all week has really begun to get on my nerves. I've been trying to keep my mouth shut to let Aerick deal with it but currently he's not within earshot and I've had about enough.

"This is slave labor at its best," he mumbles once more.

I stand up and glare at him. "Are you serious? Really? Slave labor?" I throw my hands around me to all the other people working. "Everyone here is pitching in and doing their part. Even the pregnant one is doing it, and without complaint, I might add. So why don't you keep your whining to yourself, because I'm tired of hearing it already."

"Whatever, you're just out here to ogle the eye candy."

He can't be serious. While he may be slightly attractive, his rude, disrespectful attitude completely overshadows anything else he may have. "What? You think I'm out here just to look at you? Please, don't make me vomit."

He lets out a chuckle. "Not me, Aerick! We all see how you look at him with those googly eyes."

Aerick stands up straight, his attention now on us as he has probably picked up on our conversation. "You know what? I suggest you get back to work and shut your mouth before it gets you into even more trouble," I say, trying to end this before Aerick gets involved. Skyler takes a step toward me and Aerick follows with several steps of his own so he's only a few feet behind Skyler. I slyly raise my hand a little to signal him to let me handle it, but seeing his balled-up fist at his side, I know he won't be patient for long.

Skyler's face is plastered with anger but he's not stupid enough do anything. I saw past that facade of his a while back.

He's a whole lot of talk and not much bite. He looks like he wants so bad to say something, but he merely stands there.

"Cadet, we both know it's in your best interest to walk away now, and that is exactly what I suggest you do. Get back to work and pull your weight just like everyone else." He thinks about it for a moment and then turns around to continue working. When he does, he almost runs right into Aerick's chest.

Aerick's lips turn up slightly. "That is the first intelligent thing I have seen you do since you got here." Skyler huffs and walks around him. Aerick gives me a slight grin of approval and then turns to go back to his shoveling. The small recognition lifts my spirits considerably.

Everyone keeps their heads down for the rest of the time and by a little after six we're done. It's now possible to walk around the path and into any of the buildings without fighting with the snow. I can only hope it stays that way, because shoveling snow every day is getting old quick. It isn't so much the work as it is the way I feel afterward. I'm sweaty, sticky and in desperate need of a shower. At least when I work out in the gym or run in the summer, I have very little clothing to have to worry about. Aerick calls everyone back to the stage before dismissing us all early.

The hard work has made me hungry and my stomach makes this known with a loud growl. I can smell the food already and I can't wait to get some. Tia and Andi left about fifteen minutes after we started shoveling, but I'm sure once we start eating, everyone will be grateful. The thought of food pushes my legs quicker toward my cabin, but I come to a sudden stop as Aerick steps in front of me.

"Hey, you got a sec?" he asks quietly.

I look around us and most of the cadets have already gone back inside while everyone else is close to being back to their cabins. "Sure."

"You handled that thing with Skyler very well. He was getting on my last nerve, and these days, I don't have many left."

A shy smile plays across my lips. It isn't in his nature to compliment people or to explain his feelings and you can always tell by his uneasiness. "Thanks. I, um, really want to take a quick shower before breakfast."

"Sure. I just wanted to say Merry Christmas and give you this." He pulls a small box out of his pocket and gives it to me.

"Aerick, you didn't have to get me anything. I mean, I don't have anything for you."

He lets out a huff that almost comes out as a laugh. "I have you, don't need anything else. Go take your shower and open it. I'll see you at breakfast." He gives me his signature smile and a wink before he turns and heads for the instructor's cabin. My heart flutters. I'll never get tired of seeing that, even when I can see the unease and tension behind it.

I head back to my cabin with a grin on my face. I don't appreciate that he spent money on me again but it's Christmas and it was extremely sweet of him. It sucks, though, because I can't return the gesture. Lord knows when he had time to go get anything. He hasn't left lately that I'm aware of and to my knowledge no one else has either because of this ridiculous snow we're having this week.

Terrie is in the shower as I enter the cabin, so I sit on my bed and begin undressing. When I'm down to my underclothes, I have nothing else to do but wait for Terrie to finish. I turn and pick up the black box that Aerick gave me. Untying the red ribbon, I open the box to find another box inside and a small note, 'A princess for my princess'. He can be so sweet. More curious, I open the velvet blue and silver box and my heart stops.

I have never seen anything so extraordinary in my life. It's a heart shaped-necklace with blue stones clustered together to make a beautiful heart, while a ribbon of white diamonds tie around it, splitting it into three parts. Elegant writing describes it in the lid, 'Princess Cut Blue Diamond. Past, Present, Future Heart Pendant'.

WOW! I am speechless.

"What are you staring at?" Terrie asks, coming out of the bathroom, but I still can't say anything. She comes to sit next to me and grabs my hand holding the box to steady it. I didn't even realize I was shaking as I tried not to burst into happy tears.

"Whoa, that is crazy beautiful! Is that what Aerick got you for Christmas?" I nod slowly. This one piece of jewelry has put so much hope into my own heart. He's still thinking of a future – a future with me.

"Well, at least he has some taste. Maybe he should give Paulo some pointers." A burst of laughter escapes me.

"What did you get?" I ask her.

"I don't know yet, he said he would give it to me tonight. Knowing him, it isn't a necklace. With him it is more likely to be sexual in nature." *Oh my gosh!*

"T.M.I. Terrie! I really don't need to know what you and Paulo do behind closed doors." She laughs and I quickly put the box in my drawer with the other necklace Aerick gave me.

"I'm going to take a shower and try not to imagine what the hell you're talking about."

"Come on, Nadi, don't act like you don't know. We all know Aerick is a freak in bed. It's no secret." My almost happy tears turn into a happy smile, because yes, it's true. I'll never forget the first time he tied my hands together or any of our many impromptu meetings while I was a cadet. Not that I would tell her any of it, other than maybe some loose details. I roll my eyes at her, hoping she will drop it.

"Terrie, enough. I'm not talking about my crazy sex life with you." She laughs as I realize what I've just said.

"So, it's true! You said it yourself, or at least you didn't deny it, which means it must be true."

I feel my face turning as red as a tomato. "I did not say that. You tricked me. You're so horrible!" I say, all flustered, and grab my clothes to go take a shower as I try to hide the grin on my face.

✳ ✳ ✳ ✳

"What are you so smiley about?" Jeff asks as I sit down at the table next to him.

"Nothing," I say, trying not to let my embarrassment show. "Terrie and I were just talking about something." Terrie hasn't let up trying to find out the secrets of Aerick's and my relationship. Naturally I avoided most of it, but my blushing was more than enough of an answer to some of her questions. She definitely isn't all innocent like she plays out to be.

"Care to elaborate?" He looks at me expectantly.

"Definitely not!" I push the heat away from my cheeks. I don't need him to start this either.

"Definitely not what?" Aerick asks, sitting down next to me.

"Oh, she was just telling me that her and Terrie were having an interesting conversation that had her smiling like a fool."

"Really! Well, am I privy to that conversation?" He looks at me with that damn trademark smirk, so I squeeze his leg under the table.

"Maybe later." I give him a quick wink to hopefully placate his curiosity for now.

"What? Why does he get to know?" Jeff whines at me and his curiosity gets on my nerves.

"Because the conversation was about him – now drop it!"

He stares at me for a moment before it finally clicks in his head. "Oh, oh! Yeah, on second thought, maybe I don't want to know. Never mind."

"Well I do, and I can't wait to hear it," Aerick says in my ear as he runs his fingers up the inside of my thigh. I have to use all my strength to sit still. I grab his hand to stop him from moving it any further up because I'm two seconds from exploding.

"Keep that up and I won't be telling you, I'll be showing you," I whisper to him.

With a curious smirk he goes back to eating his breakfast and I'm glad he seems to be in a much better mood today. "So, what's on the agenda for tonight?" I ask quietly.

"Everyone is getting together for a little poker, but we don't have to go if you don't want to."

I look up at him. "Why wouldn't I want to?"

He looks a little confused. "I wasn't sure you were up to drinking and poker. We can go if you want to."

Maybe I sounded a little more defensive than I thought. "I'm fine, Aerick. We can go. I think it will be good for us to go and relax with everyone."

He eyes me suspiciously. "Okay," he says simply, before shrugging his shoulders and passing off whatever thoughts were just going through his head.

I want so badly to ask him what he's thinking but I know it will get me nowhere. "So where are we having this get-together?"

"We figured we would have it in the instructors' dorm so everyone can play and be around each other, since it's Christmas. Luther already okayed Shannon to spend the evening here."

I haven't been around a large group of people in a while. It'll be nice to sit and chill out with everyone. "Is everyone coming?" I ask, curious about Luther and Ayla. They don't usually join us, but it would be a shame for them to spend it alone. It also hasn't slipped my attention that I have not seen them at breakfast.

"Actually, Luther and Ayla are leaving in a little while to spend the day with their families. They will not be back until tomorrow and I'm in charge while they are away." I hear a bit of pride in his voice as he says the last part. He really does enjoy having power, but not in a bad way. "I'm not sure about Gavin. As far as I know, he's sticking around camp. I doubt he has anyone around here." The smugness in his voice is really disheartening.

"Well, did anyone tell him we were getting together?" Aerick merely shrugs his shoulders, completely not caring. I purse my lips, a little irritated at him, and turn to Jeff.

"Did you tell Gavin about tonight?" I ask Jeff, not caring to hide my frustration at Aerick.

"Uh, no, not yet. I'll make sure to mention it to him."

Aerick gives Jeff and me both an irritated look. "Good, I wouldn't want anyone to feel left out, it's Christmas after all." Aerick turns his head away from me, no doubt he's rolling his eyes at me. He isn't a big fan of Gavin, but he doesn't need to be a jerk about him hanging around. Other than the few times he has made me a little upset, he does seem to be a caring person, and it's only right we show the same back to him.

"Hey, Nadi?" I turn around at Andi's voice. "Can you help me with dinner this evening?"

"Uh, sure. No problem." It'll be a nice break from the evening classes. Besides, generally I like to cook, so I don't mind helping out with meals.

"Great," she says, before walking back to the other table to sit with Brand and Tia.

Tia is probably getting tired of being on her feet. It's the only thing I can think of to explain why she asked me instead of Tia. Tia has begun to show a lot and her little round belly is so adorable. So far, she has only gained weight in her stomach, so it looks like she has a little ball under her shirt, which is awesome. Whenever I decide to have kids, I can only hope to look as good as her.

✳ ✳ ✳ ✳

"Andi, do you really think we needed this much food?" I'm trying to balance five different trays on top of each other as we walk over the slippery snow to the instructor's dorm. Terrie's beside me with just as many trays, and Andi has four more.

"Yes, now stop whining!"

"I'm not whining," I say, looking at her pointedly. Granted, a few of the trays are for the cadets, but the majority of them are for us. I'm not sure how she managed to talk me into helping her set up after we spent most of the afternoon and evening helping put them together. This is what I get for being so nice.

"Besides, they aren't all for us. Some of them are for the cadets."

"Andi, four of them are for the cadets, fifteen of them are for us. That's almost one per person."

"So, I bet you the guys finish almost all of them." Then again, she may be right. These guys eat a ridiculous amount of food. I imagine it's because they all work out a few hours a day. Although today, Aerick informed everyone at dinner that we would not have evening P.T. tonight since it's Christmas. The cadets were really excited to hear that but of course he had to follow it up by telling them they were confined to the dorms after seven tonight, which they weren't too happy with. Just one more thing for them to complain about. In my mind, they got the best part of that deal.

We get into the dorms and I nod at Jeff and Jake, who are setting out chairs. I begin to lay out the platters while Andi takes several over to the cadet dorms. I continue to spread out the trays on the table and rearrange the few that Andi just threw down before scurrying out of the room.

"OCD getting to you, hun?" Terrie says as she walks in behind me, carrying a few bags.

"Shut up!" I say as I continue fixing the trays.

She is followed by Trent and Paulo, who are also carrying bags, mostly filled with alcohol. Looks as if they plan on really having fun tonight. I hope they realize it's Friday, not Saturday, and that we still have classes to teach tomorrow.

"Hey, hey! It's almost party time," Paulo says as he starts unloading the alcohol on to the table.

"Did you get enough?"

"Yep," he says, smiling at me. "Well, for me, anyway." He

shoves my arm softly and I let out a laugh despite the quick sudden spike of my heartbeat. Sometimes I wonder how these guys have a job with the way they act. It's almost like I'm around a bunch of teenagers sometimes. Well, technically a few of us still are, but that's beside the point.

"Are we ready, or what?" I turn around to the sound of the voice that can set my heart on fire. His eyes meet mine and the corners of his lips turn up before setting the poker chips down on the table.

"Of course we are. Everything is done and perfect as always!" Andi pipes up as she re-enters the room.

"Jeff. Did you check on the cadets? Are they all in the dorms?" *Man, can he ever lighten up?*

"Yes, Aerick. They've been locked in for the last twenty minutes. I already gave them the ground rules and did a head count five minutes ago. We're good to start having a good time."

Aerick picks up his tablet off his desk and starts tapping on it. When he seems satisfied, he sets it down and nods toward us.

"Alright, the warden has given his okay. Now, let's play some damn poker." Everyone laughs and snickers at Paulo's outburst. Everyone except Jeff who merely rolls his eyes before turning around so Aerick can't see the scowl on his face. I swear these two never quit.

"Actually, before we sit down, I wanted to tell everyone something," Tia says as she steps in the middle of the room with Brand right behind her. We all turn and give her our attention.

"We just wanted to tell everyone that we had an ultrasound today." She pauses and turns back to look at Brand. The cheesiest grin spreads across his face as he looks into her eyes.

"Stop ogling your man and say it already!" Andi shouts and Tia looks down shyly as her face turns red.

With a shake of her head, she regains herself. "We wanted you guys to be the first to know... we're having a boy!"

The room erupts into cheers from almost everyone. The guys make their way over to congratulate Brand while us girls gravitate toward Tia. I give Tia a big hug when it's my turn and congratulate her. As I move to the side to give the next person a turn, I catch a glimpse of Aerick, who's looking at me with such an odd expression from the edge of our little crowd. *I really wish I knew what was going through his mind.* I make my way over to him with the intention of finding out, although I know from experience it probably won't happen; but you can't blame a girl for trying.

"Hey, you okay?" I look up in his eyes as I grab his hand.

"Yeah, why?"

"The way you were looking at me. What's going through your head right now?"

His lip turns up a little and he bites lightly on his lip which is a look he typically reserves for when we are alone. "It's just nice to see a real smile on your face."

"I smile."

"You smile, but it's been a while since it has reached those unforgettable eyes of yours." He runs his thumb down the side of my cheek before he gives me a sweet quick kiss on the temple. My body fills with warmth at his perfect words.

"Come on, let's go play poker so I can win these dumbass's money," he says with a quick chuckle, as he grabs my hand and leads me over to the table.

CHAPTER THREE

(Thursday, December 31th)

"IF YOU DON'T knock off this damn mood, I'm going to stop hanging out with you," Andi whines at me

"No one is stopping you. You can always go hang out with Lauren."

"Ugh, no thanks. Her and Brayden's constant flirting is making me sick. I mean, they aren't even together anymore and Lauren's leaving to go to Chicago soon. What are they thinking?"

"Why don't you go hang out with Jake?"

"I was, but then he started explaining the advantages of the tracker upgrades we're getting to Gavin and it totally bored the crap out of me. That's why I came over here."

Lucky me. It isn't as if I want to be completely alone, but the point of sitting on Aerick's bed was because I didn't think anyone else would be brave enough to sit on his bed with me. In fact, he's giving Andi his best death stare right now.

I try not to laugh. He's so predictable sometimes. Other times, not so much. Even more so lately. Every time I think things are getting better, he proves me wrong. It's been several weeks and yet he still barely touches me, but then acts so concerned about anything I do.

"Another Royal Fuck for the pretty ladies." Jeff hands each of us another of Aerick and Paulo's special drink. This is the third one and Aerick glances at me with disapproval but doesn't say anything, he merely turns his attention back to the game. This is the same thing he did on Christmas, although I was trying to be good that night, making it a point not to get too drunk, but after nothing happened that night and another week of him being hot, then cold, then hot again, I don't care anymore.

Everything I've tried to get us back to normal has failed. I've tried being sweet, caring, bitchy, demanding: nothing works. Sometimes he'll smile or look at me with those beautiful eyes as if I'm the most important thing in the world, but then he keeps me at arm's length.

I swear I'm so ready to give up. *Why am I still even trying?* He has obviously lost interest with me physically. I mean, it's not like I can blame him. I'm damaged goods now. He's probably disgusted with the thought of being with me intimately.

At first, the space he gave me to get used to physical contact again was nice, but then a craving for his touch began to build in me and each time I made an advance toward him he failed to reciprocate. He gives me these sad eyes or hesitates and gets lost in thought. Just like a few minutes ago when I lost the last of my chips playing poker. Everyone was happy and joking and I moved to sit on his lap, which is what I would normally do 'before', but this time he was so stiff. He didn't run his hands up and down my waist or thighs, no absent-minded kisses on my neck as he played his hand. He merely sat there like a stone as if he was uncomfortable with me sitting on his lap, which is exactly why I gave up and decided to come sit in the corner of the room by myself.

"Hello? Are you even listening to me?" Andi says as she snaps her fingers in front of me. I look up. *Shit, what was she saying?*

Several people's eyes are now on us, including Aerick's; he raises an eyebrow at me. *Ugh, I'm tired of this shit.* "Sorry Andi, I'm just not in the mood," I tell her quietly as I stand up.

Throwing back the drink still in my hand, I quickly guzzle it down. The glass comes down a little harder on Aerick's desk than I meant to, and I turn to see that everyone is staring at me. Jeff is standing next to Gavin, both looking concerned, and Aerick's eyes are scrunched together as if he's upset, but who cares. *Not me!* I need to get out of here.

As I walk toward the door, Aerick reaches out to grab my hand, but I adjust, moving further to the side out of his reach. "I need some fresh air," I explain as I grab a beer and walk toward the door. I see the battle going on in Aerick's mind, whether or not to follow me, but my guess is he won't. It's better that way. I just want to be alone because I'm feeling fucking emotional right now and I hate it. *Damn alcohol.*

Making it out the door, there is a bunch of murmuring as the door closes, but I have no desire to hear what they say even though it's clearly about me. I head for my spot behind the cabins, it seems as good as any. It's almost midnight – I'm actually surprised Aerick let me come outside by myself so late. So close to another year making its way into my life.

Another year. I made it through 2015. So much has happened this year. It's scary to think that this time last year I was contemplating whether or not I even wanted to see another year.

Flashback

Another year has gone by and it was no better than the year before. I'm alone in the apartment, so I make my way out onto the fire escape and sit with my legs hanging off. Mom and Dad went off to spend New Year's at the house of a friend who always hosts a poker party. All my sisters are off doing their own thing and my brother left a little while ago to go hang out with his friends. As per the norm, he asked me if I wanted to go and I declined. I just want to be alone tonight.

Alone. When am I not alone anymore?

Even when I am around people, I have to keep my distance. I'm there but I'm not. I really don't have anyone to talk to and even if I did, I probably wouldn't anyway. I just wish it was possible to get close to someone. To be able to feel someone's touch without completely freaking out.

I finally tried this year. Tried to be with someone; but even with someone as timid as Alan, I still couldn't do it. No matter how hard I tried. He liked me a lot, but I had to end it. He was falling for me and it became increasingly clear I couldn't ever be with him.

I'm pathetic. Seventeen years old and I can't even stand to be touched by a guy. What the hell is the point anymore?

Standing, I climb the fire escape up to the roof. At the top, near the corner of the building, I step up onto the ledge looking over our neighborhood. It's a little cold tonight but people are out everywhere. There are sounds of music coming from all around me from those having their New Year's Eve parties. Having fun with their friends and loved ones, making new resolutions for the year, ready to ring in another one that they're looking forward to.

A night everyone enjoys, but me. Standing here alone is fitting because it represents everything inside me. I hear someone laugh loudly. Looking down, the source of the noise comes into view as a young couple passes below me on the sidewalk. I've never been afraid of heights and standing here on the ledge, I feel as comfortable as I would standing in the middle of a room.

The last few weeks I've been up here a lot. Late at night after everyone is asleep, when I can't sleep and need to clear my head. Most nights it's quieter than tonight, although this place is never truly quiet. There's always something going on around here, whether it's the drug dealers hanging around the streets late at night, or the call girls looking to find their next hookup. I could stand here for hours watching the world pass me by and no one would even notice me.

I suppose this is all I'll ever be. A loner, watching everyone else live the life I can only dream of. The only thing I have going for me is my mind. I'll admit I'm smarter than most, but that's all. I could probably go to college, get a degree, get a well-paying job, and live out the rest of my life by myself with only a dog as a companion.

Is that life really worth living for?

All it would take is one step. One step and I could end it all. End all of my longing, my suffering, my pathetic little life. If a life is what you could call it. Being completely honest with myself, I died a long time ago. At least back then, I had Jeff and Patrick. Now I don't even have that. I pulled away from the only two that could ever understand – if only a little.

Pathetic.

"You okay?" I jump slightly at my brother's voice as he finishes climbing up from the fire escape.

"Yeah, I'm fine. Just needed some air."

"You've been coming up here a lot lately." He sticks his hands in his pockets and kicks at the roof. He's obviously worried about me. *At least that's one person.*

"It's easier to think up here. Being away from everyone. It's peaceful."

"Peaceful?" He raises an eyebrow. "That's a joke, right? We're in Chicago."

My chest huffs out a sarcastic laugh. "You know what I mean." He nods as he comes to stand next to me. "What are you doing here, anyway? I thought you were going to Brian's party." As much as I love him, I really wish he wasn't here right now.

"I am – forgot my backpack. Biggest night of the year, can't miss out on that kind of opportunity." He looks at me. "You should come. Our cousins will be there, you know all my friends. Come on, it'll be fun."

My eyes fall to the street below me, weighing my options. Being around people is never my ideal scene, but maybe a few beers, and even a few shots, will be enough to numb away everything I'm feeling right now. The feeling that I've about had enough of this life.

Ah shit! I'm suddenly flung backward as my brother pulls me away from the edge. Thankfully he lets go as soon as I stumble back a few feet. "Come on, you're coming with me. No arguments. That look in your eyes is giving me some seriously bad vibes and I'm not leaving you alone." I begin to shake my head, but he doesn't give up.

"Either you come with me or I'm staying home. Now, are you going to be the reason I lose out on all this money tonight?"

Fuck. Why does he have to do this to me?

It's obviously because he cares, and he knows I wouldn't keep him from making money. Anytime I need something, he's the first to give me money. Even if it's something as simple as a train fare.

"Come on, what's it going to be? Us sitting here and sulking all night, or are we going to the party?"

I let out a big long sigh. "Fine, you ass, let's go."

End Flashback

I was so depressed that night. If my brother had left me there, I might have decided to end my misery. Now I'm here, a year later, and that night is all I can think about. Granted I got my so-called five minutes of happiness, but it appears it's already over. What little bit of a life I could have had with someone seems to be over almost as fast as it began.

The thought of us being done is making my heart feel as if it's literally being torn from my chest, right through my ribs. I don't want it to end, but I'm at the end of my rope. I no longer know what to do to fix our relationship. All because I can't catch a break. My life is a series of fucked-up situations and each one just pushes me further and further into a black void that I can't escape.

How much can one person bear before they break?

Fate is determined to see me suffer. I slide down the wall as tears begin to fall down my cheeks. I knew what Aerick and I had could never last. I've never been able to keep anything happy in my life.

Again, I have nothing. I've worked so hard the last few months hoping it wouldn't end. Thought maybe if I tried harder, there would be a chance of having a happy life, even if it was only temporary. I knew it would end, but there was a glimmer of hope it could at least last for a few years. Shit, I would even have been happy if it lasted a year, but no such luck.

Great! Right now, I wish I was back home. I could go up on the roof and maybe finish what I was thinking of last year. Hot tears fall from my cheeks, soaking my shirt. I don't want to be alone again. I don't want to go back to being sad and depressed all the time. I bang my head on the wall behind me, trying to get the thoughts out of my head.

Pathetic. That's all I am.

I do it again, and again. I feel the cold as it blows on the trail of tears that are now free-flowing. I just want it to go away. Everything, I want it to go away. Again, and again, I feel the wood on the back of my head.

"What the fuck?"

I ignore him. It doesn't matter anymore. I turn up the bottle in my hand, drinking down several large gulps before I continue.

"Dammit Nadi, enough!"

I don't stop. There's no point, but obviously I'm not going to get what I want, yet again. Jeff throws his leg over my head so he's above me and slides down behind me so that I'm pushed forward away from the wall.

"Stop. It's okay," he whispers in my ear, keeping his hands barely touching my shoulders.

My head falls onto my knees and my hands go over my head.

"It's not! It's over, Jeff. He doesn't love me anymore," I tell him through my tears.

"What are you talking about? Is that a joke?"

"I'm damaged, broken. I mean, I was before, too, but he didn't know me then. He was around when it happened this time."

"Nadi, he still loves you. What happened to you didn't change that."

"I thought the same thing at first, but it's been weeks and he still won't hardly touch me. It isn't even just the physical side. He's always so distant these days. Even when he's with me, it's like he isn't there."

"He... He's having a hard time." He stutters out.

"Him! What about me? This shit happened to me! AGAIN!" I'm merely a toy for everyone's amusement." Hitting the side of my head, I try to numb some of my pain.

"Hey, hey!" He grabs my hands, crossing them over my chest as he holds me tightly to him, so I'm forced to stop. I give up and I lean my head back against his shoulder.

See? I can't do anything I want!

"Jeff, I'm so tired. Tired of everything," I say, barely audible.

"Come on, Nadi. You are the strongest person I know. Don't let this shit break you – you can get through this."

Haven't I been strong enough?

"I don't want to be alone again. I was so happy. For once in my life, I was really happy and now it's gone." He kisses my temple.

"You'll never be alone. I'll always be here for you. I promise," he says as he rests his head against mine. I take a deep breath.

"What the hell is this?" My heart jumps at the sound of his voice and I sit up, but with Jeff's arms still wrapped around me so

I can only go so far.

"She needs someone," Jeff says, still not moving.

"She *has* someone!" I don't know what worries me more, the fact that his voice is so low and menacing or the fact that he still hasn't moved.

"Does she?" *Here we go.* Another pissing contest.

"What is that supposed to mean?" Jeff lets go of me and jumps up so quickly I fall back, smacking against the wall as he takes the few steps over to Aerick.

"Jeff, stop," I say, trying to stop this misplaced anger.

"It means, if you don't get over yourself and soon, we're all going to lose her!"

"JEFF!" I shout, standing up as quickly as I can to go over and hit him for saying that, but I stop when the look on Aerick's face goes from pure anger to anguish.

His shoulders slump forward as he stares into my eyes, all anger forgotten. Jeff puts his hand on Aerick's shoulder and whispers something to him before stalking away, but Aerick's eyes never leave mine.

After a minute, he still doesn't move, and I shake my head. "I'm fine, Aerick; go back inside." I lean back up against the building. If this is going to be over, just let it be over.

He closes his eyes and takes a deep breath before coming over to stand in front of me. Seeing him with that expression is unbearable so my eyes fall to the side of him. I don't think I can handle looking him in the eye anymore knowing how this is going to go.

The weight of his forehead presses on my own. "Please tell me it isn't true."

"What?" I whisper after a minute.

"You think I don't love you anymore?" I squeeze my eyes shut because there is no way I can say it to his face. A lone tear falls down my face. "Hey?" He pulls my chin up. "You are wrong. I love you. I will never stop loving you." My eyes open and I see there's only truth in his words.

"Sometimes love just isn't enough." The words leave my mouth before I can stop myself, but it doesn't make it any less true. Even if he loves me, he's still repulsed by me. "It's okay, I understand." I pull my face out of his hand and look to the side, trying to hold in the tears threatening to break free.

"Don't say that." He puts his hands on my arms and I can't help but enjoy the small bit of contact, but there's no reason to prolong this any longer.

"Aerick, I understand."

"Understand what? Why do you keep saying that?" I can't, I can't say it. "Understand what?"

Why can't he walk away? Why do I have to say it?

"I'm damaged goods. I understand if you... you know, if you don't..." I can't finish my sentence.

"Nadi..." I shake my head, not wanting to hear him say it. *Please walk away!* "It's not like that. It's not you."

"Yeah, yeah, I know and it's okay. As I said, I understand. Just please, g-go." I'm barely able to say the last part. He squeezes my arms slightly.

"Nadi..." *Stop!*

"Look, I get it okay. You don't want me like that anymore, so stop prolonging this and just go!" The tears spill over and I cover my face with my hands, not wanting him to see me even more pathetic than I already am.

"Is that what you think? That I don't want you anymore?" I'm not sure why he's getting mad but hearing the words out of his mouth makes it hurt even more. "Dammit Nadi, fucking look at me!" I shake my head, not wanting to see the truth in his eyes. "LOOK AT ME!" he shouts, making me jump. His grip on my arms is starting to hurt. My hands fall from my face, grabbing his arms tightly.

He immediately releases my arms and his demeanor softens just as fast. "Sorry, sorry. I didn't mean to yell. I didn't mean to scare you. I only..." He looks to the sky, taking several deep breaths before looking back down at me. Gently he grabs both of my hands and brings them to his chest. "Look. I love you. I will always love you and you are wrong. You are not damaged, and I still want you just as much as I did the first night I kissed you."

He's only saying that. He can't possibly mean it. Why else would he be acting the way he has?

"I mean it babe."

I close my eyes, taking a deep breath. My body warms hearing his words, but his actions have made it clear that it's not true. I feel his lips press softly against my own. Taking both my hands in one of his, he moves his other hand to hold my face to his.

"I need you. I..." He mumbles into my lips. "I'm just..." He wraps his arms around me as he lays his chin on the top of my head. "I didn't want you to feel pressured. You went through some traumatic shit and I didn't want to push you. I can be a little overbearing and I didn't want you to do anything you weren't ready for.

"But what happened to you hasn't changed any feelings I have for you. Emotionally or physically. I have been..." He lets out a big sigh. "Fuck... I was..." I pull back, finally looking in his eyes.

I know he's struggling but his inability to communicate right now is frustrating. "What, Aerick? Just say it already." *Here it comes.*

"I'm fucking afraid, okay?" He drops his hands and takes several steps back, looking a little frustrated himself as he rubs the back of his neck. However, I'm even more confused now. When he doesn't continue right away, I give him my best 'of what' questioning look, since I'm unable to form a coherent word from my own mouth right now.

"Nadi, I don't fucking know how to help you. I don't know what you need. For fuck sake, I question everything I even think about saying to you because I'm worried I'm going to say the wrong thing. I'm not the best person to deal with my own emotional shit and I have no idea how to help someone else through theirs."

He takes a step back toward me. "I'm going to fuck this up. I can never do the right thing because every time I think I'm doing something right, it turns out to be wrong and it makes me worried that I'm going to hurt you."

He bites his lip and takes another step toward me, gently taking my face in his hands. "I'm am afraid I'm going to hurt you. I don't know how to talk to you. I don't know how to touch you. I just... I need you!" His lips are on mine once more, but this time he's not holding back.

This is what I want. This is what I have needed. I needed him, only him, in all the ways he used to. I kiss him back with all the need and want that has been building inside me.

"I need you too!" I mumble on his lips. He lifts me by my thighs, and I wrap myself around him. Without breaking our kiss, he begins walking. My heart pounds with relief, with excitement, and with hope.

I hear the door shut and almost as quickly, I'm on my bed as he crawls over me. He stops and pulls back to look into my eyes once more. "Are you sure? Please tell me if you can't handle this and..." I put my finger to his lips, effectively stopping him.

"I need you, Aerick; just please, go slow." His eyes close for a moment and a grin spreads across his face before he leans back down to capture my lips again. With all the alcohol in my system my head is spinning but this is what I wanted. This whole time, I wanted to be close to him.

His lips leave mine as he pulls my shirt up and my bra down.

I grab his hair as I try to keep my moans quiet. I don't want him to stop, I want this, but... but...

I push him off and jump up off the bed quickly, running to the toilet. I make it just in time and my hair is swept back out of the way as I expel everything I have in my stomach. His hand comes around to support me as I finish my embarrassing episode.

When I've finished, and flush the toilet, he pulls me back against him. "I warned you not to drink more than two of those and not only did you have three, but you drank one down in less than three seconds," he jokes as he slides his arms under me and picks me up, taking me back to my bed. He turns around once I'm lying down.

"Please don't go, I'm so sorry..."

"Hey, I'm not going anywhere, Princess." I watch as he goes in the bathroom and wets a wash rag before rummaging through my cabinet. He returns with some Advil and a glass of water.

He quickly removes my shoes and pants before getting me a clean shirt and putting me into it. Of course, he pauses momentarily as he removes my bra. "Scoot," he demands, and I move back toward the wall. He removes his own shoes and then slides into bed next to me. He pulls me over to lie on his chest, moving my hair off my neck and laying the cold rag there.

"Sorry, I really did want to," I tell him with all honesty.

"I know. Maybe when we haven't had so much to drink. Now get some rest, we still have to work tomorrow." Instructor Aerick is back. My eyes are so heavy.

"Yes, sir."

I feel his chest rumble. "Good night, Princess. Sleep well."

"I love you, Aerick."

He kisses the top of my head. "I love you, too." I can only hope he hasn't changed by tomorrow.

CHAPTER FOUR

(Sunday, January 3rd)

YOUR LOVE'S A fire, it's alive and I'm burning in it… I fall hard and you carry me away, I fall apart so you can set me free…

"Now, what did that bag ever do to you?"

I jump back, startled by Gavin's voice. Quickly I pick up the remote and turn down the blaring music. Since I left my iPod in the cabin, I decided to listen to what was on the stereo in the gym. It actually has a pretty nice sound system and, based on the music that was on it, my guess is that Aerick was the last one listening to it.

"Guess I got a little carried away." My hands are a little sore, but I was wearing gloves, so the damage is minimal.

"I came to work out, but if you want, we can spar for a while."

Aerick was supposed to meet me here. The bag seemed like a good way to pass the time until he got here, but he must have gotten held up because looking at the clock, I realize I've been here for almost thirty minutes already. The longer it took him to get here, the more my frustrations grew, the harder I began punching.

"Aerick is meeting me here," I tell him, wondering what's kept Aerick this time.

"Last I saw, he was talking to Luther and Christian."

That doesn't surprise me one bit, always working hard and, much to my delight, after the other night, he has mostly gone back to the old Aerick.

Flashback Friday Morning

"Hmmm. Good morning, beautiful."

Aerick nuzzles at my neck and a giggle bubbles up in my chest. Even going one day without shaving, he has a good amount of stubble and it tickles like crazy. Ignoring my pounding head, I open my eyes to see that it's still dark, but my watch says five-thirty in the morning.

"I have to get going but here, I brought you some Advil and water." I turn around to see him sitting on the bed waiting to hand me my Advil. I prop myself up on one arm and take it, quickly popping it in my mouth before he hands me a glass of water. I take a quick drink and go to set it back down, but he doesn't let me.

"Nope, drink it all." *Bossy!* I groan internally and roll my eyes, displeased at being treated like a five-year-old, but drink down the rest of the glass.

"Better," he says as he takes my glass. "Now go back to sleep,

I need to go get ready for today."

Did he stay with me all night? "Do you have to?"

A smirk spreads across his lips. "Well, as much as I would love to stay here in bed with you..." He leans down and begins kissing my neck, causing me to let out a low hum.

"Yes, my vote is for you to stay," I say full of the lust that is building up at the remarkable feeling his mouth is causing. I pull his hair to show him my appreciation and I'm rewarded with a delicious groan.

"And my vote is, don't you two even dare!" Terrie says loudly.

I feel Aerick silently chuckle against my neck. "Go back to sleep, Princess. I understand if you skip P.T. today," he says as he nips at my ear, teasing me.

"You keep that up and I'll be kicking Terrie out," I tell him as he pulls away with a sly smile.

"Yeah, that isn't happening, so Aerick, get your ass out. You aren't supposed to be in here anyway." She's clearly irritated with me if she's pulling that crap. *Since when is she against bending the rules?*

Aerick gives me one last kiss on the head and grabs his jacket as he walks out the door.

End Flashback

He's pretty much been like that since Friday, but we haven't had any alone time since then. Mostly because yesterday was the trip up to The Lookout. It shocked me that they even go in the winter, with all the snow, but Aerick assured me that it isn't that bad. All the equipment they have is more than adequate for the temperatures and they only go if the weather is expected to be agreeable.

Aerick tried to convince Luther to let me go since Terrie had to go, but that only made Luther rethink the hiking party. In the end, he kept Paulo back at camp while Jeff and Gavin went on the hike. Aerick was less than pleased, as was Paulo.

In the end Tia, Brayden, Andi, Paulo and myself stayed at camp while the others went to The Lookout. During the day, Luther took me to take one of my CLEP tests over in Ellensburg and then he treated me to dinner. Last night we ended up playing poker and drank a little while Luther and Ayla went out. I must admit, it was fun to relax and not worry about anything for the evening. Brayden and Paulo had us girls laughing for hours and Andi even made us some delicious country fried steak for breakfast. Aerick was jealous when I told him about our breakfast when he got back from the hike a little while ago.

"Nadi?" Gavin pulls me out of my thoughts.

"Hmm?"

"You okay?"

"Yes, I was... lost in thought. Sorry. What were you saying?" He raises his eyebrow but decides not to question it further.

"I was asking how the book was that you've been reading."

"Oh yeah. It's pretty good. I think it would make an excellent gift. I'm almost finished with it."

Aerick also wasn't happy to find out that I've been

disappearing to read in Jeff and Gavin's cabin, but to my surprise, he didn't make more of a deal about it. He saw me coming out of their cabin to workout yesterday and I explained I was reading. He gave me an odd look before looking irritated but then left it at that. No argument, not even any questioning, but it clearly bothered him. I'm still wondering if the argument is coming or not.

"...I'll talk to you later." I look back up to Gavin. I totally missed whatever he said to me, so I merely smile and nod before turning around and beginning to punch the bag again.

I watch Gavin pick up the remote I abandoned on the bench and turn the music back up, then go over to the weights. I could use a little sparring but after yesterday, I figure I shouldn't push Aerick too far. He dislikes Gavin already and I don't want any reason for Aerick and I to fight. What I really would like is to find a way to have some alone time with him.

"Hey."

I'm startled once more by a voice, but this time it's the one I really wanted to hear the first time. My lips turn up as I turn to see his gorgeous eyes. He seems to be in an okay mood, which is always a good sign.

"Sorry it took so long. I got caught up with Luther and Christian."

"Any problems?" I ask out of curiosity.

"Alex has been causing some problems in the dorms at night, but nothing too major. I wouldn't worry about it. Also, Christian wanted me to remind you that he expects to see you after his last appointment." He bites his lip.

"I didn't forget, and I have every intention of going." His lip turns up slightly.

"Good. Now I would very much like to spar with you." I can't help but laugh a little at his eagerness, but he obviously doesn't think it's funny by the way his brows pull together.

"What? It's the only time I can openly touch you without being questioned." Even as he says it and it makes sense, he still seems a little off.

"Okay, okay. Let's go!" I turn and head for the ring while he grabs his gloves.

When we're both in the ring, he takes off his shirt before putting on his gloves. He glances over at Gavin, who's currently bench pressing an impressive amount of weight, and I would bet a hundred bucks he only took off his shirt to show off. *Guys!*

I watch him a little curiously as he puts on his gloves. It's been a while since Aerick has full-on sparred with me. Usually he gets the hand pads on and I practice attacking. We have been working on my speed, not so much my technique, but it's pretty clear that's not his plan today.

Once we're both ready, we begin to circle each other. "Are you ready for this?" he asks, almost as if questioning himself.

"Yes," I say, taking my first swing at his side. He easily sidesteps and I miss, but he doesn't try to take advantage and strike back. I try again and this time he has to use his elbow to block me from hitting his side, but again he doesn't attempt to hit me.

"You know, this usually works both ways," I say with a roll of my eyes.

Giving me a dirty look, he attempts a simple punch that I easily avoid by ducking and rolling away. I want this to be an actual fight. There's no point if he isn't going to at least try. He makes another ridiculously slow attempt to hit me and all it does is piss me off more so as I duck around this time, I use the opportunity to hit him hard right in his side.

He immediately grabs his side and frowns at me.

"What? This is supposed to be a sparring session. That means I hit you, you hit me; you know, actually fight!" I tell him and I see the wheels in his head turning. *What is his deal this time?*

Getting back into his fighting stance, we start circling once more. This time as I punch, he grabs my wrist and steps behind me, pinning me to his chest so he can whisper in my ear. "I would much rather be loving you than fighting you."

I feel the heat rise in my cheeks. "I couldn't agree more." It feels so wonderful to be caged in by his arms, but this isn't the time or place for this. Especially with Gavin only a few feet from us.

I elbow him in the stomach, successfully breaking his hold, and I move out away from him. "But since we have to behave during working hours, and I need to burn off all my pent-up energy, let's do this." I smile and he gets that heart-stopping smirk on his face.

"Okay," he says, transforming into his serious stance, and I know now that he's in instructor mode. We might actually get to spar now.

* * * *

After an intense hour and half of sparring, Aerick and I are both soaked with sweat. I wipe my forehead and neck with my towel. I feel Aerick's fingers run down my shoulder and I let out a quiet moan. Gavin left a little while ago and it's only us in the gym now.

"Man, I wish I could join you for a shower. You have no idea how hot you look, all sweaty and flushed from our workout."

"As much as I would truly enjoy that, I have to hurry and get to my appointment with Christian."

He groans. I really wish I could spend some alone time with him. He walks over to the bench, dropping his gloves and then picking up a bottle of water. *Fuck!* My hormones are going crazy right now. Watching a sweaty, shirtless Aerick chugging down water is a breathtaking sight. He catches me staring and raises an eyebrow at me.

"Hey, you're the one ditching me for another man," he jokes with a smirk.

"Whatever, you know it isn't like that."

He walks back over to me, lifting my chin up to make my eyes meet his own. "I know. Go and hurry before you're late."

"Is that an order?"

"Hmm. Is that what it takes for you to do what I want?"

"Huh, no!" *Absolutely not!*

"Okay. In that case, it was a request." He leans down and gives me a quick kiss on the lips. As he pulls away, I grab the back of his neck and pull him back down to me, giving him a much slower and more sensual kiss that he gratefully returns.

He pulls back again, and I let him. Looking down at his watch, his face gets very serious. "Now, get going. You only have fourteen minutes to take a shower and get there."

I chuckle. That time, there was no mistaking that it was an order. "Okay, since you asked oh-so-nicely," I say with dripping sarcasm. Giving him a grin, I turn and walk away and he smacks my ass just hard enough to sting a little.

"Hey!"

"What? I can't help that you have a great ass."

I shake my head and head out to go take my shower, almost running back to my cabin. It's freezing outside. It hasn't snowed lately but there's still plenty of snow on the ground and the temperature is only in the mid-thirties today. My shower is quick and without any time to spare, I settle for throwing my hair up in a messy bun while it's still wet. Without cleaning up my mess, I leave the cabin and hurry over to the classrooms.

Paulo tries to talk to me, but I merely hurry past him letting him know that I'm late for something and promise to catch up with him later. I make it to the classroom only a few minutes late.

"Good afternoon!" Christian greets me as I enter the

classroom. He comes over to me and I go to shake his hand but instead he engulfs me in a hug, causing me to freeze. The heaviness begins to spread across my chest and he quickly moves back, giving me a curious look.

"And what is that all about?" I question.

"It was an experiment of sorts. Come sit and let's talk." We go over and sit on the couch. "So, how have you been doing, Nadi?"

"I'm okay. No better, no worse."

"I would beg to differ. My little experiment just now, when I hugged you, you immediately froze and stopped breathing. Now, while I realize that happens to you with most people, we were at a point where your reaction to my touch wasn't quite so... intense."

"Okay, so what does it matter?" *Shoot!* I really should have tried not to react so harshly. I really hope he doesn't take it too personally.

"With what you have been through, and please keep in mind, this is expected and completely understandable, you have regressed." I can't deny it because it's true. I'm much jumpier and I have to work even harder not to react to people touching me, including those closest to me.

"But it isn't as bad as it was," I say plaintively. "That has to count for something."

"Of course it does. It only means we need to step back a little and maybe start working on some things we thought you were past."

A thought flies into my head. "How did you know?" I think I

already know the answer, but it doesn't add up.

He looks out the window for a moment. "Aerick told me." *Since when does Aerick talk with Christian?* "Luther, Aerick and I sat down to talk for a little while today." I shoot him a dirty look at this news. "Luther was concerned about you, and also about Aerick. It seems he hasn't quite been himself since everything happened to you." *Did you really expect him to be?*

"And?" I don't trust myself to say anything else with all the emotions that are running through my head right now, but I would really appreciate some insight to what's going on with Aerick.

"Nadi, you have to understand that with Aerick, things can be difficult. Aerick has never been good with his own emotions. I don't know his whole story, but it's clear to me that he had a rough childhood himself. I suppose that's also obvious in the fact that he once was a cadet here, but Luther has let me in on a few small details I was previously oblivious to."

I bet Aerick was pissed about that. Very few people know much about him. He likes his personal life to stay pretty private. "Does Aerick know?"

"Luther told him today. The point here is that you both are going through a difficult time. Two people that both happen to have that same stubborn and headstrong mentality."

"He's going through a difficult time? This shit happened to me, not him," I retort, a little irritated, but I immediately feel bad.

"That's true, but please hear me out. First, you two have a very strong bond. Please don't take this the wrong way, but you're the first woman he's ever desired to be exclusive with, in addition to having what he calls an "unexplained pull" to you. For someone who's not typically the emotionally loving type, these emotions are difficult for him to grasp. This has led to a horrible fear in him." *Fear?*

"I don't think I've ever seen fear in Aerick. Ever!"

"Do you really believe that? Think about it hard."

Have I ever seen him afraid? My thoughts flit around the few short months Aerick and I have been together. Christian raises an eyebrow at me as my mind focuses.

"Now think even harder, what do those times each have in common."

There was the first time that I was stabbed. It was the first time he told me he loved me. It was the same look I saw when he found me at the pier after I was attacked and also when he found me at the maintenance shack. That's the connection.

"It's me," I whisper, more to myself.

"Now, don't put this into the wrong context but yes, I believe you're right, but most likely not in the way you're thinking right now."

"His fear is because of me. He thinks I make him weak and that's something he fears, being weak." Thinking over our conversations, that's the one thing he really does fear. With his past being what it was, he never wants to feel weak or inferior again.

"Okay, I'll give you credit for that, because you're partially right. His fear isn't really because of you, though, it's for you. He's afraid of losing you, as you fear losing him; but it isn't his love for you that he feels is making him weak."

I stop playing with my fingers and look up at Christian. "What do you mean?"

"He feels as if he can't protect you. In the short time you've known him, several things have happened to you and he blames himself for not being strong enough to protect you. You put that together with a man's natural instinct to protect and it's caused him to feel weak; useless, even."

"He's not useless. He's helped me in so many ways. I've felt more alive in the last few months than I have in almost ten years. Merely having him around the last few months is the only thing that's kept me sane enough to deal with what's happened."

"I believe that, but it's taking some convincing to get him believe that, which is why Luther and I sat down with him."

He did seem a little different when he met me at the gym.

"What exactly did you say to him?"

"I really don't think that's important. What's important is, did he listen? Have you seen him in the last few hours?"

"Yes."

"And what did you observe?"

"He seemed… I don't know. More himself, I guess. We sparred for a while, something he hasn't done with me for a while, but he went pretty easy on me."

"So, he was touching you?" *Where is this going?*

"Yes. He's always been able to touch me, but... wait. That's part of the problem, isn't it?" My mind is reeling at my sudden clarity. "When he found me, and I flinched away from him. I wouldn't let him touch me. Does he think I'm afraid of him? Of his touch?" My hands are beginning to shake. *Is this my fault too? Did I make him feel this way?*

"He doesn't think you're afraid of him, but he does believe that the trauma you've suffered has caused you to become sensitive to his touch and that's what has him so worried. His feelings for you haven't changed, but he's suddenly not sure of how to act around you. He wants things to go back to normal, but he's worried about doing something that will trigger your fear. It's pretty clear that his one true fear is losing you."

My chest feels heavy. I can't imagine being without him. I realize that my biggest fear is losing him and if I lose him, it's going to be my own fault.

"Hey Nadi, breathe." Christian gets up and kneels in front of me, taking my face in his hands so I'm forced to look at him. "Breathe." He takes deep breaths and I mimic him. "That isn't going to happen. As I said earlier, you two are the most stubborn and headstrong people I know. If anyone can get through this, it's you two."

I nod my head as I try to calm myself down. He's right, he has to be. "I can't lose Aerick."

"You're not going to lose him. You need to understand him.

Step into his shoes and see things from his point of view, which is, by the way, the same thing I've recommended to him. You two need trust each other and work through this. Talk, and not only when your drunk and pissed off."

"He seriously told you about that?"

"Actually, Jeff did. Don't be mad, but he didn't leave you two completely alone after Aerick found you." *Christ! What the hell is this – a damn intervention? First Luther, then Jeff.* "He hid around the corner and listened to you to make sure you were okay. And by the way, I'm disappointed that you didn't make me more aware of the situation."

I push Christian back as I stand up. "Well, that's just great. I think I've had about enough for now."

"Wait, Nadi, don't be upset. They're merely looking out for you."

"Whatever. As far as I'm concerned, everyone needs to just back the fuck off." I quickly move to leave. I can't believe that everyone feels the need to be all up in my business.

"Please think about what I've said!"

He shouts at me as I exit the room. I give him a half wave without looking back. I really shouldn't be mad but I am. Aerick did seem a little different after they talked with him, but I don't like people talking about me behind my back.

I begin walking around the track. It's cold but right now I need this. I'm really starting to hate all this snow. If it was warmer, I could run off all this irritation and aggression, but right now I have to settle for walking really fast around this damn frozen pathway, trying not to slip on the melting snow in the process. Damn I need my iPod right now.

"What's wrong?"

I almost slip and fall on my ass as I quickly turn around, startled; I didn't even realize someone was behind me.

"What the fuck, Aerick?" My heart is going about fifty miles an hour.

"Sorry. I didn't mean to scare you."

"You didn't scare me, you just startled me."

He huffs. "Kind of the same thing isn't it?"

I really wish he wouldn't raise his eyebrow at me like that.

"No. It's not." *Not really.* Besides, he needs to understand I'm not afraid of him.

"Anyway. So, what's the matter?" He obviously doesn't believe it.

I shake my head. "Nothing."

He tilts his head to the side, looking at me with total doubt. When I don't change my stance on the subject, he raises both his eyebrows, pursing his lips in frustration.

"Fine, a little pissed at everyone right now," I relent.

"Does that include me?"

Maybe a little, but I'm not opening that can of worms right now.

"No, but Luther and Jeff are definitely on the top of that list, along with Christian."

"Why do I get the feeling we're both irritated at the same thing?" he says with a heavy sigh. I turn and start walking, but this time I know he's right behind me.

"Because we are. You didn't appreciate everyone getting into our business either?"

"Do I ever appreciate anyone in my business?" he says angrily, grabbing the back of his neck and looking at the ground, but then glances back up at me. "Aside from you, of course."

Well, I guess at least there's that.

"What did you and Christian talk about?" he asks, looking away. I'm sure he knows already, and I have questions of my own.

"Why did you spar with me today?"

The look on his face tells me that isn't what he was expecting. "I needed to... I wanted... I don't know."

I stop and turn to him. He's not telling the truth. "You're lying. Just tell me."

He bites his lip. "I needed to see your reaction to my touch." He runs his fingers lightly down my arm as he says it. I don't flinch at his touch, but I quickly look around, making sure no one is watching us.

"Why?"

Christian already told me, but I need to hear it from him. He did say we needed to talk, so I see no better time than now.

He thinks for a moment before answering. "In the last few months, I feel as if I've become sort of a sanctuary for you. Someone you come to when you want to be held, when you're upset, and when you're in my arms, I thought you felt... safe."

"I do feel that way, Aerick." I tried to hold my tongue, but he has to know I do feel that way.

He looks around us. "Can we go inside and talk?"

We're almost to my cabin and Terrie is over at the infirmary. We walk the short distance to my cabin and go inside. I immediately go over and grab the bottle of whiskey that's sitting on the mini fridge.

"What are you doing?"

"Something tells me this will be easier if I'm buzzed," I say honestly.

"I'm sure it would be, but I would prefer if we stay completely clear-minded this time." He takes the bottle and cap out of my hands, setting it back down.

"Fine!" I say, frustrated, as I go sit on the bed. There he goes making me feel like a damn errant child again. He follows, sitting next to me, staring down at the ground.

"Then why?" he asks quietly after a moment.

"Why what?" There are so many why's right now.

"Why wouldn't you let me that day? Was it because I failed you or was it because you were afraid of me? Why wouldn't you let me make you feel safe?"

"It's not what you think, Aerick."

"Then what the hell is it? Because I can't for the life of me figure it out. I've gone over it, over and over in my head, and it's driving me nuts."

"Do you think I was afraid of you?"

"A lot of thoughts went through my head in those moments, but mainly yes, or at the very least, you no longer felt safe in my arms."

"It wasn't that, Aerick. I wasn't afraid of *you*, I was afraid you wouldn't want me anymore. I felt ashamed and, with everything else I had just been through, I was most afraid that you'd reject me when you found out the truth. So, I pushed you away before you could push me away."

He moves to kneel down in front of me, grabbing my hands between both of his own as I continue.

"I pushed you away thinking I could handle it and it would be better that way, but I realized after you went to jail that I couldn't do it. I couldn't stay away from you. I still wanted you, I still needed you and then you began keeping me away and it was like all my thoughts were coming true. I did want to be in your embrace, because that's the only place I feel safe."

He closes his eyes and breathes in deeply. I slide down, straddling his legs and taking his face in my hands. His eyes open, looking deep within me. I lightly kiss his lips, holding him to me. "You are my sanctuary," I whisper on his lips and his arms wrap around me, pulling me tightly to him as he lays his head on my chest. My arms wrap around him, holding him to me.

"I still want you, Princess. I never stopped wanting you." He begins kissing me across my neck and the feeling is incredible. His lips finally find mine as his words pass into actions. He lifts me as he stands and sets me on the bed, not breaking our kiss.

It only takes a second for him to unzip my jacket and I help him to remove it as I begin taking his off as well. The warmth of his body radiates off him, helping to keep me warm as he removes my shirt. Feeling the cold at my back and the heat at my front sends shivers across my body.

"You okay?" he whispers.

"Yes, please, don't stop," I tell him, yearning to feel much more of him.

He bites that sexy lip again, giving me a half smile. "I'm all yours."

I moan as his lips attach to mine once more. All my worries, frustrations, and fears begin to fall away. His hands massage my breasts as his kiss turns more insistent. Pulling down my bra, he moves his lips down and begins to tease each of my nipples. The hurt, pain, and anger disappear until it's only us the way we were. Loving, enjoying each other as we used to.

His lips move further down until he reaches my pants. Giving me a lustful smirk, he undoes my pants button with his teeth, causing a throbbing between my legs. I love that feeling almost as much as I love him.

Grabbing the top of my pants, he slowly peels them down, not taking his eyes off of me. I kick off my boots before he can reach my ankles and he doesn't pause, removing them the rest of the way.

He stops for a moment as he begins to crawl back over me,

looking at me from head to toe, running his hand along the length of my side. He reaches one hand around, unclipping my bra and slowly removing it, allowing it to drag across my front. "You have always been the most amazing woman I have ever known, and I would rather die than lose you. You are mine!"

His lips find mine once more and I'm so overwhelmed by his words that it makes my heart feel as if it's going to explode. So demanding, so much yearning that it leaves no room for question. His words fade as they are replaced by his touch. His fingers slide into my panties, massaging circles over my clit. The throbbing intensifies as a low growl escapes his mouth which is immediately muffled as his lips capture my breast.

He moves back slightly as he peels my underwear down. Sucking his lip in with his teeth, he leans down and kisses me between my legs. I hold my breath at the intense feeling it sends through me.

"You okay?" he asks quietly as he pauses.

"Yes," I whisper, praying he doesn't stop.

"Good." His lips are on me once more. I let out another moan as he begins using his tongue. "Do you miss that?" He doesn't give me time to answer as I feel his fingers enter me. I moan louder this time, not able to control myself. "That's right baby, let me hear you."

His tongue picks up speed as do his fingers and I moan louder, so overwhelmed with feeling right now I want to scream. It doesn't take long for me to reach the edge and he must sense it because he begins humming, pushing me over the edge into a mind-blowing orgasm.

As I come down, a smiling Aerick kisses his way back up my body, resting to the side of me. "Yes, I definitely missed that," I tell him, finally being able to answer him.

"And did you miss anything else?" he asks, rubbing his naked self on me, making it clear that he's already ready. Somewhere along the line he discarded his boxers.

"Most definitely."

Suddenly he moves over me and kisses my nose. I freeze for the slightest of seconds when I feel his weight come down on me. I don't mean to and I pray he doesn't notice, but the look on his face gives it away.

I immediately grab his face, trying to keep his attention. I lean up to kiss him, but he barely moves. His body has gone stiff. I don't want this to end. I want him; I couldn't help my reaction. I can see the hurt on his face as I pull back. The wheels are turning in his head and it's clear that I'm losing him.

"Please don't. I want you; I want this. Please don't stop," I beg. I try pulling him down to me but he's an unwavering brick wall. "Please baby. Don't pull away. I need you Aerick, I need you now!" Tears pool in my eyes as my heart constricts in my chest.

His eyes suddenly change and my Aerick is back. "I'm right here. I'm not going anywhere." I grab his face again, placing a hard, passionate kiss on his lips. It only takes him a minute to match my feverish lips.

Grabbing my waist, he slowly pulls me over the top of him until I'm straddling him. A position we're not in very often. I've learned that he loves control in all things, including in bed. This is him trying to make me comfortable and I love him for it.

I kiss him harder. His hands begin moving over me again and I feel both of us become more relaxed as we mold to each other. The growing bulge hardens beneath me and it seems our moment of crisis has passed. I rub myself along his length, enjoying the feeling of him against me which is heightened when he moans into my mouth.

Grabbing my hips, he lifts me slightly, allowing him room to enter me. He does it at a slow, agonizing pace, letting me feel him inch by inch. Sitting up, I take deep breaths in and out, enjoying every part of him as he continues his control of me, moving me back and forth. His eyes stay trained on me, I think watching to make sure that I'm okay, but right now I'm more than okay.

I lean back down and kiss him again, letting him keep control of our pace. As he continues to make love to me, I get more and more lost in him. Once again, the outside world disappears and it's only us. No problems, no emotions other than pure love.

As I come undone once more, he follows, and I collapse in a heap on his chest. Nothing in this world matters more to me than him. He's seen me through the worst possible heartache, and for the smallest moments in time, helps me feel as if there is the slightest bit of hope. I close my eyes and drift asleep with only him on my mind. *I fall apart so you can set me free...*

CHAPTER FIVE

(Saturday, January 9th)

THERE IS SOMETHING extremely gratifying about being able to make it through P.T. when Aerick is leading it. While it gets easier after a while, Aerick's constant changing of the workout never lets your muscles get bored and you always finish feeling the burn. I never really minded the workouts, even as a cadet. Other than the cold chill in the mornings it always made me feel better during the day. It's been a definite plus that workouts have been inside the gym most of the snowy days the last few weeks.

I pick up a bottle of water while the cadets leave to go back to their cabins. We've made it halfway through the winter session and it seems like most things are going to finally calm down. There were hardly any problems this week with the cadets and I'm starting to see subtle changes in many of them.

Thinking that I've had something to do with that gives me

hope that I can make a difference. I'm not stupid enough to think this will fix them all, but if we can manage to affect just a few of them, then it's worth it. *It helped me.*

I have wondered many times in the past why Aerick enjoyed this job so much. He's a natural at being a dick so this job fits him well, but it isn't as if he shows that he really cares about what happens to these kids. Knowing him better now, combined with my own recent feelings, I think he enjoys the gratification of knowing he helped them. Knowing that their lives may be better because of him. Of course, I would never say that to him because he would most likely deny it.

I think being excited about the day is helping my mood, too. I can't believe Luther is letting Aerick and I leave for the majority of the day. Not that we're getting completely out of work. We still have to run errands and I have two more CLEP tests today, but we get to spend the day together, just us.

With my school classes starting back up this last week, I don't have much to do this weekend, and after today's CLEP test, I only have three left. Seeing the light at the end of the tunnel has given me my second wind. If I can only get through this last little push of school and tests, I'm home free.

"Meet you out front in thirty?"

I down the rest of my water as I turn around to my man, who's barely broken a sweat. "Yeah okay," I say as I walk past him, giving him a wink. I see his lip pull slightly at the corner. *Just the reaction I was hoping for.*

I don't bother to question why we're not staying for breakfast. I'm sure he has a plan, he always does. I head back to my cabin to take a shower.

"Good luck today," Jeff says as he comes up from behind me once I get outside.

"Thanks! Sorry you have to take over Aerick's classes today."

"It's okay. I don't mind. Besides, I need the practice if I'm going to take over for Brand or Aerick next session."

"How crazy is that? Next session, I'll be taking Tia's spot and you're taking one of the guy's spots. It's definitely going to be interesting and I'm sure you guys will drive Aerick nuts!"

He raises his eyebrow at me. "Do you know something I don't?"

I stare at him confused for a second and then it clicks. "No, no of course not. Luther hasn't said anything about who's taking Ayla's position, but it isn't as if Brand is even fighting hard for it. Getting that job would mean so much to Aerick and I'm sure Luther knows it." I'm suddenly not so sure of my thought process. "Do you think Luther would choose Brand over Aerick?"

"No, not really. Other than Brand being a little better-tempered, I think Aerick would be better suited." I look at him a little surprised. "What, I think Aerick is a better leader. While Brand is better-tempered, he's quieter and more laid back. I already heard Luther say that he wants whoever gets it to be more involved in the day-to-day things with the cadets."

I'm surprised that he sees Aerick so highly, but his reasoning makes sense. "Well hey, I got to hurry and take a shower before we leave. I'll see you later."

"Alright." He gives me a little nod and a wink as we part ways.

✻ ✻ ✻ ✻

"Hey beautiful," Aerick says as he opens my door. I look down at my normal low-key clothing and give him a questioning look. He rolls his eyes at me and ushers me to get in as he shakes his head. He grabs my chin and gives me a chastising kiss. "You always look beautiful to me, so stop giving me those looks." He stares into my eyes for a few more seconds before letting go to start up the car and focus his eyes on the road.

"So, what's on the agenda for today?" Luther didn't bother to divulge this information to me but I'm sure Aerick is well aware of it.

"We have to pick up a few things for Andi, Terrie and some office supplies that we're running low on, but first I would like to have a good breakfast and later this evening I have a surprise for you."

"A surprise?" He sure doesn't seem happy or excited. *Aren't those normal reactions when you're surprising someone?*

"Yes, it is a surprise and it will remain a surprise so don't bother asking."

Geez, what a grump. "Fine, grouchy."

He grabs my hand and brings it to his lips where a smile is tugging at his lips. "Let's not fight today." He kisses my hand and then lowers it, holding it in his lap. "Besides, you need to focus on your test later."

"Oh yeah, let's get me to focus by making my mind run rampant. Good call, slick." His lips turn into a smirk. "You just love doing that crap to me don't you?"

He chuckles this time. "I am sure that I have no idea what you are talking about."

Two can play at this game. I release my hand from his and start rubbing the top of his thigh. He pauses for the slightest of moments but pretends it doesn't affect him, so I move my hand toward the inside of his thigh as I increase the pressure. Slowly, I work my hand further and further up his thigh, but his face stays perfectly composed.

As I'm about to touch his manliness, I stop and drag a single nail along the entire inside width of his thigh as close as I can get without touching it. I see his jaw clinch and feel the twitch in his pants. I press my lips together tightly to keep from laughing. I go to begin again and he grabs my hand.

"Knock it off," he growls.

"Frustrating, isn't it." He raises an eyebrow at me and then looks me up and down.

"You know, two can play this game."

On second thought, maybe that wasn't such a good idea. Staring down at my leg, his face gets serious and intense. He sucks his lower lip in and I'm already squirming in my seat. His eyes travel up my torso to my face slowly, stopping when his eyes are on mine, and he bites his lip as it slides slowly out of his mouth.

I feel as if I'm going to explode and he didn't even have to touch me! I can't sit still. I cross my legs tight to relieve the ache that's developing. All of a sudden he starts laughing as his eyes go back to the road.

I can't believe he can do that to me merely by looking at me; this is ridiculous. I fold my arms across my chest, knowing he has won this round. *And how the hell did he do that without crashing the damn car?* Somehow, we've already made it into town, and he parks the car at the Cottage Cafe.

It's pretty quiet for a weekend morning as we walk in. We head toward the back to the booth that has become our normal seat. There are some teenage kids looking a little ragged at several of the tables. At this early hour, my best guess is they're eating and drowning their hangovers with coffee before they have to go home to face their parents. Even in the winter, these kids seem to party every weekend.

"Good morning, Aerick. The usual?" I look up to the annoying voice that immediately irritates me. I swear she never changes. She's here almost every time Aerick and I come in and it's always like I'm completely invisible.

I feel Aerick's arm rest across my shoulders and he kisses my temple. "You pick this morning, babe. What sounds good?" I pick up on his game. He's doing it to keep me from exploding.

I smile up at her, handing her back the menus she had just set down. I already know Aerick's favorite and he obviously trusts that I will order it for him. "Hi Kate, we'll both have the country fried steak and coffee. Oh, and also bring Aerick a large orange juice. You know he needs to stay big and strong." My voice is dripping with sarcasm and I feel Aerick chuckle silently beside me.

She bites the inside of her cheek and writes it down in her notebook. "Okay. Anything else?"

She looks to Aerick as if I would have forgot anything, but Aerick is smooth and doesn't miss a beat. "Nope. She knows what I like," he says simply, and she immediately turns on her heels and walks off.

"Crap. Is my whole life going to be like this?" I say, mostly to myself.

"What do you mean?" *Seriously.*

"I mean, girls always being rude to me because they are crushing on you."

"Aww, don't be jealous, babe. My eyes are only for you." He leans down and kisses my neck to reiterate his point.

"I know. Sorry, I guess I'm a little on edge today."

"How come?" He asks seeming genuinely curious.

I'm not really sure myself. Despite my good mood today, I've felt a little pent up lately. Maybe being out in the woods so far from civilization is finally getting to me.

"Is there something I can do to help?" he asks, nibbling on my ear when I don't answer.

I let out a quiet moan, moving my head to the side, giving him better access. "That always helps."

71

I jump as our coffees are carelessly dropped down in front of us. Kate doesn't even spare a second glace to make sure she didn't spill; she's already headed off back behind the counter.

"Apparently someone else is grumpy too," he says with a chuckle. I have to admit, it's pretty funny.

"Hey Nadi, Aerick." I look up to see Eddie and Clara standing there. "Mind if we join you?" Clara says and I shrug my shoulders, not minding some company outside of the camp staff. I only know a few people.

They sit down and Kate comes back over to take their orders, not bothering with the menus. I guess most people already know what's on it. Aerick remains oddly quiet, not greeting either one of them and, as I put my hand on his leg, I feel that he has become very stiff. There seems to be tension between Aerick and Eddie and something tells me I'm about to find out why.

"How are you doing, Nadi?" Eddie asks.

"How do you think?" Aerick barks. *Yep, definitely tension.*

After a second, I understand that Eddie obviously knows what happened to me. Great, a small town like this, everyone probably knows by now. I just want to get past that.

"Yeah, sorry. I just wanted to say that I had no idea. Sean *was* my good friend, but I had no idea he would ever do something like that. I haven't talked to him since I found out. I mean, he's always been a little crazy but..." He shakes his head. "Anyway, I wanted you to know I have no intention of ever talking to him again and I hope we can still be friends."

It didn't really occur to me before now that Sean and Eddie were pretty close friends. Both times I met them they were together. I had also grown really fond of Eddie when we hung out at the party. He's very nice and sweet, nothing like...

"It's fine Eddie, you didn't know, and yes we're still friends," I say to stop my thoughts. Aerick huffs beside me.

"Aerick dude, I'm sorry. I would have never stuck up for him in the bar that night if I knew the real story. In fact," he glances at me and then to Clara, "I probably would have help you beat him to death if I knew why you were so mad."

"Yeah, well I didn't need help. How is your jaw, by the way?" Aerick asks smugly.

"It's better these days, but seriously dude, I'm sorry. We cool?"

I look to Aerick expectantly. *Come on, if I can forgive him, then you can too.* Aerick takes in a deep breath and the blows it out again in dramatic style. "Yeah, I suppose."

"Good, because the last place I want to be is on your bad side," Eddie says, rubbing his jaw, and I feel Aerick relax. Our food comes and we all settle into comfortable conversation.

* * * *

"Hey babe," I say, getting into the car and leaning over to give him a kiss.

We ran a few errands together this morning before he dropped me off for my test. I took two ninety-minute tests with a ninety-minute break between the two, so he should have had plenty of time to finish getting supplies. Looking behind me in the back seat, it looks as if he accomplished his tasks.

"Hi," he says, mingling our fingers as he takes my hand. "How did your test go?"

"I did awesome. I got a ninety-one percent on one and the initial grade for the other was a ninety-three percent. I won't get the final grade until they grade the essay section, but I feel good about it." Aerick gets a look of pride on his face. "So how was your afternoon? Did you finish everything?"

He raises an eyebrow. "Of course I did."

"Yes, of course you did," I say, mimicking him. "So, do I get to know what the surprise is now?" I ask excitedly.

"Nope." *What?*

"Come on, you told me after I finished my tests."

"No. What I said was it was a surprise and I didn't want it to distract you from your test. I never said I would tell you after. You will have to wait to find out."

I cross my arms over my chest. "Ugh, you're so frustrating!"

"I know." *Yeah keep it up buddy.*

He pulls out of the testing center but he doesn't head toward the freeway, so we must be going somewhere here in town. I sit as patiently as possible and my irritation starts to wane as my excitement grows. As much as I hate surprises, I secretly love them, too. Especially when they're from Aerick. He never disappoints.

I haven't forgotten his reaction to telling me this morning either, which is making me even more curious. Thinking about it actually did distract me for a while today. It was like he was on edge about this, whatever it is. We pull into a parking lot and I look at the sign on the building.

"Wing Central's Roadhouse Grill. My surprise is dinner. I love getting to eat out with you babe, but you could have just said that." I actually feel a little disappointed now.

"Just come on." He's beginning to get a little tense and I begin to get the feeling this isn't going to be a normal dinner.

He takes my hand as we meet around the car and we go inside, where we're greeted by the woman behind the counter.

"I have a reservation," Aerick tells her and gives her his name.

"Yes sir. Your table is ready, right this way." She takes off in front of us and we follow.

"Wow, you even made reservation!"

"It's the weekend and we're here during the dinner rush. I wanted to make sure we got a good table."

I open the menu and start looking, but Aerick doesn't bother. When the waitress brings out our drinks, she also sets three sets of silverware on the table. I look to Aerick, confused, but he doesn't bother to look at me. He's just staring out the window, seemingly deep in thought.

"Are you going to tell me who's joining us?"

He finally looks toward me, without actually looking me in the eyes. "You'll see."

Now my stomach is all in knots. *Who could be joining us that would be making him act so strange?* He looks at his watch and bites the inside of his lip. I wonder if he's worried whoever it is, isn't going to show up. We've only been here a few minutes but Aerick hates being late and therefore hates when others are late.

"Do you know what you want?" he asks, looking at the abandoned menu in front of me. My appetite is now gone; I just want to know what's going on.

"I'll just have a salad. I'm not really hungry."

He rolls his eyes at me.

"Did you guys want to order, or did you want to wait for the rest of your party?" The waitress hovers nearby with her order pad. *Party? Is there more than one person?*

"No," Aerick says quickly. "We'll wait, but until then can we get two Corona's with lime and an order of mozzarella sticks."

"We're drinking?" I look at him cautiously. This isn't his normal style, not when we aren't close to home, and not when we're driving the camp's SUV.

"Only one. I thought it would go well with our appetizer." I look away, rolling my eyes. *Yeah, keep telling yourself that's the reason, because I don't believe it for one second.* He resumes staring out the window and this time I join him.

"Long time, no see!" Aerick and I both look up to see a gentleman with darker hair. He seems older than Aerick, but not by much. I immediately recognize a similarity between him and Aerick; the dark hair and those eyes. I thought I would never see those gorgeous eyes on another human being.

"About time." Aerick rises from the table across from me

quickly and shakes the man's hand.

"You sure haven't changed much. How long has it been?"

He grabs my hand and pulls me to my feet. "It's been almost six years. Good to see you. This is my girlfriend Nadi. Nadi, this is my Uncle Davy," Aerick says with a small grin on his face.

"Wow, Aerick," his uncle says, with a quick glance to Aerick before looking me up and down. "You are absolutely gorgeous." He says to me making me blush.

Without warning, he pulls me into a hug, and I freeze. Aerick's hand is immediately on my back and I reach back with one hand, grabbing his hand tightly, using it as an anchor to my emotions. I hold my breath, waiting for his uncle to let go, which he does in short order.

"Aerick has told me a lot about you. I'm glad we're getting to finally meet."

I look to Aerick as we sit back down, Aerick sitting next to me this time. "You talk about me?"

"Ignore him, he's exaggerating. I've only talked to him twice since I met you, and one of those times was the five-minute conversation we had yesterday. He was in the area and wanted to see me. Since he's the only family I have left, I figured you would like to meet him as well."

"Aerick, your dad is still alive. He's a selfish, greedy, arrogant dick, but he is still alive," Davy bites out.

"Not to me," Aerick says coldly.

"Fine. I didn't come here to argue. If I wanted that, I would have gone to see him. So, how have you been?"

Aerick takes a deep calming breath and then looks at me. "Things are getting better every day. How about you? Enjoying the house? I miss fishing up there during the summer."

"Yes. It is rather peaceful. A little bigger than is needed being it's only me, but you won't hear me complain. Maybe one day I can find me a beautiful someone to share it with." He looks down at his hands. "I miss fishing with him too. Sorry I didn't come to his funeral. I knew it was better for me to stay away. It wouldn't have ended well." He laughs a little. "But from what I heard, instead it didn't end well for you. Man, the only part I regret is not getting to see his face when he found out he didn't get anything. Greedy bastard. And Nadi, standing up to the wicked witch of the west and the big bad wolf..."

"Where did you hear that?" Aerick interrupts.

"Your brother called me the next day. He had me rolling on the ground laughing." He is smiling from ear to ear.

"I have to say, it was priceless," Aerick agrees with a chuckle.

Thankfully the mood has lightened and they both begin to relax. The waitress comes to take our order. Aerick doesn't let me order my salad. Instead he orders me the crab cake dinner and I ignore his unnerving need to control things. The guys start discussing some renovations Davy has done to the house on the lake and Aerick tells him about the prospect of him being promoted.

Aerick goes on to tell his Uncle about all I've accomplished, and I sit quietly, watching them talk. I don't mind sitting back and not being the center of attention. It's also nice to see Aerick relaxed and enjoying himself. From what he's told me, he never really got to know his uncle.

"You know, Aerick, you remind me of Dad when you talk about Nadi. It's the same way he used to talk about your Grandma."

Aerick smiles at me, but then something shifts in his eyes.

"So, Uncle Davy. I know you didn't only come here to have dinner. What's going on?" This is news to me. It seemed like that is exactly what this was.

"What? I can't just stop by to visit my nephew?"

"It's been six years. I find it too much of a coincidence that you just happen to be in town and were thinking of me."

His uncle huffs and smirks at Aerick. "No matter what your Dad says, you are highly intelligent and in saying that, I will confess this trip wasn't entirely just to have dinner. However, I think I would enjoy doing this a little more often in the future."

"What's going on?" Relaxed Aerick has disappeared.

"I spoke with Grandpa Scott last week. He is accepting some prestigious lifetime achievement award in the business sector. He has been given several tickets for his family, but you and I both know the extent of family for him is very limited. You know your father would never go, your brother wouldn't go knowing it would upset your father, which only leaves us. He didn't know how to get in contact with you, so he asked if I would get a hold of you and ask you to come. You and Nadi both."

"That could have easily been done when you called me."

He's still suspicious and he must be rubbing off on me because so am I.

"True, but after I heard about your spitfire girl here, I wanted to get the chance to meet her. I also thought a thank you in person was warranted."

"For what?"

"Your brother told me you paid for the funeral out of your inheritance. Dad would have been proud of you. You know he always hated how my brother treated you and paying for that, it made you the better man.

"Because of that I would like to offer to pay your expenses for the two of you to fly out to Chicago with me for the weekend to show our support for good ol' Grandpa Scott."

"You really don't have to do that, Uncle," Aerick says quickly as he shakes off the shock of what he's heard.

"Please Aerick, let me do this one thing. I never really got a chance to be an uncle to you. Besides, I hear Nadi is from Chicago. Maybe she can show us around."

Aerick thinks for a long moment. "Fine. When is it?"

I'm surprised he's giving in so easily, but I'm sure he has his reasons. Davy and Aerick talk out the details. It's extremely short notice. We would have to go this coming Friday and that's only if we can get Luther's approval to leave camp for a few days. I'm not sure, but Aerick says he doesn't think it will be a problem, as long as we come back by Sunday evening.

Listening to them discuss it gives me butterflies. *Chicago!* I'll get to see my family. Just thinking about them has made me realize how much I miss them. I haven't talked to my dad since I was sent here, and I only talk to my mom and brother every once in a while. By the time we leave, I'm really excited!

✳ ✳ ✳ ✳

"He said yes, really?" I ask Aerick as we finish stocking and entering data into the inventory reports. He went and talked to Luther as soon as we got back while several of us unloaded all the stuff we bought today from the trunk.

"Yes, we leave early Friday and we'll get back late Sunday." This actually makes me a little nervous. I'm not keen on the idea of flying and I wish we could spend more than just a few days there, but I'm grateful to be going.

Aerick's uncle already made rental car and hotel arrangements. We're staying in some really nice hotel across town from where my parents' apartment is.

I look at Aerick, who has become quiet. He's deep in thought, concentrating way too hard on straightening the bottles in the cabinet. "What's wrong?" I abandon my inventory count and go over behind him, wrapping my arms around him and laying my head on his back.

"Nothing."

"Come on Aerick, I know you. Please tell me what's going on." He pulls my hands apart and turns in my arms. He sits down, bringing me with him until I'm straddling his lap.

"It's nothing. I get a little wary when my family actually shows any sort of kindness. I don't think he has a hidden agenda, but I'm really not the trusting type."

I huff. "Yeah, so I've noticed. I was a little surprised you gave in so easily. Care to explain?"

"The first thing that popped into my head is that I would get to spend a semi-quiet weekend with you. It has been a while, and I figured this would be the perfect opportunity. Luther is all about family, so I knew he would agree."

"But you agreed to let him pay for everything."

"Yeah, about that. I don't think he would ever hold it against me, so I figured what the hell. I just don't like feeling indebted to people."

"So what, you don't let me pay for anything because you would be in debt to me?" I raise my eyebrow. *Is that what he really thinks?*

"No, no, that's different. You're my woman. It's my job to provide for you. That is, when you aren't trying to take my manhood away from me," he teases, pulling me down by my face to kiss him. *Hmm, I love when he does that.*

Suddenly the door opens, and I jump off Aerick's lap to see Luther standing at the door. "Um. Sorry Luther," I stutter, picking up my abandoned tablet and starting the counting again. Aerick remains in his seat, looking slightly amused but quiet.

"Aerick, I need to see you in my office to discuss next

weekend." Aerick gives him a disapproving look and then looks around at everything that still needs to be put away.

"It's alright, Aerick. I'll do it," I tell him and even though he visibly does not want to leave me with all this work, he nods his head and follows Luther out, giving me a tight smile.

CHAPTER SIX

(Friday, January 15th)

"WE COULD HAVE shared a car," Aerick says irritably to his uncle. It almost feels a little weird calling him that. I mean, his uncle looks as if he could be a friend of Aerick's or even an older brother. In fact, several times I caught them chatting away like they were old-time buddies that haven't seen each other in years.

I suppose that's pretty similar to the truth. It's nice to see Aerick relaxed around him. It's something that I don't see often, but with his uncle, it seems natural. He and Aerick are very much alike, very blunt and straight forward, but I pick up a much more laid-back and joking attitude from Davy. He had us both laughing most of the way to Chicago.

On the plane, they both told me a little about spending time with Aerick's grandpa, and Davy told me a few embarrassing stories about Aerick growing up, like how he was afraid of clowns. Aerick insisted it was a moot point since his parents didn't believe being a clown was a worthy profession, so he didn't have to deal with them often, but the way he glared at Davy told me he would rather I didn't know that bit of information. I find it funny that of all things he could be afraid of, that's it. I didn't give him too much grief about it though, wanting us to continue to enjoy each other's company, but it didn't stop me from trying to get Davy to tell me more.

After a few minutes of bickering at the car rental counter, Aerick gives in, grabbing my hand and leading us over to sit while Davy fills out the paperwork. I take Aerick's hand in both of mine, hoping to break his irritation. It took a lot for him to let his uncle fly us out here and pay for our hotel, but he's really pushing Aerick's patience. He doesn't move, so gently I tug on his hand. He finally looks at me and I raise my eyebrows and give him a pouty face.

After a moment, he takes a deep breath and then brings our entwined hands to his mouth, kissing the back of my hand – his form of an apology. I accept it with a smile, and we sit quietly as we wait for the rental company to ready our cars.

So far, this trip has been great, other than the fact that we have to get back on Sunday morning now. When Luther interrupted us the other day, it was to inform Aerick that Visiting Day was on Sunday and we would need to be present. Apparently, it's usually more eventful than it was when I was a cadet. It's understandable, being all of our families were all the way in Chicago, while our current cadets are mostly from the Seattle area. Luther had let it slip his mind when he first talked to Aerick, so Aerick called and made arrangements with this uncle, which turned out to not be a big deal since our upgraded seats allowed us to change times with no extra fees.

Today has already seemed like such a long day, even though it's only eleven in the morning. We got up super early this morning to make the ninety-minute drive and our five a.m. flight. I lay my head on his shoulder as the exhaustion begins to kick in, but I don't get long to rest. Davy walks over to us and hands Aerick a set of keys.

"I got you a Charger," he says with a grin, but Aerick looks unimpressed. "Hey, at least it isn't a bright red clown car." I giggle at the reference.

Aerick glares at him. "Come on," he says as he takes the keys from his uncle. "Let's get to the hotel and get checked in."

We walk outside in silence and two cars pull up as we walk out. A yellow Mustang convertible, and the other looks similar to a red Dodge Charger, only my face falls in confusion because it's also a convertible. "Wait, Dodge doesn't make a Charger convertible."

My eyes glance to Davy, feeling his stare and see his eyebrows raised as he looks toward Aerick. "She knows cars, too?"

"I know enough. I grew up poor. We fixed our own cars and dreamed about the ones we couldn't afford," I say simply, and he lets out a bellowing laugh.

"She's a keeper, Aerick. It's actually a custom car that they bought for the non-average renter. Nice, huh?"

"You can say that again. I love powerful cars." My enthusiasm is taking over and both Aerick and Davy chuckle.

"Oh, I can show you power," Aerick says in my ear but the grin on Davy's face says he heard it quite clearly. I smack Aerick's arm as my face turns as red as the car.

Taking the opportunity of his inattention while he laughs at my expense, I snatch the keys out of his hand and start toward the car. "Fine, I'm driving."

It only takes a moment before Aerick catches me, picking me up from behind. "Not today, Princess." He grabs the keys out of my hand and sets me down next to the car, opening the door to the passenger side.

I press my lips in a line and proceed to get in, but not before he smacks my ass, leaving a little sting. I sit down, glaring at him.

"There's my good girl," he says sucking his lip in his mouth and biting it as it slides back out, making me forget why I'm irritated. *Hmmm.*

He comes around and gets in. Looking around the car, the inside is just as beautiful as the outside with a top-of-the-line stereo and navigation system, custom-stitch leather bucket seats and impeccable carpeting. He starts the car, revving up the powerful Hemi. *What is it about guys and muscle cars?* Whatever it is, the excitement is noticeably building in me. With the look on Aerick's face, I would say as pissed as he is, he's going to enjoy driving this car. Although he has a Charger, this one has obviously been modified.

"What?" he asks, catching me staring at him yet again.

"Nothing." *Except how crazy hot you look right now.* I smile sweetly at him. He grabs the top of my thigh and squeezes. His signature smirk appears as I squirm in my seat.

"What time are we meeting your brother?"

"He had to go to school today so sometime afterward, or if you don't mind, we could pick him up." I'm dying to see him as soon as possible after being apart for so many months.

"I don't mind."

"Awesome. I'll text him. What do you want to do until then?" He bites his lip as he looks at me with his eyebrows bouncing up and down.

"All afternoon? I thought you wanted to see the city?"

He laughs. "I would much rather be locked in a room all weekend with you."

"Well, I'm back in Chicago for the first time in six months, and I would like to get out and do something. Besides, we have all night and weekend to do that."

He gets a pouty, irritated look on his face. "Fine. Do I at least get a little before we have to pick up your brother?"

"Maybe, if you're good," I tease and he grabs my thigh again, making me jump. "Aerick!"

"What? I'm behaving," he laughs. I can't wait to get to the hotel.

* * * *

Aerick drags his fingers up and down my arm and places light kisses in the wake of his fingers. It feels absolutely incredible. His fingers move to my stomach and down further until they are at the top of my pelvic bone. He places a kiss on my stomach and looks up at me with a half-smile, half-smirk.

"What? You didn't get enough the first time?"

"I will never get enough of you." I get up, throwing his black tee shirt on over my naked body.

"Hey, where are you going?" He whines as he moves to the edge of the bed.

"Sorry babe, but I need a shower and we have to pick my brother up in forty-five minutes." An animalistic growl comes from the bed as I turn and walk into the bathroom. "I'll make it up to you later, I promise," I throw over my shoulder before I turn the shower on.

"Or I could just join you for your shower." His arms wrap around me from behind and he begins kissing my neck. As much as I don't want him to stop, my warring mind is pushing to go see my brother.

"If I don't stop you now, we'll never get out of here." I try to get my heart behind my words but it's becoming increasingly hard as his finger trails between my legs. His fingers begin rubbing me in circles.

"Do you really want to stop me?" he whispers, nipping at my neck.

Damn that feels so good, and hell no, I don't want him to stop. I grab his forearms firmly but don't move them.

"We can be fast. I already got you on edge. Do you want it?" Words evade me as his fingers begin to speed up. "Come on, tell me you want me, Princess. Tell me and I'll help you with that ache that we both know is building inside you." I grab the back of his neck as my head rolls to the side on his shoulder. "Say it." Only a tight moan escapes as he continues. "Say it, babe." The ledge is so close, but I would much rather have him in me when I reach my peak.

"Please," I moan finally. He pushes me forward, stepping us both in the steamy shower and under the water. My shirt is soaked in a second, but he doesn't bother removing it. His chest on my back pushes me to lean forward and instinctively I support myself on the wall with my hands. Without stopping his assault on my clit, he slides into me from behind and I instantly feel the part of me craving him relax as he pushes me to hit my peak. I hear him breathing hard as his forehead presses against the top of my back. He begins slamming into me hard and his fingers move quicker. My legs begin to shake and it impossible to hold off any longer. I let go, moaning Aerick's name, and it only causes him to move quicker and makes my orgasm peak for several more seconds.

After several more thrusts, I begin to come through the end of my release. He grunts loudly and stills inside of me. He's breathing hard and as he slowly pulls out of me, aftershocks shooting through my body threaten to collapse my legs. Feeling his tightened grip around my stomach holding me up, my head falls forward, resting on the wall as I try to regain my composure.

"See, now don't you feel better?"

I laugh, knowing we know that was just as much for him as it was for me. He straightens me up, pulling my arms up before removing his soaked shirt from my body. Turning me around, he places a kiss on my lips. I wrap my hand around his neck, pulling him back down as he begins to lean back and attach my lips to him once more. When we pull apart a moment later, he's wearing that adorable smirk. "Now hurry and wash up before we're late."

Aerick hands me the soap and we quickly begin to wash up, standing side-by-side under the double showerhead. Afterwards we get out and dry off, shooting flirtatious smiles across the room; it's not usually Aerick's style, but I'm loving this carefree side of him. I don't get much time to enjoy it, as we still have a twenty-minute drive to the school. I quickly put on my black skinny jeans, long sleeve shirt and throw my hair up in a wet messy bun. Even as fast as I am, Aerick is already finished, sitting on the bed watching me as I put my Chucks on.

When I finish, he gets up and grabs my hand, pulling me up to him. He engulfs me in a hug, and for a moment, everything falls away. I would be so happy if we could be wrapped in our own bubble forever. He lets out a sigh and kisses the top of my head. "We better get going or we'll be late."

"I know," I say, but don't bother to release my hold. He laughs and shrugs out of my grasp and I pout at the loss of contact

"Come on," he says, grabbing my hand and pulling me out of our room into the living room of our two-bedroom suite. I can hear loud snoring coming from the other room. I had almost forgotten that Davy was in the same suite. It was cheaper this way according to him, but it also gave us the advantage of having a living room and kitchenette. Thankfully, the bedrooms are on opposite sides of the suite. If not for that, I may not be able to look at Davy for the rest of the trip. I really need to learn to quiet down, but with Aerick I find it almost impossible to be quiet.

We leave quietly and our car is waiting for us when we get downstairs. I don't know when he called down to the valet, but I'm grateful because we're running a little late. Using the navigation, Aerick quickly makes his way through the busy Friday traffic to the school.

It's a bit surreal to be back here. Watching the buildings pass by the window of the place I grew up in, I try to hold in the sadness that I'm feeling. As much as I love Aerick and my new job, I still miss this place. We pull up to the school and we've managed to get here right as the last bell rings.

I'm so antsy I can't wait in the car. I jump out of the car and lean up against it, but Aerick doesn't bother. Kids start flooding out of the high school. Had things been different, I would have been a senior this year. Funnily enough, that's the one thing I don't miss. Things like prom, senior trip, and being the leaders of the school never excited me much. I always hated school despite being a good student.

Finally, I see my brother come out the front door, closely followed by Patrick, who starts running toward me as his eyes find mine. When he reaches me, he gives me a quick bear hug before passing me off to my brother. I try hard not to tear up as my brother's arms wrap tightly around me. I've missed him a lot the last few months. For so long, he was the only person I had that understood me.

"Missed you, kid," he says to me before looking down to Aerick. "Aerick."

"Evan," Aerick volleys back, neither sounding too enthused about being around each other.

"Hope you guys don't mind, but I invited Patrick along. What are we doing anyway?" I've already planned everything for this afternoon, wanting to get out and show Aerick the city, since our stay here is extremely limited.

"That's great. I missed both of you. I thought we could take Aerick to Willis Tower and then catch a dinner boat tour. He hasn't ever been to Chicago."

"Sounds good to me, but only if I can pay," Evan says with a smile, but I instantly know that isn't going to go over well after the argument Aerick already had with his uncle.

"Yeah, that's not happening. So, either get in and deal with it, or go home."

Okay, not necessary. "Aerick, knock it off." I turn toward my brother. "Please let him pay, alright: it's our treat, no arguments."

He doesn't look happy but concedes, nodding his head, and I wave my hand toward the car.

"Nice car. Bet it cost a pretty penny to rent this baby," Patrick says. Aerick doesn't say anything but he does rev the engine before pulling out. He gives me that look, making me blush. Thinking about his comment and show of 'power' earlier, I know exactly where his mind is. I'm also fairly certain that knowing he can exert his 'manhood' by picking up the bill is ultimately making him feel better.

✳ ✳ ✳ ✳

"What flavor would you like?"

"Chocolate chip mint, please."

The woman behind the counter makes up my ice cream cone and hands it to me as Aerick orders his and pays for all of them. Our afternoon has been perfect, even though he's been slightly on edge for some reason. Part of me thinks it's because he's not in his element. He can be very particular about things and when things aren't to his liking, it shows.

Evan, Patrick and I head back outside from the ice cream shop and walk over to the railing to wait for Aerick. It's nice that they instinctively keep me out of crowded places. Things have been better, but I still feel uncomfortable when too many people are standing so close to me.

"What now?" Evan asks, stealing a bite of my ice cream.

"Hey brat, knock it off." I pull my ice cream away from him, trying to keep from dropping it. *Brothers!*

"Nadi?" Startled hearing my name unexpectedly, I turned around quickly and instantly freeze. *Oh, shit.* "It is you." He walks up to me with a shy smile. "Hey guys," he says to Evan and Patrick, who both instantly seem more alert. Leaning in, he gives me a quick kiss on my cheek, but I'm too shocked to move away from him. *What are the freaking odds of this?*

After a moment, I shake off the shock. "Uh, hi. How are you?" I need to think of how to handle this situation and quick.

"I'm good. I was sorry to hear about you being shipped off to Washington. That had to have sucked."

"It wasn't too bad; in fact, I'm still living there." *Think, think, I need to end this conversation.*

"Yeah, Evan told me you got a job there. I was a little sad to hear you weren't coming back. You look great, by the way. Not that you didn't look great before. You've always been beautiful," he stutters out.

"Yes. She has." *Shit!* Aerick steps beside me, wrapping his arm around my waist and kissing me on my temple, but his face and tone are a cross of agitation and anger. "You going to introduce me to your friend, babe?"

Taking a deep breath, I attempt to calm my nerves. The last thing I want is for this to get out of control. "Um, yeah. Aerick, this is Vince. Vince, this is my boyfriend, Aerick." *Crap, did I ever tell Aerick about him?* I can't remember. *Crap, Crap, Crap!*

Aerick takes his hand from around me and shakes his hand very firmly. I see Vince bite the inside of his cheek as he shakes

Aerick's hand. He looks to me and back at Aerick several times before he says anything.

"Boyfriend? Wow, um, that's great." Aerick wraps his arm back around me. "Glad to see you have gotten past your, um, issues."

I feel Aerick's glare on me, but I can't bring myself to look up at him. "How exactly do you know Nadi?" he questions. Obviously, not very many people know specifics about my issues.

"I... I... Nadi and I sort of dated for a while last year."

Aerick's grip around me tightens and his fingers dig slightly into my hips. "Really. I don't think she ever told me about that."

Vince seems at a loss for a moment before ignoring Aerick's comment. "So, what are you doing here? Your brother didn't tell me you were going to be in town." I look to my brother, but he merely gives me a slightly apologetic smile as he gives a little shrug. He didn't tell me he had become good friends with Vince or anything.

"We're only in town for a few days." Aerick's short clipped statements are making me a little nervous.

Vince turns his eyes back to me and it seems he doesn't get the point that Aerick really doesn't want him here. "Wow, so you're working and going to college now? Your brother told me you even live at the bootcamp where you work. You really enjoy living at a bootcamp?" He does seem genuinely curious.

"Actually, we only live there part of the year. Nadi moved into my condo on the waterfront just south of Seattle. That's where we live when the camp isn't in session."

Vince's eyebrows shoot up. The longer we stand here the worse this is going to get. "Well, it was nice to see you Vince, but we have to get going. We're on a tight schedule since we're only here two days."

He nods his head. "Alright, maybe I'll see you around next time you're in town."

"Don't bet on it," Aerick murmurs and I can't help but roll my eyes.

"Bye." He looks as if he wants to say something more but thinks better of it. He turns to my brother. "I'll see you guys around." My brother and Patrick both say goodbye and the four of us start walking down the pier in the opposite direction.

Aerick is quiet but he hasn't let me go. Today has been such a good day; I don't want the last few minutes to ruin it. We spent the last few hours going all around Chicago. We went to Willis Tower and went up to the sky deck. Aerick held me from behind as we looked out over the city. For a moment just standing there, it was as if we were alone, flying high in the sky.

Then we went on a boat tour and had dinner. I spent the whole time pointing things out to him and telling him about the city. We told Aerick stories from our younger days, like how we used to play tag in the big hotel and sneak into the pool on hot summer days. It was nice to get to show him where I grew up.

I don't think he's mad at me and really, he has no reason to be mad at me for having an ex-boyfriend – he's had more than his share of ex-girlfriends; but then again, with Aerick, I never can tell. I love him, but sometimes his logic is a pain in the ass. I fight with the idea of whether or not to say something, but I'm probably better off giving him a minute to think through his thoughts so he doesn't say something he doesn't mean. I decide to slide my hand in his back pocket and keep walking. *Umm, he has such a fine ass.*

By the time I've finished my ice cream cone I can feel that he's relaxed just a bit, but I can tell we're heading back for the car. I wasn't ready to leave; I was merely trying to get away from Vince before something bad happened. The sun is setting but I really can't think of anything else we could go do. I'm not ready to leave my brother. Tomorrow evening we're spending with his family, so this is it.

I look to my brother. "It's Friday night. What is the plan?"

Evan looks at me, a little surprised. "We're actually supposed to go to the club later." *Crap.* Supposed to go, meaning they're going to be selling. "But we can do something else if you want to."

I don't want to ruin their night either, especially if it's getting in the way of him making money. "No, that's fine. You go have fun."

"What are you guys going to do?" he asks, seemingly conflicted.

"I was thinking I'd show Aerick around the neighborhood." I see Aerick glance at me for a moment out of the corner of his eye.

"Alright, but please stay out of trouble," he jokes and I kick the side of his leg, making him laugh.

We make it back to the car and I take one more look at the dying sun before getting in. It's beautiful reflecting off the water all the magical colors but even as pretty as it is, it doesn't have anything on the sunsets I see at our condo. Funnily enough, it's making me miss it, but I don't know if that's a good thing or a bad thing. Just because I moved away, doesn't mean I want to forget where I came from. This place is me. It made me who I am and even as fucked-up as that is, I wouldn't want it any other way. This place and the things that happened in it are the only reason I met Aerick. They say what knocks us down makes us stronger and in my case it's true, but I was lucky enough to find someone who could catch me when I was no longer able to get back up by myself.

I hear Aerick say my name quietly and I'm brought out of my thoughts to see that I'm the only one not in the car yet. I quickly slip into my seat and shut the door, a little embarrassed. Aerick gives me a questioning look but I shake my head and punch my address into the GPS.

"Patrick? We taking you home?" I ask quickly, trying to get the attention off me, since everyone in the car is currently staring at me.

"No. Just back to your house." It isn't my house anymore, but I don't bother to correct him. I turn around and stare out of the front as Aerick pulls out and heads south.

As we head further out of the main touristy area of Chicago, I watch the scenery change. For someone who didn't grow up here, you may not notice some of the differences, but I know better. As in any great city, there's always the bad outlying areas and Chicago is no different.

It actually makes me curious. Seeing the faces of the young people on the streets. *How many of them are going to end up in a camp like ours?* Gavin's camp is opening in only a few short months. I'm curious to know if their camp will get the same results as ours. I wonder if some of those kids that end up there will be people I know.

I don't think I could work there. I don't know how I'd be able to deal with that. It's one thing to act tough and like a bitch to strangers, but to people I've known? People I've grown up with? It would be too weird. Working at the camp, you almost have to be a bit of a bully, which is completely opposite to my life here. I was always the protector, the one who stood up to the bullies. People here may look at my life now and say I'm not who I once was. Really, they're right and again, I don't know if that's a good thing or a bad thing. I'm dying to relax and want clear my mind – I know the best place to do it.

We pull up to the apartments and Aerick parks the car but doesn't turn it off. "Are mom and dad here?" I ask, looking back to my brother.

"Nope. Dad's working a double and mom is spending the weekend at her cousin's. Why?"

I turn to Aerick. "Come on. I want to show you where I used to live." He raises an eyebrow at me, turning the car off, and we all get out. Going inside, we head straight to the stairs. Living here, you learn quickly, the elevator is never a safe option. It breaks down more than my uncle's old Chrysler. When it is working, there's usually someone there charging people to use it. My brother would get us through with his reputation but with Aerick's temperament right now, it's better to avoid it anyway.

When we finally reach our floor, several stories up, Aerick lets out a half chuckle. "No wonder you were in decent condition when you got to camp." We all laugh as my brother lets us into the apartment. It isn't much, but it was home for what seems like forever.

Patrick says his goodbyes after covertly getting something from my brother's room. I take it that he's back to his old ways and the smell coming from his backpack as he walks past me only solidifies my assumption. It's clear Aerick is having a hard time holding his tongue but he somehow manages. Feeling the tension, my brother quickly excuses himself saying he needs to get ready, so I give a quick tour.

Aerick's expression doesn't give away much as I show him around the small three-bedroom apartment. "But my favorite place isn't actually inside," I explain as I finish only a minute later. He gives me a confused look and I grab his hand and head for the fire escape. I feel the hesitation in his grip, but he follows. Once outside, I let go of his hand but don't stop as I head up toward the roof without looking back. I make my way up on top and walk over to my favorite spot, stepping up the half a foot onto the ledge as I have done so many times before.

"What are you doing?" Aerick asks as he steps onto the roof, but I don't answer. I look out at the neighborhood. It only makes everything that's happened seem even more surreal. It feels as if I haven't been here in years instead of months. Barely a year ago, I was standing in this exact spot debating if I even wanted my life to continue and now, I'm so grateful it did.

I feel his arms wrap around me. "Hey. You okay?"

A deep breath fills my lungs. Even the air here is different. I have gotten so used to the fresh air of the mountains. "Yeah. It's kind of nostalgic."

"Do you miss living here?" Worry laces his words. I don't know why he's always doubting that I'm happy with him.

"No, not really. I love living with you. It's just, this is where I grew up. This was all I knew for so long. It's weird being back here. It feels like I've been gone for so long." His arms tighten around me and I look down, leaning forward slightly, trusting him to keep me from falling.

"This used to be my favorite place to come. Whenever I was mad, or sad, or lonely. I'd come sit up on this ledge. Sometimes I'd sit here for hours and watch everyone go about their business. It gets pretty interesting this time of day, in fact, and Friday and Saturday are usually the most eventful."

The sun has recently set, and you can see everyone starting to come out and make their way to whatever festivity they have planned. Aerick still hasn't said anything and even being in my favorite spot, it's making me feel on edge. Without thinking twice, I step forward off the ledge, only to feel Aerick instantly yank me back. "What the fuck?!"

"Oh good, you're still there. With all this silence, I was starting to think I was up here by myself." I tighten my arms over his, still tightly gripped around my waist. "Come on, sit with me." Still not saying anything, he lowers me slowly so that I can sit down and still keeps his one arm around me as he sits next to me so that our legs dangle over the edge.

"Well, this explains your non-existent fear of heights." A bit of relief floods into me as he finally speaks, but I only shrug my shoulders. It isn't that I'm not afraid of heights, I just don't let them bother me too much. Standing up on the lookout certainly took my breath away, but when I got over the initial shock, it allowed me to see the beauty around me.

I lean against his shoulder and look up. "It's so amazing how many more stars you can see when you're in the mountains. I mean, I used to think how crazy that there were so many stars in the sky when I sat up here at night, but the first time I looked at the sky from camp, it was mind blowing."

"Mind-blowing, huh?"

I sigh. "Seriously? Of everything I said, that's all you heard?" *Men!*

"I was just saying. I can think of a few other things that were mind blowing."

I let out an exaggerated huff. "Yeah, such as?" I feel him turn his head toward me, so I look up at him.

"Well, for starters, your confidence." I raise my eyebrows at him. "Seriously. I had my doubts when I first saw you. You seemed like this little girl and then that attitude and confidence appeared, it shocked me. I couldn't believe it. You seemed completely immune to my intimidating and overbearing nature and carried yourself like you had no doubts. Then I saw that blush on your cheeks, and I was hooked. Yet another completely unknown and mind-blowing emotion." He kisses me lightly.

His voice deepens and his face gets completely serious. "Then I started falling for you: mind blowing. Falling in love with you: mind blowing. The first time we made love, so much more than mind blowing. And I could probably keep going for the next hour." He bites his lip, giving me that look, and I swear I'm going to spontaneously combust. *How the hell does he do that to me?*

His lips are suddenly on mine, taking away all my thoughts. I grab his face with my one free hand, trying to pull him impossibly closer. I gasp as he grabs my waist without breaking our kiss and pulls me onto his lap so that I'm straddling him. My heart quickens knowing there's a very long drop behind me. I tighten my legs around his waist, only making him grab my ass tighter. My adrenaline is going crazy with all my senses on high alert.

Pulling his hair hard, I deepen his kiss, rewarding me with a loud groan that resonates deep in his chest. *Ahhh fuck!* His hands slide just beneath my shirt without exposing anything to anyone, but right now I couldn't care less even if the whole neighborhood was watching. The feeling of his hands on me, right here, right now, is definitely mind blowing. "How about this? Does this register as mind blowing for you?" I whisper on his lips.

"Hell fucking yes." Kissing me more vigorously, he rolls his hips up and I feel the bulge in his pants making me moan.

"Really, you guys?" My brother's voice screeches through the air. Aerick's irritated growl matches mine as our perfect moment is ruined. "I was coming to say goodbye, but we can skip it if you want."

I rest my head on Aerick's chest. "No," I grumble. "I love you, brother, but right now I really, really dislike you." Aerick and Evan both chuckle, irritating me more. *Fine.* I push all my weight forward quickly, causing Aerick to lose balance and fall backward onto the roof, taking me with him. He looks up at me in shock. "Keep laughing," I say and I hear my brother break out in another bought of laughter as I stand up, leaving Aerick lying on the ground.

"Got to be careful with her, Aerick."

"Trust me, you don't need to tell me." He jumps up and brushes himself off.

"Come give me a damn hug," I tell my brother as I walk toward him.

The minute my brother leaves I'm dragging Aerick back to the hotel, where we can hopefully be uninterrupted – Davy is out hanging with some old friend tonight. I hug my brother tightly and we say our goodbyes. He promises to come visit on his next break from school and then leaves us alone once again on the rooftop. The neighborhood is getting louder as people begin enjoying their Friday night.

"Let's get back to the hotel so I can give you something to write down on your 'mind blowing' list." *Oh Christ.* That fucking smirk is going to be the death of me. At least our minds are in sync. I grab his hand and pull him quickly toward the fire escape, wanting to get back to the hotel as quickly as possible.

CHAPTER SEVEN

(Sunday, January 17th)

Aerick POV

"PLEASE, MAN! I need you to do this for me." This is such adolescent behavior. It's not right that someone so tough is whining at me like a little girl.

"Paulo, I don't want this responsibility. Why don't you ask Brand to do it?"

"You're joking, right? I don't trust him to hold on to it. Come on, please?" I let out a low growl in displeasure. He has been pestering me for the last hour about this and I have no time for it. There is a stack of paperwork that needs to be finished before people start to arrive. The only bad thing about taking a few days off is that you come back to twice the work.

"Fine." I must be crazy to do this. I'm actually agreeing to hold onto his engagement ring. *What the hell am I thinking?* "You owe me big time. I can't even believe you're going to propose. You guys really haven't been together that long. How do you know you want to be with her for the rest of your life?" Not that I haven't had a thought or two about proposing to Nadi, but it's a huge step, and Paulo has never really been the tied-down type, which is why we always got along so well.

"Dude, there's no way I will ever find someone like her. She's incredible, smart, and for some crazy reason, she actually loves me. I've got to do something to hold her down."

"Do you really think she would break up with you?"

"I don't know, but I sure in hell ain't gonna wait to find out. I'm going to lock her down before she has a chance to run. You know what they say, if you like it, put a ring on it!"

I can't help but chuckle. "Okay, whatever you say."

"Do you really think it's too early to ask her?"

"You're asking me? How am I supposed to know? The only long-lasting monogamous relationship I've been in is with Nadi, and our relationship is far from normal."

"Fuck man, I don't know. I love her, and I just don't want her to slip away."

"So, you're telling me that you're only marrying her because you're afraid she's going to leave you?"

"No. That isn't the only reason. I love her and I can see us spending the rest of our lives together. Don't you ever feel the same about Nadi?"

Hell yes. I've thought about what our lives would be like if we got married, but we are still struggling to get over what happened to her. "Yeah, maybe, but I don't think it would be a good idea to go down that road right now. I think we need some normalcy before we think about those things."

* * * *

"Wow, you were right. This is a lot more people than when I was here." Her soothing voice speaks up beside me.

I really try hard not to look at her as we do a perimeter walk. After a small argument with Luther, I got him to agree to keep Nadi from walking around by herself today. The last thing I need is for something else to happen to her. She bumps my arm with her own and when I look at her, she has a questioning look on her face.

"What?"

She smiles in that adorable way, causing a small twitch in my pants that I hope she doesn't notice. "I asked if this is normal."

I look around and there are a bunch of people roaming around with whichever cadet they are visiting. "Yes, this is pretty typical. During your session we were all pretty bored. Normally it takes all of us to keep an eye on things, which is why Jack and Shannon chose to visit today. They get to spend the day with their loved ones in exchange for helping out for a few hours. It's a win-win for Luther. "

She nods her head and looks around at the various small groups scattered everywhere. I take the time to do the same. Luther didn't want her distracting me today and I have no intention of giving him a reason to say no in the future.

My attention is drawn to an older man and Skyler; they are walking back toward the far side of the dorm building. I wouldn't usually think of it as odd except Skyler looks off, shoulders slumped, staring at the ground as he walks. Way out of character for him. *This can't be good.*

I slightly tug at Nadi's sleeve to get her to follow and start walking in Skyler's direction in a roundabout way, so they don't notice that we are following them. Nadi doesn't question me and it only takes a second before her eyes light up in understanding. It is so nice to be with someone who can just look and understand me without words. Sometimes I wonder if she is psychic; it's as if she knows what I want and merely does it – well, most of the time. Then again, if that were true, she would do what I ask and keep the bad shit from happening to her, but it is nice when it works.

Focus! I look up to see Skyler glancing back with apprehension as he rounds the corner and then disappears behind the building. Seeing his face puts all of my nerves on high alert. Every year there is something. Someone tries to get away or tries to sneak something into camp. Fortunately for me, I tend to pick up on people even when they're trying not to be suspicious. It is not happening on my watch.

As we approach the corner staircase I slow and wave to Nadi to get behind me. I need to get a sense of what I am dealing with before we go after them. On rare occasions people to try to get weapons in here and the last thing I need is Nadi in danger again.

She gives me a questioning look but complies. We stop when we reach the stairs.

"Are you fucking joking me? What kind of Brady Bunch shit is going on here?" The older man's voice is harsh but low. "This looks more like a fucking weekend outing then a bootcamp. How are you ever supposed to learn shit here? What do they do here? Probably sit around the campfire singing nursery rhymes."

Skyler is silent but I have yet to hear anything too concerning. Most parents don't get the point of this place. They just get to see the aftermath when their child comes home, typically better behaved than when they left. My father would probably be saying the same thing. Then again, he never even bothered to visit when I was here – nor did my mother. They would rather try to hide the fact that I had even gotten in trouble.

"What the hell, you little shit? I asked you a question." My nerves are back on edge again as his voice turns menacing and slightly louder. Nadi goes to walk in front of me but I grab her wrist. She obviously is uncomfortable with his tone too. Still, we shouldn't interfere unless he is in danger. "Boy, you better answer me!"

"It's, um it's..." Skyler reaches for words barely above a mumble.

"It's what? Speak up, you retard. I see they haven't even taught you proper speaking skills." *Asshole.* I am starting to get a good idea about what kind of man he is. He reminds me too much of a man I know all too well.

"We do a lot of stuff here. They keep us pretty busy. We go to classes, and we exercise a lot."

"Classes? What good does that shit do? Sounds like a cakewalk to me. This place ain't gonna change nothing with you. It's just another hole for them to stick screw-ups and pretend they're trying to help. Mark my words, this place will never help a kid like you. You will always be a fucked-up troublemaker who is too stupid to not get caught. What a fucking waste of my tax dollars. They even got girls in your damn dorm. Not that any of them would ever give two bits about you. What a joke."

"That's not true."

"You calling me a liar, boy?"

"No sir. I'm only saying this place isn't so bad." Wow, you could have fooled me. I was under the impression he hated it here.

"Isn't so bad. What the fuck? You turning into a sissy? Is hanging out with all those girls turning you into a weak little pussy?" *What the hell is wrong with this guy?*

"I am NOT a pussy," Skyler says loudly.

"Who the fuck do you think you're talking to, you little shit?" Immediately I start to move and I hear something slam against the wall. "Better remember who you're talking to, you little bastard!"

"Hey!" I shout, but it is a second too late as he swings and hits Skyler square in the jaw. He doesn't even try to block it and his head snaps to the side, but his body is pinned against the wall, keeping him from falling down.

"This isn't your business, just walk away. This is between me and my son." *Not today!*

"This is my camp, he is my cadet, and that makes it my business. Now let him go." He slams Skyler hard against the wall before releasing him and taking a step toward me. Nadi goes to take a step toward him. I can see the rage in her face, but this is no place for her. I quickly step in front of her. "Nadi, take Skyler into the dorm please while I talk with his father."

"I'm not done here."

"Yes, you are. Skyler, go with Nadi." Skyler moves toward her, but his father grabs his arm as Nadi steps out from behind me toward Skyler, making me a bit nervous, but I focus back on the asshole in front of me. "Remove your hands from him now."

"Or what? This is my fucking kid and if I think he needs a smack here or there to keep him in line, then that is what he's going to get."

I take one more step so that I am directly in front of him. "I will only say it one more time. Remove your hand from him."

"Fuck you, asshole. If I want to beat the shit out of this sorry excuse for a son, then that is what I'm going to do, and there isn't anything you or this little bitch can do to stop me. He deserves everything he gets, so back the fuck off." He pulls at Skyler's arm, moving him back toward him.

I warned him. Without another thought, I swiftly punch him in the jaw in the same manner I saw him do to Skyler minutes ago. He goes down to one knee, letting go of Skyler, and looks up at me shocked, as does Skyler.

"Skyler, go inside with Nadi. That is an order, cadet." I keep my outside composure, but on the inside, I want to beat this douche bag to a bloody pulp.

He stands up straighter and looks at his father in disgust. I can't help but feel how much I would have loved to do that to my father when I was his age. "Yes sir." He turns, heading toward the dorm, and Nadi falls in behind him.

"You son of a bitch. You think that you're saving that boy. He'll be out of here soon and then he won't have you to fight for him."

"I don't need anyone to fight for me." I look over my shoulder to see Skyler and Nadi have stopped at the corner.

I look back to his father but speak loud enough for Skyler to hear. "You're right. You don't, because this will never happen again. If by some chance it did, you now know how to protect yourself and I damn well expect you to. No matter who it is, you have the right to protect yourself. Is that clear, cadet?"

He glances at his dad and then nods at me. "Good. Now go." As they turn around and head for the stairs, I watch his father get up, looking half angry, half confused. I lower my voice and glare hard at him as I lean in. "As for you, if I ever hear about you touching him again, and trust me I will hear about it, I will find you and next time I won't stop at just one punch." *Stupid fucking child-abusing, sorry excuse for a father.*

"Are you threatening me?"

"Threatening you," I shake my head and frown mockingly.

114

"No." I straighten up and give him a small smile as if we are having an everyday conversation. "Only stating a fact. Now get the hell off my property before I call the police." He gives me a dirty look but smartly stalks off toward the parking lot.

I let out a deep sigh and head inside to check on the kid. As much as I disliked him, things are starting to come into perspective. According to his file, he lost his mother to a car accident when he was five and is being raised by his father, a suspected drunk that may have a drug problem. No wonder he has so much aggression.

After pausing to watch him walk between the buildings toward the parking lot, I walk into the dorm. Nadi is sitting on a chair in front of him as he sits on his bed. They are talking quietly, but he seems calm. "Are you okay, cadet?"

In a rush, he stands and turns toward me. His bad guy act is back in full swing. "I didn't need you to step in. I could have handled it." I push back the irritation at the fact that Nadi had to jump up to avoid his sudden outburst. I also don't believe for one moment that he would have 'dealt with' his father, but I do believe his pride is hurt. With that in consideration, I take a quick calming breath.

"I know. I figured it was better for me to get in trouble for hitting him instead of you." I shrug my shoulders, playing it off as Nadi presses her lips in a line. She is obviously pissed, but I know kids like him. He wouldn't have hit him. He would have merely stood there and taken it, but it isn't my job to sit here and put him down, it is to help him build confidence in himself so he can become a better person. "Now, go to the infirmary and get some ice for that jaw."

"I don't need–"

"Don't forget who you are talking to. I stepped in because your father was wrong to do what he did. I, on the other hand, am not him. I have done nothing to earn your disrespect and I will not allow you to act as such. I would never stoop as low as to hit you, but I will discipline you if you continue in this current manner. Don't let your pride overpower what is right. Do you understand, cadet?" He stares at me for a few more seconds before he walks off without another word. As much as I dislike the fact that he didn't answer me, I watch him walk out of the dorm with his head hung low. He has been through enough for the moment.

Nadi barely waits until the door closes fully. "What the hell was that?" I don't face her because with that tone I can already see her face in my head. "Luther is going to be pissed!"

"Luther doesn't need to know," I say quietly, hoping she will calm down.

"Luther knows everything that goes on here. He'll find out. Why would you jeopardize your job?"

"What was I supposed to do, nothing? Let him be knocked around by that piece of shit?"

"Absolutely not, but you didn't need to hit him."

"Well, he deserved it."

"I'm not saying that he didn't, but you're supposed to be the responsible adult here. What you did was childish."

"Are you calling me a child?" Anger rises in me quickly and I turn toward her.

"I'm not calling you a child; I said your actions were childish. How many times have you preached control to me, and then you pull something like that?"

"Because you needed it, making you the least qualified person to stand here and lecture me about it!" I shout, instantly regretting it as I see sadness and anger filling her eyes.

She walks up to me barely containing in her own ire. "Glad to know how you really feel," she says quietly, without looking me in the eyes, and steps around me, heading for the door. *Fuck!*

"Babe, stop." But she doesn't even pause. Great, this would be one of those times she takes what I said the wrong way. "Hey..." I grab her shoulder quickly trying to keep her from opening the door. She instantly becomes tense under my hand, making me drop it immediately. *Double fuck!*

I know better than to do that when she is being emotional. At least she has stopped, but she makes no attempt to speak or to even turn to face me. I didn't mean what I said. I'm more irritated that she's right. I really didn't think my actions through before I acted.

She remains quietly facing the door with her back to me. I have to say something, I don't want to fight with her. We had such a good time in Chicago, we have been on a natural high since we got back. I have been feeling up in the clouds, kind of like I felt standing with her at Willis Tower looking over the city from the sky deck. I felt as if it was only us, in our own little shell, looking out over the city below.

"I didn't mean to shout at you. I was frustrated. Don't be mad at me." She doesn't say anything, so I risk it and lightly run my fingers down her arms. I feel her relax slightly under my touch, a good sign.

Pulling her hair to the side I kiss her gently behind her ear, trying to kiss away the last few minutes. She takes a deep breath and leans back into me.

"It just worried me. I know you want Ayla's position. On top of that, what if Luther decided to fire you? I've worked my butt off to be able to get this position here. So that I could be here with you. I did this for you… for us."

Shit. She's right again. I didn't think about that. Actually, I really didn't think at all, which is the real problem, and she's right on both counts. I know better not to act on a whim like that and I should have realized that my actions don't only affect me now. It is my job to take care of her; it's not only my life anymore. She put a lot of faith in me by giving up her life and staying here with me.

"I suppose it probably wasn't a good idea to hit him."

"You think?" she says sarcastically as she turns around and wraps her arms around my neck. "Please, keep your cool in the future." She lays her head on my shoulder and I wrap my arms around her, hugging her tightly to me. "Apology accepted."

My eyebrows shoot up. "Apology?" *Where did she get that*

from?

"Am I mistaken? Should I still be mad at you?" She pulls back with her lips pressed into a line.

"Well no, but..."

"But what?" I am at a loss for words. She totally pulled me into that.

"Nothing." *Ugh,* this woman is so frustrating. I shake my head with a little chuckle and give her a peck on her lips. "We better get back to patrolling before we really do get into trouble." A grin spreads across her face. She grabs my hand and we head back outside.

As we pass through the doorway, I pull my hand out of hers. After a brief moment of pouting, her smile returns. I scan my surroundings again and everything seems quite normal, or as normal as can be expected. Visiting only lasts another hour and then we can relax a little since there is no evening P.T. The only part that sucks is I'll have to spend most of the night going over the surveillance videos to check for suspicious activity.

In the past, I didn't mind going through them while everyone else sat around drinking and hanging out with each other. Big groups aren't my thing. It would have been nice to hang out with Nadi tonight, though. I suppose it is only fair being we got the last few days off. The next few months can't go fast enough. I can't wait to have her all to myself again.

Nadi slows and I follow suit. Following her gaze toward the staff cabins, I don't see anything out of the ordinary. Luther and

Gavin are talking in front of them, and an older couple is walking with one of the cadets, but that's it.

"Do you see something?" I keep scanning the area in that direction, but she doesn't answer. "Nadi?"

She stops and hesitantly looks up toward me. "Huh?"

"You okay?"

She shakes her head as if to clear it. "Yeah, I'm fine." She's off, almost looking confused, and it puts me on edge.

"You're sure?"

She smiles up at me, but it doesn't quite reach her eyes. "Yeah. Just tired, spacing out a little. I need some coffee."

"We can go get some."

"It's okay. You don't have to come with me, I can grab it and meet you back out here."

Yeah right, that is not happening. "It's alright, I could use some myself. It's going to be a long night for me." She nods her head and we start moving toward the mess hall.

Once we get inside, she relaxes a little, but her arms are wrapped around herself. I press my lips in a line. "Where's your jacket?" I scold her lightly as I notice she only has her sweater on.

"I left it in the dorm. With all the adrenaline running through me, I was hot, so I took it off and left it on Skyler's chest. I didn't even realize I was cold until now."

Geez. She really doesn't have any sense of self-preservation. I slide my jacket off and put it around her shoulders. I make our coffees as she slides her arms in the sleeves, her smile returning.

Paulo walks up to us as I finish and hand her a cup. "Hey guys. What's up?"

"Not much. Mister Macho over here decided Skyler's dad was a douche bag and hit him, but other than that it's been fairly uneventful."

"What, are you kidding me?" Paulo looks at me expectantly.

This is not the time or place and I glare at her. "I'll tell you...."

Nadi suddenly spits her coffee all over the front of Paulo, cutting me off.

"What the hell?" Paulo yells, jumping back. My face is scrunched up, trying not to laugh, until I see her hand.

Her eyes are wide staring at the little box she's holding. Paulo finally stops trying to brush himself off and looks to see her shocked face before looking at me.

"Babe, it isn't what you think," I try to explain quickly.

In less than a second, she hands her coffee to Paulo, puts the box back into the pocket, takes the jacket off and hands it to me. "Nadi, I..."

"I'm sorry. I shouldn't have been going through your pockets. Sorry." She turns and runs out the back door of the mess hall. *What the hell was that all about?* I mean, I know it must have been a shock and I can imagine what she thought, but her reaction leaves me flabbergasted.

"I fucking told you, Paulo. This is just my luck."

"Does she think...? Why is it in your pocket? Why was she wearing your jacket?"

"Not now."

She's freaking out. I don't even know how to process that. Shoving my coffee at him, I take off after her, not caring that I spilled my coffee on Paulo.

"Dammit, Aerick!"

It only takes two steps out the door before I see her crouched down with her back against the building and her hands covering her face. If I didn't know better, I would say she was hyperventilating as I hear her trying to take deep breaths. I really wish I knew what was going through her head right now.

"Hey." Not wanting to freak her out any more than she already is, I crouch down in front of her instead of trying to touch her. I understand her being upset but I didn't ever think she would react this way. *What if it really was for her? What if I had decided to propose?*

"I'm sorry. I don't know what to think right now. I wasn't expecting something like this. I'm so sorry, Aerick."

"You don't need to apologize. It's not what you think." But now I'm a little worried about my thoughts. She doesn't want this. That hurts a bit, since I couldn't imagine not being with her. Marriage is an eventual and logical next step. Maybe she needs a little time. I can only hope it's that and not something else.

"We're young. Are you sure you've thought this through? I mean, this is a big step. It hasn't been that long and there's so much, so much... Me, are you sure you want this with me?" I put my finger on her lips to quiet her rambling. She is talking so fast I can barely understand her, and she is two seconds from hyperventilating again.

"Nadi, please calm down. That ring isn't mine." She looks at me horribly confused. "I'm holding it for Paulo, he is going to propose to Terrie."

"You mean this wasn't..."

"No, but do you really not want to marry me?" I try to keep my voice even but I am not successful. Now that I've asked the question, I'm not sure I want to hear the answer. My heart constricts painfully at the thought that she might say no. I've thought about it, and I do want to, but I was afraid that she would react just like this. Well, not this dramatically, but that she would think it is too soon to get married.

"It's not that, Aerick."

Could have fooled me. "Then what is it?" Because that is exactly what it seems like.

"Aerick, I'm probably the most fucked-up, unlucky person in this state. Hell, maybe even the entire country. Do you really want to go through life constantly worrying about me? I'm broken, damaged, and you deserve so much better than me." I hate hearing her voice so weak, so self-deprecating.

Thinking about it more carefully, I suppose the problem really isn't me. I wish she would stop doubting herself. I carefully grab her shoulders and pull us up to standing, but she keeps her head down, so I pull it up as well. "Hey, I love you and want to spend the rest of my life with you. You're not ready to take that step and that's fine, I'm okay with that. It doesn't make me love you any less, and one day when you are ready, we can take that next step together."

She grins and a tear escapes her eye. "I think I can handle that."

"Good, because it wasn't up for discussion. One day you will be my wife," I say playfully.

"Really? You know, I could always say no." If it wasn't for the sarcastic grin, I would be hurt.

"Yeah, but would you really want to?"

"Hmm, spend the rest of my life with a protective, intelligent, hot boot camp instructor, or live the rest of my life alone? That's a hard one."

I love it when she's playful. "Well here, let me help you choose." I take her face gently in my hands and kiss her, letting her melt between my hands. When I stop, I sense that she is much more relaxed. "How about now?"

"I don't know, you think you could show me again?" she says breathlessly.

I happily grant her request. Spending the rest of my life doing this? Yes, I would be perfectly content with this. I can only hope when I really do ask her, I get a much different response.

I break our kiss much sooner than I want to but know I have to. "We have to get back before anyone realizes we're gone and for the record, I want to thank you for getting Paulo back. I never wanted to hold on to that ring to begin with. The look on his face was priceless."

"So, you've really thought about marrying me?" she asks shyly.

"All in good time, Princess. I'm in no hurry, and I'm not going anywhere." I give her one last kiss and grab her hand, leading us back inside.

CHAPTER EIGHT

(Saturday, January 23rd)

I WALK SLOWLY down the aisle toward Aerick, who's standing patiently waiting, for once. I don't think I have ever seen him look more handsome. The sleek black suit shows off his perfectly sculpted body. A navy-blue vest peaks out from under his jacket along with a matching tie, brightening his eyes, which are frozen on me. I'm incredibly nervous, even though I know I shouldn't be. This is the man I want to spend the rest of my life with.

Paulo, Trent, Jeff, and Aerick's brother Greg are all lined up next to him in matching suits with smiles on their faces. Terrie, Shannon, Andi and my oldest sister are lined up on the opposite side. Blue and white flowers are beautifully laid out on the stage and throughout the room, accented by ribbon and lace. It's everything I've always wanted, small and personal but breathtaking.

Staring at me are the faces of people closest to us. My mom, brother and sisters, Aerick's Uncle Davy and Grandpa Scott, Luther and everyone from camp. My dad tightens his arm around mine as we reach the end of the aisle and the music stops.

As the pastor starts to speak, I see his lips move, but no sound comes out. My father moves beside me and gives me a kiss on the cheek before leaving me standing there by myself. Gesturing, the pastor waves for me to join Aerick but my feet are stuck. Again, I try to move forward but it's as if I'm stuck in cement. I yell out to Aerick, whose expression has turned confused.

What's going on?

Just a few more steps and I'll reach him. I want this, to be with him. I want to spend my life with him.

Why can't I move?

I try again, finally moving slightly, but instead of taking a step forward, I take a step back. I don't want to go back; I want to go forward. I want him. Putting more strength into my legs, I lift my foot again to move forward but only succeed in taking another step back. Please, I want to go to him!

Panic explodes in me as I lose the last bit of composure I was holding onto. I put all my energy in moving toward him, but the more I struggle to go forward, the further away from him I get. Tears begin streaming down my face and my heart breaks as his expression turns to sadness.

Please, please – I want this, I want him. He lowers his head as Paulo lays a hand on his shoulder. This isn't how it's supposed to be. We were going to be happy, finally happy. I scream for him once more as I move back out of the room and the door slams shut in my face.

I wake up in a pool of sweat. The clock on the nightstand reads four in the morning. *Why can't I ever have a happy dream?*

Terrie is still sleeping soundly in her bed and it's still pitch-black outside. In the back of my mind I know I should go back to bed, but my body is tingling. I need to get up and move. Getting out of bed, I slip on some sweats and a hoodie. I grab my jacket and leave my cabin quietly, so I don't wake Terrie.

It's been a crazy winter and it's still freezing cold outside. There's still some snow on the ground but it hasn't snowed in over a week. Only the low temperatures have kept the snow around. As I stare at the stars that are so bright in the sky, I quickly put on my coat. The cold, fresh air awakens my body, making me feel a lot better as the remnants of my dream begin to fade away.

I really only have two choices: I can walk around the track or I can go to the gym. Aerick would probably have a heart attack if I was outside this early all by myself, so I opt to go to the gym and avoid a potential argument. It's irritating to make a decision based on his reaction but in hindsight, I don't tend to make the best decisions. Actually, that may be an understatement. I need to start thinking things all the way through instead of acting on pure emotion.

As I almost reach the gym, I decide there is no way that I'm going to survive the day without caffeine and detour to the mess hall to make some coffee first. I have plenty of time to drink a cup and get in a quick workout on the bag before everyone gets up. I stifle a laugh as a thought comes to mind. I'm even starting to act like Aerick, working out before working out.

Inside, the mess hall is awkwardly quiet. There's usually someone in here all day long, whether it's prepping meal, stocking supplies or organizing meal schedules. Now that it's winter, many of the cadets come in here just to get out of the dorm since the weather isn't suitable for being outside. I come in here often to find one sitting at the table working on their assignments.

As expected, the pot is ready to brew. Waiting for it to brew, I stand at the window looking out at the stars. Time seems to be flying by. Visiting day was last week, marking the halfway point of the session.

I can already see subtle changes in the cadets. Several of them are starting to show characteristics of wanting to succeed, showing more respectful behavior, even the desire to better themselves. It makes me proud that I've been a small part of that. Although my part is not as prevalent in camp yet, I know it will come, and that feeling of accomplishment will be even more fulfilling.

It'll definitely make up for this ridiculous schooling regiment. All these late nights up studying for tests and doing homework will soon be over and I'll have finally accomplished something to be proud of. A degree in education, an awesome job, and an amazing boyfriend. I'll have all that and a whole lot less stress. I have no delusions that the rest of my life will be a cakewalk, but with everything that has gone wrong, I can only see them getting much easier for me.

The coffee pot beeps that it has finished, and I pour my cup of coffee. As I turn around, I'm startled by a figure standing inside the door staring at me. I fumble my cup in my hand and somehow manage not to spill any.

"Couldn't sleep?"

"Bad dream. I would ask you, but I already know."

Aerick smirks at me. The only time he sleeps more than a few hours at a time is when we're sleeping together. I turn back around and begin making him a cup of coffee.

"You know me well. Better than anyone else on this earth. Do you want to tell me about your dream?"

I shake my head. Really, I just want to forget the whole thing. "How about we go get a workout in together before PT?"

"Okay, if that's what you want." He smiles, taking the offered coffee cup and giving me a kiss on the cheek.

He grabs my hand and we head for the gym. The lights are on now; walking in, I see Gavin is putting on is gloves. I try to release Aerick's hand, but he doesn't let me. We're still trying to keep our relationship professional but Aerick has taken a dislike to Gavin again after he gave me another book. I really don't think it's anything other than being friendly but of course, Aerick has to take it personally.

"Good morning," Gavin says, looking up at us. "Nadi, don't see you much this early in the morning."

It's true, I'm not much of a morning person, other than when my nightmares get to me. Aerick huffs beside me and I ignore

130

him. I'm assuming this isn't the first time these two have crossed paths in the morning.

"I couldn't sleep. I thought I'd join Aerick for a quick workout."

"You don't want to spar this morning, Aerick?" I didn't know they did that. Aerick has never said anything to me.

"Don't let me mess up your routine. I can hit the bag for a while. In fact, I think I would prefer it this morning," I say.

Gavin looks at me with an odd expression but understanding crosses Aerick's face and I'm grateful.

"Alright," Aerick says simply, giving me a quick kiss on my forehead and handing me his iPod before he heads over to the ring. I'm not sure how he knew I didn't have mine, but I'm not going to ask.

"Everything okay?" Gavin questions with a lifted brow.

"Oh yeah. Just part of my therapy," I say with a giggle, walking away toward the glove cage, because it really is for me. It's been my go-to since I first came here.

I put the ear buds in and put on my training gloves. I glance back at Aerick for a moment and he gives me a wink as he and Gavin begin to circle each other. I grin and turn back to focus on my bag.

There are so many things circling my mind. This week has been fairly busy. Tia has been sick again and I've been in the classroom a lot by myself. As much as I appreciate the practice, it also comes with a lot more work. Having to grade the papers, teach lessons and grade behavior for everyone, in addition to my own studies. The work has kept my mind busy, so I haven't really had to confront a lot of the things that happened last week. Apparently, it isn't going to go away on its own. Obviously, I haven't confronted the fact that I thought Aerick was going to propose to me. My dream was extremely vivid and while I feel a little better, I can't help but wonder what the heck it meant.

I know it shouldn't have been a big deal and I'm not sure myself why I overreacted so badly. I always think of our relationship in the long term. If he asked me, I'd likely say yes and be perfectly happy and content with that. The small amount of time that I've tried to justify my actions, I have come to believe it was only the shock of knowing, or at least thinking, that he wanted it too. I never thought I would be with anyone for an extended period of time, and in no universe ever did I think that I would get married.

With everything we've been through, I wonder how he still wants to be with me. However, I can't discard his words or his actions. He's not always the most vocal person, but he tries when we're alone, as infrequent as that is. His actions, on the other hand, are loud and clear. As much as I hate him being jealous, it also gives me a little relief because it makes me feel as if he still wants me.

I'll admit, it can be overbearing sometimes, but he's getting better. After we ran into Vince back in Chicago, he was very tense for a short period of time, but he reigned it in and we continued to have a great time afterward instead of letting it ruin our whole trip. The next night he did just as well, toning it down and acting like a proud boyfriend.

I don't think I will ever forget that night. It was so wonderful to go and support his Grandpa Scott. After making a big deal about how great I looked in the dress that his grandpa sent over for me, we had a very nice and normal night. As people throughout the night complimented me on how beautiful I was, he smiled, putting his head up and shoulders back like he had won the prize himself. I don't know if I've ever felt so wanted, so loved; it was unforgettable.

Why would I ever have doubted his love for me or the want to marry? He has stuck by me this whole time. Broken, used, and even a little crazy, and he acts as if he's the one who has won the prize. I need to do something to show him that what happened was nothing more than the messed-up nerves of an over-emotional day.

I feel a tug and one of the ear buds pops out of my ear.

"Your phone keeps buzzing," Aerick says with a lifted eyebrow.

Crap. I didn't stick it back in my pocket. I hurry over to the bench and check to see what's so important. It's only Tia with the same thing she has texted me several times this week.

"Tia is still not feeling good. She asked if I'd take over yet again and then sent four more messages to apologize for being sick. Like she can help it or something. It's not a big deal, I don't mind."

"Yeah, I let Brand go spend the night with her last night. She was puking a lot and he's been a pain in my ass all week worrying about her. I have Terrie keeping an eye on her too. She says as long as she doesn't get dehydrated, she should be okay, but there is no telling Brand anything. Really, I merely wanted him out of my hair."

Sure! He would never admit it, but he cares too, and that was really nice of him. "I guess it's a good thing I got everything put together for today. She didn't look good when I stopped by to visit her yesterday, so I kind of expected it. You know, Jeff could probably take over for Brand today so he can stay with her. If it's that bad, she really shouldn't be alone."

Aerick stays quiet so I glare at him. I don't know why he always has to act like such a hard-ass to him. "You know, Brand did cover for us while we were gone last week."

"Covered? Jeff taught my classes. How did he cover for me?"

"Aerick!" I scold him. He and I both know there's more that he does than just teaching classes and there's no way Jeff did it all by himself. I don't even think he knows how.

"Fine." He puts his hands up defensively. "Fine, I will give him the day off to take care of her, okay? Happy?"

I give him a smirk. "Yes, very." I pull him down to me and give him a quick kiss. "I need to go get changed." Aerick is already in his uniform but I'm not and P.T. starts in fifteen minutes.

"I guess I should go let the guys know our change for the day."

"You're a good man, Aerick."

He huffs. "Only because you're around."

I smile giving him another kiss. "See you at P.T."

✳ ✳ ✳ ✳

"Hey. Would you like to go into town with me?" Aerick asks, walking into the classroom. I just dismissed my last class of the day and we have a little time before dinner and P.T. but I also have to do today's paperwork. I suppose I could always do it later.

"Sure. What are we going for?"

"Terrie wants us to pick up some electrolyte water for Tia. She's getting dehydrated and Terrie is getting a little worried, but Tia is refusing to get hooked up to an IV. Of course, she's acting as if she's fine. I swear, sometimes you women just need to admit when you can't do something."

"Whatever. She's trying to stay strong. Similar to you, she likes to show she can handle anything." He lets out a little huff but wisely doesn't say anything back.

I grab my phone and keys and we head out to the car.

"How were classes today? Any problems?" Him asking me about my day. This seems so normal and it's very welcoming.

"No, not really. I've been taking over for Tia so much lately that I think they've learned not to mess with me. Although, in a surprising twist, Skyler seems to be much more interested in doing well. I think what happened last week really put his future in perspective for him."

"Really?"

"Yeah. I graded some of his work earlier. I can't tell you how much it has improved, and I think this week is the first time I ever saw him actually participate in an open discussion." A discussion he helped start, no less. It shocked me; I was almost speechless.

"Well, I guess that's what we do all this work for. Maybe he'll be one of the lucky ones that actually makes something of themselves."

He's holding back something. I can see the wheels turning in his head. "Stop acting as if you don't care. I know you've been keeping an eye on him this week."

He huffs. "I guess he reminds me a little of myself. He obviously hasn't had the best upbringing. Maybe I think he deserves a second chance; and you're right, I've noticed the change in him, too."

His admission surprises me but it's also completely understandable. I see the parallels that he's drawing, and it makes sense. Crappy parents, getting into trouble as a form of self-medication, and it was this place that turned Aerick around. Gave him something meaningful to work for.

"Do you really think he'll change?"

He shrugs. "I hope so, but it is really up to him. I was lucky enough to have Luther."

"Well, with Gavin opening a new camp, maybe he would be interested in taking him. Giving him a new start, away from everything."

"Maybe, but he would really need to have a good second half

of camp. He hasn't been terrible, but he is sitting in the bottom half right now. We'd need a major improvement."

We get out of the car and head into the store. Going down the aisle, I start looking for the best deal on the tiny selection that is available. "Did she say what flavor?"

"I have no idea. I'm in the mood for an energy drink, you want one?"

"Yeah sure. What should I get Tia?"

"I don't know, just grab something." Well that doesn't help me any. I decide on a six-pack of light orange ones. Hopefully she likes this kind. I walk over and meet Aerick who's picked up a couple of zero calorie energy drinks and we head to the checkout.

"Do you think six is enough?"

"If not, it merely gives us a reason to leave camp to be by ourselves again." He gives me that adorable smirk as he hands the money to the cashier and I pick up the bag from the counter.

"Yes, it would be great if we took advantage of that."

He takes the bag from me. "That could be arranged." He stops and in an uncharacteristic move, he grabs the back of my neck and gives me a deep, passionate kiss.

"That sounds good to me," I say, looking around to see a few people staring at us and I feel my face turn red. He laughs at me and grabs my hand as we head for the door.

Continuing to look around shyly I slow and stop as I complete another scan of front of the store. My eyes focus on the other side of the store. *This can't be real. There's no way.*

"Nadi babe, what's wrong?" I feel the tightening in my chest and my vision is cut off as Aerick steps in front of me. "Hey, hey!" My eyes focus on him for a fraction of a second before I take a step to the side, focusing on the figure that was near the flower section, but no one's there now. *Did that really happen? Did I really just see who I thought I saw?*

I don't know how it's possible. My chest is getting heavier as my memory of visiting day flashes back into my head. That figure, I swear I saw the same person that day, too. Merely a flash in my vision. I convinced myself it was all in my head.

"Dammit Nadi, talk to me. Are you okay?"

Am I going crazy? Have I finally snapped? I can't tell him, not now, not as things are finally starting to get back to normal. Right as we're beginning to be happy again and I go crazy and start seeing things. I try to take deep breaths to calm down as spots appear in my vision.

"I, um, I'm kind of dizzy. Maybe a little dehydrated." I focus on breathing as I begin losing the battle. I lean against Aerick, almost unable to hold myself up anymore.

"Nadi, you're freaking me out here."

"Please, just get me back to camp." He bends down slightly and grabs me under my arms and legs, bride-style. I feel the rush as I'm swooped up right as I fall into the darkness.

* * * *

My eyes flutter open to the all too familiar sight of the infirmary at camp. *What the hell happened?*

"Hey, you okay? You scared the crap out of me," Aerick says as he picks up my hand and sits on the edge of the bed.

I try hard to focus on what happened but it's fuzzy. I saw something, a person, someone I never thought I would see again. I can't tell him. I'm still not even sure if I really saw what I think I saw. Maybe after all these years of bad shit happening, I'm suffering from PTSD or something. Maybe it's all in my head and I'm punishing myself for finally being happy, finally getting to have a semi-normal life. I don't want him to know that I'm going crazy. I look up to his eyes as he waits for an answer.

"I, um, I'm not sure. I got really dizzy and then passed out."

He bites on the inside of his cheek. "You mentioned that you may have been dehydrated."

"Maybe. It was kind of weird." It really was, but not in the same way I'm sure he's thinking.

"I had Terrie look you over and she said you seemed fine. Babe, I don't think you were dehydrated. It was as if you were having a panic attack, but I've never seen you react that way. It was as if you were fine one minute and the next minute, you're pale white and your chest was heaving. What freaked you out like that?"

Damn, he's good. I shake my head. "Nothing, I didn't see anything. As I said, I just felt weird all of the sudden, but I'm feeling much better now. What time is it? How long was I out?"

"It's only been thirty minutes."

I see the doubt on his face. He isn't buying it. I sit up and crawl into his lap. He told me not too long ago that he felt like he was my sanctuary, a place where I felt safe. He was right. In this moment, with this dread looming in the back of my mind, I want to be in his arms and I'm grateful when he allows me to.

He wraps his arms around me, and I bury my face in his chest. "Sorry I ruined such a perfect little outing. Maybe it was that amazing kiss that did it," I try to joke with him.

He pulls my chin up and looks into my eyes. "Are you sure you're okay?" His eyes are drawn together in doubt.

Pulling his face down, I give him a kiss on the lips, trying to push away my horrible thoughts. "I'm fine. Please don't worry," I mumble on his lips. "We're alone again you know, right here, right now."

"Always so hungry." He kisses me and I moan into his mouth. When he pulls back, he has a wicked look on his face. "Which is good, because dinner has already started, and you need to eat."

"Really?" I whine.

"Really. You just passed out, now I'm going to make sure you eat a proper meal and stay hydrated."

Great. That completely backfired on me. He stands up and puts me on my feet, making sure I'm steady before letting me go. He takes my hand, leading me out of the room, but I can't help the nagging feeling in the back of my mind.

CHAPTER NINE

(Sunday, January 31st)

I JUMP UP to pounding on the door. *What the hell?* I run over to the door and throw it open to find Andi freaking out. She only speaks in single words repeating 'Terrie' and 'Tia'. My stomach drops as I look over to see Terrie already throwing on her pants.

Tia has been sick for over a week. She started to feel better on Monday but then two days later she started throwing up again. By Thursday, Luther made her go to the clinic in town, but they said she was okay other than being a little dehydrated. They even monitored the baby for a few hours to make sure he was okay. The doctor concluded that she had a bad case of the flu, giving her strict instructions to stay hydrated and stay in bed until she could keep food down.

She managed to go all day yesterday without getting sick and even ate some soup. I thought maybe she was past the worst of it.

Apparently, I was wrong. *God, I hope she's okay!*

Terrie bolts out the door but stops as I follow and turns to me. "Wait! I need you to go get Luther and then quietly get Brand. Please don't freak him out. Just tell him he needs to come now. I don't need him being a menace but whatever is wrong I'm sure she needs him there. Okay?" I nod my head and take off to Luther's cabin.

I pound on his door, probably making him jump out of bed the same way I did. He answers the door quickly and I look away as I notice he's in nothing more than a pair of boxers. "Nadi? What's wrong?"

"Um... yeah, there's something wrong with Tia."

"What do mean something is wrong?" He grabs my shoulders, forcing me to look up at him. His eyes get large and full of worry. I mentally kick myself realizing I have a job to do and being an emotional idiot isn't one of them. I need to get a hold of my emotions here.

I take a deep breath and square my shoulders. "I'm not sure what it is. Andi woke us up and was so panicked she couldn't talk." Luther turns away as I begin to speak, rummaging through his things. I turn my head to stare at the door jamb when I realize he's putting on pants but continue explaining. "Terrie asked me to come get you and then go get Brand."

"Good. Go get him quickly. I want Aerick, Trent and Paulo up too, just in case. Trent and Paulo are to stay in the dorm and watch the cadets. You and Aerick get Gavin and meet me at Tia's cabin as fast as you can. Can you do all that?"

"Yes sir."

"Good. Then go quickly, and for heaven's sake stay calm. I don't need a panic on my hands."

"You got it, boss." I run off quickly, heading for the dorms. I run up the stairs two at a time and flip the light on as I go through the door. Aerick sits up immediately but I ignore his confused look and run straight for Brand's bunk, shaking him awake.

"Brand I need you to stay calm, do you understand me?" My emotions are under much more restraint this time. He goes to talk but I cut him off. "Just get some pants on and go to Tia's cabin as quickly as possible. She's okay, but you need to go now. She needs you." He jumps up and I quickly turn to Trent and Paulo, who are already awake from the commotion. "Trent and Paulo, you need to stay here and watch the cadets. Luther's orders." Aerick appears by my side, already dressed. Brand takes off through the door and I follow him as Aerick follows me.

"Aerick," I say as we get outside and I head back toward the other end of the row of staff cabins. Thankfully Aerick gets the point to follow me.

"What's going on?" he asks quietly.

"I don't know anything other than there's something wrong with Tia."

"Where are we going, then?"

"Luther asked me to get Gavin." Which is almost pointless to say, since the words are barely out of my mouth as we come upon his cabin's front door. Again, I'm banging on another door, waking someone up in the dead of night, which reminds me that I don't even know what time it is. Glancing at my watch I see that it's almost three-thirty in the morning, but I have no time to process it as Gavin opens the door in his boxer briefs. *Geez. Do these guys all sleep in their underwear?*

I don't have time to say a word as Aerick steps in front of me, blocking my view of yet another near-naked man. "Gavin, get on some pants and meet Luther at Tia's cabin." Grabbing my wrist, Aerick quickly pulls me away and toward our final destination before Gavin can ask any questions.

When we reach the door, I can hear Tia's softened cries inside. Aerick stops but I continue inside. Luther is standing there, seemingly waiting for something, while Terrie is feeling around Tia's stomach and looking at her watch. Brand is holding Tia's hand, looking like he's going to explode any minute, while Andi sits impatiently on the couch, her leg bouncing so fast it might fly off.

"Terrie?" Luther asks impatiently.

Terrie shakes her head and lays out the situation. "She's running a fever and is in labor, but the baby's heartbeat is strong." She looks up at him. "We need an ambulance."

Without saying it, her face tells the seriousness of the situation. Luther gets it immediately and shouts, "Aerick!"

"On it..." Aerick volleys back, obviously listening in on what's transpiring in the cabin.

"Labor! What do you mean labor? She isn't due for another ten weeks," Brand shrieks.

"The contractions are strong and consistent..."

Tia moans in pain, grabbing Brand's arm tightly.

"Crap, they're too close together. Everyone except Brand, out now. I need to check her." She jumps up, pushing us out quickly, but we don't go more than a step out of the door.

Aerick is already calling the hospital and explains the situation. "Fifteen minutes," he says quickly to Luther. *How is he so damn calm?*

I really want everything to be okay, but I have a bad feeling in my stomach. "NADI!" I hear Terrie yell and I quickly run back into the room.

"There's no time; listen carefully." She puts up her fingers and starts counting off as she says them. "I need clean towels, warming packs, clamps, scissors, and an oxygen tank with the smallest mask they can find. I need you to stay and help me." Incredibly, I get the meaning of her words and short clipped tone, and I react before the full implications can cross my mind. Running back out, I start spouting off orders for the guys and Andi to gather the things Terrie needs before going back inside.

"Hurry. Wash your hands really good. This baby is coming now." Tia whimpers again as Brand whispers in her ear.

"It's too early," I say, stupidly out loud, as I quickly wash my hands. *We already know that.*

"Well, this baby doesn't care, and I'm counting on you to help me. Tia doesn't want the guys in here and Andi isn't reliable in these types of situations." Brand already grabbed the few towels from the bathroom and put them under Tia. Terrie is giving Brand instructions to sit behind her head and prop her up when I turn back to see what she wants me to do.

"Nadi, I need you to assist me. As soon as he comes out, we need to give him oxygen and get him warm. He's extremely premature..."

"Can't we wait for an ambulance?" Brand says, cutting her off.

"No, Brand! He's crowning!" I don't know what that means but it makes me realize she hasn't moved an inch. She has been right in front of Tia the whole time. I haven't seen her hands once. "That's it, Tia, short labored breaths. Just for another minute. You can do it."

I'm about to ask what 'crowning' means when fists banging on the door make me jump and I quickly open it just to have Luther and Gavin barge in with their arms full of towels and warm packs. Luther tries to hand them to me, but I motion for them to put it all on the table, only to have Terrie yell at them to wait outside. As I'm closing the door, Aerick comes in with the oxygen tank and medical supplies.

"Crap. Nadi, her water just broke, more towels. Aerick, start breaking those warm packs and put them between two towels." I grab several towels and take them over to her.

"Put them under my hands." I spread several of them out as she instructs and I see for the first time the top of the baby's head that Terrie appears to be holding in. "Alright Tia, on the next contraction you can finally push. You're going to grab the back of your knees and pull them toward you while you bear down. Nadi, help her."

"But it's too early, he can't come yet," Tia whines, like she didn't realize her labor was this far along.

"Tia, this is going to happen, and I need you to be strong and help me help your baby, okay?" Terrie puts a hand on Tia's stomach. Tia looks terrified but she shakes her head and I'm a little afraid that Brand is about to pass out.

"Aerick, don't leave yet," she tells him as he lays the towels with the warm packs at the end of the bed. She must see the same thing as she looks up at Brand. "Get that mask hooked to the oxygen tank and turn it on. Alright, Tia. Here we go."

Tia's face scrunches up and she moans as she pushes. I help her pull her legs back. As odd as it sounds, I cannot look away from what's going on. I'm completely entranced. "Again Tia, I need another really good push – he's almost here." Terrie's far away voice comes through and a second later a small, thin baby slips out into her hands. The room is completely silent.

Terrie quickly grabs a suction bulb and starts cleaning out his mouth and nose, but he doesn't cry. Grabbing a towel, she starts rubbing the baby all over, coaxing him in a soft quiet voice to breathe, but he doesn't cry. When he still doesn't breathe, she flicks his tiny feet and aggressively rubs his back again. I feel a tear fall down my cheek as I stand there for what feels like eternity. *Come on little one.*

Large strong hands engulf my closed fists that are now at my sides and my legs feel similar to jelly. He's so tiny, and I know that color is not normal. *Breathe baby, please breathe!*

"Please..." Tia's soft voice fills the room and a second later a small noise comes from the tiny person in Terrie's hands.

"That's right, buddy. Keep it up," Terrie encourages him excitedly as everyone in the room seems to let out the collective breath we were all holding. "Aerick, oxygen," Terrie says. "Nadi, get the warmed towels."

I scoop up the laid-out towels in my arms and turn to Terrie. She nods for me to move my arms closer and as I do, she places the tiny little boy onto the towels and quickly covers him up as she continues to rub his back.

I can't breathe again. I have a tiny little person lying in my arms. *I'm holding a baby that was just born into this crazy world.*

I barely notice Terrie clamping off the umbilical cord and having Brand cut it. My heart literally feels like it's warming up inside my chest. It's the most amazing thing I've ever felt. Like a color-blind person seeing the sunset through new eyes for the first time.

Once the baby is free, as much as it pains me, there's someone else who wants him more. I gently lay him on her chest. "Keep rubbing his back, Tia. Keep him stimulated," Terrie tells her as she sets the mask next to his face. It is almost the size of his whole face.

"Why isn't he crying?" Tia asks, full of worry. He's making

small sounds but hasn't fully let out a loud cry.

"His lungs aren't fully developed, but he's breathing, and that's what matters."

The sirens of the ambulance finally hit my ears right as several firefighters burst through the door. The sirens sound as if they're almost here so I must have been tuning them out before. I move back into the corner to let them have more room as Terrie starts to explain the situation.

Somehow, I back right into Aerick's chest and he wraps his arms around me, which is good because I'm feeling a little weak in the knees. *I can't believe I just witnessed that.*

"That was amazing." I whisper and feel Aerick kiss the top of my head. He's silent, having nothing to say.

As soon as Terrie finishes delivering the afterbirth, the EMTs quickly load both Tia and the baby on a stretcher and haul them out of the room, whispering they need to get the baby intubated. We all softly give our congratulations as they exit with Terrie and Brand in tow. The words of the EMTs really worry me, but at least I'm confident that they have the proper tools to take care of the baby from here. I still cannot fathom what just happened. What a beautiful and heart-wrenching experience it was.

Luther gives orders to Aerick and Gavin, saying that he'll be going to the hospital. Then they all start to clear out. Andi goes to the guys' dorm to fill them in on what happened, while Gavin takes off somewhere else, leaving only me and Aerick. I'm feeling way too amped-up to go back to my cabin. I look at Tia's bed; it's a mess.

I walk over to the bed and start to strip off all of the blankets and sheets. Once I get it all off, I tie it all inside the sheet. As soon as I finish, Aerick's there with clean sheets and we quietly put fresh sheets on her bed. He doesn't say anything but there's something on his mind. His eyes seem so far away and I'm not sure I should interrupt his thought process; after a minute I decide on just letting him mull things over in his head.

When we finish, he comes around and picks up the bundle of bedding. He grabs my hand and pulls me out of the cabin, walking toward the laundry. The silence between us isn't uncomfortable, it's actually the opposite. The air is cool and crisp and we both watch the stars as we walk hand in hand.

✳ ✳ ✳ ✳

"Good morning, Princess," Aerick whispers in my ear.

I fell asleep in his arms when we finally got back to my cabin, but the clock shows it hasn't been more than an hour. "Come on. I need you to help with P.T. this morning since Brand's gone."

"Ugh! Can't Jeff help you? It's his job." My body is utterly exhausted.

"He could, but I would rather look at you," he says and even though I don't see his face, I can see the smirk on it. He nuzzles my neck when I remain mute. "Please," he says in a sexy, soft voice.

I don't want to, but who can refuse that? "Fine, but you owe me."

"And I look forward to repaying you."

Lord, please tell me why I fell for someone so 'awake' in the morning. Dragging myself out of bed, I search for my clothes, only to see he's already laid them out at the end of the bed. I turn to stare at him, and he gives me a knowing look before walking out of the cabin to go wake up the cadets.

That man is going to be the death of me. Death; maybe the wrong word to use today after what happened just a few hours ago. I'm anxious to know how everything is going with Tia and the baby. Just the thought motivates me to hurry up and get ready so I can talk to Aerick more before we start. Knowing him, he's already talked to Luther.

I throw on my clothes and jacket and head outside. Slowing down a bit, I notice there is no cloud cover. Hopefully it will be a nice day. The snow is pretty much all gone around camp and the green is beginning to return.

Aerick is on stage so I jog over to join him. "Good morning, sleepy head," he says with a grin.

"Keep laughing, buddy," I sneer. "So, what did Luther say? How's Tia?"

"How do you know I talked to Luther?" He raises an eyebrow at me, but I glare at him, not in the mood for games, and he drops the act. "Tia is doing good and she was sleeping when I talked to him. The baby is doing better, too. They have him on a ventilator because his lungs are underdeveloped, but they say it's normal with how premature he is. He isn't completely out of the woods, but the doctors say he is looking good. Do you want to see him later?"

"We can go?" My heart is jumping at the opportunity to see him again.

"Luther says we can go in groups of two. So as long as you want to wait until later when I can go then yes, we can go. Or, if you want, you can go with someone else."

Geez, that pouting face is priceless. "Of course I'll wait for you. When are we going?"

"Around dinner. Actually, I need to meet with you and Jeff this morning. You both will be stepping in sooner than expected and while you've been covering a lot anyway, Jeff hasn't. He's going to have to get moved into the instructor's dorm today and take over classes starting Monday."

Wow. I haven't even really had time to think about that. We have about six weeks left still and now Jeff and I are a bigger part of that. I feel as if I'm ready to take over fully for Tia, but it feels like I'm a bit outside of myself. Like it's not me standing in front of those kids. It's a little crazy and even makes me a little nervous.

"Hey." Aerick draws my attention back to him. "You both will do great. Stop worrying about it."

"I'm not worrying," I sulk. I wish he didn't read me so well.

"Yes, you are. I know you." He pulls my chin up so I have to look at him. "You are ready for this and you'll do great as always. You're a natural at it."

The recruits start coming out. "Stay here, I want you to help lead P.T. today." *Huh. That's different.* He steps forward and we wait for everyone to file in.

When everyone gets into position, Aerick gives a short explanation of what happened in the early morning hours and the changes that the cadets can expect. After his speech, he backs up so we're side by side and begins our workout.

I really enjoy the fact that we're leading this together today. It makes me feel like things are supposed to be this way. It feels normal.

✵ ✵ ✵ ✵

Sitting on the bed, I finally finished the prep work for tomorrow's lesson. It's taken me the better part of the day to get it done. Jeff and I met with Aerick after breakfast and he explained how we were going to run things going forward. As Aerick said before, there's not too much change for me, but Jeff is making a huge leap moving into Brand's position.

Things are going to start getting hectic for me too now that I have to balance out school and work again. Before, when Tia was merely sick and I was filling in, she gave me everything that I needed. Now there's much more prep work that I have to do, and it isn't something she really worked with me on, so I'm trying to go with the flow with the information I already have.

"I'm heading out. I'll be back in an hour or so," Terrie says as she walks out the door.

Her and Paulo are going to head over to the hospital before visiting hours are up. Aerick and I just got back after dinner. It was so amazing to see the baby again. Tia and Brand decided to name him Sam. Not Samuel, only Sam, and I think it's beautiful, exactly like him.

It was hard at first to see the wires and pumps he was hooked up to, but he was sleeping so peacefully under the blue lights. Even though he just lay there, I felt as if I could watch him for hours. I stood there looking at him with Aerick holding me from behind and thought of so many questions and fears of my own.

It wasn't that long ago that I thought Aerick was proposing to me. I thought at one point in time it was possible that we would also have a child. Granted, the thoughts originally came because I was getting my shot; it made me realize the other things that could happen if that was a path we chose. *Life is so precious, but my luck is terrible.*

You never know if your body can handle going through labor. Tia is blaming herself for having the baby early and, even though I know it's stupid, I understand how she feels. Even though she really has no control, she thinks the early labor was brought on because her body wasn't strong enough. *What if I'm not strong enough?*

These are basically new fears that pile onto the old ones. I don't know if my body is strong enough for growing another life inside of me. Mentally I'm already drained and I'm not even pregnant. I don't know how I would be able to deal with something like that. I want so much to be a perfect wife and perfect mother, but in reality, I know I'm far from perfect. In fact,

I'm royally screwed up. I suppose Aerick's nickname for me is really fitting in that sense.

I look up as Aerick walks in. "Hey. You okay?"

"Yeah. Just finished tomorrow's lesson. What's up?"

"I wanted to check on you. Today has been a little crazy and you've been pretty quiet since we left the hospital."

"I'm fine." My notorious words flow trying to placate his concerns.

"I know. I just thought you could use a little time away." He runs his fingers down my arm and I close my eyes at the tingling running through my arm.

"Time away?" I ask in an unsteady voice.

His lips press softly against my neck and he begins dragging them lightly across the length of my jaw. "Yes. Away from reality." *The best thing I've heard in a long time.*

CHAPTER TEN

(Saturday, February 6th)

"LUTHER, IT'S NOT really necessary."

"I'm saying it is. Nadi, you have been acting a little weird lately – even for you." He pauses, thinking better of his words, and backtracks. "I'm not saying that you're weird, but you have always acted a little different than others. This is stressful for you and you've been through so much since we first met. Christian says you've been skipping your sessions. You have been busy, so it's understandable, but I think you will benefit from sitting down and talking to him."

I'm sure he's right, but there's so much to do and very little time to do it. Next week's lesson plans need to be worked out, daily paperwork needs to be filled out, and I'm still doing my classes online. All this and he wants me to drop it all to sit down and 'talk to someone.'

"Would you rather talk to me?" he asks, raising his eyebrow.

"No!" I all but shout. *Not just no, but hell no!*

"Well, then the least you can do is to go, since your weekly sessions with him are already paid for."

Crap! It sucks when he's right. He'd already told me he paid a little more than normal so that the counseling sessions would cover me, too. I'd also promised Luther to go to them when he set up the arrangement, but that was before all this work was thrown on me unexpectedly. It was never the plan for me to teach any classes on a permanent basis this session.

"Good. I am glad you see things my way." My eyes shoot up to his, but he has already started going through things on his desk and it's clear there is no more arguing about this. "That will be all, Nadi. You better hurry before you miss breakfast. I don't need Aerick in here whining that you're not eating."

My interest is piqued through my irritation. "Does he really do that?"

He looks up. "What do you think? It is rather annoying, so go, and I will see you later."

"Fine." Letting out a huff of irritation, I leave the office and go out into the cool morning air.

It's cloudy but it isn't supposed to rain today, which means Aerick's and Jeff's cabins will be taking a hike this afternoon. I've been a little worried ever since Vincent and Charlie got into a fight earlier this week during a self-defense class that Jeff and Gavin were leading.

The class was supposed to be Trent and Jeff, but Gavin wanted to help out, so he took over while Trent went and did some paperwork. Not the smartest thing in the world to leave those two alone with the class, but leadership in this camp seems to have a sink or swim mentality and often throws people into things.

Aerick never did tell me what the fight was about but he watched the video after the fact and only said that 'Jeff did good'. He appeared confident about it, but I wasn't convinced. Since Jeff is walking around with a bruised rib that he received trying to break up the fight, I'm fairly certain they both played down the severity of it.

After a lot of thought, I realized the cadets were doing really well up until Brand left. It seems a few of them are pushing Jeff and Gavin a little just to see how much they can get away with. All that considered, I'm more at ease that he will be with Aerick this afternoon. Jeff can take care of himself, but Aerick is more experienced around here and he knows how to handle things when there are 'incidences'. It's one less thing I have to worry about.

Worry...

Something that is a constant loop in my head these days. I really thought things were going to get easier for me, but it's like as soon as I finish something, or find a way to put a problem behind me, something new pops up in its place. There's so much on my plate these days, it has my mind running a thousand miles an hour.

Trying to teach kids while I'm still trying to finish school myself is a whole basket of headaches in itself. I'd been helping out Tia with teaching for the last few weeks, but she was putting the lessons together herself; now I'm responsible for all of it on my own, and it's so much more than just standing in front of the kids and talking.

Tia is the type of teacher that actually shows an interest in teaching. I had teachers back in school who would just give out information for students to copy or chapters to read and expect us to do our homework without direction. I learned absolutely nothing in those classes. Tia is the opposite: always very animated, walking around the room, talking and answering questions, wanting the cadets to actually interact. I think that's why I did so well in her classes. Now I have to do that, because I'm not going to be one of those teachers I hated in school.

Tia offered to Skype for a few hours to help me with the lessons, but I told her I could handle it. She needs to be with her baby and focus on getting better herself. The day after she got to the hospital, they told her she had developed pneumonia. I felt so bad for her. With the baby being so early, she already had enough to worry about. It's as if my luck is rubbing off on her.

Aerick and I visited again for a little while yesterday and got to see the baby. He's so small still and it's so hard to see him hooked up to a bunch of wires and tubes. The doctors said his lungs were developing well but he'll likely have to be in the hospital for a few more weeks until he can breathe on his own. Even though he looks so small and helpless, he's so strong just to make it at such a premature age. He'll definitely be a fighter. I sat next to his incubator for almost an hour, watching him and rubbing his little arm. *So precious.*

There have been other things on my mind too. I've tried to shake it, but it won't go away. Searching through my mind over and over again, trying to decide if what happened a few weeks ago actually happened. I'm torn between which reality is true. Neither one makes me feel any better.

On one hand I'm crazy, and on the other hand, well, it's almost too frightening to consider. I've also been struggling with the fact that if I'm not crazy, it only took a blink of an eye to lose everything I've accomplished and built up. It literally took a blink of an eye to go from being completely fine, to being that frightened little girl again.

So far, it's more practical that I'm crazy. The possibility of even seeing him under these circumstances has to be a one in a trillion chance. Which brings me to the reason why I'm so afraid to talk to Aerick about it. I try my best to not worry about it around him because he notices more than most people, but it's been a losing battle.

Anytime there's a strange or loud noise, it startles the crap out of me and I'm constantly looking over my shoulder, just to see nothing there. I've become paranoid all over again, which in turn has made my other reactions change. The other day I actually flinched at Aerick's touch and then instantly regretted it when I saw the look on his face. I hadn't meant to, but I had drifted off into my own world again, debating all the crazy shit going on in my life, when he ran his fingers down my arm to get my attention.

Jeff attempted to talk to me about it a few days ago too, but I asked him to back off, that it's nothing and he did. Unfortunately, Aerick isn't so easy to shake. However, it's completely ridiculous and uncalled for him to get Christian and Luther involved. He's making me feel like a child again. He'll likely try to tell me he's only looking out for me, but it still isn't right.

I work hard to keep my cool as I enter the mess hall to get some food. Everyone is already there eating and, considering Aerick didn't look up at me when I walked in, that gives me the impression he knew exactly the reason for my tardiness, which only infuriates me more. He's being completely unreasonable.

I move quickly to get myself a small plate of food now that I've lost my appetite. I'm not going to give Aerick anything to complain about, so I get just enough to be considered acceptable and sit down next to him, leaving a usual amount of space between us.

"Good morning." His timid tone is another confirmation, making me even more frustrated.

"I don't know about the 'good' part, but it's morning." He presses his lips into a thin line but doesn't look up at me. "I take it from your lack of response and no questioning as to why I'm late that you know exactly why that is." Again, silence. "Seriously

Aerick. What the hell?" I say a little louder than I mean to, forcing a small reaction out of him as he looks around to see who's paying attention to us.

"Nadi, can we talk about this later when there aren't so many prying ears around?"

"Later? What for? You obviously can talk to Luther about your concerns before you even bother to talk to me. Why not let everyone else know as well?" Terrie and Paulo are staring at me in obvious shock at my forceful tone with Aerick, but at this point my control is all but non-existent. Besides, it isn't the first time.

"Nadi, please."

Calm down Nadi. I take a deep breath, trying to slow my rushing blood. "What-fucking-ever. Forget it." I put my head down to force some food into my body. I hope he knows it wasn't that sweet pleading voice that's making me give in. I don't want to fight with him on this right now because he's right, there are a lot of other people within earshot.

"Nadi?"

"I said forget it." I drop my fork mid-bite and glare at him.

"Alright, alright." With a heavy sigh he turns back to his plate and starts eating again, focusing way too hard on his food.

When I'm sure he isn't going to say anything else, I inhale the rest of my small plate of food. Once I'm finished, I don't bother saying anything to anyone, including him, just get up and leave. Today has been exhausting already and I've barely finished breakfast.

UNBROKEN

✽ ✽ ✽ ✽

Somehow, I've managed to get through classes today without snapping at anyone. My morning really put a damper on my emotions, and I've had to try hard not to take it out on the cadets. It isn't their fault that people around here are too nosey and can't let me be.

What's irritating me even more is that Aerick didn't stop at only talking to Luther. He also talked to Paulo about it. From what I understand from everyone else, he's always been a private person himself, but it appears my privacy is not a factor in his mind, because he doesn't seem to be extending the same courtesy to me. I wonder how he would feel if I did the same thing to him.

Although Paulo didn't outright say it, him coming in earlier between classes and asking, 'how are you doing', gave it away pretty clearly. He never just drops by to see me and when he said that Aerick's really worried about me, I literally shoved him out the door. His pleas to me were cut off when my hand pulled the door shut in his face.

Maybe I'm a little more edgy lately but it only makes it worse that everyone is making a big deal about it. *Who cares if I'm moody?* Andi is worse than I am, and no one bothers her about her attitude.

The door creaks open, getting my attention, and Aerick walks in. He gives me a half smile as he walks over and gives me a kiss on my cheek. He says 'hi' in a voice that is low and guarded as if he's testing the waters. *Let me answer your unasked question!* I ignore him and turn around to start erasing today's lesson notes off the white board. It takes a moment, but he eventually presses himself against my back and wraps his arms around my stomach. *God, I love when he does that!*

I refuse to give in so easily though, and keep erasing the board. More determined, he pulls my hair from around my neck and starts placing kisses there. *Damn, that feels good.* Internally growling at myself for my weakness, my hand slowly comes to a stop and my eyes close, soaking up the warmth radiating from his body as he continues.

"It's only because I care about you, babe. I'm worried. I admit I should have talked to you first, but please don't be mad at me. I hate it when you're mad at me." With a heavy sigh, my hand drops and I lean back into him, relaxing my body. Just feeling him against me helps bleed away some of my irritation.

"It would be nice if you would keep everyone else out of it next time and just ask me. I value my privacy too, you know," I mutter quietly. He nods against my neck and it seems to be enough for both of us at this point in time. We stand there for a while holding each other as he occasionally places soft kisses on my neck.

Finally, he turns me so he can look into my eyes. "So, do you want to talk about what is bothering you so much?"

"Well, now that I have to talk to Christian tomorrow, I think I'll wait," I say sarcastically, letting out a fake chuckle.

"You just said to ask you."

"I said next time. Now that you had to go and get everyone else involved, I have to talk to a shrink and I really don't feel like repeating myself." I'm also a little worried about how to tell him some of the things that have been going through my mind.

He glares at me.

"Don't even. This is your fault, not mine," I say, putting the last of my things on the desk away. "Come on, let's go eat dinner."

"That is the first reasonable thing you have said today." He grabs my hand. "Let's go."

* * * *

"You needed me, Luther?"

"Yeah, can you run into town for me please?"

"Sure, Luther. What do you need?"

"I need you to pick up some certified mail that is being held over at the post office. I need those contracts for our meeting in Seattle. I would go myself, but the post office closes in twenty minutes and I have to get this stuff done before I have to leave to go meet up with Ayla and Gavin."

With my mind being everywhere else all day, I almost forgot they were all going to be gone for the night. They have some important meetings with the Chicago investors who are flying into Seattle. Ayla and Gavin left this morning to make sure the investors make it and to greet them at the hotel. "I know you are busy, but I don't trust Brayden to pick them up, and everyone else is busy." He doesn't seem altogether happy with me having to go. I'd bet a hundred dollars Aerick and our conversation this morning has something to do with that.

"It's fine, Luther. I've got this." It's running into town, not rocket science.

"Thanks." He gives me the slip of paper with the information on it and hands me the keys to the SUV as he gives me instructions to pick up the camp mail too.

I don't bother to tell Aerick I'm leaving. It should only take me a few minutes and I doubt anyone will know I even left. I head for town, trying to remember where I've seen the post office. If I remember correctly, it was somewhere in the middle. I spot it on the opposite side of the street across the street from the Dairy Queen.

Grabbing the paper Luther gave me, I go inside and am totally blown away. It's nice inside, like any other post office, but this one is almost empty. Living in Chicago, there's a minimum thirty-minute wait anytime you go. I grab the mail out of our box and then wait in line for the one person in line to finish. It takes less than three minutes to get the certified letter: that has to be some kind of record.

The lady behind the counter is extremely nice. She doesn't look at me like some little hooligan or troublemaker, just smile politely and asks if I'm new to working up at the camp. It's odd knowing everyone in this town knows everyone. It's even more crazy for people to be openly nice to me.

I walk out of the post office and head to the car when I hear my name. Looking up, my eyes find a familiar figure across the street and I freeze. *Not again!*

I close my eyes tightly, praying that it's all in my head. *Go away!* It only takes a second before his hands are around my arms. "No!" I scream, spinning around as I stumble back, almost tripping over my own feet until I slam back up against the SUV.

"Nadi. Hey, hey are you okay?" My eyes fly open to see Casey. "Chill out, it's just me, Casey. You know, Aerick's friend that has the cabin. What's wrong?" Ignoring him, I turn back around, looking across the street, but he's gone again. I have to be going crazy. *What the fuck?*

"Nadi?" I turn to Casey, worry etched on his face. "Should I call Aerick or something?"

Hearing Aerick's name is enough to focus my thoughts. "No, no. I'm fine. I thought I saw something." I glance over my shoulder again but still nothing. I work on trying to get my breathing under control as heaviness still sits in my chest.

"I'm sorry I startled you. Aerick has warned me about doing that." He lets out an awkward laugh. "I was walking and thought that was you. I don't think I've ever seen you around without Aerick attached to your side. How are you?"

"I'm good, thank you. I was picking up something important for Luther at the post office." Thankfully this gives me my out. "I actually was on my way back. He's waiting for me and he's in a bit of a hurry."

"Oh, well, sorry. I don't want to keep you. I know how business trips can be." I look up to him in shock.

167

"How do you know he's going on a business trip?" I question. He grins and puts his hand out, gesturing for us to walk around to the driver side of the car.

"I already talked to Aerick today. We normally hang out when I'm in town, but he said Luther and Ayla were leaving for the night, so he had to stay at camp." He opens my door for me, and I slide into the driver's seat.

"Oh." I guess that makes sense.

"Are you sure you're okay? You're still really pale. I can drive you back if you want." He looks down to my hands that are still shaking, and I clasp them together quickly to hide it.

"Like I said, you just caught me off guard. I'm sure Aerick's told you I get a little jumpy when people touch me. I'm okay." As much as I hate it, it's giving me a pretty good cover at this point.

"Okay. Well it was nice to see you. I hope you and Aerick can come hang out sometime soon."

"Sure, I will make sure we do. See you later."

He smiles and closes the door, lingering for a moment before he walks around the car back to the sidewalk and continues on his way. I can't help but look one more time across the street just to find there's no one there I recognize. "Fuck, what the hell is wrong with me!" I yell to myself.

An older couple passing the car stare at me, startled. *Crap!* Now I really am crazy, yelling at myself. I take several deep breaths to calm myself down and try to shake off the creepy feeling I have.

After a minute my body calms a little, but not entirely. I need to get back to camp. Starting up the SUV, I quickly pull out and head back, being careful not to speed.

The closer I get to camp the less freaked out I am, but it still feels as if I've just finished a ten-mile run. Now I know I've gone completely crazy, right over the deep end. There's no way I saw him. It was only a few seconds from the time I closed my eyes; it isn't like he can just disappear. This isn't some kind of fucked-up fairytale where the villain has magic powers. This is real life and it's obvious that I'm cracking under all the pressure I have on me. *Why does this have to happen to me now?*

As I pull into the camp, Aerick is standing out front with his hands in his pockets and an irritated look on his face. *Great!* I can only hope that he's standing out here like this because I didn't tell him I was leaving, and he's upset that Luther sent me alone.

I pull into the parking spot and grab Luther's mail, which I'm only now realizing I threw onto the seat next to me without any thought. I don't even remember doing it. I take a deep breath, pulling myself together, and get out to face Aerick.

I plaster a smile on my face as I walk up to him and give him a quick kiss. "Hey, you didn't have to wait out here for me. I had to run and pick up something...." He puts his finger over my mouth, cutting off my words and pursing his lips. Things are clearly not okay, and he isn't merely standing out here to greet me. Not that I actually thought that or anything.

He takes a moment to compose himself. "What the hell

happened? And don't lie. I just got off the phone with Casey."

Shit. Of course, luck isn't on my side. "He startled me." It isn't a lie; he really did. Why is it my stupid damn luck that I ran into someone that knows Aerick? *Urgh!*

"Bullshit," he growls at me, grabbing my arm. *Whoa! Upset, very upset!* "If that was it then you would have hit him, not freak out like you were scared shitless to the point my friend nearly didn't let you drive back alone. Now tell me what the fuck happened? Is it the same thing that happened a few weeks ago? What the hell is going on with you?" His hand has tightened almost painfully.

Words evade me. I can't tell him that I'm going crazy, I just can't. "Aerick, Nadi, is there a problem?" We both turn to see Luther and Aerick drops his hand to his side quickly. I almost rub my arm where Aerick was holding it but stop myself, not wanting Luther to be any more concerned then he already looks.

"No," I say quickly, hoping to keep him out of this. "I just got back and was coming to find you. Sorry if it took too long."

He's looking back and forth between Aerick and I. "No, actually, you weren't gone long at all. I was coming to find Aerick. I need to speak to you for a moment before I leave, Aerick."

It isn't really a request and I can see the wheels turning in Aerick's head. He's not ready for this conversation to be over but he really can't tell Luther no. "We aren't done. I'll catch up with you in a few minutes."

Here we go again, treating me like an errant child. I shake my head at him. "You know what? Don't bother. I have stuff to get done and, thanks to you, another appointment on top of all the other shit I have to get done by Monday. As far as I'm concerned, I don't have time for anything else until tomorrow night," I hiss, trying to keep it low enough Luther doesn't hear me.

He sighs and his intensity comes down a few notches at my blatant anger toward him. "Nadi..." He says softer but still with obvious frustration.

"I said tomorrow. Now if you'll excuse me, I've got more pressing matters. Good night." I walk past him toward my cabin, only pausing to hand Luther his mail.

"Thank you," he says as I pass. "Everything okay?"

I only nod and keep walking. There's no real reason why I should be so upset right now. He's worried about me and I understand that, but it makes me so mad. Not at him, but at me. It's not fair that I'm taking out on him, but I can't help it. He wants answers and I want nothing more than to forget it. Unfortunately, that isn't likely to happen on its own and now I have to face it, because there's no way Christian is going to give in. If I walk out of his office, his first stop will be Luther's office. Yet another person I don't need to know I'm going crazy.

I let out a heavy sigh. *How the hell am I going to fix this?*

CHAPTER ELEVEN

(Sunday, February 7th)

"CODE RED, ALL cadets remain in the dorm. Camp is on lock down until further notice. Code red, all cadets remain in the dorm. Camp is on lock down until further notice." I nearly fall out of bed at the loud noise screeching in the room.

I jump up and start throwing on the first thing I grab out of my drawers. This feels eerily familiar and I know right away what's going on because this happened when I was a cadet.

There's a cadet 'off grid,' meaning someone managed to get their bracelet off without activating it. My memory recalls that all staff members are supposed to meet in front of the cadets' dorm immediately. In the few seconds it takes me to get ready, Terrie is ready just as quick, and we grab our jackets and run outside.

Somehow several of the guys are already out there and we're joined by mostly everyone else by the time we reach the group where Aerick is already shouting out commands.

"Jeff is on dorm duty. Brayden, Trent, Paulo you're with me. Terrie, prep the infirmary and call Luther to let him know what's going on. Vincent is off grid and you all know we only have a short amount of time to find him. I want this done and done right."

"We're short people," Paulo quips looking around our circle.

"Yes, I'm aware, Paulo. Jake…."

"On it!" Jake says quickly and takes off toward the front buildings.

He turns to me. "Andi and Nadi." He quickly scans the foreground, then the woods, as if he's trying to make up his mind about something, before his eyes finally find mine. "I need you two to do a quick but thorough check of the immediate area. Stay within the main camp and check inside, around and on top of all buildings. When you are done, get to the control room and help Jake. Please, be careful and watch each other's backs." His eyes bore into mine and the worry is at the surface, but he only hesitates for a moment longer before taking off toward the woods.

"Come on, this is my normal post. We got this," Andi says, breaking my attention as I watch the guys run away from us. Turning, I follow as she starts toward the instructors' dorms.

"What does he mean by 'short people'?" I ask as we run.

"Normally Luther is with me. We've been through this many times and know exactly what to do. You, on the other hand, are new, and the one time we practiced in our pre-camp week, we had more people. With the higher-ups gone, Tia and Brand are still not here, it leaves the main search party two people shorter than normal and creates a weak front in the main camp because one of us is a rookie."

At least she's honest, and it's taken me until now to realize that Luther, Ayla and Gavin are indeed gone. That moment of hesitation in Aerick's eyes, that was because of me. He was either debating whether to pull me to go with them or debating the fact that he's leaving two girls, one of whom is inexperienced, to sweep the main camp.

My mind is tugging at the first thought. I suppose only leaving one in camp wouldn't have been the smartest idea either, even if Jeff and Jake are nearby. Then again, maybe he didn't want me trampling around the woods in the dark when he's already worried about my mental state.

Well, the least I can do is make sure we do it right in this moment, so I focus on what we were trained to do. After checking around the fire pit to make sure no one is hiding there, we start at the first building in the corner closest to the main dorm. Quickly checking each building, going in a counter-clockwise motion, we only skip over the cadet's dorm and the infirmary, which should have already been done by Jeff and Terrie.

When we finish, we still haven't gotten the all clear, so we go to the control room, which is really just Jake's office. It's pretty quiet as we walk in and Jake is typing away, looking around his multi-screen setup. I walk behind him to see if I can make sense of any of it.

"Any word?" I ask as I see several dots on the screen with a map on it. He's tracking the guys as they search the woods.

"They're on his trail. He tripped one of the sensors and they should hopefully have him soon." I watch as the dots start to converge. "Don't worry, Aerick is pretty good at tracking people. His attention to detail gives him a big advantage."

My thoughts begin to raise questions that have nothing to do with the present. "Are the sensors on all the time?" It never occurred to me before now to ask about this.

He looks up to me and after a second, I see the understanding in his eyes before he turns back to the screens. "They're only turned on during emergencies, to conserve power. You know, because the animals would be setting them off all the time. Unfortunately, Liz was privy to that information. She would have known how to avoid them."

In the next moment, all the dots are suddenly in the same spot and not moving. The others notice it too and it only takes a millisecond for the room to become ice cold. We all stay completely silent for at least an entire minute; you could probably hear a pin drop. Finally, Jake's phone springs to life, vibrating itself almost off the desk. Answering it, he nods several times but doesn't say anything before hanging it up again.

"They got him. They will be back in about ten minutes. He's unconscious. Nadi, please go give Terrie a heads up and have her call it into Luther to let him know the situation is under control."

I nod and head out the door to the infirmary, happy to get out and take a breath. It seems like everything happened so quickly; my mind hasn't had much time to process anything. Once outside, the cold helps slow the adrenaline rush and extreme tiredness washes over my body like a tidal wave. Looking at my watch for the first time I see it's only three in the morning.

We had headed back to our cabin around midnight after playing poker in the instructor's dorm. It was so nice to have just a normal night, or what's considered normal around here. I put my issues with Aerick aside for the night and spent most of the night sitting on his lap while he touched me every chance he got.

He ended the night in a pretty good mood, too. I'm sure part of it could have been my better attitude, but I'm sure the seventy dollars he won helped, too. Also, with both Brand and Gavin gone, he really didn't have much to complain about. My only wish was that I had a personal cabin so he could have spent the night with me. The few times we manage to have alone time are too scarce and short. I miss having him in bed beside me.

When I walk into the infirmary Terrie looks relieved, but it only lasts the amount of time it takes me to explain the situation. She tries to hide the look of dissatisfaction on her face before picking up her phone and calling Luther. The 'unconscious' part obviously doesn't make her very happy and she oddly leaves out that part when explaining things to Luther. I lean patiently against the wall and wait for the guys to get back while Terrie pulls out some additional supplies.

Thankfully, they don't take too long. Paulo walks in a few minutes later with Aerick close behind him carrying Vincent over his shoulder. I'm momentarily shocked by his appearance. He's dirty from head to toe, twigs and leaves littering his clothes as well. He goes right to the room and plops Vincent on the bed.

"Are you okay?" I ask, letting my concern show more than I prefer.

He lets out a little huff. "I'm fine. That fucker is fast and doesn't listen. I had to tackle him to get him to stop."

"Why is he unconscious?" Terrie questions as she shines a light in his pried open eye, moving the light up and down several times before checking the next.

"He hit his head on the hard ground. He regained consciousness once on our way back, but he was still pretty out of it, just mumbled for a minute or two and passed out again. He's got a pretty good knot on the back of his head."

As if Vincent heard him, he starts to move around, and his eyes flutter open.

"Hey Vincent. Can you hear me?" Terrie asks, but he only groans instead of answering her. "Vincent, open your eyes and look at me."

"Ugh, fuck you! Why is my head pounding as if it went through a cement wall?"

"Watch how you talk to her or your head *will be* going through a cement wall. But while we're on the subject, you hit your head on the ground, which is just as good as concrete this time of year." Only Paulo could start a sentence so angrily and end it laughing.

Terrie examines the back of his head with several hisses escaping Vincent, but he smartly says nothing else.

"He looks like he will be okay. I will keep him for observation for a few hours and make sure he doesn't have a serious concussion, then you guys can have him."

"Good. We're looking forward to it," Aerick says threateningly. I know how this will go and feel sorry for him already. "Paulo, come get me when he is ready and get Jake over here to get another bracelet on him ASAP."

Paulo nods and Aerick walks to the door, pausing once it's open, and looks at me. Taking the hint, I follow him out. "Good luck, Vincent," I say over my shoulder. "You're going to need it." A smirk tugs at Aerick's lips as he shuts the door behind us.

We walk for a minute before Aerick finally speaks. "Mind if I lie with you for a while?"

I raise an eyebrow at him. "Maybe after a shower. I would prefer not to have a bunch of dirt in my bed." I pick something off his shirt. "Or pieces of tree."

It's enough to put another half-smile on his face. "I have clothes in your dresser. I'll take a quick shower in your cabin. I miss sleeping with you next to me."

How could I deny that? "Alright."

We get inside and I immediately strip back down to my pajamas and crawl into bed before turning to see Aerick watching me. "What?" I yawn.

"Nothing," he says as he grabs clean boxers out of my drawer. "I'll be out in a few minutes."

I hear the water turn on and as much as I don't want it, my eyes force themselves shut.

✳ ✳ ✳ ✳

"Hmmm." Strong familiar arms tighten around me and kisses feather my hair line. I absolutely love waking up this way.

"I have to get up, babe."

My eyes fly open only to see a very dark room. I must have fallen asleep. I push myself back against him and wrap my arms over his, holding him tight to me. "Shit, Aerick. I'm sorry, I didn't mean to fall asleep."

"It's okay. I was happy to get to catch a nap with you. Go back to sleep, I'll set your alarm. You can skip P.T, but don't forget you need to help Brayden collect the laundry today before breakfast." He gives me one last kiss before crawling out of bed.

My eyes scrunch closed, too tired to argue that I hate laundry day. "Okay. I love you."

"I know, babe." Satisfied, I pull the blankets tightly to me and fall back asleep.

✳ ✳ ✳ ✳

I've been dreading this all day. I knew my day was only going to drag on knowing I had to see Christian this afternoon and drag on is exactly what it did. Even though I slept in and there was plenty to do today, the day seems to be lasting forever. Listening to Jake going on and on about how Vincent shorted out his bracelet for the last hour hasn't helped, either. Now I have to deal with this.

"It's about time you came and saw me." Christian gets up to greet me at the door.

Luther insisted both yesterday and over the phone this morning, which didn't leave much up for discussion. "It's not like I had much of a choice," I mutter as I shake his hand.

Giving him a tight nod, I move toward my normal seat on the couch in the corner. Thinking about it now, it's a little odd to have a couch and recliner sitting in the corner of a classroom. It looks out of place to me.

I shriek away from the sudden heaviness on my shoulder, spinning around on my heels. Both Christian's hands immediately go up in front of him, palms facing me with a worried look on his face. Not only worry, but a hint of fear. After a moment, I quickly take several deep breaths, realizing there's no threat. *Calm down!* Christian stares at me for another minute before lowering his hands.

"I'm, uh, sorry," I mutter, quickly moving toward the couch again. I don't want to look at his face. The fear that showed, no matter how briefly, is embarrassing. *Why can't I get a hold on this?*

"Nothing to apologize for, I startled you. It was my mistake for not being more careful with my actions."

The last few weeks, I have been slowly retreating back into

my shell that I lived in for so long. As I sit, I stare down at my fidgeting hands. I focus on my breathing and try to relax. It's Christian; no need to be so tense right now.

"It appears there has been a little setback."

I chance a quick look up at him only to be disappointed that his expression shows clear irritation.

"Apparently," I whisper, mostly to myself.

His tone lightens as he begins to speak again. "Regression is normal. It happens, and there's nothing to be ashamed of. You've been doing great these last few months. It was only natural for there to be a hiccup. You of all people should know that nothing is ever perfect."

He speaks all truth and he's right that this isn't the first setback, but it seems to be the worst. None of which I blame on him. Christian has been nothing less than remarkable in helping me. Makes me wonder a little to why he works here at all.

He's brilliant and probably has a much more prestigious practice than he leads on. I have thought on more than one occasion that this may be his charity work. Even though I know Luther pays him decently, it's probably way under his normal charge. The drive up here alone is an hour each way, which he does every Sunday.

"Are you still with me?" he questions and I look at him, dumbfounded. He must have been talking to me. Great – now I'm tuning him out, probably not inspiring much confidence.

"Sorry, what were you saying?" I ask, trying to focus.

"I asked how things have been this week," he asks again; calm, no judgment on his face at all.

"Mostly okay."

"Mostly?"

I bite my lip at his confidence in that one word and the no bullshit expression he's currently wearing. There's no doubt he's already talked to Luther. Luther told me that much yesterday. What I'm wondering is if he talked to Aerick, too. I wouldn't go as far as to say him and Aerick were close friends, but at the very least they're good colleagues. It wouldn't be the first time those two have ganged up on me.

When I don't say anything, he continues. "You can't just shut everyone out, Nadi. Shutting people out was what got you in trouble to begin with. We got through this by talking. Even if we didn't focus on what caused it. You instead opted for learning coping methods, but that doesn't mean it's always going to work that way. Regression, like anything else, is typically caused by a trigger. Now, while you may not want to talk about your past, you are going to need to divulge what has triggered this more current issue. It's the only way to not only help you now, but to keep it from being a problem again in the future."

It's really not that simple. "And if I don't?"

"Come on, we've gone through this. I cannot help you if you don't accept my help. I'm here for you, to help you, but you have to be willing to accept it. If not, then I'm wasting my time."

He says the end with such sadness that it makes my stomach

cramp with regret. He's invested a lot of time talking with me and teaching me how to deal with my problems. More than he did with the others, and he sure didn't do it for the money. I've never questioned his motive that he really wants to help me. Well, other than when I first met him, but I had reasons to be skeptical of any shrink at that time.

"You're not wasting your time. I want your help, it's just – not always easy."

"Understandable, but in my experience, nothing is ever easy. It takes someone strong, smart, and willing to get through the problem. These are all qualities we both know you possess."

"You don't understand."

"Then please try to explain it."

"I can't."

"Can't or won't?"

My legs push me up quickly and I start pacing as my frustration begins to boil over. I can't utter those things again. Even trying to explain what has been going on lately would mean me talking about my childhood. My biggest fears.

"Can't," I say confidently.

"That's a lie!" he almost shouts at me and my body freezes in shock. "You've talked about it before."

Aerick. He's talking about when I told Aerick. "That was different."

Anger spills over. That day is still clear in my memory and I distinctly remember telling Aerick I couldn't tell him, too.

Unfortunately, Aerick never stopped, he just kept pushing and pushing until I broke down. As much as I hated Aerick when he got me to confess my secret, I've long forgiven him for it, but it isn't something I would like to repeat anytime in the future.

"Different how?"

I shake my head. "Because I didn't tell him. Not really." *That's the truth!*

"Then how does he know?" He presses.

Urgh! "Because he tricked me."

"What do you mean 'tricked' you?"

I increase the speed of my feet as I try to hold my overflowing emotions back. "I never meant to tell him. He used his hold over me to get it out of me. I didn't even say most of it out loud."

"What do you mean you didn't tell him out loud?"

"He guessed most of it, okay? I… I only confirmed or denied his thoughts! I can't talk about it. I just can't!" I scream, exhausted at this intense questioning.

"Okay! Okay. Take a deep breath." His voice is calm and soft again drawing my attention back to him. He has that look of fear in his eyes again even though he's trying to hide it. My chest is heaving, and I only now realize that I have backed into the corner, my white knuckles fisted at my sides, ready to lash out.

He starts counting off slowly and I close my eyes, leaning my head back against the wall. I begin breathing deeply, matching it to his counting, and I slowly begin to calm down as the heaviness in my chest begins to ebb away only to be replaced with a flood of emotions at what just happened. I lost control, lost complete control. I cover my face in embarrassment as a tear falls down my cheek.

"I'm so sorry. I didn't mean to..."

"As I told you before, don't apologize. I pushed you, I knew the risk, you reacted, it's what I do."

His slightly joking tone helps. I lower my hands and look at him and his mouth turns up slightly. He gestures for me to come back to the couch and I take the few steps out of the corner, sitting back down.

"I guess there's no question now as to how far back you have fallen." My head nods in agreement, there's no denying it. I knew the minute I began flinching at peoples' touch again, but that doesn't mean that my words a few minutes ago are any less true. I don't think I have it in me to tell him any details.

As if reading my mind, Christian cuts into my thoughts. "You don't have to tell me today. If you're okay with it, there's only a few more questions, nothing about the past – I promise." I nod my head in acceptance.

"What have you experienced?"

"All of it," I answer slowly, knowing exactly what he's referring to. It has all come back: the heaviness in my chest, the fear of touch, nightmares, it's all back.

"When did it start?"

"A few weeks ago."

"What about Aerick?"

"What about Aerick?" I ask, confused.

"Well, we know that he's always been an exception to your issues. Have your most recent ones caused you to act out toward him? More specifically, to his touch?"

There were a few times I flinched at his touch. "Yeah, a little."

"But when Casey startled you yesterday, you didn't act out violently. As I was told, it appeared that he scared you. That's quite a contrast in your reaction."

I sit quietly, thinking about that. That line of questioning is pushing back into our first conversation and I don't want to go there right now. He must sense it because after a short silence, he changes directions.

"So how is everything else around camp? You'll be finishing school soon, isn't that right?" He gives me an encouraging smile and I hope it's signaling that we can stay off the previous subject.

"Yes, I'm almost done with school. The last quarter is about to start, and I have pretty much finished up the CLEP tests and intern hours. As of now I'm teaching the class, even though I'm not certified yet."

"How is that going?"

"It's okay. It's a lot of work to have to contend with. I still have all my schoolwork and am basically working full time. Most nights I'm up until at least midnight. Unfortunately, we have several more weeks of class, so I won't have much relief until then."

"So, you feel a little overwhelmed?"

I don't want Luther to think I can't handle it, but Christian hit the head on the nail, and I'm afraid that it's why this is all happening to begin with. I'm afraid to express that to him too. I enjoy my job and I want to keep it. Luther is counting on me to be able to do this.

"It's okay to feel that way, Nadi." My hesitation has answered his question for me. "It doesn't make you any less of a person. We all struggle at some point in life. It's important to learn to take some time for yourself. This added stress could be part of the problem." *Good, at least we're on the same page.* "Stress is an awful thing and tends to intensify already bad situations. How about other stress? How is your relationship with Aerick going?"

"Not stressful, but definitely frustrating." Then again, being frustrated is making me a bit stressed.

"Let me guess: he wants to talk to you about what's been going on and you don't?"

"Precisely."

"I don't want to sit here and lecture you on how that could actually help, because it's clear that you don't want to, but, well, there it is, I said it anyway. All that aside, it would be helpful to find ways to have a little 'you' time. You were always a fan of isolating yourself and listening to music to clear your mind, if I recall correctly. I think that, in this case, it would be really helpful. While I don't want you to completely cut yourself off, because that would be counterproductive, try taking thirty minutes to an hour each day and just get away from it all. No people, no work, no school. Give your mind a chance to rest and recuperate."

That actually sounds great. Granted, I do find a few moments to forget everything, those moments are few and far between and have only been thanks to Aerick helping me forget about everything in the world. Those moments are the only ones I've been able to enjoy lately.

"Well, it's about time we go get some dinner. What do you say?" He stands and offers his hand to help me up, which I graciously take. I feel worn out mentally.

"Sounds good."

* * * *

Leaning against the wall behind the instructor's cabins, I look up at the beautiful, colorful sky as the sun sets. It's been a long time since I sat back here and just relaxed. This was my refuge when I was a cadet here, but it appears no one else has figured that out. Or perhaps they don't value the silence and being able to get away from others.

So many things have been racing through my mind today and the last thing I want to do right now is see anyone. More specifically, I don't want to run into Aerick. I'm not in the mood for more questioning about what's been going through my head.

I want nothing more than to forget all the bad shit going on in my life right now. I haven't had enough time to get away and give myself a chance to forget everything, even if it's only for a while. It always made me feel a little better afterward, no matter what I had to come back too. Back in Chicago, I had the roof. No one ever came up there; well, except for Jeff. Anytime my mom would worry, she'd call him, and he would immediately go to the roof. I never did get out of him why he didn't just tell her I was up there.

Instead he would check on me and tell me to get home. Now I know it was because he probably liked me, even then. I can't complain, either. Seeing his smile, making sure I was not thinking anything stupid, it was always comforting.

Flashback

"Hey you!" Jeff pulls the cheapo headphones off my head. "You okay?"

Even as mad as I am at him for interrupting my 'quiet time', I can't help but grin at him. "Yeah, I'm fine." I sit up from my spot where I was lying down looking up at the few stars that you can see at night in the city.

"Come on, don't lie to me. You only disappear when something is bothering you. What happened today?"

I can't lie to him. He's only going to find out anyway. "Patrick was walking me back after your mom called you inside. A group of older boys were walking down the street messing around." It seems so stupid looking back at it. "One bumped his shoulder into Patrick as we walked past them, and he started yelling at Patrick and pushing him, so I started yelling at him to leave him alone. Then two of the other boys grabbed me."

I stop for a minute, just remembering that feeling. Jeff grabs my hand and coaxes me to continue. I let out a heavy sigh.

"I was fine for a second and then you know..." I pull my hand back, embarrassed that I'm so weak. "I lost it. I tried to get away but couldn't. Then I started screaming... and crying. They threw me down, but I couldn't stop crying and I couldn't... breathe. They said I was a stupid baby; said I was a freak."

A tear escapes my eye and I wipe it away quickly. I hate feeling like this. Jeff scoots over in front of me, grabbing my face so I'm forced to look into his eyes. "You're not a freak. You're stronger than anyone I know. I'm sorry I left you guys; I should have asked if I could walk you home. I know better than that."

"Jeff stop, it isn't your fault." I have to be strong. It's not fair for him to beat himself up over this, it was my fault, not his. I was the one that was weak. "You're right Jeff, this is stupid. I can't let this bother me. I'm stronger than that."

His lips press in a line for a moment, staring deep in my eyes, but then he gets up and pulls me to my feet. "That's right; you are." He gives me a quick hug before grabbing my hand again. "Now, let's get you home before your mom sends out a search party for both of us." His smirk melts away my sadness and I already feel better.

End Flashback

Those were the simple days. Where it really was just stupid boys being boys. Now things are so much more complicated. Maybe, just maybe I can find a little bit of peace, even if it's only for a while.

I slip my earbuds in and turn the music up, tuning out the rest of the world in an attempt to quiet my mind.

CHAPTER TWELVE

(Sunday, February 14th)

"WHEN ANGELS FALL with broken wings, I can't give up, I can't give in…"

My eyes draw open as I feel a shadow pass over me, and I grin up at the gorgeous smile that shadows above me.

"Feeling better, are we?" Aerick asks with his cute half smirk as I pull my blaring earbuds out.

"Actually, I am." Taking Christian up on his advice, I've found some time to be alone. It's had a major relaxing effect on me this week. Not that much has happened, but it has been a good way to 'deflate' every afternoon. Coming and sitting behind the cabin, listening to loud music and not thinking about anything has given me a much-needed boost of energy.

Aerick reaches to my outstretched hands and helps me up. Looking deep into my eyes, his lips attach to mine giving my spirits a little extra kick, but he releases all too soon. "You ready?"

"If I say no, do I get another kiss?"

He smirks at me. "No."

"Well then, yes I'm ready," I say letting my excitement get to me. This morning at breakfast Aerick told me that he, Paulo, Terrie and I have been granted permission to go out for Valentine's day. Gavin has agreed to lead PT tonight, and since there isn't much else to do, Luther said the rest of them could hold down the fort.

I'm very excited for Terrie, too. She hardly ever gets to leave. When she does it's never for very long, because she's the camp nurse and there's no telling when something might happen that will need her expertise. In all honesty, I'm still not sure how the guys talked Luther into it.

Both Aerick and Paulo have been overly excited all day and neither of them are giving Terrie or I any indication of what we can expect. Another reason I decided it may be helpful to have my quiet time before we leave. I have no idea what they're planning, and I don't want my stress from the week making me edgy.

Aerick gives me another other quick kiss on the cheek and pulls at my jacket for a moment to get me to follow him. When I asked Aerick how to dress, since they wouldn't tell us where we're going, he said nice but warm, so Terrie and I both decided to dress in cute skinny jeans, nice tops and cute boots, as opposed to our combat boots. Terrie, being the lifesaver that she is, also lent me a nice jacket.

We stop by our cabin to grab Terrie and then head out to the car. I'm getting giddy with excitement and Terrie seems to mirror my emotions. To make things even more intense, my hormones are also on edge as my eyes keep drawing back to Aerick's outfit. Even as many times as I've seen him in his designer jeans, button-up shirt and leather jacket, it never gets old. Paulo is waiting at the SUV, dressed similarly to Aerick, and holds open the rear door while Aerick opens the front passenger door for me. *Such gentlemen!*

Not that it's abnormal for them to be so polite, but both of them seem to be a little off today. Even last night something wasn't quite right with them. It was a bonfire night and both of them spent a lot of time sitting together talking. At the time I chalked it up to them just being guys, but then I found out we were going somewhere today, and now I'm certain they were planning something. Neither Aerick nor Paulo are really the romantic type but who knows, maybe they'll surprise us.

Despite both boys keeping to themselves last night, Aerick made it a point to keep sneaking glances and sexy smiles at me when he thought no one was looking. He was talking to Paulo mostly, but I have no doubt he was thinking of us. Bonfires tend to be special nights for us because it's a reminder of my eighteenth birthday, basically when we first got together. Typically, even on our not so great days, we put things aside on bonfire nights. It's nice to just forget everything that's going on and have a nice night by the fire.

Besides that, we both drank last night. I didn't overdo it, but I got pretty buzzed, again heightening my longing for him when he would do things like biting his lip as he stared at me. I think Paulo was getting fairly annoyed that he didn't have his full attention. His irritated facial expressions kept making me giggle.

As we get on the freeway and head out of town my curiosity is piqued again. We're obviously not staying in town. Aerick is concentrating on driving but has that smirk on his face. Probably feeling my stare, he looks over to me and brings the hand he's holding up and kisses the back of it with a grin.

He's backed off a lot since last Sunday. I saw him talking to Christian after our session last week. I'm hoping he told him it would do no good to push me and that he's better off to let me figure things out and I would tell him in my own time.

That's how much of the week has played out. As in most weeks, we don't have much time to spend alone, but we mostly fall back into our normal routine of working out together, stealing kisses and hugs when others aren't around. However, since a few cadets have started working out at night, our moments seem to be even more rare. With the start of the new quarter at school, there isn't a whole lot of work yet, so mostly I'm focusing on the work of teaching, which is also getting easier.

It's also made me feel a little better about taking my 'me time'. Aerick has picked up on these away times the last few days and has begun meeting me back there at the end of them to bring me back to the real world after so we can share a few moments together. I figure it was also his inspiration for last night's little detour.

Flashback

Finally, we're done putting away the bonfire supplies. Today has seemed like a really long day and I'm ready to get into bed. Tonight Aerick, Jake and I were on clean up duty.

I pack the last of the supplies into the bags and Aerick grabs the table that all the s'mores supplies sat on. "Jake, if you want to take this table to the supply room, we'll get the rest of the food and soda to the kitchen," Aerick says.

"Sure." Jake takes the table and heads off.

I smile at Aerick as he puts out the last of the fire before picking up the cooler and the bag of garbage. I grab the few bags of leftover food and he nods his head to start walking back. It's been a nice evening with no clouds in the sky. It's a bit colder without the clouds to hold in the warmth, but the stars are shining brightly, a sight that never ceases to amaze me.

Once we put the stuff away in the mess hall and head back outside, Aerick grabs my hand and pulls me toward his dorm. I quickly look around to make sure no one's there but it's well after lights out and almost all the lights in the buildings are off. There's little chance that anyone is still up, except maybe Jake.

I give Aerick a questioning look, but he ignores it and keeps walking. There's no way Aerick would actually be taking me to his dorm. I haven't slept in there since the end of the last session, and even then that was a little awkward, but there's no way Terrie would be okay with him sleeping in our cabin, either. I decide I'll go along with it for now because it means spending a little more time with him.

When we reach the stairs leading inside, he merely moves around them and keeps walking. It only takes a minute to realize where we're going. He keeps his eyes on the cameras, just like he did that night many months ago.

"Can we sit for a while?"

He turns me around so my back is to him and slides down, bringing me with him. I'm now sitting in his lap, giving me a big deja vu moment. I let out a giggle at the warm feeling that presents itself and he kisses the back of my head. Leaning back on his shoulder, I can see him looking up at the trillions of stars blinking down at us.

"It's been too long since we have done this. Wouldn't you agree?"

"Yes. I miss just getting to sit with you, too."

He leans down and gives me a sweet kiss before looking back up the stars.

End Flashback

We sat there for some time until I finally fell asleep in his warm arms. The next thing I knew, he was laying me in bed, assuring Terrie I was okay and that he wasn't staying, just dropping me off – literally. In keeping his word, once he stripped me down to my tee shirt and panties, he tucked me in with a kiss and left, much to my disappointment.

We exit the freeway in Ellensburg and go down the street to the hospital. Looking to Aerick, I give him a questioning look. Not that I would mind, but this isn't even close to what I thought we would be doing.

"Only a pitstop."

Paulo jumps out, telling Terrie that he'll be right back, and gets into the back grabbing out a bag.

"Brand asked us to drop off a few things for tomorrow," Aerick explains further while we wait.

Luther told me earlier today that Tia is finally getting released tomorrow, even though baby Sam will still have to stay for at least several more weeks. Luther is helping Brand pay for a hotel next to the hospital so they can stay near the baby. Although their new house in Cle Elum has officially been theirs for a few months, they want to stay in Ellensburg until they can take the baby home. Tia can't bear to be away from him, and I can completely understand that. I don't think I could leave my baby, either.

It'll be nice once they can all go home though, and I've been keeping my hopes that he'll get to go home sooner rather than later. Each time we've visited, the doctors have said how impressed they are with how quickly he's coming along. After the first week, he was pretty much out of the woods and it settled a lot of people's nerves. I had Terrie explain a lot to me about the ins and outs of premature babies. Once she seemed confident he was going to be fine, it calmed my nerves, too.

Paulo jumps back in the car and we head off again, but we

don't go far. We pull into a cute Italian restaurant. I can smell the food as soon as I exit the car and it's mouthwatering. Aerick comes around and wraps my hand around his arm before we head inside, with Paulo and Terrie trailing behind us.

"Reservation for four. It should be under 'Aerick,'" he tells the hostess. She smiles at him, trying to covertly look him up and down, and turns to take us to our table in a quiet corner of the restaurant.

We take our seats and the hostess tells us tonight's special. Aerick orders a round of rum and coke for us while he orders himself a Corona, presumably since he has to drive us back to camp. The host gives him an overly sweet grin before excusing herself. *I'm not going to get irritated tonight!*

My eyes begin scanning the restaurant while everyone else begins to look over their menus. It's pretty nice, maybe a little more upscale than anywhere I've ever been. They definitely went all-out for an expensive dinner.

A cute little waitress, probably a college student, comes over with some water and introduces herself, letting her eyes linger on both of the guys a little longer than appropriate. Aerick kindly lets her know we need a few more minutes and she leaves.

"Have you ever been here before?" I ask Aerick.

"Yes. Casey and I have been here a few times. They have really good Chicken Parmesan."

"That actually sounds really good. I think I'll have the same." I look to Paulo and Terrie to see if they have made up their minds, but Paulo seems to be concentrating way too hard on his menu.

"Paulo, you okay?" I ask. He's awfully quiet. Aerick pulls out his phone and does something. I look at him strangely when Paulo pulls his phone out and reads something on it.

"Actually, if you ladies will excuse me a moment." We both chime in with 'okays' and he gets up and walks to what I'm guessing is the bathroom. Guys can be so flipping confusing sometimes. Aerick is back on his phone texting and I give him a questioning look at their behavior, but he merely shakes his head, saying that it's nothing.

After a few minutes Paulo finally gets back, but he still doesn't seem any less awkward. In fact, he seems downright scared and my nerves go on high alert, but Aerick grabs my hand under the table. I quickly look at him and he's trying to hold back a smile while he keeps his phone resting upright on the table.

"Terrie, can you come help me with something please?" She looks up from her menu slightly confused but grabs his offered hand and stands up. Aerick's hand tightens on mine and Paulo sinks down to one knee. Terrie instantly freezes and her eyes go wide. My heart stops along with my breathing.

Paulo wipes the back of his neck. "You know I love you more than anything in this world, babe. I know I'm not that romantic, smart, rich guy that you deserve. Hell, I'm also not that guy who's always prompt and responsible. In fact, most of the time I don't take anything seriously, like ever." He laughs and Aerick quietly coughs.

"Yeah, but this is serious. I'm being serious right now." He clears his throat and recovers his blushing face. "I have thought about this for some time and I'm positive that if I could spend my life with you, I would die a happy man, and I only pray you feel the same."

He grabs a box out of his jacket pocket, the same one I pulled out of Aerick's pocket not so long ago. He fumbles to get it open and looks back up to her. "So here it is. Terrie, will you make me the happiest man on this earth and marry me?"

Tears begin streaming down her face and she nods her head 'yes'. Paulo's face breaks into a huge grin and he puts the ring on her finger before standing, picking her up and giving her a very passionate kiss. The few people on this side of the restaurant break out in applause and even a few whistles. The waitress immediately appears with a bottle of champagne and several glasses instead of our original drink orders.

"Ou te alofa ia te oe," he tells her with another kiss. They finally sit back down, and champagne is passed around the table.

Aerick picks up his and raises it. "To you guys, and a lifetime of happy marriage." We all raise our glasses and clink them together before taking a drink. Terrie is still trying to wipe under her eyes to keep her mascara from running.

"Well, let me see!" I hold out my hand and she shows me her ring. It's a simple but beautiful three-stone ring. "It's so beautiful Ter, congratulations. I'm so happy for you."

Even though I knew he was going to do it, I had no idea that was why he was acting so nervous the last twenty-four hours. Aerick and Paulo share a manly, goofy smile with each other and Paulo looks a hundred times better. *Did he think she would say no or something?*

"Oh, come on Aerick, please tell me you are not filming me messing up my makeup with my tears," Terrie says.

"Of course I am. It may be the only time I ever see it again. I don't think I have ever seen you so emotional," he teases and I slap him on the leg as he laughs, finally putting his phone down. I'm surprised when he grabs my face with both hands and gives me a passionate kiss of his own.

When we break apart, he gives me a half smile. "Just so you know, that is how you should act when I decide to ask you that question," he whispers next to my ear.

"I'll keep that in mind." I pull him back in for another kiss, but we're broken apart by our waitress returning to our table now that things have quieted back down a bit. Terrie is obviously still too out of it to really think straight so I tell the guys to order for us and pull her to the bathroom, grabbing her purse as we leave.

Once in the bathroom, she turns and engulfs me in a tight hug. Although I tense significantly at the contact, I just concentrate on breathing, knowing she needs this right now.

"I'm so happy for you! I guess moving in with him totally works in your favor now," I tell her, trying to ease the tightening in my chest. She finally pulls back with a laugh and my airways open back up.

We go over to the counter and she rolls her eyes, looking at her smeared makeup. She immediately takes her purse and starts to straighten it out. I take the time to use the toilet and get my bearings after our extended close contact.

"I can't believe he actually did it," she says as I come out of the stall. "He was right about one thing – he is never serious about anything. I never thought he would actually take on such a big commitment. I wonder how long he really thought about it."

I really hope she's not doubting that he really thought this through. "He's been planning it for a while."

She looks at me. "How do you know?"

"Don't be mad or anything, but I kind of found out a few weeks ago." Her eyes squint together. "I sort of found out by accident." She waits for me to continue. I don't want her to be mad at me for not telling her or anything.

"Well, the thing is, he asked Aerick to hold on to the ring. It just so happens that I got cold the same day, before Aerick could put it in a safe place. He gave me his jacket to wear and I sort of found it in his pocket. Let me tell you, I completely freaked out. I actually thought he was going to propose to me."

"Seriously? That wouldn't have been so bad; Aerick loves you."

"I sort of shut down and ran off. I wasn't prepared for that to happen. I know Aerick loves me and all, but we haven't been together more than a few months. It's too soon for all that."

She laughs at me. "Sweetie, trust me. It isn't something he

would do on a whim. Aerick is very calculated and if he did propose, know he has thought long and hard about it." My lips turn up, it actually makes me feel a lot better about it. My reaction was kind of stupid.

"So, how long have you known?"

"That was almost a month ago," I say, a little shy.

"Wow, he really planned this out, didn't he! That's a first!"

The rest of dinner goes off without any more surprises. We spend the next several hours talking and laughing about all kinds of things. They tell me about how they got together and how hard it was to hide it from everyone, including Luther. Aerick tells me that him finding out was also by accident but, as it turns out, it has been to their advantage since he could help Paulo sneak around. He admits he was pretty upset at Paulo for not telling him.

Aerick keeps a tight hold on me and is overly affectionate. I don't know if it's because Paulo and Terrie can't keep their hands off each other either or if it's something else, but I don't mind. Once we finally finish off the bottle of champagne, we decide it's time to get back.

Once back at camp, Luther and Ayla are waiting out front. For a moment I think something is wrong, but the moment we get out, Ayla runs and gives Terrie a big hug before passing her off to Luther.

"Geez, did everyone know except me?"

"No, just us. Paulo had to get permission for you guys to leave for a few hours and he also had to ask me for your next surprise," Ayla says beaming.

"And what would that be?" Terrie asks, almost nervous.

"I agreed to switch cabins for the night so you two could be alone. It's only right, but please be respectful that you're borrowing my cabin," Ayla says with a sly smile.

"I still vote that Nadi stays in the instructor's dorm for tonight," Aerick pipes up from next to me.

"Absolutely not."

"Come on Luther, nothing will happen, I promise."

"I know nothing will happen, because she is sleeping in her own bed, as are you." I hold in my laugh. *Did he really think Luther would agree to that?*

"Fine. But if she can't stay with me, then I'm going to hang out there for a bit before lights out, if that's alright."

"That is okay, but you guys are all back in camp, so keep it professional outside the cabin. Paulo and Terrie, that goes for you two as well. Tomorrow I know you will be tempted but you need to remain professional around the cadets."

They both nod and Aerick takes my hand, pulling me away from them as we say our goodbyes. He releases my hand after a few steps and we just walk side by side. Not thinking, I rub my sore hip as it begins to hurt more.

"You okay?" Aerick asks.

"Yeah, I got my shot today. It tends to hurt for a day or so after."

"You mean your birth control shot?" I nod yes. "Well, that means I still have free access anytime." His eyebrow jumps up and down and I laugh. "Well, we better hurry before Ayla gets there. I would really like to give you my Valentine's Day present."

I look quickly over to him. "Aerick, please tell me you didn't spend more money on me."

He bites his lip and gives me a devilish grin. "Oh baby, this won't cost a thing."

My core heats up and I pick up the pace, eager to get back to the cabin.

CHAPTER THIRTEEN

(Sunday, February 21st)

AERICK POV

DAMN!

Picking myself up off the mat, I internally curse myself. That is the second time he has knocked me on my ass today. "Maybe it's time I stop sparring with you. Where the hell did you learn that move?"

Gavin smirks at me. "What can I say? Nadi was right."

Nadi? Using every ounce of restraint, I somehow manage to keep the grimace off my face and keep my tone level. "What exactly was she right about?"

"She told me you're a good teacher." I frown at him. I wonder when she told him that; but the thought is quickly replaced with anger at the realization he is thinking about her. I really don't like that he thinks about her at all. *She's mine!* Part of me doesn't appreciate that she was talking about me to him, either.

For the last few weeks, early in the morning, I have been sparring with Gavin; but that doesn't mean that we're friends. It is a mere convenience. Next to Paulo, he is the closest match for me, and Paulo isn't much of a morning person so I have to settle for this; it is what I have been in desperate need of. Gavin is a way for me to get back the edge that has begun slipping as I have become more distracted by a certain woman.

Much to my dismay, Gavin has been slowly getting better and becoming an even better sparring partner. It isn't that I have been teaching him, more like he is very perceptive. Something that I pride myself on to overcome my opponents. As he has become more familiar with my fighting style, he has been able to find ways to counter my strikes, and like just now, picked up on a few new moves for himself.

He's not the only one who has been paying attention though. One of his lingering weak points is that he is easily distracted especially by her. I want to growl at the thought but hold it inside. The day she woke up early and decided to join us in the gym, I knocked him on his ass several times. It didn't take a rocket scientist to realize her presence was to blame. *That I can use.*

"She told you that huh?" I ask as we circle each other again.

"Yeah a while back. How has she been doing lately?" Mentally, I groan again at his words. Maybe this wasn't the best form of distraction. It may be to my detriment as the weakness applies to both of us.

"She's fine." *Not that it is any of your business.*

Shit! I barely miss his right hook. "She's seemed a bit up and down the last few weeks."

Yes, she has. Much to my disappointment, whatever it is that is bothering her hasn't been shared with me. She's internalized everything and any time I try to get her to talk, she insists it is nothing. Then again, she is a woman, and not just any woman. I don't think any woman on this earth can compare to her. I can't help but laugh, but immediately stop when he raises an eyebrow at me.

"You're mistaken; that's just her. She is the most confounding woman – ever." I hold back the smirk that threatens to show through.

A question is etched in his eyes. "Ever?"

"I know women. Usually they are pretty easily pleased. You just have to know how to see their needs and make sure you satisfy them." A simple formula.

"But not her?" His head turns slightly to the side.

I can't tell if that was a question or agreement, so I explain further. "No, not her. She is much more… complicated than most women." Although I'm not sure 'complicated' fully describes her.

"She does seem very intelligent." *Is he suggesting most women aren't intelligent?*

"She is, but that isn't it."

He waits expectantly as he slowly relaxes his stance. I'm not sure I know how to explain this. For the first time in a while I fumble for words to describe it, but I try anyway.

"I don't know. I guess she just has so many sides of her that fight for dominance. It's hard to judge which one is there at any given time, and it tends to change at the drop of a hat. It makes keeping her satisfied a little more difficult."

Gavin is clearly trying to repress a laugh and I throw a punch, landing it in his ribs. *Distraction!* He lets out a satisfying grunt. "I didn't say I couldn't satisfy her, asshole. That isn't what I meant; I satisfy her plenty. Thankfully, that is one side of her that is easily brought forward." *Choke on that, prick!*

"Hey, I never said you didn't." He puts his hands up in surrender.

"Good."

He'd better stay the fuck away from her. I see his game and I'm not stupid. The way he looks at her, always finding a reason to be around her, giving her those books, I know what he is doing. I see his game because I have done the same thing myself with other women. It's funny how quickly women warm up to you when you pretend not to be interested; make it seem as if you only want to be friends, and they fall right into your lap.

Now that Jeff has moved into the instructors' dorm, it makes me even more uncomfortable. At least when Jeff and Gavin shared a cabin, he was able to keep an eye on Gavin. I am extremely grateful that Christian has been pushing Nadi to have her 'alone time' which means less time she has to just sit around and read. Outside of that time, I have been really careful to either keep her busy or make sure Gavin is busy.

I look down at my watch because my desire to continue our match has waned. "I need to head out. There's some stuff to get done before P.T."

Geez, she really does distract everyone; that's why I'm here and instead of getting my workout in, I am walking away to end our conversation. *Idiot!* I can only blame myself.

Thankfully he shrugs, accepting my withdrawal from our match. "Yeah, sure."

Grabbing a bottle of water, I chug it down quickly and grab my things. This day is not starting off very well and I'm not sure if I'm merely irritated with Gavin's constant interest in Nadi, irritated at myself because my plan backfired on me, or irritated at the fact that Christian wanted to talk to me before his sessions started.

Things with Nadi have been good since Valentine's Day, so I really can't blame her for my foul mood. As a matter of fact, I would love nothing more than to have had her working out with me this morning. Last night, as we played poker in the cabin, she seemed more relaxed than she has been for quite some time.

A groan escapes my throat as I remember feeling her sitting on my lap, running her fingers along my arms as I continued to play. I need some alone time with her soon. Maybe I can borrow Casey's cabin; he won't be up here this weekend. Unfortunately, I will have to wait a few hours to text him; it's Sunday, there's no way he's up yet. *I hate having to wait to do shit!*

✳ ✳ ✳ ✳

"Hey, Christian. You wanted to see me."

I always talk to him before his sessions to give him a rundown of the weeks' activities and any problems we had with the cadets or possible revelations to share. But this morning he texted me asking me to come in a little earlier to discuss something. *More like to discuss someone.* I wonder what it is this time. Luther has been making Nadi go to her appointments lately and I wonder what he has gotten out of her that he feels he needs to share with me.

"Yes, sorry to call you in early. I know you're busy."

I have no patience for stupid small talk on a typical day and he should know that by now. Just say what you need to say. Today I have even less patience and I have a half of mind to turn around and walk right back out.

"What can I do for you?" I don't bother holding back my irritation.

"Well, I know this is a little unconventional, but I was wondering if you would sit in on mine and Nadi's session today."

Yeah, right. Nothing good can come of that. "Does she want me to?" I eye him skeptically, hoping he picks up on my disdain for the idea.

"I haven't said anything to her about it yet." His words are quiet, reserved, but almost curious, which piques my own curiosity.

"Why?"

"I think I may be able to get her to open up a little more if you're here." I see what he is getting at. He's talking about her past. She doesn't like to talk about it, plain and simple.

"Yeah, probably not such a good idea."

He interrupts before I can refuse any further: "You know more about her than anyone. Apart from you, she has never shared her past with anyone."

That isn't true; I know otherwise. Patrick and Jeff were there when it happened. They are the ones who helped her through it and I'm pretty sure Jeff knows more about that time in her life than even I do. Of course, not by choice, but because he was there. It bothers him as much as it bothers me.

As much as I dislike Jeff because of his feelings for her, I'm grateful for him at the same time. Not just because he was there for her back then, but that he is still there for her even now. Especially when I am being my dick-ish self and she needs someone to turn to, like the night of the party. Better him than Gavin, but it's not my place to tell Christian any of this. She has been pissed off enough at me for talking about her with others and I'm not in the mood to fight with her. Nor do I want to rehash the bad shit that she has told me.

"Christian, you don't understand. When I got her to admit that shit..." *It was horrible.*

The things she admitted, her crying in my arms, exposed and broken. It was just as bad as when I saw her physically hurt. The grief and pain that she had shown was so raw. I made her relive that in her mind and it pained me to see it. I shudder at the thought. I think it is really the only time she has fully let her guard down. A couple of times she got pretty close, but I feel as if there is always a small part of her that keeps me at an arm's length.

"Let's just say I have no desire to relive that day." Even if it was the first time, she let me in.

"But the fact is that you did get her to admit it. She feels more comfortable around you than anyone else."

"She has a wall up around that shit that you're trying to get to and it almost never comes down. It isn't something she openly talks about. I simply got to see through a small crack in that wall for a brief moment. Unfortunately, it was long enough for me to find out she had some pretty fucked-up things happen to her. She isn't going to start singing like a canary just because I'm here."

Combine that with the fact that she has been more distant lately and I'm pretty positive he won't get her to admit anything about her past. *Then again...*

"Are you looking to talk to her about her childhood or what has been going on lately?" My wheels are turning.

His eyes shoot up in curiosity. "Do you think she may be more willing to talk about that instead?"

Maybe this is how I can get my own answers. She isn't going to like this, but I'm at a loss here. I've been trying for weeks to figure out what is going on with her. Something is off and I'm determined to figure out what.

"Yes." I say, putting my confidence behind my words even though I still have my doubts as to whether or not this will work.

"Okay, well, we can work with that. So, you'll come?"

Bad idea, bad idea, bad idea. I try to shut out my subconscious and nod my head. She will be mad, but sometimes you have to give a little to get a little.

Christian is satisfied and he points to the cadets' folders in my hand, effectively dismissing our conversation about Nadi and we move on to our normal conversation about the cadets. Thankfully, I have a few hours until her session. Now, I just have to prepare myself for her ire.

✳ ✳ ✳ ✳

By some miracle, I have hidden from Nadi for most of the day. My leg bounces up and down nervously as I sit on the couch waiting for her to show up. Christian waits by the door, biting his nails, clearly worried about how she is going to react to this. He insisted on not telling her because he believed she would flat out refuse to show up.

I talked to Casey earlier. He confirmed that he wasn't up for the weekend and that I was more than welcome to use the cabin this evening. Convincing Luther was the more difficult task. We have been spending a lot of time together outside the camp and he's worried that others might start complaining that it's unfair.

In the end, I had to throw the fact at him that for the last few years, I was the one who always stayed behind while everyone else did their thing. Not once did I complain that I was pulling more weight than them and it pissed me off a little that he even needed the reminder of that. He agreed, but said that I would have to pick up a few more duties these last few weeks of camp. If that is what it takes, I'm okay with that. Besides, in a few weeks Nadi and I will be on our way home to spend eight weeks together alone.

I'm drawn out of my thoughts by the figure that has paused in the doorway. It's like a deer frozen by the headlights. She looks to me and then back to Christian several times before speaking.

"What is this?"

I can't tell which emotion is more present, fear or anger. "Nadi, if you would please just sit, and then we can talk." Christian gestures for her to join me on the couch, but his tone is too soft.

She takes a deep breath and takes a step to the side and crosses her arms in front of her. She doesn't enjoy being talked to like she is weak or a child. "I think I'll stay right here, and you can tell me what the fuck is going on here."

This wasn't my idea, and I plan to let Christian try to pick his way out of this. "Nadi, I only want to talk, as always."

"And you feel he needed to hear what we're talking about?" She nods my way.

"Not necessarily hear what you have to say, but to be here more as support. Please can we sit down." She looks between us again as she chews on the inside of her mouth.

Instead of responding she keeps the pissed-off look on her face and walks over, joining me on the couch, but she leaves more space than normal between us. *Great.* Christian follows behind us and before he has fully taken his seat she speaks up.

"So, talk."

He works to contain his amusement. "How was your week?"

"Fine."

"No problems this week?"

"No."

"Anything new?"

"Nope."

"Are you having a good day today?" She tilts her head, giving him an irritated glare. "Okay, let me rephrase. Were you having a good day before coming here?"

"Yes."

He lets out a slight chuckle. "Are all your answers today going to be monosyllables?"

"Maybe." I turn away trying to hide my smirk as she says a word that contradicts her answer, but I'm sure she is fully aware of that.

"Do you have something to add, Aerick?" I turn back, throwing daggers at him with my eyes. *What the hell?*

"Nope. This is your show. I'm here per your request, although it seems my presence is hurting more than it is helping." I don't need her thinking this was in any way my idea.

She looks at me for a moment before turning her attention back to him. "Well?"

It takes him a minute to get his thoughts in order. "Okay, let's start easy. Have you been able to continue to have some personal time to yourself?"

"Yes." She seems to calm at the new direction he is taking her, and I finally get a glimmer of hope that this may work.

"Does it seem to be helping?"

"Yes."

"Good. I want you to continue to do that. Have you taken any time to reflect on what has been causing your regression?"

Her eyes fly to me, then down to her lap. "I told you, I'm fine."

"Come on Nadi, you need to be honest. If what you've said the last few weeks is true, I'm sure Aerick is just as aware that you have had a slight setback." I don't know if slight is really accurate, but maybe he is saying that for her benefit.

"I don't want to talk about it right now," she mumbles, and my mouth opens without a thought.

"You mean you don't want to talk about it in front of me." My hurt is barely contained and regret instantly hits her face, making me feel bad. We are pushing her into this and that isn't fair to her. I so badly want to know what is going on with her. My dueling emotions are getting the best of me. *Fuck!*

"Aerick," her voice is so small, but I don't want to hear it. I feel ridiculously emotional right now.

"No, forget it. She doesn't want me here." I swiftly get up and leave the room.

Nadi yells out to me as the door closes behind me, but my feet keep moving. I know I shouldn't be so upset, but I am. Right now, I really want to punch something, so I do a U-turn and head for the gym, ignoring a crazy look from one of the cadets.

When I get inside, there are several people around doing various things, but I just head straight for the punching bag and lay into it. I just want to know what the fuck is going on with her. My mind has been running in overdrive for weeks. I have imagined fifty different issues, including me, as being the problem, but the more I think about each one, the more each seems unlikely.

She is scared, worried, angry, lost and nothing explains where it is all coming from. She was doing so well, we were doing so well, and then all of the sudden a few weeks ago something changed. At first I thought I was over analyzing things, but then whatever it was progressed, and even other people started to notice.

I have gotten her to talk about her biggest secret, the most painful time in her life, yet she won't talk to me. I have stood by her as she went through hell, never once giving her a reason to question my love or loyalty to her. *WHY THE HELL WON'T SHE TELL ME WHAT'S WRONG?!*

The bag swings several feet out as I put all my anger and frustration into my attack. I grab onto the bag as it swings violently back into me to keep it from knocking me over. Suddenly my mind feels so tired and worn out. My hands cling to the sides of the bag and I shake my head, letting it come to rest against the bag. *Why can't I figure this out?*

"Aerick?" Her timid voice behind me almost makes me jump.

I can see her face before I even turn around. Taking a deep breath, I try to compose myself. When I turn to see the expression that I knew would be there, she is very wary and seems to be questioning if she should be here or not. *Crap!* That is all she needs; me being more unstable. She's got enough issues without me being a dick.

"Come on." I give her a ghost of a smile before turning and heading out of the gym.

Once outside, I glance back to make sure she is following, and she is, but she still looks unsure. She doesn't say anything as we cross the courtyard and she stays several steps behind me, only pausing once we enter the instructors' dorm. I know she's confused by my emotional state and there is no denying the irony.

"Just let me change my shirt and then we can get out of here," I tell her as she opens her mouth to talk. I would rather wait until we are more alone before we start talking. She walks further into the room, sitting at the edge of my bed.

"Where are we going?" The continued timidity of her voice pulls at my heart; it's not like her. No doubt she is questioning my words before leaving her and Christian. Reality is that it hurt me just as much to say them as it probably did for her to hear them. Another debate begins in my head as to whether or not I should apologize for my harshness, but again, it's the truth.

Though, I am pushing her yet again to tell me something she isn't ready to tell me. I yank on a clean shirt and hold my hand out to her, but she stands on her own. My hand falls to my side and I let out a sigh. It does no good to push her into things, and I know better.

"Look, I needed to get out of here for a while and figured you would like to join me. It's up to you, I don't want to force you to do something you don't want to." Well I want to, but the rational side of me will not give in to those thoughts.

She doesn't answer right away. Just as I'm going to tell her to forget it, she takes a step toward me. "Yeah, okay." I release a heavy breath in relief, pick up my jacket and we both head for the door.

For a moment there I really thought she wasn't going to go, which just adds to all this confusion. In the past she would have answered that question in an instant. It's almost as if she is questioning our relationship, and it's making me even more worried. I can only hope that she isn't going to pull away from me again, thinking some delusional thoughts about why we shouldn't be together, which seem to stem from her complete lack of belief that she deserves to be loved.

Wait! Is that it?

It all clicks into place. All this basically started after she found that ring in her pocket. She started acting a little off after that day. Why didn't I make that connection before this? I'm so fucking stupid. *Is that what this is all about?*

Okay, now I know the 'what', I need to figure out the 'why'. I can think of several right off the top of my head. One of the most logical, well her kind of logic anyway, is she is wondering why I haven't proposed to her, which would explain why she is pulling away. She is likely thinking that I don't want to marry her and is pulling away before I can leave.

Of course, that is total bullshit, because I do want to marry her. Looking over to her, she is deep in thought as I start up the SUV. I want to pull her onto my lap right now and tell her to stop over analyzing her thoughts, but I don't. We can talk when we get to the cabin; then there will be no one to interrupt us. Putting the car in drive, I set off for our destination.

Another logical reason would be that she doesn't want to get married, although that would bring up a whole new list of 'why' questions. I don't question her love for me one bit, but her inner turmoil is controlled by her fear. It could be that she wants to get married but is afraid that I will tire of her and leave. Several times she has expressed that insecurity. Again, she is completely wrong, but she is stubborn just like me and it is hard to make her believe things.

I have so completely fallen for this girl and there are times when she is so clueless. Sometimes I think it's because she didn't know me before. She didn't understand that before her, I didn't care for anyone. I just existed. Those who have been around me longer consistently hint at how she has changed me or joke around with me by saying she has made me soft.

Fingers lightly skim along the back of my hand that I only now realize has made its way to her thigh. My eyes momentarily close at the feeling of her touch. She grabs my hand with both of hers and brings it to her mouth, kissing it gently. Sighing in delight, I take a peek at her face, only to pause several seconds longer than I should have by the confused look on her face. Understanding hits quickly as I notice her staring at my knuckles and again running her fingers over them lightly.

They are all red and scraped up. I wasn't wearing gloves when I was beating the hell out of the punching bag. I was too hyped up to even think about stopping to put on gloves. She looks at me with sad, worried eyes.

"It's okay, babe. It doesn't hurt."

I pull my hand out of hers and grab her hand, bringing up to my face, skimming it lightly across my cheek before kissing it. Thankfully, she doesn't pull away, and I don't bother letting go of her hand, just rest it lightly back on her leg. Her lips turn upwards, slightly relaxing some of the tension that has built up in my shoulders.

We both seem a little more relaxed once we pull into the driveway to the cabin. I get out and go around the car, taking her hand as we walk up toward the door.

"I figured we could use some alone time."

"When did you decide this?"

"After my early morning workout. I couldn't get you off my mind." I give her a quick kiss before we go into the house. The contact makes me twitch in my pants. Yes, it has been far too long since we had some unrushed time to ourselves, but I am still longing for answers.

Taking her hand, I lead her over to the couch and then grab us a few Corona's out of the fridge. She eyes me skeptically as I return to the couch, handing her one and then sitting next to her. I make no move to touch her because right now I know it won't take much for me to give into the animalistic side, but I have no doubt she has an inkling of my intentions.

She takes a long drink and sits back looking up at the ceiling. "Are you okay?"

My beer freezes halfway to my mouth and I put it down on the coffee table then rest my elbows on my knees. I am hesitant to tell her what I'm feeling right now, but my mind and body are tired of holding it all in. Maybe if I lay it out on the table for her, she will open up to me.

Staring at the ground, I take a deep breath. "Nadi, I'm not going to lie and tell you what you implied didn't hurt, because it did. I know it's stupid and petty and that you didn't intend for it to hurt me." She tries to say something, but I put my hand up. "Please, just let me get this out."

She nods and I continue. "I feel like this," I gesture between our static bodies, "us, I feel like we have completely gone back to the beginning of our relationship. It's as if you have lost all trust in me. I can't pretend to understand everything that is going on in your mind, but I thought you knew me enough to know I'd never judge you or think any less of you because you feel a certain way."

"Aerick –"

"Nadi, we've been through so much, and I don't understand

why you wouldn't talk to me about this. I really think you are over-analyzing things. I finally figured out that this all began when you found Paulo's ring in my pocket and I know whatever is going on with you is because of your feelings from that." She opens her mouth again, but I stop her.

"Babe, it really isn't a big deal. I need you to know that I do want to marry you, but I want to wait until you're ready. I figured when you froze that day, that even though my mind had thought about it before, it was too soon for you, and that's okay with me. If you're scared, if you want to wait and get to know each other more, that's fine. Even if you wanted to just up and get married right now, I'm completely fine with that. I need you to tell me what is going on in your head, because I'm at a complete loss and going out of my mind trying to figure out your stance on this. Please, please just tell me what you want, and I will make it happen. I swear it to you."

Grabbing her hands, my lips graze them with a kiss, begging her with my silent gaze. Her eyes are glossed over as the wheels turn in her head. "Please, baby, tell me what's bothering you."

"I..." Her mouth opens and closes several times before she looks down at our tangled hands.

"Nadi, we can work through whatever it is, I promise."

She stares into my eyes intensely looking for something. "I... I... I love you."

In an instant she moves onto my lap, straddling me and kissing me fiercely. I'm frozen in shock for about a tenth of a second before my lips move in sync with hers. All the intense, held-back emotion that has been hanging between us is poured into our kiss. At this moment, I realize I need this, I need her. Yes, I have been craving her touch, but it is her raw emotion that has me caught up in this moment.

I feel her need for me, not just her lust or her need to forget the world around us. I feel her need for my touch as much as I need hers. My lips begin to move on their own accord down her neck and I reach down, pulling her shirt up, catching her bra on the way up over her head, losing contact with her skin for the slightest moment. She clings to me, pulling me impossibly closer to her at the moment of lost contact.

Moving my lips to that point on her neck, I elicit a moan out of her. My pants are getting uncomfortably tight. Grabbing her ass, holding her tight to me, I pick her up and she wraps her legs around me. I pull the throw off the back of the couch, putting it down across the couch, and lay her gently down, settling myself above her. My eyes linger for a moment on her bare chest before I devour each peak. Her sounds cause the bulge to grow even more in my restricted pants but before I can complain, her hands are deftly undoing my pants to release me.

I grunt into her ear as she firmly grabs my manhood. "Fuck baby, I'm not going to last if you do that again," I warn.

Grabbing her hands, I pin them above her head to keep her from ending this before I'm ready. The pout on her face makes me smile and I reciprocate with a kiss to her nose to take away the disappointment because I have no intention of making this fast. We are finally alone, and I'm determined to take my time.

I begin kissing down the side of her face, then move slowly down her neck. Her breathing has picked up, but her body continues relaxing more and more with each passing minute. This is one side of her I know well and have never had a problem satisfying. As my lips reach her chest, I give ample attention to each of her nipples, causing her to moan loudly into the cavernous room.

She's so close already and I've barely even started. Moving both her hands into one of mine, I skim the other hand lightly down her body, taking my time in getting to my destination. My fingers slide into her pants, under her panties and as they slide between her legs, it only confirms my thoughts. In an instant my fingers are dripping with her excitement and I almost lose it. *Fuck, that is a wonderful feeling!* I groan, my lips still attached to one of her nipples, causing her to squirm beneath me, intensifying my need to be buried in her. I wanted to take this slow, but it seems that is no longer possible. Spending a moment to bring her to the edge first, my fingers quickly move inside her, making sure to hit the right spot.

When I'm sure she is barely holding on, I begin moving my lips further down her body. Quickly I undo her pants, peeling them down, along with her underwear, making sure to scrape what little bit of nails I have down her legs as I rid her of her clothing. Pausing again to appreciate her beautiful form, I slowly run my fingers along her thighs before removing my own clothes as swiftly as possible.

Her eyes beg me, and I'm all too happy to oblige. I settle between her legs and admire the view of her face as I sink into her. The sight of her eyes squeezing closed in lustful satisfaction pulls deep down in me and I begin moving with purpose before she even fully adjusts to me.

After only a few minutes she begins to flutter around me, and I pick up the speed, chasing my own release. Her screams fill the room as her orgasm rips through her. After milking it, I can no longer hold off mine and I slam into her one last time. My body stiffens as I pour into her, then collapse.

We both are breathing heavily, and she begins running her fingers through my hair, massaging my scalp. I hum appreciatively.

"So, am I forgiven for crashing your session today?" I ask lightly, hoping to get her to forgive me in her heavenly state.

"Hmmm, I may need a little more convincing," she jokes playfully, still beaming at me.

"Well, let's see if I can accommodate." I grab her ass again, holding her tightly to me as she wraps her arms and legs around me. Pulling myself back up into a sitting position, I swing my legs off the couch, so we are sitting back on the couch with her on my lap. "Go ahead baby, I'm all yours." Her face brightens in delight, no doubt by the control I'm giving over, as she brings her lips to mine.

We take things much more slowly this time and by the time I find my release for the second time we are completely dripping in sweat and exhausted. She collapses on my chest as I lie on the overly soft rug in front of the couch, running my fingers up and down her back.

"Am I forgiven now?"

"Hmm."

I chuckle. "Is that a yes?"

"Hmm."

She is so fucking adorable. I glance out the window: darkness has fallen, and I let out a sigh at the meaning. "We have to get back, babe, and by the way since you can't form a coherent word, I'm taking that as a yes."

She lazily sits up. "Kay." *Hmm.* What a wonderful sight: all mussed up and completely sated.

I sit up to join her, wrapping my arms around her. "I wish I could stay right here forever," I whisper into her neck.

"Me too."

I grab her face, giving her one last passionate kiss before moving her and standing up, bringing her up after me. "Come on."

We both dress quietly, completely happy in our blissful bubble. As we head back, I debate whether I should try talking to her again. She was so close to finally talking to me about it.

"Not tonight," she says, guessing at my thoughts.

I look over to her and she looks so happy right now. *How can*

I deny that face? I pick up her hand, kissing it and hold it to my chest. "Okay." Besides, she said not tonight, which means she intends on telling me sometime, which is good enough for me.

It isn't lost on me that she has picked up on the weakness which I apparently share with Gavin and used it to avoid my line of questioning. *Distraction!*

CHAPTER FOURTEEN

(Sunday, February 28th)

THE SOFT HUMMING behind my ear wakes me up. It's too early but there's no way I can deny the warmth that comes from the man pressing against me. "What are you doing here?" I breathe groggily. If he wakes up Terrie, she's going to be pissed.

"Don't worry, she's gone, but I can't stay. I just wanted to be the first person you see today." He kisses behind my ear down to my shoulder.

Waking up to him is such a nice way to start my day. Rolling onto my back, I reluctantly open my heavy eyes. He comes into focus and leans down. giving me a soft kiss. "Morning, sleepyhead."

"Morning. Where is Terrie? I didn't hear her leave." Which I don't always, but lately I've been waking up at the slightest sounds.

"One of the cadets has the stomach flu. She's giving him some fluids and nausea medication. Are you too tired to join me for an early morning workout?"

Again, how can I deny this man? "I'd love to." His mood since last week has been rather upbeat, even despite the lack of admission of my little problem, but I'm not complaining.

I crawl over him to get out of bed and he helps with a slightly stinging slap to my ass. "Knock it off, it's too early for that," I say, trying not to grin at his playfulness. He holds in his laugh as he watches me throw on some workout clothing. It only takes a minute for me to dress, brush my teeth, and we're out the door. This morning is chilly, but it's been slowly getting warmer each morning. Some nights it barely gets below freezing and that thought excites me; I hate the cold.

We enter the gym, which is dark and quiet; not what I expected. "Not that I'm complaining, but where is Gavin?"

Obviously not what he wanted to hear, because he gets a sour look on his face. "Him and Paulo had a late night. He texted me that he wasn't going to make it to our workout this morning."

"Ahh, so you decided to pull me out of my sweet sleep." I start walking toward the gear.

His chest is suddenly against my back as he wraps his hands around my waist. "Yes, because I would much rather have my hands on you." Moving a stray hair that didn't make it into my ponytail, he plants a kiss on my neck. I lean my head back against him as his light kisses wake up my insides, but as soon as I start enjoying it, he moves out from behind me.

"Hey!"

He laughs at me. "I said 'workout' and that is what we're going to do."

"What if I want to do something else?" I tease, and immediately there's that dark look in his eyes. It doesn't take a genius to see that he's entertaining my thoughts. It has been quite a few days since we were alone, and he feels it too.

"Behave," he says finally. "We don't need to be giving anyone a show."

Of course, the camera in here. "Fine. What are we doing this morning?"

I let him take control of our workout. While we don't do anything naughty, he finds as many ways as possible to touch me as we stretch and do weight training. By the end, we have both worked up a sweat. We behave ourselves for the most part, though we do stop a few times for some passionate kissing. As we are putting away the equipment, Terrie comes in.

"This can't be good," Aerick murmurs. "What is it?" he almost growls at her. Elbowing him, I give him a 'be nice' glare.

She doesn't look happy either, and something tells me she's already having a bad day without his attitude. "Jeff brought two more cadets into the infirmary."

"Great."

"That's not all. He said there's another one in the bathroom throwing up and so is Trent. I think we either have a serious case of the stomach flu going around or possibly food poisoning."

"Fucking wonderful. Which do you think is more likely?"

"Considering our very rigorous steps to prevent food poisoning, and the fact that each person I have talked to started exhibiting symptoms over the course of the evening and night, my bet is on the stomach flu."

"Are they all from the same cabin?"

"All but one. They are all from Trent's dorm, except Asa."

"Let me guess, Clarissa is one of the other sick ones in Trent's dorm," he says tersely.

"How did you know that?"

"I had Jeff bring Vincent in earlier. Those three have become rather close. My bet is the stomach flu as well. Makes the most sense. What do you recommend? Isn't this fairly contagious?"

"Yes, more than likely it is very contagious. Quarantine for twenty-four hours is probably the best thing. More than likely, it's a normal stomach flu. You can expect the ones who get it to run high fevers accompanied by vomiting, weakness, and possibly dehydration. Depending on if it spreads further, you may want to call off classes tomorrow."

"Have you talked to Luther yet?"

"No."

"Good."

He takes another moment to put his thoughts into order, but quickly goes into instructor mode. "I want to get all the cadets already showing symptoms in one dorm. Check all the other cadets for symptoms; if they have even one, they are to be quarantined in B dorm with the others. We can put extra mats on the floor if needed in either dorm. All medical checks need to be done in the dorm. Let's try to keep the numbers down as much as possible. I'll go wake Luther and get him up to date. I want all staff members in the mess hall in fifteen minutes except Trent, he can stay his sick ass in the dorm with the sick cadets. Nadi, get changed and help Terrie get the sick cadets to the dorm and round up the staff."

I nod, ignoring his demanding tone. It's just this side of him and I have mostly gotten to know it well. It also helps that as he exits the gym, he winks at me with that freaking adorable smirk.

"Well, since you have to change, how about you round up the staff and I will get the sick ones back to the dorm. The less contact people have with them, the better," Terrie says, not at all enthused.

Then again, she has been around them already, maybe she's worried she's going to get sick. I will have to remember to stay away from her and Jeff today. The idea of getting the stomach flu doesn't sit well with me.

I change and head to the cabins to wake up everyone. I start with the instructor's dorms and work my way back toward the mess hall, quickly getting everyone up. As I get to Gavin's cabin, I have to knock several times before he opens the door, in only his boxers, rubbing the sleep out of his eyes. I look down to the floor immediately and quickly tell him we need to be in the mess hall in a few minutes. *Why can't this man ever wear some damn clothes?*

Quickly I turn around and it's just in time to see Aerick glaring at Gavin's almost naked form. *Great!* Things have been going so good for us this week. Ever since our little getaway to the cabin for the evening, things have smoothed out between us. Although I haven't talked to him anymore about what's been going on, he hasn't pushed me to tell him. He's backed off considerably and we've just been enjoying each other.

The more I think about it, the more I'm certain, I was too stressed and emotionally drained. Things have been fine, and nothing has happened in almost a month. We've been busy this week, but without Aerick pushing for answers and us releasing some of the tension that was built up between us, things are going so much better.

Christian has been saying for the last few weeks that stress may be part of my problem. Even though I didn't tell him specifically what has been going on, he could very well be right. Just the thought that I may not be going crazy after all is a huge relief and has lifted my spirits considerably.

I hurry into the mess hall before anyone else gets there and find Aerick still talking to Luther. "Aerick, can I speak with you for a moment before we get started?" I look to Luther and he excuses himself before Aerick can say anything.

"What?" he snaps, and it takes all my effort not to flinch.

"Babe, please don't be mad. It's not a big deal."

"I'm not mad," he says, still not looking at me.

"You are, and you're snapping at me for something I have no control over. I have no interest in him and I don't want this to put another wedge between us. Please. This week has been so good. Don't do this; let it go." I place my hand on his cheek and move his face so that he's looking directly at me. "I love you, only you."

After a moment he lets out a loud sigh. "I know, Princess. I'm sorry." He glances around and then takes my face in both hands, giving me a deep passionate kiss that he ends entirely too soon, leaving me wanting more. He smirks at me before going over to stand with Luther.

I turn, a little taken aback by Aerick's out-of-character show of affection, until I see Gavin looking at Aerick with raised eyebrows. I let out a sigh. *Boys!*

I let the irritation from Aerick showing off his possessiveness fall away. If that's all it took to make him feel better, then I'm fine with that. Luther doesn't seem bothered by it, so why should I? Others start filing into the room, so I take a seat and wait for everyone else to get here.

✳ ✳ ✳ ✳

Today has been a nightmare. This morning I figured since we were locking down half the camp that it would be an easy day; boy, was I wrong. With half the cadets puking their guts out and confined to one room, there has been plenty to do.

I've been running around as an errand girl all day. Terrie has been spending most of the day in the dorm with the sick cadets while Brayden and I run back and forth getting supplies for her.

With Andi needing help and only a limited number of cadets being able to help clean up, staff had to help out.

Then halfway through the day, Paulo and Gavin both joined the land of the sick. I found out Trent went out with the guys last night. After those two fell, I deduced that the source must have been Trent. It makes the most sense. I told that much to Terrie and Aerick and they agreed, with Terrie cursing under her breath that she was going to make him pay for this.

I'm almost finished helping Terrie replenish her supplies so she can go check up on the sick when Luther walks in looking pretty grim. Aerick looks up from his tablet and stands when he sees Luther's face. "Nadi. You have a long-distance call holding."

"Me?"

"Yes, it's Patrick. He's calling via Skype." My lips turn up momentarily until my mind processes that something is obviously wrong.

"He's on in the office. Aerick, go with her, I'll help Terrie finish." *Something is definitely wrong!*

I quickly drop everything in my hands, not caring where it lands, and rush out the door. When I get into the office, I can see Patrick already on screen waiting impatiently. His head snaps up as the door slams open and I throw myself into the chair in front of the desk.

"Hey, baby girl."

"Cut the shit, what's wrong?"

"Nadi, you need to calm down first." His concerned words

make me even more jumpy. I feel the weight of Aerick's hands on my shoulders, but I just shrug them off.

"Tell me what's wrong. I know something's wrong or Evan would be calling..." *Wait...* "Evan, oh my god–where is he, Patrick?" My voice falls into a small whisper as a lump forms in my throat. It continues to swell as Patrick allows silence to balloon between us. "Patrick, where is he...?" I can't finish my sentence out loud.

"Sweetie, calm down, he's alive." His concerned look moves behind me to Aerick and arms wrap around me.

"Baby, calm down or you're going to pass out. He's alive. Just take some deep breaths." Aerick's words barely register. My chest is so heavy it hurts. Closing my eyes and concentrating on the feeling of Aerick breathing behind me, I inhale deeply, slowing my breathing to match his, but my anxiety is still through the roof.

"Okay, I'm calm, now tell me what's wrong," I say, trying to keep my voice steady. Aerick lifts me up and slides between me and the chair, holding me tightly to him.

"Evan is in the hospital."

"Oh god!"

Patrick holds his hand up to me to stop me. "He's going to be okay, but he's in really bad shape."

"What happened?" I almost scream, and Aerick's grip tightens.

"He was jumped this morning. We don't know much. He was on his way home from a party we were at last night when two men beat him up and took his backpack."

"They wanted his backpack. The drugs!" I think out loud. That stupid idiot. I've told him time and time again that selling that shit was a bad idea. Patrick's face flashes with momentary panic as he looks at Aerick. *Have I ever told him that?*

Patrick must assume I did because he continues, "Well if the drugs were what they wanted, then they are pretty stupid. First, anyone willing to steal something that belongs to Marcello must have a death wish or is just plain crazy. Second, he'd already sold most of it the night before at the party and they didn't even bother to take his wallet that had all the money in it. It doesn't make much sense to any of us."

He has a point. Marcello is one of the most well-known guys in Chicago. Everyone knows any drugs you get in our part of the city belong to him, and he can be ruthless. Another reason I hated that my brother worked for him.

"Did you tell the cops?" *His scholarship.* He'll lose his full-ride scholarship if he ends up with a criminal record.

"No, of course not. They think it's a random mugging, but they are suspicious because of the brutality." *What?*

The large lump in my throat comes back three times as large; I can't even ask. Thankfully Aerick does it for me. "Exactly how bad is he?" he asks cautiously, keeping one eye on me.

"It's pretty bad; one of the guys had a bat. He has a broken jaw, several broken ribs, his right wrist is broken, and he has a concussion."

My head falls into my hands as tears begin streaming down my face.

"It was a little touch and go for several hours, but the swelling stopped and he stabilized. They did surgery on his wrist and had to wire his jaw shut. They say he will recover but he has been in and out of consciousness."

"Where are my parents?"

"They're in the room with him. Neither of them wanted to leave him. I'm out in the waiting room." He moves the camera around so I can see the room and it stops on Mike.

"Mike?" *What is he doing there?*

"Hey, Nadi. We're so sorry we weren't with him," Mike says, full of sorrow.

I shake my head. "No, don't say that. You would probably be there right next to him if you had." I hate how broken my voice sounds. "Mike, what are you even doing there?"

"Oh, well, Patrick and I kept in touch when we got back. He introduced me to your brother."

"Yeah, without Jeff here, I needed a new wingman," Patrick says, shrugging his shoulders.

I shake my head. "I need to be there. I'll be on the next plane as soon as I can make it down to SeaTac."

"No, Nadi. He doesn't want you to leave work." The camera turns back so I'm looking at Patrick. How could he possibly think I shouldn't be there?

"What do you mean?" The feeling of hurt replaces a bit of my sorrow.

"He doesn't want you to see him like that. He'll be spending the next week or two here in the hospital and there's nothing you would be able to do for him. Your parents are here taking care of him, he's stable, and he promises he'll call you soon. He wanted me to call you to let you know what happened and that he loves you and doesn't want you to worry about him. I'm supposed to remind you that he's your 'bigger, little brother'," he says, quoting my brother's favorite words to me, but I can't find it in me to find it funny right now. My internal conflict begins pulling at me. I really want to go, but he doesn't want me there. What would I really be able to do there? Maybe he's right.

"Patrick, you're sure he is going to be okay?"

"Yeah, of course. He's a fighter, same as you. He promised he will call you soon. He's pretty heavily medicated right now. He has a hard time staying awake for more than a few minutes."

Thinking about how much pain he must be in for them to put all those pain killers in him makes more tears fall down my face.

"Fine, but he has two days. If I don't hear from him, I'm on a plane, understand?"

"Okay, I'll let him know." I wipe my tears away but more keep flowing out of my eyes; I've lost control over my emotions.

"Aerick, be sure to take care of her."

"I will."

"I'm serious. Or I will be on the next plane to see you."

Aerick huffs behind me. "And do what?"

"Oh my god, will you guys quit!" I yell, no longer able to deal with their bickering, even if it is friendly.

"Baby, calm down. We were just messing around." He kisses my shoulder and I turn into his chest, trying to hide my over-emotional face. I don't enjoy others seeing me like this.

"Patrick, I will take care of her, I promise."

"Alright. Talk to you guys later." The call ends and I let my tears turn into sobs. Aerick doesn't say anything, just lets me cry until no more tears come.

It appears my terrible luck has rubbed off on my brother. It was bound to happen sooner or later, and I have even warned him, but it doesn't make it any easier. My only hope is that he'll learn his lesson and quit selling drugs. Not that I have a lot of room to tell anyone how to behave.

We sit there, Aerick holding me tight to his chest, until Luther comes in. I stand up, wiping off the already dried tears from my face. "Sorry, Luther. We'll get back to work," I tell him, moving toward the door.

"That's ridiculous, Nadi. Take the rest of the afternoon off." Luther's word's set me off because that's the last thing I want to do right now.

"What? No. I'm fine, and we have too much to do around here."

"Nadi..." I stop Aerick before he can even get started.

"I said no. I'm not going back to my cabin to sit and sulk while I run through my head just how bad he really is. We have entirely too much to do with half the camp sick and I'm not going to sit around while everyone else picks up my slack." Without waiting for either of them to say more, I push past Luther and go out the door. Right now, a distraction is extremely welcome; I'll take it, even if it means cleaning up and caring for a bunch of sick people.

✻ ✻ ✻ ✻

My stomach is in knots when I finally make it back to my cabin. I tear off my dirty-sweaty clothes and get in the shower. The hot water feels wonderful as it washes away the day.

This afternoon was even more busy than this morning. Two more cadets have joined the quarantined cabin, along with Jeff. I've not felt great either, but I'm fairly certain it's today's events more than it's me catching this stomach flu. Terrie insisted I wear a mask when I went into the cabin and I've gone through a half bottle of sanitizer. Unfortunately for Jeff, he had more contact with the cadets before we really knew what was going on. I also skipped dinner, much to Aerick's dismay. We argued for at least five minutes before he finally gave in and let me be. We don't typically argue with others around but there weren't many left when dinner time came around.

Luther decided classes are cancelled for tomorrow, so tomorrow is going to run similar to today. We are going to keep everyone quarantined until we know it has fully passed. Several of those that got sick first are already showing signs of getting better, which makes it even more likely that this is only a twenty-four-hour flu.

I haven't seen a whole lot of Luther today. He has been locked away in his office majority of the day and didn't bother coming to dinner either. He's probably trying to avoid catching this too. Not that I blame him, I'd avoid it too if it was possible.

Unfortunately for me, there are only a few people to run the camp. Terrie and I have stopped several times to complain about Trent. We've agreed we will be getting back at him for this. It's not fair, he gets everyone sick and then just because he is one of them, he gets waited on hand and foot while all the rest of us work our butts off. He's normally the prankster, but he'd better watch his back the next few weeks, because he's not getting off scot free.

Once my skin is red from scrubbing it, I shut off the water and quickly get into my sweats. I'm too tired to dry my hair, so I settle with putting it up in a high bun and I will deal with it tomorrow. When I get out of the bathroom, Aerick is sitting on my bed with a half-smile gracing his lips.

"Hey," he says, carefully testing my current mood.

I go over and sit next to him. The work has been successful at blocking out all the bad of the day and I don't want to bring those feelings forward, nor do I want an argument with him. "I really want to go to bed. It's been a long day and I'm exhausted."

"I know, Princess. Do you want me to stay with you until you fall asleep?"

"Yes please. Is that okay?"

"Yeah. I brought my tablet." He picks it up off my desk and brings up the dorm cameras before setting it on my nightstand.

I pull back the blankets, sliding under them, and he gets in behind me, pulling me tightly to him. "I love you, Aerick," I whisper when he turns the lamp off.

"I love you too babe, always."

I know he does, and it's the only thing holding me together today. He's been hovering most of the afternoon and I did snap at him a few times to let me get my work done; yet he's still here, even after the way I treated him. If that doesn't say love, I don't know what does.

Cuddling into him more, my exhaustion happily takes over my thoughts and I drift off to sleep, feeling the occasional kisses on my head.

CHAPTER FIFTEEN

(Saturday, March 5th)

WHERE DOES THE time go? A few months ago, I was as scared as a five-year-old starting their first day of school. *Not that I would have admitted it out loud.* I was so worried about leaving my old life behind and starting a new one; a life I was going into completely blind, but somehow, I've managed to get through it, and all in one piece. *Well, sort of.* Despite the roadblocks I had to get through, I'm proud of how far I've come.

Since Tia had to leave suddenly, I've completely taken over for her. While it was hard in the beginning, I've been able to get myself into a good routine and feel comfortable in my position. Once I finish this last quarter of schooling, I'll be a fully certified teacher. Now that I'm done with my CLEP tests and we'll be out of camp in a week, it should be a breeze.

It's almost sad that camp is ending in a week, but today there will be no sadness, because tonight is capture the flag. Outside of the realm of 'Aerick', it was probably my favorite part of camp while I was a cadet here. The only downside of playing as a staff member is that we have to help setup. Thankfully, I got out of most of it because I was in the classroom teaching all day. Unfortunately, having just dismissed my last class for today, I have to report to Paulo to help out with the final details and then later we have a staff meeting.

I'm putting the last of the homework in my bag to take back to my cabin and grade when Aerick walks in.

He comes over to me without a word, wrapping his sweaty arms around me, and nuzzles my face. "Yuck, babe." I push him away and wipe his sweat off my face.

"Whatever, you know you like it when I'm all sweaty," he says, grinning at me as he grabs the front of my shirt, bringing me closer to him. His playful attitude instantly makes me weak in the knees and I gladly go into his sweaty embrace.

"You're right, I do." I grab his face and bring his lips to mine for a quick toe-curling kiss. "I thought I was reporting to Paulo."

He kisses me again and I have to push him back to get an answer. "You are, but if you keep kissing me like that, you may not make it."

He tries to kiss me again, so I push at his chest with a raised eyebrow. "So, did you actually have a reason for coming here other than to attack me?"

The frown that spreads across his face has me itching to break out in laughter, but I continue to hold him back.

"Actually, I'm supposed to tell you to meet him in the supply room to help bring the supplies out to the field." Using his strength against my weaker arms, he brings himself inches from my lips. "But as I said, you may not make it there."

Finally, I give in and let him kiss me. His muscles relax as he realizes I'm no longer putting up a fight and I use the opportunity to my advantage. I quickly slide out of his relaxed grip and grab my bag, not stopping until I'm at the door.

"Okay, thank you for letting me know. Love you, babe." Giving him the sweetest sarcastic smile, I walk out the door, leaving him still stunned.

Laughter erupts out of me as I head over to drop off my bag in my cabin and then head to meet up with Paulo. I get a few curious looks from cadets who are still lingering around and immediately try to harden my face but it's so hard when I manage to get the best of Aerick. It doesn't happen often, so I have to enjoy it whenever possible.

Paulo is lining up all the paintball guns when I get to the supply room. Like Aerick, he's all sweaty and you can tell the guys have been working hard to get all the boxes set up in the back field for tonight.

"Hey, little sister. Word is you're stuck with me this afternoon."

"Yep; that's the word. What do you want me to do?"

"We need to refill the paintball guns and pack the supplies out to the two teams' posts. Here," he puts a box of paintballs on the table, "you fill half the guns with this color, and I'll do the other half; then we can pack all this stuff out to the field. If we're lucky, it won't take long and we can relax this afternoon until the game."

"You guys already finish setting up the field?" I figured with their classes it would take them a few hours more to finish it up like it did during my session.

"They're finishing it up now. Between Aerick, Gavin and I, we got most of it done faster than normal. I think a lot of it was Aerick and Gavin trying to show off but whatever, at least it's almost done. Besides, with Brand out, I get to set up supplies."

I roll my eyes at the thought of Aerick and Gavin. They go at it any time they get a chance. In the beginning, I thought it was them trying to show off to me, but even though Gavin has backed off from me, it's still a pissing match anytime there's a chance to show off their strength. Both of them are ridiculously competitive.

"Have you gotten to talk to your brother again?" His voice comes out quieter and more serious like he's worried bringing up the subject.

"Yep. We video chatted last night." Well, not technically talking, as it's impossible since his jaw's wired shut. We did a video chat, but we had to type everything to each other. Seeing him the first time on Tuesday was a terrible shock; he was hardly recognizable. The guys who mugged him really did a job on him, but I was relieved to see he really is going to be okay…*eventually*.

"How is he doing?"

"A little better. He seemed a lot more awake this time and he was really happy to get to see Jeff." I had waited until the next day to tell Jeff, since he got sick before I could talk to him. Same as me, he completely freaked out at first until I managed to get through to him that he would be okay.

Aerick surprised me again by being very understanding when Jeff wrapped me in a tight hug and didn't move. He merely walked outside and gave us some room. No dirty looks, no heavy sigh; he frowned with sadness in his eyes and left. When he didn't say anything afterward, I knew that the look and sadness was for the situation with my brother and not Jeff's actions. Aerick understood that Jeff just needed someone close to him at that moment.

Paulo breaks me out of my thoughts. "Did they find who did it?"

"No. They really didn't have much to go on and it isn't unusual in our part of the city. A poor kid from the wrong side of town getting beat up doesn't tend to draw a lot of extra attention."

Surely the lack of information they were able to get out of my brother was part of his own situation. He couldn't exactly go tell the cops that he was robbed for the drugs that were supposed to be in the backpack. It's also a good bet that some of the cops are on the take too. Even though I've had some run ins with them, I don't think all cops are bad. In fact, I've met a few decent ones when I'm not getting busted by them, but there are always going to be the bad apples. All it would have taken was for my brother to say the wrong thing to the wrong cop and Marcello would have found out. Everyone knows you don't cross him. My brother probably wouldn't have made it out of the hospital.

I think about telling Paulo the real reason my brother was mugged but then I think better of it. The less people that know the better. He nods and we fall into a comfortable silence as we work.

It doesn't take long for both of us to fill all the guns. When we're done, we grab them, along with the vests and glow sticks, and head out to the field. By the time we drop off the vests in the instructors' dorm, we still have plenty of time to go catch dinner. We knew we might miss dinner but figured it would be better to just hurry up and finish so we could have the afternoon off. As it turns out, we finished even quicker than we thought and still had time to eat.

*** * * * ***

We walk out to the field and it's set up exactly as it was the last time I played. Luther already gave his speech regarding the rules and split us up into teams. Since Brand is not here, Luther let Gavin lead the second team. Unfortunately for me, whatever contest is going on between Aerick and Gavin is still in full force. Gavin picked me on his first pick of staff and Aerick was pretty pissed. He didn't let it show much, but I know that look.

Gavin is not as familiar with the cadets as Aerick, which gave Aerick the advantage, and it showed on his face as we split up. Our team is definitely not the one I would have picked, but we got what we got and we need to make the best of it. As we fall into a loose group next to our flag, Gavin turns to the cadets.

"Alright, you've got a few minutes to work out a plan amongst yourselves."

"You're not going to help?" Vincent asks.

"No. This exercise is for you guys. The staff are just here to have a little fun." He looks at me, wagging his eyebrows and smirking. *Great!*

The cadets start bickering between them and I take the opportunity to satisfy my curiosity. "How come you didn't want to referee the game with Luther?"

"Luther gave me the choice but I really wanted to play. Maybe get a chance to beat your man at something." Quickly I cover my mouth trying to control the laugh that bursts out of my mouth. Gavin and the rest of our team look at me questioningly.

"Stop gawking at me and get a plan in place, we're about to start," I snap, then lower my voice to Gavin. "And good luck with that. I'll try my hardest, but Aerick has the advantage, the experience, and he hates losing."

"We'll see." *Yes, we will.*

The cadets actually formulate a pretty decent plan quickly. They choose to split up in two groups, leaving a small group behind to guard the flag while the rest of us go after the other team's flag, breaking up into two person teams. We let them split people up and thankfully they don't stick me with Gavin.

In fact, Vincent suggested they match one staff member with a cadet, which is pretty smart. It's not the same strategy we used the last time I played, but this is for them, not me. We hear Luther's shot to start the game and get in position.

I get matched up with Karen and we move off toward the other side in the middle of the group. Moving quietly, I let her lead us as we duck and weave in between the boxes. It doesn't take long to hear the other team moving around us.

Shots start flying around us. Grabbing the back of Karen's vest, I get her to lower herself so it's harder to get hit. Unfortunately, we're ambushed from both sides within a few minutes. Two shots hit me in succession, making me jump at the stinging in my ass. *Fuck!* Focusing, I see Skyler and Alex snickering and Luther calls me and Karen out of the game.

Well that just sucks!

Karen and I take our seats and we wait. Listening to the pops of the shots and the shouts, it's hard to tell who has the upper hand. Several more people join the hit group and I'm starting to get antsy when I hear Gavin curse loudly. There were several quick shots right before his outburst and I would venture to say he was hit. My best guess would be he was shot by Aerick.

Another few minutes pass before Skyler raises the flag announcing their win. I'm not surprised but I am irritated at being on the losing side. Others from my team share their displeasure a little more vocally as we begin to gather back into one group.

Luther quickly pipes in with his speech, trying to make everyone happy again, and Aerick sneaks up behind me. When I look up to him, he's wearing a smirk that he's clearly trying to hold back.

"What's so funny?"

"How does your ass feel?" A small laugh escapes his control.

"You think that's funny, do you?"

"Well, I did warn them they better not leave a bruise on you."

"Warn who?" *So, this was planned?!*

"Skyler and Alex; they said they were going to get you and I kindly told them they better not bruise you." He lets out another laugh. "I suppose those ass shots won't really leave a bruise, but it might hurt to sit for a day or two."

Those fucking brats, and Aerick, thinking this is funny. I find no humor in the fact that my ass hurts and that there's a chance it may still be sore tomorrow. Aerick bumps my arm, trying to bring my attention back to him, but I just elbow him hard in his side.

"Glad you think that's funny. Thankfully you won't know what's sore because as far as I'm concerned, you won't be spending any private time with me for the next few days."

"Oh, come on. I was looking out for you. I can't help that they found a loophole in my orders." He gets a bit of a smug look for a moment before his smirk returns. I want to laugh because he's just realizing that means they found a way to do exactly what Aerick was trying to prevent. I roll my eyes in his full view and go to stand next to Jeff on the outside of the group.

Luther dismisses the cadets back to the cabins and Aerick puts in his few words quickly before following me. "Babe, don't be upset. You know I love you. It was only a game and I did have your best interest at heart." While he's right that he was trying to protect me, he's also standing here laughing at me.

"Whatever. We've got work to do. Come on." I join the rest of the staff to start cleaning up. I hear Jeff and Aerick whispering behind me, but I'm not interested in what they're saying. I just want to finish so we can go relax. It seems that I'm not the only one that was thinking that: it doesn't take long for everyone to get to work and, after a minute, Jeff and Aerick join us too.

"Aerick, Gavin?" We all stop and look up to see Luther walking toward us.

"I would like both of you to join Ayla and I for a few drinks tonight." Aerick looks at Luther, seemingly confused. This must not be a normal request.

"Luther, it's pretty late."

"I am aware. We will not be long, just for a little while. I want to discuss something with you and tomorrow is an easy day."

Aerick shrugs his shoulders, not seeming bothered. "Okay."

"Great. I will see you two out front in ten minutes." Luther turns and walks back toward the cabins.

I look at Aerick, who's still looking at Luther. "What was all that about?" I'm completely confused. I don't know if I should be more concerned about the fact that Luther wants to talk to him, or the fact that Aerick seems almost speechless.

"I have no idea." He finally looks down at me then, to Gavin, who's still standing near us finishing up with whatever he was putting away. "Walk me to the cabin really quick."

I look around to the stuff we still need to get put away and to Jeff and Paulo who are still working to get things packed up.

I turn toward Jeff and say, "I'll be back in a minute." He rolls his eyes at me but doesn't say anything, only nods acknowledgement.

We walk quickly to the cabin and I'm stopped at the base of the stairs by Aerick grabbing my hand. I fall back into his chest as he wraps his arms around me. As I melt into his hold, he starts kissing my neck. Not that I want him to stop, but it isn't the time or place for this, and I'm supposed to be mad at him. "Aerick…"

"Sorry, but I can't help myself. Tonight made me think about the last time we played this together. It was so hot watching you that night."

"That night was awesome, but don't you have to meet Luther out front?"

He takes a deep breath. "Yes." I'm spun around to face him. "I just wanted to give you a good night kiss without prying eyes watching us."

Leaning down, he kisses me, taking my breath away. When he finally pulls away, he has that grin that I love so much plastered across his face. "Good night, Princess."

He gives me another peck on the lips and then goes into the dorm. Just when I think I can't love that man any more, he goes and does something incredibly sweet. After a moment of being frozen in thought, I decide I should get back to help Jeff and Paulo. Now that Aerick and Gavin are leaving, we have even more to get done. Trent was lucky enough to get stuck watching the cadets.

When I get back to the field, the guys have almost finished getting together all of the equipment. Jeff pauses to give me a knowing smirk. "Stop looking at me like that and let's get this stuff done so we can go inside; it's cold out here." I shove him with my arm and start stacking the vests that are covered in paint.

Once I've gathered all of them, I take them over to Paulo, who has clean ones. "Here you go. Need anything else?"

"Nope. The others took a lot of it and I told them they could call it a night after they dropped it off. We should be able to get this all back in one trip if you guys can handle those bags over there. I'll take all this stuff."

"Sounds good. Go ahead, Jeff and I will get the rest." There are only the two bags left which are not very heavy, only a little bulky since they have all the guns in them. Paulo picks up the vest and another large bag and walks off, awkwardly holding the paint covered vests away from his body.

By the time I get back over to Jeff, he's done packing up the guns.

"Okay, we just need to grab these two bags. Paulo got the rest."

"Good, I'm ready for bed."

"Ready for bed? It's not even midnight yet. Man, you must be getting old."

"Shut up. I'm the one that actually has to be up early every morning, even on Sundays."

"Are you joking? I'm usually up every morning for PT and I have an obsessive muscle-bound boyfriend who likes to wake me up to work out before the morning workout, so stop complaining."

"Okay, good point, but I'm not old; more like 'being responsible.'" He laughs and we grab the bags, heading back to the supply cabin.

Today has been a good day. Other than being a little concerned about why Luther wants to talk to Aerick, I'm happy. Things are finally looking up again. Camp will be over in a week and hopefully Aerick and I can start fresh again without all the drama of my past.

Something flashes behind the cadets' cabin, drawing my attention, and I stop walking. I look at Jeff; he's still walking in front of me talking. My eyes go back to the cabin: someone is there. There's no way it's a cadet; their tracking bracelet would have triggered when they took a step off the stairs. My feet carry me a little closer.

The person comes into focus and I stop in my tracks. *IT'S HIM!*

No, it can't be. Please – this can't be happening, not again.

The figure takes a step forward and I can see his face more clearly. *Oh God, it's him!* A smirk grows on his face and I feel the heaviness bearing down on my chest.

"Nadi, Nadi what the hell is wrong?" I turn to Jeff as his voice becomes a shout.

"Look," I whisper and point to the man, but as Jeff turns to look, he's gone. That can't be; I know I saw him.

"Look at what?" Jeff puts his hand on my shoulder, but I shake it off. He was there; I know he was there. I was not hallucinating, dammit! Not this time.

Dropping the bag, I take off, running toward the cabin. As I round the corner, there's nothing. I look around, but all I see is the cabin and the woods. I listen for any movement, but there's only the sound of the forest. *What the fuck?*

"Dammit, you're freaking me out. Tell me what's wrong!"

"I... I don't know. I... I need to check something." I have an idea. Turning quickly, I walk toward the offices. Jeff mutters out something, but I don't bother to ask what it was. As I get into the office, I go straight to Jake's desk and pull up the surveillance cameras. There's no camera that looks directly at the back of the dorms, but there is one on each end. Aerick and I have the cameras memorized, a must when you're trying to keep your relationship on the down low.

I pull the two cameras onto the main screen. "What are you doing?" Jeff asks, but I ignore him.

If I really saw something it should show it on here, either him or the light. I saw a flash; he must have had a flashlight. Rewinding the video slowly, I look for the light to cross either camera.

My heart begins to sink the further back in time I get. Nothing. There's nothing. No one crosses in front of the camera except Jeff and me. That's it, it's official: I've gone crazy.

"If you don't talk to me right now, I'm calling Aerick."

"NO!" I shout, turning around to face Jeff. "Please don't." Aerick can't know. I don't want him to know. What will he think? I'm already a handful; he won't be able to deal with this, not with me being completely crazy.

"Then tell me. What's wrong?" He pauses a moment and then wraps his arms around my shoulders. He looks at me confused when I unintentionally flinch at his touch. "Come on; you know you can tell me anything. I promise I won't tell anyone, just tell me what it is."

I don't want to tell him but right now I don't have a choice. If I don't, he'll tell Aerick. Jeff follows through on his promises. I guess if I have to tell someone, then he's my best choice. Melting into his arms, I wrap my arms around his waist and his grip tightens.

"Jeff, I'm going crazy," I whisper, keeping my face buried in his shoulder.

"What do you mean 'going crazy'?" His voice is soft and full of confusion. How do I explain this to him? I don't even understand it.

"I'm seeing things; things that aren't really there. It's freaking me out. I don't know what's real anymore."

"Is that what's been going on with you? When you freaked out in town with Aerick, or when you ran to the post office for Luther?" I look up, wondering when he heard about that. "Aerick told me. He was worried about you; don't be mad." That's strange, since when does Aerick confide in Jeff? The few times Aerick actually talks it's usually to Paulo.

"I'm not mad, but yes. It's so weird, so real. I swear it's real, but every time I see it, it disappears almost as fast as it appears."

"Sweetie, you have to talk to someone."

I push back from him. "No, I don't want anyone to know."

"You can't keep this bottled up inside; there has to be a reason."

"I don't want anyone to know. Please don't tell anyone. I finally have a halfway normal life. Please – I don't want this to ruin things. Promise me you won't tell anyone."

"Hey, calm down." Quickly he wraps me back in his arms. "I promise I won't tell anyone, I already said that. But you should. Nadi, you can't fix it if you try to just ignore it. If you don't want to tell Aerick, then talk to Christian. You're already making progress if you're admitting you have a problem, right? Maybe he can help you get to the bottom of it, help you work through it."

"I don't know. I'll think about it."

He stares long and hard in my eyes as if he's in a silent debate over whether or not I'm telling him the truth.

"Alright. Come on, let's get this stuff put away." I look down and both bags are sitting there; he must have grabbed mine before following me into the office.

"Okay." I shut down the computer and pick up the bag. As always, nothing in my life can ever just go right. Maybe I will never have a normal life. I can only hope Jeff keeps his mouth shut. Normally I can trust him to keep his word, but I wouldn't put it past him to talk if he was overly concerned.

Aerick can't find out about this. It would break me if Aerick left me, but I can't expect him to want to stay with a person like me – a crazy person.

CHAPTER SIXTEEN

(Sunday, March 13th)

WOW, IT'S OVER! Standing here watching the bus drive away, taking the kids back to the city, is a bit saddening. It took a lot to keep my emotions in check as we said goodbye. I never thought that I'd get so attached, especially after all the grief they gave me the first few weeks. It's funny how much some of them have changed in the last few months. There's real hope for many of them.

It's likely I'll never see any of them again. Either they will shape up or they won't. Whichever way, they won't be back here. Due to all the changes already going on, Luther decided not to offer a position to any of the cadets. With the improvement in Skyler, he had a chance at getting a position here, but it wasn't the right time. I'm glad he left here on good terms. It makes the chance of him making it as a law-abiding citizen go up that much higher;

or so say the statistical records Luther keeps.

Jeff gives me a small smile that doesn't reach his eyes and starts back inside. He has been avoiding me most of the week. I've tried to act normal as if nothing has changed, but it's pretty clear that things have been tense between me and Jeff.

Aerick gives me an equally confused half-smile before following Luther back toward his office. We have a mandatory meeting in fifteen minutes. Aerick hasn't been oblivious to the tension between me and Jeff, but it seems that Jeff has kept his promise so far, because Aerick is still clueless. His continued badgering me for answers when he manages getting me alone has convinced me of that.

Avoiding being alone with Aerick has become more and more difficult as the week has gone on. On the few occasions he's managed to talk to me without others around, I simply told him it was the stress of the final week coming to a close, but he isn't stupid. While that explains my behavior, it doesn't explain why Jeff and I have been avoiding each other like the plague. After I dodged Christian all day Sunday, after saying I would talk to someone, Jeff was pissed. I tried to tell him I would talk to Christian, but he knows me well and didn't believe a word I said. I'm not ready to talk yet.

I'm not sure if I can get through our post week without giving Aerick a more believable answer. Now that the cadets are gone, it isn't going to be so easy for me to avoid him. It's only a matter of time before he corners me and there won't be any other choice than to explain myself.

Unfortunately, I haven't thought of any other way to talk my way out of this. Lying isn't something I want to do, either. It's only going to drive the wedge further between us. I wish I could be honest, but the risk of his rejection is too great. It's a double-edged sword threatening to split my life in two no matter what I say. The dilemma is trying to decide which way will hurt less.

A hand lightly squeezes my shoulder and I jerk around to Paulo with his hands up in defense. "Hey little sister, it's just me. Come on or we're going to be late. You know how Luther is." My eyes finally take in the front of camp that everyone else has abandoned. I give Paulo a reassuring nod, but he doesn't move; he quietly waits for me to come with him.

One day I'll have to figure out a way to thank him. In Jeff's absence this week, Paulo has stuck close by me. I'm not sure if Jeff said something to him or if it was Aerick, but he's kept me in his sights nearly every waking hour. His presence is the only comfort I've managed to get with everything else going on. He didn't press about why I'm avoiding Jeff or Aerick; he's kept everything simple and light, which I greatly appreciated. The more I think about it, he's become like another brother to me.

I'm not stupid. It's obvious that he's watching over me likely at Aerick's request, but it doesn't seem to bother him. If he doesn't mind, neither do I. At least I can put it off for as long as possible.

We walk over to the mess hall together in silence. We're the last ones to enter the hall. Brand and Lauren greet me as I come in. They've come for the meeting as per the norm, leaving only Tia absent from the group, but Luther rightfully excused Tia so that she could stay with the baby. We quickly sit, as Luther seems ready to start our meeting.

"Good afternoon," Luther begins and a hush falls on the room. "Another session is done, and I'd like to congratulate everyone on another successful completion." Everyone claps, including me, although they seem in much better spirits. "Now for some announcements. As I mentioned at the start of the session, Lauren and Ayla will be leaving us to join Gavin in Chicago." He turns to Gavin, who's standing next to him, and shakes his hand. "Take care of them."

Gavin nods and steps forward. "I promise they're in good hands, Luther. I just want to take this time to thank you for all your hospitality during the last few months. There's so much I've learned from everyone here, and I'll gladly take it back with me and apply it in our new camp. This has been time well spent and I'm truly grateful for this opportunity."

Gavin moves and takes a seat with the rest of us as Luther moves back to the center of the room. "With these departures, I know there have been some questions as to who will be replacing Ayla. After much thought and consideration, I have finally chosen. Aerick, will you please join me up here?"

Aerick rises and goes to stand proudly beside Luther. "I've spoken to Aerick and he has agreed to take the position starting next session. Congratulations, Aerick." Luther shakes his hand before Aerick retakes his seat. "Next session will be a little more challenging, with many changes. As planned, Jeff will be taking the opening for the new instructors. Brand will be moving into the Lead instructor position and Nadi will be officially taking the position as the camp's teacher. Congratulations to each of you on your accomplishments and thank you to the rest of the staff for all your support along the way. I will be meeting with all of you throughout this closing week, so that we can talk more in-depth about these changes. I think we still have a great team and that things will run smoothly come May."

Luther continues to go over details for the rest of the week, but I draw back into my own head. Hearing him say it out loud only makes it more real. I'm officially part of the team. Not that I wasn't before, but there's a certain gratification to hear him say it. All the hard work finally coming to an end. *I did it!*

* * * *

"Come on, it's too early!" Andi whines at me again as I try to leave our little get-together. When Luther announced that he was taking Aerick, Brand, Gavin and Ayla out for drinks, Brayden insisted we have a little party of our own. Of course, that meant playing poker and drinking in the mess hall without any senior staff around.

It isn't that I'm not enjoying myself; my mind is too caught up in what I'm going to do about Jeff and Aerick. I agreed to at least come and try to have a good time, but even after a few drinks, my mind is too consumed to concentrate. When even alcohol doesn't drown out your problems, it's a real problem. No point in staying here and losing all my money, too.

Thankfully, today was extremely busy and eventful as we started getting things straightened up before we go on break. There's a lot to get done and even more to prepare for now that several of us are taking on new positions for the coming summer session. Aerick was especially busy, running around all day on the heels of Luther and Ayla. It barely gave him a minute to even say hello to me in passing.

The few minutes we got before Luther pulled him to leave a little bit ago was the most we had all day combined. It wasn't wasted with irritating talk. It was filled with a lustful kiss, stolen in the corner of the room before we were discovered. For those few short moments, things were perfect again; but like always, it didn't last.

"Andi, it's late and I'm tired. I got up early this morning and my body is just spent. Luther is going to have us up bright and early and I don't want to be dragging all day. Besides, I still have schoolwork that needs to get done."

"Let her go if she wants," Jeff sulks from the end of the table. "If she doesn't want to socialize, that's her choice." This little attitude he has is getting on my last nerve. Although he hasn't told anyone, he is making it quite clear that there's something wrong, which is almost as bad.

"Do either of you want to explain what the hell is going on between you two?" Brayden questions, looking between us.

"Nothing is going on," I say quickly. "As I said, I'm just tired." I get up and head for the door.

Paulo quickly follows me. "Paulo, I can walk myself back to my cabin."

"It's dark and late. I'm walking you back, no arguments."

"Whatever." No point in arguing; besides, it can't hurt. "Goodnight everyone. See you tomorrow." Everyone else chimes in with their goodbyes, grumbling that I'm not sticking around, as we walk out the door.

Once we hit the bottom of the steps, Paulo's cool façade breaks. "Okay, I'm not getting anything out of anyone and it's driving me nuts. What the hell is going on between you guys?" So much for him keeping to himself. I guess I couldn't expect it to last forever, he's way too curious for that.

"Paulo, I'm really tired and I don't want to get into this right now."

"Oh, come on. Not even a hint?"

"Not tonight. But thank you for being there for me this week." We reach the steps of my cabin and I stop and face him. "It means a lot to me."

"I'll always be here for you, little sister. Even when Aerick and Jeff are being a bunch of dumbasses."

"I know." He can be such a sweetie. I give him a quick tight hug. "Thanks for walking me back."

He gives me a kiss on the top of my head. *Damn tall people.* "Night, little one. Terrie's joining me tonight, so don't wait up for her."

"Thanks Paulo; for everything." Smiling, I turn and walk into the cabin. I close the door behind me, leaning back against it with my eyes shut and take in the silence. *What a fucking day!*

"Well, well, well. Aren't you the popular one?" My face falls – along with my heart. Heaviness hits me like a ton of bricks, all the air deflating from my lungs instantly.

It sounded so real; I can almost hear his breathing. I don't want to open my eyes, but I must. It's the only way to get this out of my head. Slowly my eyelids open and I move my head toward the cold voice.

No, it can't be!

It's real…

He's real…

And he's here!

Shaking my head doesn't help, my vision doesn't change. Sitting at the table in the dark corner is the man I have feared half of my life. The one that caused me to become a social outcast so many years ago. The man who haunts my dreams, who used and abused me as a child. He's here, my imagination is not playing tricks on me, this is real. I don't know how or why but he's here, in my cabin, sitting only a few feet away; his eyes staring icily into my own.

I'm frozen in place. For a moment, I debate whether to scream. Paulo couldn't have made it back yet. He would hear me; he would save me. My chest is already heaving trying to take in the air, there isn't going to be much strength in it. Just as I'm about to yell out to him, the air gets stuck in my throat. My eyes are drawn to the knife sitting on the table and the man's head is shaking back and forth.

"Now you wouldn't do anything stupid, would you? I really don't want to hurt more innocent people because of you." My breath slowly deflates from my lungs. *More?*

Slowly I shake my head. No one else gets hurt, but who did he hurt? Please let Aerick be okay. "Well, don't be rude, get over here and sit down." I'm still stuck in place, not sure what to do. I can't scream, I can't run. It's only a few short steps to get to the table and there's no way I can get out the door before he reaches me.

My lack of movement must anger him, and he picks up the knife. "I said now! Get over here and sit down."

My whole-body trembles as I slowly move forward to sit directly across from him. "Now that's better, isn't it?" He lays the knife back down on the table, but it does nothing to help the dizziness swimming in my head or the pain in my lungs from the lack of air.

How the hell do I get out of this? Is this it? Am I going to die here?

"It seems you have all these boys around here wrapped around your little finger, don't you, whore?" He runs his fingers along the tabletop as he continues. "I see you dragged along that little piss ant who used to crawl into bed with you just to spite me.

I knew I should have taken care of him a long time ago."

Opening my mouth to defend myself, he glares, and it automatically snaps shut. For once I need to control my mouth or it may be the death of me. "Then there is that poor boy that walked you to the door, pretending to be all brotherly. But that couldn't possibly be, because your brother is still laid up in the hospital back in Chicago now, isn't he?" My eyes shoot up – my brother!

"Yes, I know about Evan. That was absolutely brilliant work on my part. Let it serve as a warning. I can get to anyone at any time. You see, I have become quite the little social climber myself. I have connections you couldn't even imagine."

It's his fault; he did that to Evan. All this time we thought it was some idiot's misguided plot to steal something, but something always seemed off. There were too many unanswered questions left hanging. We never considered it was a message, not until now. It was a message for me. *It's my fault!*

"Finally, there is that sorry piece of meat that calls himself your boyfriend. Someone you can whore yourself out to. You have really let your standards drop, haven't you, *Princess?*"

Oh god! Hearing that single word out of his mouth drops my stomach to the floor. That's a word Aerick rarely says in the hearing distance of others. It's something special that we share. How long has he been watching us? I try to think back to the last few times that he said it to me, but my head is too full of haze as my chest still heaves.

"Oh yes, I know all about you and him. He has you so

wrapped up, so twisted up in la la land that you are completely blind. Do you really think he loves you? Do you think anyone could ever love someone like you? A whore like you? You're broken, you're used, useless to anyone. Well, except for me.

"You see, you were mine first. Mine and only mine. My claim kept that little piss ant back for all those years and no macho wannabe is going to move in on what's mine."

That's impossible, he couldn't have been watching me all these years. He disappeared after that summer. I never saw him again; only in my dreams. "How did you find me?" I whisper before I can stop myself.

"That is the wonderful part. See, you found me. That's how I know this is so right. This was meant to be. I admit, I lost track of you after the summer camp ended and my new job took me away from the city. Years gave way into more, and eventually my job brought me back to Chicago. It's funny how things come full circle. All those years working with kids and the various charities bringing me right back to you." His voice drops low, sending a jolt of fear in me.

"Even though there were others, I never did forget you, and I always knew you would come back to me eventually. You were special. It's that dirty whore in you that you won't let admit you loved every moment we spent together, but you did love it." Chills run down my spine at his words, but I remain frozen to my seat, trying to understand where he's going with this story.

"Then I saw you again for the first time and it was as if

everything fell into place. Only it wasn't as perfect as I had imagined because you walked into the room on the arm of another. My fury ran straight through the roof and man I was ready to snatch you away right then, but pulled back as you greeted the guest of honor. My moment of shock that you knew him gave me enough time to get myself in check and formulate my plan to get you back. See, I knew it was fate that you showed up to that award ceremony in Chicago."

Shit. The trip to Chicago with Aerick for his grandfather's award ceremony. He was there watching us.

"You disappointed me. I didn't like what I saw that night. That boy's hands on you, his lips, it's not right. No one's hands belong on you, only mine." Tears finally break the barrier, falling in streams down my cheeks. He found me and it's my own fault. I can't go through this again. I can't deal with being in this room.

"You've been a bad girl, letting another man touch you. You remember what happens to bad girls, right sweetness?" No… no I'm not going through this again. Jumping up, I run to the door, but I'm slammed against it before I can reach the handle. He's still as strong as I remember.

"Now, let's not do anything stupid." His harsh voice spits in my ear as he pins me between him and the door. His fingers run along the back of my head and bile rises in my throat.

"Please don't do this!"

"Hmm, I love hearing you beg. I think I'll enjoy this more than I thought. But not just yet, I have my own plans. You see, this time you will come with me willingly. Things are better that way. You need to show me you deserve my forgiveness."

I shake my head 'no'. There's no way I'm doing that, no way I'll ever go to him willingly. *Never!*

Grabbing my hair roughly, he stops my head from moving, pain shooting down my body at the force. "Oh yes you will," he growls. "You will because if you don't, I will hurt everyone you ever cared about. I already got to Evan. How hard do you think it would be for me to get to your family back in Chicago? Or your precious Jeff, or these little rugrats around here that you call friends? What about that boyfriend of yours? You don't think I haven't found out where he lives? That condo down in Des Moines seems awfully comfortable. It's a shame there's no security at all. Just look at what already happened to you."

My breath catches. He knows where we live, he knows about my attack. "Oh yes, I have connections that reach all over. It would be far too easy for something bad to happen again. Although I hardly think it was fair, how was that man supposed to resist you flaunting yourself around?" The pressure lets up from behind me as my hair is pulled back to the base of my neck.

"So, here is what's going to happen. Tomorrow, you're going to tell your little boy toy you don't want any part in this little whore romance anymore. You're going to tell him you want to go back to Chicago and then you are going to leave with me." *NO! I can't. I can't.* He yanks on my head, stopping it from shaking in disagreement, and slams my body hard into the door again.

"Yes, you will, or you can say goodbye to all of them and I will take you by force. I told you, you are mine and only mine. I'm leaving here with you either way. Whether those you think you love make it out alive is entirely up to you; you decide."

What am I supposed to do? How can I leave here with him? Will he really hurt them?

A sharp point presses against my neck and begins to drag down my spine. "Have you seen your brother? I made sure he was left just alive. The baseball bats were a nice touch. It was so easy to take him by surprise. I will have no problem getting to them, too. Don't doubt me. You have until eight tomorrow night. Be out front or you will regret it and so will they. They will regret ever knowing you. And Aerick, I'll make sure to pay special attention to him for putting his hands on what's mine."

His mouth presses on my neck and his voice softens. "Oh, I have missed you. That smooth skin under my fingers, that perfect body begging for me to do dirty things to you, I can't wait. Time to come back where you belong. Eight o'clock, don't make me wait." Then all the weight against me is gone. I slide down the door, unable to hold myself up on my own two feet. Too afraid to move, to turn, to speak.

I didn't imagine it. It's real, he's real, and he's found me. All those times I thought I was going crazy. He was really there, following me, watching me, waiting. Now everyone I love, everyone I care for, is in danger.

My mind struggles with what I want to do and what I should

do. The right thing would be to leave, go so that those I love are safe; so Aerick will be safe. But the selfishness in me wants to stay and forget this ever happened. I want to hide away and believe Aerick will save me. That everything will go back to normal because I know now, I'm not crazy. Sobs wrack my body as the full weight of the last few minutes bear down on me.

Whack! The window shades slam in the wind, making me jump up and turn around. No one is there, just my window wide open. Stumbling across the room, I throw the window closed, locking it and pulling the shade closed. My feet give out again and I fall to the floor next to my bed, even more exhausted.

I'm so lost... I'm so scared... I'm so alone...

CHAPTER SEVENTEEN

(Monday, March 14th)

MY WORLD HAS stopped, time has stopped, there's nothing I want more than to die where I sit now. Of all the things in my life, for it to come to this, like this. *What was the point?* A life of grief, loneliness, and now extreme heartache. At least I was able to find love, even if it was for such a short time.

Apparently, it's not in my future to ever be happy. It was only a cruel joke life played on me to show me how happy I could've been if I was normal. Although normal is relative, even a small circle of normal is all I wished for. Unfortunately for me, my circle doesn't go on forever. It stops abruptly, turning my infinity into an acute triangle.

Maybe it was never normal at all. In the few short months that I've considered myself to be happy, it was filled with the craziness of Liz. Then the craziness of when we were back at Aerick's condo.

Was I ever destined to merely be happy and content with Aerick? Is it possible we could ever have a normal life?

Even if I stay, there's no telling what might happen in the future and there's no telling if everyone will even make it out of this alive. The attack on Evan was so brutal. My gut tells me that he's telling the truth. He won't hesitate to hurt those I love. If I stayed and something happened to them, how could I live with myself knowing I could have prevented it? Most of them do have happy and normal lives. It's not fair for me to ruin it for them.

Aerick, too. He deserves better than this. He's worked so hard to have a normal life of his own. He worked through his struggles and now I'm bringing it all to a halt. His love for me puts him in danger more than the rest of them.

My heart aches at the thought of being without him. I know his love is true, that much I'm sure of. It may be the only thing I'm sure of right now.

I'm not sure what to do. I have two choices and no matter how much I try to work it out in my head, neither of them works in my favor. The seemingly endless amount of time I've been thinking it through has done nothing to make up my mind, although I'm leaning toward just going and saving everyone else the grief. The grief that would be all my fault. The only thing holding me back is Aerick. Having to tell him goodbye, having to watch the sadness and pain in his eyes will be unbearable. A third option has found its way into my thoughts a few times, but I have no idea how he'll react. While it will end my misery, it will still hurt

Aerick that I'm no longer part of this world.

Then there's the worry that my loved ones may still be hurt out of spite for finding a loophole, but it's the only option where my pain and suffering will end indefinitely. The unknown is the reason that option is not a reasonable option. I can't leave everyone else here to deal with my mess.

My mind hurts. The painful thoughts completing endless laps in my brain have done nothing to help me decide. I'm not sure how long I've been sitting here, but it seems like an eternity. My tears have long dried up even though there's still an overwhelming urge to cry.

I can see a few stars peeking through the shade from the window above me. They're so beautiful, so peaceful, so powerful. Everything I wish I was right now.

Exhaustion has finally taken its toll on me. I don't think I could move to the bed if I tried. Tilting my head back further to better see the stars, I begin counting to clear my head. Maybe if I can clear my head for a while, I can think about this again with a refreshed mind.

One, two, three, four, five...

One hundred, one hundred-one, one hundred-two...

Five hundred, five hundred-one, five hundred-two...

One thousand...

Five thou...

Click. My heart drops at the sound of the door handle releasing the door from the frame. Fear takes my breath away. *He came back to take me now! I'm not ready!*

The dark silhouette figure steps inside closing the door behind him.

"Babe. Why are you on the floor?" *It's not him, not him.* I feel tears well up in my eyes as he shuffles over to me quickly.

"Nadi? What the fuck?!" *Aerick!* Words elude me. He gently takes my face in his hands. "You're freezing and you look as if you've seen a ghost. What happened?"

His eyes are so beautiful. Eyes I could fall into forever. His arms pick me up and he sits on my bed with me on his lap. All I can do is cling to his chest. My tears spill over as he engulfs me in his tight embrace.

"Babe, what's the matter? You're freaking me out here." I pull him tighter to me. I just need him right now, to feel him hold me. "Seriously, talk to me." *How can I?* I don't want to say goodbye. Now that he's here, the weight over my heart is crushing it.

Suddenly he pulls me back, forcing me to look at him, and I flinch back from him unintentionally. I see his concern at my actions and try to gather my thoughts.

As he looks back and forth between my eyes, the wheels turn in his head. "What the hell is wrong? Talk to me, please! Do you want me to go get Jeff?"

I finally find my voice. "No!" I say, a little more forcefully than I meant to. "Please don't leave me right now."

He takes a deep breath, wrapping his arms back around me. "Okay. I'm not going anywhere."

"Please, just hold me."

Another deep sigh raises his chest. "Babe, I'm not going anywhere, but you have to talk to me."

"Aerick, I'm…." I begin, but he cuts me off, already knowing my answer.

"Don't! Don't you dare say you're fine. I walked in here at five in the morning to find you curled up on the floor pale as the dead, looking as if you didn't sleep all night. For fuck sake, you are shaking uncontrollably, and you just flinched away from me. You are *not* fine."

I should do this now. It'll be easier if I get it over with and if I hurry up and say it, maybe I can go through with it. *Distance.* I unwrap myself from him and move to sit at the top of my bed.

"Aerick." He turns toward me with raised eyebrows. "I uh, I have to, um." I close my eyes, trying to concentrate on my words. "I have to go. I'm moving back to Chicago."

He stares at me in shock for a moment. "Whoa, whoa, wait a minute. What do you mean 'leaving'? What the hell happened? Where is this coming from? Nadi, did something happen with Jeff? Is that why you've been acting so weird and avoiding me all week?"

"No, it's not that. Jeff and I merely had a misunderstanding. But I have to leave. I can't stay here anymore; I have to go away."

He rubs his hand across the back of his neck. "Okay, then we can go. If you miss home, we can move to Chicago."

Chicago is not my home; my home is with you. It's what I want to say but I know I can't. "No, you don't understand. I have to go, but you can't come with me." The tears blur my eyes so I can no longer see him straight.

"What do you mean I can't go? If you're leaving, then I'm fucking going with you," he growls.

The pain that shoots through my heart is unbearable. "I have to, Aerick, and you can't," I whisper, losing my conviction.

"No, you don't." All traces of his anger have disappeared. He slides onto the floor, pulling me over in front of him so he can wrap his arms around my waist and look into my eyes. "Baby, whatever is wrong, you can tell me. We can work through it. I promise."

I'm torn again. I know he believes what he says, I just don't know if we can work through it. I shake my head to tell him no.

Fear spreads across his face and he pulls me into a crushing hug. "Please don't leave me. Nadi, I love you. I need you. Please don't do this."

Sobs rack my body at his pleas. The pain in my heart is ripping it in two. *How can I leave him?* Maybe I can change his mind. If he knows, maybe he won't want to be with me anymore. He must be getting tired of my fucked-up shit. Perhaps my past coming back to haunt me will be enough to push him away.

"Aerick, I have to tell you something." *How do I even explain this?* He leans back to look at me, but my eyes fall to my hands.

"You can tell me anything. You know that, right?"

Here goes nothing. "He's back. He found me when we went

to Chicago, and now I have to leave with him. If I don't go, bad things are going to happen. I need you guys to be safe; especially you."

"What do mean 'he's back'?" He pulls my chin up, forcing me to look at him. "Who's back? And what do you mean 'bad things'?"

I shake his hand off and look down again. It's too hard to concentrate looking into his eyes and I'm too ashamed. More tears fall onto my hands. "The teacher," I whisper.

"Teacher?"

Heaviness falls around me and my hands begin to tremble. "The one from summer camp."

The silence in the room is deafening.

After an endless silence, his hands cover my own. "What do you mean by bad things?" His words are soft, almost comforting, if it wasn't for the reminder his words brought to my head.

"He's responsible for Evan being in the hospital. It was a warning to me. If I don't leave with him, everyone I love is in danger. The only way to keep you all safe is for me to leave. I have to go."

"How did he find you in Chicago?"

"He saw us when we were there. He followed me back here." No point in telling him where in Chicago it was. That will only make him blame himself and this isn't his fault.

"That was months ago..." He pauses as the puzzle pieces begin to fall into place. "You fainting, acting scared, it's all connected, isn't it?"

"He's been watching me. Up until now I thought I was going crazy – hallucinating. I never imagined it could really be him."

"What changed that? Why are you so sure he isn't a hallucination?" Now he does think I'm crazy. I guess this is what I wanted.

"He was here."

In an instant he's on his feet looking around the room. "Here where?"

"When I came back to the cabin last night. He was here waiting, but he left. He told me I have to go or everyone I love will suffer. I can't do that to you guys."

"Fucking Christ! You're not leaving here with him; over my dead body."

"Exactly, Aerick! If I don't go, he's going to kill you and take me anyway. I don't have a choice here."

"The hell you don't!"

He starts walking toward the door and I jump up, pulling back on his arm. "Don't, Aerick."

He swings around, pulling up to his full height. "No, you don't. You are not leaving with some child-abusing psycho to try and protect me. Did you really think I would just let you go after everything we have been through in the last few months? I finally found someone I love; someone I want to spend the rest of my life with. I'm not letting you go without a fight."

This is not how I imagined this going. "But what if he hurts you? I couldn't live with myself if something happened to you."

"Don't worry, nothing is going to happen to me or to you. I'll keep you safe, I promise." He pulls me into a crushing hug. My plan backfired and now I'm no better off than when I started. It seems Aerick has made the choice for me, but it still doesn't make me feel any better. At least I have him. He's choosing me over all this stupid over-the-top heap of shit that makes up my life and showing his true, unrelenting love. I begin to relax in his protective embrace.

"What are you going to do?" I whisper.

"We need to call the police."

"No, please," I beg. "I can't go through that. Telling people over and over again. Being dragged into court for everyone to hear what he did. I can't do that." A shiver runs down my back. "Besides, he has friends in high places, it may never even go to court. With the right friends, he could probably make a call and have it all swept under the rug."

Pulling back slightly, he looks into my eyes trying to decide on the best course of action. "Fine, but we have to tell Luther." I open my mouth to argue but he silences me with a finger. "I know you don't want people to know. I will tell him the edited version, but he needs to know. If there is a chance that we're in danger, then we need to tell him."

I nod my head. He's right. I have to protect everyone, and to do that, Luther is going to have to know.

"Get dressed." He releases me and starts pulling out my

clothes from the dresser.

"Wait, we're telling him now?"

"Nadi, he was in your room last night. Yes, we are telling Luther now. Go get dressed."

I'm not sure if I'm completely okay with this, but it's too late now. I've made up my mind. I'm staying, and I need to do what Aerick thinks is best. I trust him.

✼ ✼ ✼ ✼

Luther stands on the stage looking out at all of us. We spent the last hour in Luther's cabin. Thankfully, Aerick skipped over the details of my ordeal, and Luther was extremely understanding. After a little bit of an argument over whether to call the police, Luther gave in. I had to explain a little more about my brother and the fact that he has influential contacts that could protect him.

Instead, Luther decided to put the camp into a lockdown until we decide what we're going to do. Again, my life is causing problems at the camp. For the life of me, I can't understand how Luther can even stand me when I keep becoming a wrench in his smooth-running camp.

"Good morning, everyone. Sorry about the late start, but we had something come up that is cause for concern. Until further notice, I am asking everyone to stay in camp. No one is to go anywhere by themselves, and anything suspicious needs to be reported to me immediately. After dark, no one is to be walking around alone."

"What's going on?" Gavin asks.

"I had a threat on the camp staff. While that happens often considering the juvenile delinquents that come through here, I also have reason to believe this threat may be credible. The staff's safety is my number one priority, so I will expect everyone to take this seriously and keep your eyes open."

Satisfied with the answer, we begin our workout. Luther promised to be discrete about the situation, but he made it clear that he was not going to do anything that would put his staff at risk, either. If it becomes necessary, he'll tell the police. It makes sense and I can't fault him for that. Hopefully we can figure this out without having to resort to that.

We discussed ending the week early, but Luther insisted he didn't want us going home and having to deal with this alone. Especially because we didn't want him to call the police. He isn't sure what we're going to do next, but he promised that we'll figure it out. Though, I'm not sure how much it's going to help. I don't see a way out of this. I suppose we won't know how bad it is until tonight when I don't show up out front.

As we finish, I grab Jeff to keep him behind. No point in him still being mad at me, and he should know the whole truth. Besides, he's in just as much danger as Aerick.

"What's going on?" he snaps at me, rightfully guessing I'm in the know.

"I told Aerick. About the things I thought I was hallucinating."

"What do you mean *thought*?" His demeanor changes

immediately.

"Jeff, I told you I'd been hallucinating, but I never told you who." It would have sounded even more crazy.

"Who? And you still didn't answer my question. What do you mean 'thought'?"

Here goes nothing. "All the times I thought I was seeing something that wasn't there, well it turns out I was really seeing him. It wasn't all in my head; I'm not going crazy."

"Him who... just tell me."

I take a deep breath. "It was Mr. Redding. He's back."

"Wait. Mr. Redding? The Mr. Redding from..."

I cut him off, "Yes."

"How is that possible and what the hell is doing here?" He stands up straighter and begins to look around us.

"He saw me when Aerick and I went back to Chicago. He's here for me, and he told me if I don't go back with him, the is going to hurt everyone I love."

"Nadi, there's no way he's going to hurt anyone; he's trying to scare you into thinking..."

"He already did. Evan's attack wasn't some random mugging. That's why it never made any sense. We know no one is stupid enough to steal that stuff from him. That's why Marcello still hasn't found out who did it. No one on the streets knows because it wasn't someone from the streets."

"Why though? What was the point?"

"He was sending a message. Showing me what he would do

to those I love if I didn't obey him."

"You didn't consider it, did you? Aerick will protect you. We all will. You know that, right?"

"I'm here, aren't I?" He gives me that stupid look, telling me he knew I did. "I promise I'll let Luther and Aerick handle this," I try to assure him.

"What are they going to do?"

"I don't know yet. We told Luther the whole story. Well, we gave him a quick overview of it. I couldn't tell him everything, but he knows enough to understand my issues." Which is way more than I prefer, but things are out of my control now.

"And this lockdown is because of him. How do you know he's even here? That it isn't all in your head?"

Great, him too. Everyone would rather think I was crazy, than to believe that I'm telling the truth. Luther asked the same question too, and even Aerick. Glad to know everyone is on the same page. I take a deep breath. "Yes. When I went back to my cabin last night he was there."

"Holy fuck." He grabs me, pulling me into a bear hug. "Are you okay? Did he hurt you?"

"No, he didn't do anything. Just threatened to hurt everyone I love if I didn't meet him tonight."

"Now that Aerick knows, he isn't going to let that happen, and neither will I." That's the hope. All I can do now is hope my worst fears don't come true.

* * * *

"You can't possibly think I'm going to sit here while you go out there," I shout as Aerick unwraps his hands. We spent the last hour punching at bags trying to clear our heads, or at least that's what I was doing.

"No. You are going into the instructor's cabin and staying with Paulo while Luther and I go out there."

"Aerick, I'm not going to sit around while you put yourself in danger." In what universe does he really believe I'd sit around and do nothing?

"Yes, you are."

"No. I'm. Not," I seethe.

"I'm not letting you walk into another dangerous situation," he shouts as he begins to lose his temper. I flinch a little but recover quickly, standing up straighter.

"Neither am I and if you're going out there, so am I." At least if something happens, I can try to bring the focus to me so he doesn't hurt Aerick. His eyes soften a little as he reigns himself in.

"Babe, you need to trust me. I can't concentrate if you're not safe. Chances are he isn't even going to be out there."

"But what if he is?" I take his face in my hands. "I can't live without you."

He leans down, kissing me softly before pulling back. "I promise nothing will happen to me."

"But what are you going to do if he's out there? If he doesn't see me, he probably won't even let you see him. You won't even have a chance. You don't even know what he looks like."

"What are you suggesting, I just let you walk out there and give him a chance to hurt you?" His hands grab at the back of his neck in frustration. I know this has got to be hard for him.

"Not let him hurt me, but use me as bait. If you let me go out there and you and Luther hide in the shadows, it will give you both a chance to catch him." The wheels begin turning in his head. He's considering it so I continue trying to gain the upper hand. "At the very least you will be able to see him, then you'll know what he looks like."

"I don't know, I don't want you out there." He shakes his head as if trying to shake off a different thought blooming in his head. My hope isn't shot down yet again.

"Aerick, I'm not the helpless little girl I was all those years ago. You taught me well."

His face contorts. "Well, I can't say it has all been me. You have an awful amount of rage built up inside you."

"Yes! Rage he created. I would love nothing more than to make him suffer for what he did."

"That would be fine and dandy, except you freeze and panic every time you see him." He turns away, picking up his gear.

"I won't this time, not with you there. You'll be there to protect me. This is your chance to get him and end this before it even begins."

Taking a deep breath, he turns back toward me. He looks deep into my eyes as if trying to read my soul. I stand up straighter and meet his stare head on. I'm not backing down on this.

He begins shaking his head and backs down first.

"Fuck!" he growls and then gets right up in my face. "Fine! If we do this, you listen and do exactly what I say; and I'm not giving in because you asked. I'm doing this because if I leave you in the cabin, you will try and run off on your own and do it anyway. At least this way, I can have an eye on you at all times."

Yessss! I won; well, sort of. There really isn't any winning in this situation, but at least I can keep an eye on him too.

"Come on. We need to go discuss this with Luther. Something tells me it is going to take some convincing."

* * * *

Aerick was right. Luther was livid when he first heard the plan; but similarly to Aerick, in the end he couldn't deny the fact that this is the perfect opportunity. After a little discussion, our plan was put into place. Unfortunately, he insisted Jeff also be there.

At first he suggested Gavin, but that would mean explaining what was going on, which I argued with until my face was blue before he agreed on Jeff instead, since he already knew the situation. It didn't make me happy, but it was hard to argue. The more people there, the less likely anything will happen to us.

By the time we brought Jeff up to speed, we only had twenty minutes before I had to be out front. Luther dismissed us, telling us to meet him back here in ten minutes so we could go change. The plan is to wear our uniforms so that the black will help conceal the guys until the right time.

We drop off Jeff but Aerick doesn't bother going inside. He still has a spare uniform in my cabin. As we get to the cabin, I'm starting to get worried by Aerick's silence. He hasn't said a word since we left Luther's office.

He goes straight to his clothes and starts changing, so I follow his lead and do the same. There isn't a reason for me to wear black too, but after our workout I was all sweaty, so I figured I might as well. Grabbing the brush, I put my hair up into a ponytail and quickly braid it. If something does go down, I don't want it in my way.

As I turn back around, Aerick is standing leaning up against the wall staring at me, but this time his gaze isn't challenging me. This time there's nothing but concern in his face; maybe a little bit of uncertainty.

"Promise me."

I look at him confused. "Promise you what?"

"Promise me you will do exactly as I say. That you won't stray from the plan." He walks toward me and only stops once he's mere inches from me. His eyes beg for me to follow his command.

"I promise."

He takes my face in his hands. "I'm serious, babe. You can't freeze up. I need you to be fully compliant. If I tell you to move, you need to hear me and act. Promise me you will be focused."

"Everything is going to be okay; I promise." I don't know if I'm trying to convince him or myself. I'm praying the words I tell him are the truth. That his presence will help me stay calm and not freeze in fear.

His lips cut off my thoughts. Instead of tender and sweet, it's hard and lustful. Since this might be the last time he sees me. My hands find his hair and I'm lost in him.

He lifts me and pins me to the wall as I wrap my legs around him. "I can't lose you. I swear I'll keep you safe." His breathless voice breaks our kiss.

"You're not going to lose me and I'm not going to lose you. This is going to work."

He looks deep into my eyes. "I love you, always. No matter what."

"I love you, too."

Our foreheads fall together, and we breathe each other in. It almost feels like goodbye, but I refuse to believe this is it. We're going to get through this.

"Come on. We're going to be late." He breaks away first, slowly lowering me back to the ground. "I'm serious, don't stray from the plan, not even a little bit."

"I won't. I promise."

Finally satisfied, he takes my hand and we head back toward Luther's office, picking up Jeff on the way. The closer I get to going out there, the more my nerves make themselves present. This plan will work, I know it. We get to the office and Luther is all ready to go. He was already in uniform, he only had to put on his jacket.

"Nadi. If this starts going downhill, you get behind us. Do not hesitate, you do not get near him, and if he comes at you, I expect you to fall back. Do you understand?"

"Yes, Luther. I'll be careful, I promise."

"Alright, it's time."

I move to walk out the front door but I'm stopped by Aerick.

"Be careful and don't forget, I'm right behind you." Completely out of character, he gives me a soft, comforting kiss, causing me to freeze and look to Luther and Jeff, who both turn away quickly. "Give us thirty seconds and then go. Remember, no more than twenty feet from the door."

The three guys head out to the back door and walk around the side of the building where they can hide in the shadows. No turning back now. *I can do this.*

I open the front door and step outside, trying to regulate my breathing. Aerick is right, I cannot freeze. I have to stay alert.

The night is chilly and dark. The moon is hidden by the clouds, leaving only the couple of lights on the outside two buildings to light the parking lot. Peeking at my watch, it's exactly eight o'clock. Maybe he won't come.

Now that it's real, I wish it really was all just a hallucination. What's worse is that I'm putting everyone in danger now that they know. I pray this plan works and that they can capture him. Aerick is a scary man and if he gets his hands on him, there's a big chance I'll never have to see him again.

The noise is the first thing that draws my attention. The creaking pops of the tires on the rocks. Straining my ears, the low hum from the engine makes its way to me, but I see no headlights. They must be off and the lights from the building only reach about thirty feet away from the building. Likely why Aerick had pushed the twenty-foot rule. He wanted to be sure he could see me. In the dimness beyond me, a silhouette of a car comes into view, going very slowly. After a moment, I can see that it's the back end of the car. *Smart!*

He made it so that he didn't have to turn around. Just as I'm able to make out the car, it comes to a stop. My heart begins to pound stronger in my chest. The car door opens, and he steps out but leaves the car running. My chest begins to get heavy and I try to breathe through it. The guys are right behind me. They see what I see, and it would only take Aerick seconds to get to me. *I can do this!*

"I knew you would make the right choice. Come on, let's not make this a big deal. Get in the car."

"I…" I lose my words as the fear begins to creep in. *Breathe, breathe.*

"Get in the car. Don't make me wait."

The battle between my body and mind goes into full swing. "I… I can't."

"You can, and you will. Don't make me come get you, or your punishment will be severe. Now, do as you are told!"

I'm frozen in place, but it's okay, because I want him to come closer into the light so the others can see him; but he's rooted in place next to the running car. I need to draw him out, be smarter than him. I need him to get angry and come forward. Inhaling a deep breath, I take a step forward. In the darkness, I think his lips turn up into a grin and I pause. The slightest movement alerts me to Aerick's worry. He specifically didn't want me too close, but it's necessary for this to work.

I begin shaking my head and take a step back, causing him to step forward with me. "What are you doing?" he says, anger bleeding from his words. "Do you want to be punished?" My eyes follow the outline of his hands as he quickly unbuckles his belt and pulls it from his waist in one quick movement.

My chest begins to heave again. The last time it was bad. So bad it hurt to even wear my clothing. Phantom pains shoot through me as if it was yesterday. "Get. Over. Here," he commands as he takes another step closer, his face now visible in the low light.

Back! I need to step back, that's the plan to draw him out, but I'm frozen in fear, staring at the belt that hangs from his hand. I barely register as he takes another step and then another.

Move! I scream at myself, but my body is like a ton of lead. He's only a few feet from me; the plan was to walk back as he walked forward, but now I can't move.

Aerick is behind me; he'll keep me safe, now MOVE!

"Get in the fucking car or I will make you sorry." He raises his hand that holds the belt and takes another step forward but pauses and looks over my shoulder. "You stupid little whore. I told you what would happen. Mark my words, you will be mine."

Before I can comprehend what's happening, he leaps back toward the car and gets into the driver seat right as Aerick, Luther and Jeff all fly past me. Their efforts are useless, the car peels out right as Aerick reaches the back.

"Fuuucccck!" he screams as the sound of the car fades into the dark.

CHAPTER EIGHTEEN

(Tuesday, March 15th)

AERICK POV

"DUDE. WHAT ARE we doing?" Jeff asks from the back seat.

If he didn't know what this asshole looked like, I would have left him back at camp. Nadi's going to go ballistic when she finds out what we're doing, and bringing Jeff along only digs my hole that much deeper. On the other hand, he's probably just as dedicated to getting a little revenge. His love for Nadi doesn't rival mine, but there's no doubt she has part of his heart and likely always will: something I've come to terms with.

"I would be interested in the answer as well," Gavin says from beside me.

This probably wasn't the best idea, but there is no going back now. Her safety is the only thing I care about right now. With him out there, she will always be in fear, and I won't be able to function knowing she's in danger. When Luther finds out I took Jeff, Gavin and Paulo out looking for him, he is going to have my ass too, but I don't care. Besides, they didn't put up much fight when I invited them to take a ride with me. Hopefully that will divert a little heat off me when I face Luther to explain why we all left in the middle of the night. He didn't exactly say we couldn't leave, but I know him well enough to know it was implied.

Paulo hits the back of my chair. "Earth to Aerick!"

"Fuck off, Paulo." The fact that I could get them to leave with me without explanation was a miracle in itself, but I gather they already know they were going to get more information out of me. "I'm going to fill you guys in on a few details about our lockdown."

"Aerick!?" Jeff almost shouts as he grabs the back of my seat. "You can't do that."

"I don't have a choice." Jeff and Paulo both share my need to protect her, so they will understand and stand with me.

Unfortunately, Gavin wouldn't let us leave without him. Everyone decided to play poker tonight. We were the last ones up playing; everyone else had gone to sleep. Most of us are all bunking in the main dorms, since the doors have heavy duty locks on them and high windows that don't open. Security measures that were put in place to lock down cadets, not lock in the staff, but it is proving to be handy.

Ayla is staying in her cabin since Jack agreed to come and stay at the camp, but Luther requested Gavin also join us in the dorms.

Sort of a hypocritical move being that he is remaining in his own cabin, but then again, he has the one and only gun we keep at camp.

"She will skin you alive if you tell them." He's right, she's going to be pissed, but her safety trumps that right now.

"Tell us what?" Gavin and Paulo say in unison.

Focusing my eyes straight ahead on the road, I try to calm the nerves in my stomach that are telling me I shouldn't do this. Here goes nothing. "This lockdown isn't about a disgruntled cadet, it's about Nadi. Someone from her past that hurt her has come back. He's threatening her and those she cares about, which includes the staff members."

"You mean what happened when she was a kid; what causes her nightmares." My eyes dart over to Gavin, then to Jeff.

"You fucking told him!?" Anger boils up in me, even though I'm no better. He has the nerve to question me when he already opened his big mouth?

"I didn't tell him what happened to her. I only told him that something bad happened when we were kids. He was curious the night you two got in that fight at the party and she came to me after having a nightmare."

Fuck! How can I forget that night? I was so worried when I couldn't find her. Then I find her in another guy's bed, in a room with two half naked men. Not that I believed she would do anything with him, but I still didn't appreciate it.

"What the hell are you guys talking about?" Paulo almost

whines, being the only one with no clue as to what we are talking about.

Taking a deep breath, I can only hope she forgives me for this. "When Nadi was younger…"

"Aerick," Jeff interrupts. Rightfully he is worried, but this is what makes sense. If they are going to be in on this, they deserve to know the basic facts.

"Jeff, I will take her ire for this. If they are going to be in on this, they should know why we are doing it."

He lets out a deep sigh and sits back, giving in. "It's your funeral, dude."

"That bad, huh?" Gavin's full attention is on me.

"When she was younger, she was abused by a teacher at the summer camp she attended." My breathing picks up on instinct as I see Gavin's eyes grow wide and I try not to grit my teeth as I continue. "He spent the whole summer exposing himself to her, touching her, threatening her, and beating her. Very few people know about it. She's buried it deep and has tried to forget about it."

"Is that why she reacts so violently to touch?" Gavin guesses with a quiet, rattled voice. I answer with a nod. "How old was she?"

She was just a kid. A helpless little kid that now blames herself over and over for something she had no control over. It pains me to my very core thinking of how scared she must have been, how much pain she had to endure; it's sickening.

"Nine," Jeff finally speaks up when I don't answer. "She was only nine fucking years old when that bastard hurt her. The last time was so bad, I couldn't touch her for a week without her flinching in pain. She'd come to me seeking refuge after he left her room; she needed comfort as she did most nights he visited her.

"But that night, for some reason, he came back. Something he never did, or she would have never chanced it; her room was empty. He found her curled in a ball on my bed as I tried to calm her. Dragging her from my room, he locked me in. I tried and tried to get out, but it was useless. I couldn't save her; I tried so hard, but it was hopeless." A tear falls down his cheek as he turns to look out the window. "After that night, no one could even lay a finger on her without her freaking out."

"Christ!" Gavin shakes his head but stops, suddenly looking back to me. "Are you telling me this teacher is here?"

"That is exactly what I am telling you."

"But how? She's from Chicago. What's he doing here?"

It took a minute for me to wrap my head around it, too. Ultimately it was my fault. We went to Chicago because of me, because of my family. The whole situation still boggles my head. The chances of us running across him are a one in a million.

"He followed us here from the trip we took there. Somehow, he saw her and followed us back. He's been lurking around for a while. She thought she was hallucinating at first, but he's here."

He concentrates hard on a point in front of him before he opens his mouth. "How do you know she isn't hallucinating?

Abuse has been known to cause PTSD; hallucinations are a side effect."

Jeff angrily comes to her defense before there's a chance to answer. "He's not a hallucination, and she's not crazy. He threatened her and tried to get her to leave with him. We saw him when he came to take her away!" For a moment, I wonder if he is so angry because he thought she was hallucinating at first, too. Hell, I was guilty of it myself. "He's also the one responsible for her brother being beaten within an inch of his life," he adds, a little calmer.

"Damn, that is some heavy shit. So, what are we doing, and why aren't we going to the police?" His questioning is starting to get on my nerves, but it is important that he is on our side, so I appease him with an answer.

"Apparently, he has friends in high places. She's afraid she'll have to tell the world about what happened just to have him convince everyone she's a liar and sweep it under the rug. We tried to reason with her, but she is adamant it will only make things worse, and after a lot of thought I concluded she may be right. So, we are going to find him and deal with this ourselves."

"And you expect us to just go along with this." His smugness pisses me off.

I'd expected it would be only Jeff and Paulo, but I was put into a bind when it got late and he was still awake with no sign of retiring for the night. "You do what you want. But I know these two and they care for her almost as much as me."

"Yep," Jeff says.

"Damn straight!" Paulo adds.

"Why did you bring me?"

As smart as he claims to be, he always seems to be clueless. "To keep you from tipping us off to Luther. Besides, even you seem to have a soft spot for her. All that time you spent buddying up to her. I'm hoping you'll want justice just as much as us."

He is quiet for a minute as I pull into The Brick's parking lot. It's the most popular bar in the area; I figure this is the best place to start. I am sure someone must have seen or knows something.

"Fine. I'll help, but I'm here to make sure you don't kill him. It won't help Nadi if all of you end up in jail." He opens the door to exit the car. "Or in prison," he mutters as he steps out.

That's okay with me. He's right, I can't leave her and if he needs to be here to stop me from killing him, then so be it. After what happened with Sean, I'm not sure I could stop once I've started, and the more people looking for this asshole the better.

As we walk into the bar, I nod to the old man who sits at the door checking IDs. We're locals, so he lets us right in without asking for ours. It's barely after midnight but there are more people here than normal considering it's a weekday. My eyes automatically scan the room for people I know.

Matthew is working tonight so I decide to start with him. I take a seat at the bar and tell Jeff and Paulo to go check the back and other rooms. Gavin sits down beside me.

"Hey, Aerick. What can I get you?" Matthew asks as I turn

toward the bar. He gives Gavin an odd look. The town is small, and outsiders stick out like a sore thumb, which is exactly what I am counting on. With this being a tourist spot, I'm hoping he has been lurking around.

"Actually, I just stopped by to ask a few questions." His eyebrows raise at me. If I was an outsider, his lips would be sealed, but this town loves to gossip among its residents. "Have you seen an older gentleman poking around these last few weeks that seems to be more than the normal passing-by tourist?"

He smirks at me but there is irritation in his eyes. "You must be talking about that ignorant prick that has been asking about the camp."

Fuck!

I am on my feet in an instant and it takes all my strength to keep me from jumping over the bar and grabbing him. If it wasn't for Gavin pulling at my arm, I may have actually done it. This is what I was hoping for but deep down, I didn't have much hope.

"You've seen him..." Pausing, I fully comprehend what he just said. "Wait, asking about the camp?"

"Yeah. He's been in a few times asking around about it, trying to be slick or something." He pauses as a guy at the counter asks for another beer and he quickly grabs a glass, filling it with the beer on tap.

This is not a time to test my patience. "Meaning what?"

"You know, trying to act as if he was concerned a bunch of delinquents were running around over there without any security measures. Barrett quickly defended Luther's camp but the more the guy talked, the more you could tell he was fishing for information rather than just being concerned."

The manager, Barrett, is a good friend of Luther's. No surprise that he jumped to defend him. "When Barrett figured out what the guy was doing, he told him that the camp was welcome here and that he wasn't. After a few more choice words, he eighty-sixed him, and the guy left without a fight. I haven't seen him in here since, but a few other people have seen him around."

Jeff and Paulo come to stand behind us; Jeff gives me that look that tells me they didn't find anything worth mentioning, growing my frustration. "Like who?"

"He's been around The Cottage and even up at the Old Number Three asking around, but don't worry, no one's going to talk to some outsider sniffing around."

"When was he here? Do you know if he is staying around here?" I need something to nail him down. He has to be staying somewhere, and there are only a few hotels in town.

"It was about two or three weeks ago, but I haven't heard about him at the hotels. Then again, I've been working a lot and haven't been hanging out with the girls. Speaking of, now that you got a permanent girlfriend, we don't see much of you."

Completely ignoring his comment, I push to get my own answers. "Did he ask about her?"

"The stranger?" I nod impatiently. "Not her specifically, but he asked if there was a new female employee that was from

Chicago. Barrett and I both know she is, and it was what tipped Barrett off that he wasn't who he appeared to be."

"Anything else he said that didn't sit right with you?"

"Just that he seemed really interested in the security of the camp. Barrett did tell him that there were cameras before he realized what was going on. What's this guy's deal? Is he a reporter or something?"

It's probably better that most people don't know what we are up to, in case this does end badly. "We heard someone was around getting nosy. Wanted to make sure he isn't making trouble for us. Luther worked hard to get the camp a good name in this town and we don't want someone coming in and disrupting that. If you see him or hear that he's around again, can you give me a call?"

"Sure thing."

"Thanks man." We shake hands and we all make our exit. My heart is racing a hundred miles an hour. I didn't think we would get that lucky so quickly, but it isn't enough. There must be others who have seen him or know where he is staying. The urge to find him is weighing heavily on me.

"Where to now?" Gavin asks once we are back in the car. Without putting much thought into it, I head toward The Cottage. It's the only other real hangout spot outside of the bars.

Our initial luck doesn't seem to be following, because there are only a few cars in the parking lot. As we enter the restaurant there is mostly staff with a few scattered tables of customers, but Kate is on duty, lifting my spirits a little. She is extremely chatty, especially when she is shown any amount of attention. Her eyes find me and light up the minute they touch me. We all take a seat at the counter.

"Well, hello Aerick. We've missed you. It's been a while since you were in to see us. What can I get you?" Her words are laced with double meaning as she looks me up and down, almost drooling with lust. Both Jeff's and Gavin's eyes question me while Paulo grins. I've been a little more than a friend to her and another waitress on a few occasions.

The first time I brought Nadi here she was working, and when she saw me kiss Nadi, I thought she was going to jump over the counter and attack her. My thoughts weren't on her at the time, they was on the asshole sitting next to Nadi, but her face was full of hatred after seeing that. I'm not sure why. I've always made it clear with every girl I've been with that monogamous relationships aren't my thing. Some women tend to be better at accepting it than others.

But right now, I need answers and the nicer I am to her, the more likely I'll get them. Sometimes she can be a little juvenile and after the way she acted when I was with Nadi, it is going to take a little finesse. Playing it smooth, I order us all coffee, giving my signature smile.

"Coming right up." She bites her lip, grinning as she turns to go get our coffee.

"Do I want to know?" Jeff asks. I'm about to answer when Paulo answers for me.

"He had a thing going with Kate and this other waitress Sarah before he met Nadi." Jeff's eyes go wide and I punch Paulo in the arm. Not sure why he insists on airing out my laundry.

"Two, huh?" Gavin sounds impressed but Jeff looks pissed.

"Multiple times," Paulo smirks.

"Paulo, if you don't shut the fuck up, I'm going to lay you out." Looking toward Jeff, I try to placate his emotions before he ruins this. "As he said, it was before Nadi and things are different now. I would never do anything to hurt our relationship but getting answers out of Kate is going to take a little charm," I warn. While she doesn't mind sharing, she doesn't take rejection well.

Kate returns and I put my smile back on. Jeff takes his coffee and puts his head down, concentrating on the spotless counter. After all this time, he still has his doubts; or maybe he still feels it's a betrayal.

"How have you been, Kate?" I ask, trying to keep her interested.

"Better, now that you're here. What's the occasion? You don't typically stop by during the weeknights unless you need something." She hit dead on with her words, but her thoughts are totally out in left field.

"Actually, I do need something." Her eyes light up and she gets all giddy. Geez, was she always this bad? "I need to ask you some questions. It's really important to me." Lightly I run my finger over her hand and look up to her with just my eyes.

She almost melts to the floor. "You can ask me anything."

Sometimes my charm comes in handy. Jeff huffs beside me while Gavin and Paulo try to hold in their laughter, but I have her just where I want her. Ignoring the other guys, I focus on getting her to answer my questions. "Have you had anyone in here asking around about us at camp?"

"Yeah, mostly about you." My heart picks up. "Everyone knows you're up here, but no one has seen much of you." She sticks out a pouty lip. "How come you don't come hang out with us anymore?"

Let down. For a moment, I thought she had seen him. "I meant strangers, Kate. Have there been any strangers around asking questions?" Is she really this dull? It takes a lot of restraint to keep the smile on my face and not scowl at her.

"Oh… no, not really."

My patience with her is wearing thin. "Not really?"

"Well, some of the girls said there was this old geezer asking about the camp, but they mostly gave him the cold shoulder. Then last night some stranger came in, all pissed off. He kept mumbling to himself and staring at me. It was creepy. From how they described him, I think it may be the same guy they were talking about."

"About what time?"

"I don't know – maybe around 8:30 or so. He was all mad until he saw Maddie, she was hosting last night." He must have come here after leaving the camp. That was a brave move. We could have called the police or came looking for him; it's as if he isn't afraid of getting caught. Maybe Nadi is right about him having friends in high places.

"Sarah's little sister?" Paulo questions pulling my attention back. *Little sister?*

"Yeah. That's what is so creepy. She's barely fifteen and he had to have been like, almost fifty. After he saw her, he wouldn't stop staring at her. His eyes followed her everywhere she went. He was trying to act all discreet about it, but it was pretty clear he was interested in her. Like I said, creepy. Maddie was going to walk home, but Sarah called their brother to pick her up because it freaked her out too."

"Do you have a picture of Maddie?" Jeff asks.

She looks him up and down and trains her attention on him. "And who might you be, cutie?"

"Sorry, I'm being rude. This is Jeff, he's a new instructor at the camp." I clap him on the shoulder and give it a shake. His good nature gets him to beam at her. She is pretty hot and there is no way he is completely oblivious to it. Maybe she will lay off of me and he can have a good time for himself. Lord knows that boy needs to loosen up.

"Welcome," she grins kindly at him. She pulls out her phone from her back pocket and scrolls through a few pictures, selects one, then hands him the phone."

We all huddle around the phone looking at the picture. Maddie is cute: medium length, darker hair, beautiful smile, youthful face. She almost doesn't even look old enough to be working.

"She kind of looks similar to a younger Nadi," Jeff says sourly as we exchange a look. He's right, they look very similar, and it makes me sick to my stomach. Knowing the kind of man he is, it was probably a very good thing she didn't walk home by herself. She may have never made it.

"Who's Nadi, your girlfriend?" Kate asks, a little disappointed.

I push, ignoring her question to Jeff. "What happened after that?"

"After Maddie left, he sat here drinking coffee for a couple of hours. Sometimes he was texting, but mostly he stared out the window as if he was deep in thought. Then he left suddenly without a word. Didn't even bother leaving a tip; just the lousy dollar for his coffee." She rolls her eyes, frustrated. "The least the creep could have done was left me a tip for letting him stare at my ass half the night. Anyways, that was it. He hasn't been back. Why?"

"That's it, you didn't see what he was texting or anything, did you?" My frustrations get the better of me.

"No, why? Aerick, what's up? Who is he?"

"Does it bother anyone else that she looks so similar to Nadi?" Jeff asks as he still stares at the picture on the phone.

"Why does it matter that she looks like your girlfriend?" She grabs her phone out of Jeff's hands. He looks at her crazy, shocked by what she said.

"She's not his girlfriend," I snap without thinking. "She's *mine!*"

Her face falls, then molds into a 'go fuck yourself' look as she realizes my game. "I see. Well, I can't just stand around here talking; I'm busy. Let me know if you need a refill." It looks as if that is all we are getting out of her tonight. Putting the phone back in her pocket, she walks away toward one of the few occupied tables to busy herself.

"She's right about one thing. It is creepy as hell! I would hate to imagine what would have happened if that girl left here alone." Gavin shakes his head as he hits on what I am sure we are all thinking.

Feeling bad for leading her on, I leave Kate two twenties for our four-dollar coffee bill and we head out even though we barely touched our coffee. None of us seem in the mood and this new revelation just creates a deeper need to find him. If he can't have Nadi, nothing is stopping him from preying on some other young girl.

We decide to visit a few more places around town that are still open early in the morning, but we're not able to get much more information. When we stop at the only open gas station, Eddie is working, and doesn't know who I'm talking about. The girls at the Old Number Three give me a similar story to what Matthew gave me, but none of them were as open to the outsider, so they can't tell me anything. No one at the hotels have seen him either, which means he is either staying in a private rental or in a different town.

The closest one with a hotel is over thirty miles away.

Gavin smirks at me as we leave the last hotel. "You sure do get around, don't you? You hold the attention of a lot of the girls around here." We ran into another old fling at the last hotel. She didn't bother hiding her attraction to me.

"I have a past here, but it's in the past, so let's drop it." Gavin looks back toward Jeff, who seems to be at the end of his rope for tonight.

"You better hope Nadi hasn't woken up," Jeff snaps at me a few minutes later as we pull back into the camp.

"That is one thing I don't have to worry about."

"Why is that?" Gavin asks.

"She had a headache before bed, and I switched out a Valium in place of Tylenol. She'll be out for at least a few more hours."

"You drugged her!"

I figured he of all people would have been appreciative that she was getting some peaceful rest. "Jeff, she hasn't slept in two days and with everything that has happened, she was refusing to go to sleep. Hell, can you blame her? You and I both know she would have been screaming herself awake the moment she fell asleep. I had to give her something; she's exhausted and she would never agree to take it on her own. She hates taking meds; in her mind, they make her look weak."

The anger in his face softens as he takes in my words. He knows I'm right. Just thinking about the sound of her screaming herself awake sends shivers down my spine. We walk back to the dorm in silence.

Using the master key, I let us back in. Earlier I had walked around and locked up all three exits to make sure everyone inside was safe. The only other people with keys are Ayla and Luther. I also checked the cameras a few times from my phone while we were gone to make sure nothing was out of the ordinary.

Inside, everything is dead quiet. Nadi is still fast asleep on my bed while Terrie is asleep on Paulo's. Jake and Andi are passed out on Trent's bed; he graciously agreed to give up the bed to sleep in the cadet dorm along with Brayden. Part of me thinks he merely wants to keep an eye on Brayden. The kid doesn't know how to stay out of trouble and if there is danger, it's the brotherly thing to do.

Sitting down next to Nadi, I push her hair off her face. She looks more peaceful now that she is resting in a deep sleep. With everything she has been through, she deserves a little peace. It's impossible to comprehend how she continues to deal with all the bad shit that life throws at her. I've had it hard, but none of it compares to what she has been through.

Paulo, Gavin and Jeff say their goodnights and head to bed. I set up my tablet up next to the bed with the cameras in and around the dorms alternating across the screen. Then I crawl into bed, wrapping myself around her. It still blows my mind how we seem to fit together perfectly, even as imperfect as we are as individuals.

I want so much for this to be over. Her sanity is on the edge of breaking and no one would be able to blame her if she did go over. We all feel bad for thinking she was seeing things, but then again, so did she.

All I wish is for her to be happy. To be able to live without fear, without worry. Suffering through life thus far, it is only fair that she be able to enjoy life, preferably with me. I will do what I must to make sure it happens for her. Even if I have to kill this fucker to get him out of her life.

CHAPTER NINETEEN

(Tuesday, March 15th)

DAMN, IT FEELS as if I've run a marathon, and PT this morning was only a light workout. The heaviness in my whole body has kept me dragging all morning. Several of the guys look a little tired too, but they were up a lot later playing poker.

I must even look a little off, because Jeff asked how I was feeling. Maybe my body is more exhausted than I realized. On the plus side, I somehow managed to sleep without any dreams. Up to the last moment, I fought sleep, fearing what might show up; in the end, no dreams came at all. A little reprieve in my constant torment.

Everyone else seems a little on edge this morning. The staff must have taken Luther's warning to heart, but the way everyone seems to be acting is putting me off. It's bothering me that several of the guys seem to be walking on eggshells around me. I expected this from Aerick or even Jeff, but why Paulo and Gavin seem to be sharing the same concerned looks has me at a loss. Their knowledge of this situation, like everyone else's, is limited. Luther kept his promise to keep my past as quiet as possible, but it's almost as if they know I'm in danger – or maybe they have an inkling that I'm at the center of this.

Thinking about it, I haven't been alone once so far this morning, other than my shower after PT. Naturally, Aerick tried to join me, and as much as I wanted him to, it would be inappropriate. Almost everyone is staying in the dorms, which means we all share the same bathroom to get ready. If he joined me, something inappropriate was bound to happen, and I wasn't having that with others in the same room.

"I know it's my job, but I always hated doing laundry," Andi says from beside me as we fold the sheets that came out of the dryer.

She's not the only one. Living in an apartment growing up, my sister and I always got stuck doing everyone's wash at the laundromat. The washing part isn't the part that sucks; all the folding is the real pain in the ass. "Trust me, I understand."

"So, are you going to finally fill me in on the details of what's going on?" Leave it to Andi to be blunt and just come out and ask instead of ignoring the elephant in the room.

"Why do you say that? What makes you think I know?" Hopefully, the calm tone will throw her off.

"Seriously? You always know! In fact, lately, you always seem to be in the middle." She catches her tongue and quickly continues. "Not to say that you're in the middle of this. I'm only saying you seem to have some bad luck or something with all the bad things that happen to you."

Well, it's the truth. I know it, and it shouldn't surprise me that so does everyone else. As much as I wish it weren't the case, I can't deny all the trouble around lately always has me at the center. "As Luther said, there were threats against the staff here."

She purses her lips at me. "I figured that much; Luther isn't one to lie, but something tells me you have more details than that. Even if you aren't in the center of it, your man is always in the know of everything that goes on here. He acts like he owns the place half the time."

Can't deny that either. In fact, it wouldn't surprise me if Aerick was watching us right now. "Luther said he doesn't want us talking about it. I'm new, so it isn't in my best interest to defy his orders." Well, it is sort of accurate. He didn't want everyone to panic, and said to keep the details to ourselves unless he felt it needed to be said.

She glares at me and slams the folded sheet on top of the finished pile. Good, now maybe she will drop it. The rest of this week is not going to be easy; it's only Tuesday, and even though the cadets only left two days ago, it feels like a month.

It still worries me what we're going to do once we leave. Luther is hesitant to let anyone depart before they find the source of our current threat; although, I don't know how they're going to locate him. Luther has been locked in his office pretty much since he found out, no one is allowed to leave, and we don't even know if he's still around.

He can't keep us here forever, but a few times so far today, I have worried about what leaving here means. At least being here together, we can help protect one another. After that, we're all on our own, other than the few of us that have significant others.

What if he hurts them? It would be all my fault. As much as it sucks to admit it, I still have that nagging feeling that I should just leave to keep them all safe. But even trying to do that seems impossible with everyone keeping such a close eye on me. There's no possible way to sneak out of here without anyone seeing me. Jake is spending all his time in the office on Luther's order. It's probably safe to bet that he's been ordered to keep track of everyone in camp, me in particular.

Then there's Aerick's unusually pissy mood – well, more pissy than normal. He had a meeting with Luther early this morning. By the way he exited the office looking ready to blow something up, it's safe to say he got in trouble for something, or Luther is going against Aerick on something. Unfortunately for me, they're both giving me the silent treatment.

Paulo walks in as we fold the next sheet. "Andi, I'll take over here. You and Terrie can start lunch; she's waiting for you on the steps."

"Hell yes. I would much rather cook than do this."

"Hey, at least you don't have to clean all the gym equipment.

Worst job ever, and to make matters worse, I'm stuck doing it with Trent on Thursday." Paulo whines.

She laughs. "You're right, I think that's worse. I'll stick to laundry." She hands me the sheet and heads out the door.

Paulo comes around the table with the pile of clean sheets sitting on it and empties the another dryer. It's a good thing we have multiple washers and dryers, otherwise this would take weeks instead of days. Although we throw out the clothing with stains or tears, it's still a lot when you're doing a weeks' worth of laundry for twelve people, including their bedding. Throw in all the employees' stuff, and it turns into a mountainous pile of smelly laundry.

"How are you doing?" Paulo asks me as we begin folding a sheet off the pile. I don't like this. He's oddly somber and almost glum. It's also making me wonder how much he really knows. If Aerick confided in anybody, it would be Paulo, but he wouldn't have told him this. The only way to tell him how serious this is would be to explain to him what happened to me; Aerick wouldn't do that. *So, what the hell is eating at him?*

"I'm fine. Do you think these threats are credible?" If he's going to figure me out, I can return the favor. Maybe I can figure out how much he really suspects. Perhaps he's merely assuming it's me, just like Andi.

"I've known Luther long enough to know that he doesn't overact. If he's worried, there's a good reason. So, don't go off and do anything crazy."

"Me? Crazy?"

He rolls his eyes. I guess we both have a foot in that boat, but my actions are more protective, while his actions are just plain old nuts. We both jump as his phone beeps, and he rushes to read the incoming message. After a quick glance, he starts contemplating something before facing me. "I need you to stay here for a few minutes."

Confusion momentarily clouds my mind. "What's wrong?"

"I'm not sure, but I need to go next door to the office. I'll be right back, please don't go anywhere." With one more quick debate playing out on his face, he rushes out of the building toward the office next door.

What now?

How many more things can happen around here? It's all getting ridiculous. With a shake of my head, I slowly pick up another sheet and start folding. Of anywhere, I feel safest here. It's not as if something is happening within the camp. If that were the case, Aerick would be here already.

Even as I think it, Aerick enters the building. *Great, maybe I was wrong?* "Is everything okay?"

The look I just saw on Paulo's face is now mirrored on Aerick's. "We had three different maintenance shack alarms go off within a few minutes of each other. It's probably nothing, but we're going to check them out."

Fear fills my body. *It's a trap.* I feel it in my bones. He's going to split them up and hurt them one by one. This is how he's going to get back at me. "Aerick, you can't go alone, it's not safe." Especially not for Aerick.

"As much as I would love to argue, Luther agrees."

"He does?" Thank heavens; someone has a level head.

"Luther insists we go in pairs."

Finally, I can help do something. It's driving me nuts just sitting here waiting for something to happen. "Okay, we can go together."

"Wait! You're not going anywhere. You need to stay here where it's safe. I need you to go in with Jake while we spread out and check this out."

I slam the folded sheet down. "You're kidding me, right?" I'm being left behind again. Treated like a child. He takes a step closer to me, but I react by moving one back. They can't keep me locked up here all week.

"Babe, please. I need you to go next door and let us figure this out. Ayla is still in town, Terrie and Andi are in the Mess Hall. Just go next door with Jake until we all get back. Or promise me you will stay in here. Luther and Jake have an eye on the camera's; I need to know you are safe, please."

I hate when he gets like this, there's no way to say no when he pleads with me. "Fine, I'll stay here. But for the record, this is stupid."

"I know, you're probably right; likely a malfunction. It's odd for all three to trigger within a few minutes of each other. They are too far apart for one person to trip them in that short amount of time. I'll be back soon. Stay in here!"

Bossy. "Okay, okay, I get it." It's so frustrating when he acts this way.

He's probably right. I've been out to all the shacks, and there's no way someone could have triggered all the sensors in only a few minutes. Aerick gives me a quick kiss and leaves without another word.

Out the window, I can see the others waiting for Aerick, and they all take off as soon as he reaches them. Aerick, Paulo, Jeff, and Gavin go toward the trail that leads to two of the shacks, and Trent and Brayden head out toward the other one. When they are out of sight, I head back over to the stack of sheets. It's going to take them a few to get to their destinations so I might as well keep myself busy or I might go crazy.

I keep repeating in my head that it's nothing, but like the look I saw in Aerick's face, neither of us honestly believe that. It would be a smart move other than the fact that there are still several people around, and we have cameras everywhere. With Luther and Jake manning the cameras, we should be safe. Deep down I know that isn't true, either.

The clock on my wrist ticks away the minutes slowly as I finish folding the sheets. After looking at my watch for the twelfth time in five minutes, I shake my whole body, trying to release some of the tension. Why does time seem to go by so slow when you want it to speed up?

My stomach knots as I hear the door behind me that leads out to the front of camp open and close quietly. *Fuck me!* It's just Jake or Luther; it has to be. There's no way the guys are back yet, but we hardly ever use that door. My feet turn me around slowly and the urge to vomit rises in my chest as the figure that enters stands no more than a foot from me. Pain shoots through my suddenly deflated lungs.

"It's a beautiful sight seeing you working away in here. It's so... domestic. You're going to be a great little housewife. Doing what I want, when I want, and with no lip."

Is he fucking serious?

I open my mouth to tell him exactly what I think about that, but he takes a step closer and lays his finger on my lips. "Ah, ah now. Don't go and let your nasty little mouth ruin this perfect little moment. I have other plans for that dirty mouth."

The grin on his face infuriates me. How can he think after all this that I would willingly do or go anywhere with him? I smack his hand away. "Fuck off."

I'm pleasantly happy with how confident I sound, despite the bricks sitting on my chest, but dread replaces my moment of happiness as anger builds in his face. His hand shoots up before I can react. A stinging pain erupts on my cheek, and he grabs me with a death grip on my bicep.

"What did I just say to you, you little wench? You are going to learn to do as you're told. I'm tired of all this defying me. You're going to give up this act and come where you belong. Staying here is a lie. These people don't care about you, and he will never love you. He's using you."

"No, he's n..." Another flash of pain spreads along my other cheek.

"You're still a slow learner. Don't interrupt me. Neither of you is too bright, are you?" I rub my burning cheek as he finally lets go of my arm, but he makes no move to remove himself from my personal space, nor has the anger dissipated from his overbearing frame.

"I know he was out all night asking around about me. What does he think he can do? I know about his past; it would be easy as pie to bury him with what I know." His face twists into a wicked smirk that makes my stomach drop. "I'll bet you don't even know. Did he tell you what he did to get sent here years ago? He's got one wicked temper on him. The photos in his file were quite gruesome. How long before he gets angry with you and lets out that temper.?"

Aerick was a juvenile when that happened. *How did he get access to that?* I thought juvenile records are sealed.

The tips of his disgusting fingers run across my shoulder. "He probably gave you some sob story about how his daddy hit him; how he never loved him. Maybe how his mother is a mindless feeble, only after his father for the money and cares nothing for her children. Is that how he got you in his bed? Did you feel sorry for him?" Aerick never feels sorry for himself. He's stronger because of the childhood he had. He's a good guy.

"He isn't innocent, you know. Did he tell you about all the

girls he runs through; sometimes two at a time? How about tying up girls, only to beat them so he can get off? The boy isn't capable of real love. He views women as something to bide his time. He goes through them like a runner goes through shoes, sometimes quicker. He has much more in common with me than you realize. Perhaps that's why you're with him; you missed me. Deep down, you enjoy what I do to you; you know you do."

My stomach jumps to the ceiling then drops to the floor. He has to be lying; Aerick isn't that way. Yes, he's been with women, but he's never enjoyed inflicting pain on me; it's been the opposite. "Lies, it's all lies." My head shakes vehemently.

"But it's not, sweetness. You need to stop denying the truth and finally admit it to yourself. You want to be with me, and you know it. I gave you a chance to come with me, but instead, you told him. That hurt me."

He leans in, lowering his voice, though pointlessly as it's only the two of us in the room. "I shouldn't, but I am giving you one last chance to make this right. I shouldn't, but I'm going to. Meet me at the entrance of the driveway at 1 am, or everything and everybody you love will disappear."

There's no reservation in my mind that he would be willing to do it just to hurt me, but could he really get away with it? As if reading my mind, he speaks again, pushing down all doubts. "It was so easy to lure everyone away. A few time delayed contraptions that set off the alarms. Just like the game of 'Mouse Trap.' With all the blind spots in the camera's, it would be all too easy to trap each and every one of them; a bunch of little mice."

Shivers spread up my spine. My mind still can't comprehend why he wouldn't just take me and leave. There's no real reason why he hasn't, with as many chances as he's had. There have been so many times when I was alone, and no one would have missed me for hours. His insistence of me doing it myself has to be some justifying fact that if I go on my own that makes it okay, makes it right in some way. My only chance now is to stall and pray somebody comes in.

"I can't get out." I think about telling him how locked down we are, but on second thought, letting him know the details of our situation may hurt more than it helps.

"You're a clever girl. You've already proven that. You'll find a way." I open my mouth to argue, but he raises his hand to smack me again and I react, covering my face before the blow can come. But it doesn't. Instead, there's a breeze, and when I look up, he's gone.

Fuck! I rush out the door, but he's disappeared. He knows about the blind spots in the cameras. I'm well acquainted with them myself from when Aerick and I used to have to sneak around. My chest is still heaving from the stress of the last few minutes, but it's less from fear and more from anger.

He fucking got away again. *Is this shit ever going to end?*

I close the door right as the other one opens. "You okay? Just wanted to check on you." Luther says from the doorway that leads to the courtyard.

All I want is to tell him what happened, but now I know this isn't going to end until I end it. If he knows what just happened, he's likely to put me in a locked room with twenty-four-seven security, and if I am going to do something, I can't be locked down. "I'm fine, Luther. Just nervous waiting for the guys to get back." I'm proud my voice stays steady. Not wanting Luther to see my face, I stare out the window next to the door I'm standing in front of.

"Alright, stay inside. The guys didn't find anything, and they're heading back. It was probably a glitch." *Or not.* I nod my head and wait for him to take it as a cue to leave; he does.

Things are getting worse. It's only a matter of time before he gets tired of playing games and either takes me, or keeps true to his word, hurting everyone I know. Neither option has a flattering ending. I have to end this myself; on my terms.

* * * *

The rest of the afternoon went by quickly. The guys all showed up with a mixture of relief and frustration. Aerick checked on me, but his only clue that anything out of the normal was going on was when he questioned why I looked flush. Playing it off, I told him it was merely the stress making me feel a little under the weather. It seems to have worked.

As we lie in bed, I'm nowhere near tired, despite the fact that it's barely after eleven at night. Ever since the little encounter, something has been bothering me. The things he said about Aerick, although I'm sure he was lying, it still bothers me to have those images in my head.

Watching everyone else during the day didn't help some of my own thoughts. The way Gavin and Paulo were watching me, how they acted around me. For the first time in a long time, I felt uncomfortable hanging out with friends. My suspicions are on high alert.

Aerick shifts slightly behind me. It seems he's also restless. I wonder if he thinks this afternoon was a trick. Despite being in a room full of people sleeping, I need to put some of my thoughts to rest.

"Aerick? You awake?"

He grunts behind me, burying his face further into my hair. If nothing else, maybe I'm wrong.

"Where did you go last night?" His body tenses behind me, but he answers immediately.

"What are you talking about?" *HA*. Now I know he's lying. Instead of denying it, he put it back to me.

"I know you left last night. I woke up and you were gone."

"Go to sleep, babe; I know you didn't wake up."

"And how is that exactly?" I sit up and turn to face him. Something is majorly off here.

"I just do, now go to sleep." He turns away from me trying to settle into his pillow.

I attempt to keep as quiet as possible, since everyone else is asleep, or at least faking it. "Who else went with you? Where did you go? I know Jeff was one, but who else?" I bluff.

It makes sense that Jeff would have gone with him if he went out searching for him. He was the only other one that knew the truth. But I have my suspicions it wasn't only them. "Paulo and Gavin went too," I say, more as a statement than a question, letting my mind work out loud.

His silence is my answer, and my anger explodes. They all left last night after I fell asleep. "Where did you guys go? Why don't you want to tell me, and how do you know I didn't wake up?" Of this quick conversation, that is the one thing throwing up the most alarm bells in my head.

He finally turns back toward me. "Babe, it was nothing; please go back to sleep." Ugh, this is so frustrating. If it were nothing, then he wouldn't be dodging the question. It isn't as if I'd be mad if he went to the bar and drank with the guys. Those words echoing in my head come to the forefront, 'I know he was out all night asking around about me.'

It all comes into focus. "You went out looking for *him* last night." Concern fills his masculine features. "You, Jeff, Gavin and Paulo all went out last night looking for him. That means you told them, didn't you? You told them what happened to me!"

"Nadi…" I'm no longer able to hold back the anger and cut him off.

"No, you don't 'Nadi' me. How could you tell them? It wasn't your place to let them in on my past." Unwanted tears spring out of my eyes at the feeling of betrayal. "And Jeff, how could he do that to me?"

Aerick shakes his head. "Jeff didn't do anything, he tried to stop me, but they had a right to know what we were getting into going out to look for him. They needed to understand the danger you're in. They all care about you, and no one wants to see you hurt."

"Hurt? Don't you think this hurts me? You told people the most horrible, embarrassing, humiliating things about me. I trusted you, I trusted you to keep my secrets, and now everyone knows," I yell in a whispered scream. "How could you?"

Aerick reaches for me but I scramble onto the cold floor beside the bed and panic fills his eyes as my shirt slips through his outstretched hand. "Babe, please calm down," he whispers.

Like everyone, he's betrayed me. I look for an escape, but the door is locked, and everyone else must be asleep, because no one is stirring at our quieted argument. As much as I was ready to walk out of this room, I still needed confirmation to my final question.

"You didn't answer my question. How did you know I wouldn't wake up?" Defeat bounces in his eyes. He grabs my hand, trapping it between both of his, and lightly strokes the back of it with his thumb.

"I just wanted you to get some sleep without the nightmares. I swear, I didn't even think about leaving until you had already passed out."

I knew it. My tears give way to uncontrollable rage. "You gave me sleeping pills. All those times I told Terrie no, and you gave them to me anyway." His head falls in shame as it rightfully should.

"I wanted to help, but you are just so stubborn sometimes."

I rip my hand away from his. "Oh great, so you drug me and go off telling everyone my problems. In what reality does that seem okay, Aerick? Because to me it sounds like an overacting, overbearing, overprotective boyfriend that is putting his own feelings in front of mine." He remains quiet, begging for forgiveness with his eyes.

"You asshole." Grabbing his sweater that is lying on the end of the bed, I head toward the bathroom.

"Babe…"

"Don't, just don't. If you know what's best for you, you'll leave me alone for the night. I'm going to go sleep in the other room with Trent and Brayden."

My body moves on its own into the other room before I can turn around and hit him in that beautiful face of his. My heart is pounding and my stomach is in knots. Of all the things he could do, this feels as if it may be the worst.

How could he tell them those things? And Jeff not stopping him. He, above all, knows how much I hate people knowing about my private life. The feeling compares to the cliché of getting in front of a group of people only to find out you are naked. That's how I feel, naked in front of all the people I care about.

Trent and Brayden are sleeping on the beds closest to the bathroom, so I sit at one closest to the outside door. My fisted hands bury themselves in the mattress close to my thighs. The fucked-up part is I know eventually I'll forgive him, but it won't be happening anytime soon, and definitely won't be happening tonight.

So many thoughts have been circling my mind over the last few hours. Aerick's admission only throws a wrench right into the middle of them. At least it's made me more confident of my decision. It's the only way to stop all this, and it's the right thing to do. I'm surer of it now, more than ever.

CHAPTER TWENTY

(Wednesday, March 16h)

"I AM THE only one you can trust. All boys are just liars, girl. They will say whatever they can to make you do what they want. Boys don't love girls, they love to control girls, and that's why you can't trust them – any of them, only me."

His rough hand runs down my arm and it takes everything in me not to shudder. The consequences of reacting poorly to his touch are painful. I have no desire to be beaten today, or for him to find some other way to use me. My only option is to stay as still as possible and hope his visit is quick and painless. Although there really isn't such a word as 'painless.' The mental pain I'm going through is almost as bad as the physical pain.

All I want is for this to end, for the summer to end, for my life to end. Is there any reason to continue this life? I'm ruined. No one is going to want me after this. No one can protect me; I can't even protect me.

A slap to my thigh brings a wave of dread. He's had too much to drink tonight. He's always more rough with me when he gets this way. I want so much to cry, but it will only make things worse. It's not fair, none of this is fair.

Why me?

Why…

Me!

My mind is exhausted at all these old memories resurfacing. The last time it was this bad was when I was ten. The first few months after I got home were the worst. Not even my parents could touch me. Though my dad wasn't much of a hugger anyway, it worried the shit out of my mom. She asked a million times what was wrong, but I never told her – only gave her lame excuses. After a few months I was finally able to at least not flinch when my parents or siblings touched me, but there was nothing I could do about the memories.

All it took was a sound or smell and my mind was instantly transported back to a ghastly memory of him. It wasn't until I heard the whispers of my mom on the phone to my aunt that I attempted to learn to block it out. Her words hit me like a ton of bricks that she was considering sending me to a therapist and how they would get me to talk.

The threat of having to tell someone what had happened frightened me more than anything. While it was stupid to be so scared of talking, it was what made me stronger. I learned to block out my memories and the harder I tried, the better I got. Denial was my best friend.

After a while, I was able to suppress a lot of it, even to the point that my bad dreams began to go away; but it only fueled my anger problems. The more I put up walls around the memories, the more violent my reactions became. It came to a point where I merely stopped being around people whenever possible, to avoid the trouble. If no one was around to bother me, I had no reason to react. Unfortunately, I couldn't stay in a bubble forever.

The day that brought me here started similar to most days. I walked to school by myself and made it through the first few periods of the day without incident. Everything was fine until lunch came around.

Lunch was always hard for me. Too many people crammed into a small space didn't sit well with my nerves. Rainy days were worse because going out into the courtyard wasn't an option. As luck would have it, buckets of water were dumping over our city that day.

My only other option was to eat in the hallways where the choir kids would gather to practice on lunch, but I never made it that far. After carefully waiting for my lunch, I took my tray to leave, only when I moved to exit the cafeteria, a group of kids were standing right outside the door, blocking me from going down the corridor.

One of the popular seniors was laughing with his friends. Like everyone else, I knew who he was, and he had a reputation of being a 'player.' The latest rumor had upset me quite a bit. One of my few friends had told me that her best friend's little sister, who was a freshman at our school, had found out she was pregnant.

She refused to tell anyone who the father was out of fear. Only, I wasn't sure if it was fear that people wouldn't believe her, or fear because he had threatened her if she told. Unlike most people, I saw things that went on around me. In my attempt to keep people away, most people didn't notice me, giving me a chance to see what most others didn't.

I'd seen him lure her away from people so that he could be alone with her. She would look at him with longing eyes when she didn't think people were looking, and when they did sneak away, he would play the spellbound boyfriend. She was young and naïve, with no idea of what kind of guy he really was. A few of us knew who it was, but no one could prove it. Despite her life being ruined, he sat here laughing with his friends like he didn't have a care in the world.

I knew it was a bad idea to walk through him and his group of friends, but my only other choice would have been to stay in the overcrowded cafeteria, which could possibly end badly anyway. So, I took my chances. Coughing to get their attention, I gave them an irritated look to get them to move.

He spat out one of his ridiculous comments about me finally giving into my feelings for him; it was nothing new. They say men always want what they can't have. My lack of falling over him is what attracted his attention to me. I was one of very few who didn't fall for his good looks and sweet-talking personality. My constant shooting him down only pushed him further in his quest.

Rolling my eyes, I told him "whatever" and pushed through the small gap a couple of the boys made. Apparently, he was ready to push the point that day. Perhaps he needed someone else to pass his time with, now that his old play toy was pregnant and he couldn't risk being seen with her.

As I walked past, he stepped up next to me to whisper in my ear, "One day soon, I'm going to get in those pants. I promise you."

I tried to brush it off and to not let it bother me. "Not in this lifetime."

I attempted to keep walking, moving away from him, but his friend stepped in my path as another one moved to my other side, blocking me in. My chest started heaving as I felt his fingers move my hair back from my ear. "What is a little girl like you going to do to stop me?"

I'm not sure if it was his devious tone or the words, but everything in me snapped. I don't remember a lot of those next few minutes, only my tray disappearing out of my hands and banging his head onto the ground before my brother pulled me off him.

❊ ❊ ❊ ❊

My ass hurts from the lack of movement since I sat down. Part of me wishes Aerick did come after me, but he knows better. When I'm this mad, I need my space. Besides, even though I didn't plan it out quite the way it went, it worked perfectly.

As quietly as I can, I slide Aerick's sweater over my head, being careful of the keys in the pocket. When he locked up, he put them in his pocket. Normally he puts them in the nightstand beside the bed, but he has been distracted all afternoon.

I unlock the door as quietly as possible, trying not to wake the others in the room. A part of me is screaming to stay, but this is it. If I don't do it now, this is only going to continue.

I've had so much time to decide what to do. My mind has played with so many possibilities and yet I'm still not sure about what I'm about to do. Facing him is going to be hard enough but fighting back is going to be the ultimate road to my redemption. This may not work, but if there's even a small chance I can end this, it's worth a try.

Quietly, and careful to avoid the cameras, I make my way to the supply cabin to pick up a few things. It would be stupid to go completely helpless. Using the master key, I help myself to a few things in the supply cabin before I go out front.

By the time I get out front, there's only a few minutes to wait. The deadline comes and goes as I start to get more antsy. Maybe he won't show up, maybe he gave up and left. *Yeah, right!*

Dread spreads over my body as taillights appear down the driveway where the tree line meets the parking circle. Heaviness falls on my chest, but I shake it off before my breathing can get erratic. *Here goes nothing!*

With no moon in the sky, the darkness of the night reflects the blackness working its way through my body right now. I force my feet forward until I'm at the passenger side of the car that's waiting. It takes a heavy breath of fresh air to get my center, and I get in the car.

"Hmm… 'bout time you came to your senses. We could have avoided all this trouble if you would have just done what you were told. I hope you learned your lesson." Unable to speak, I nod slightly and look down at my knotted fingers that sit in my lap.

He seems satisfied and drives off. The car smells strongly of alcohol and it's starting to seem as if this was a bad idea. *What the hell was I thinking?*

Too late to back out now, but more panic arises as we immediately get on the on ramp for I-90, heading toward Seattle. We aren't sticking around, and the chances of me being able to get away are decreasing with every mile that falls behind us. There really wasn't a plan per se, but this was the least favorable outcome that ran through my mind. My trembling lips quietly attempt to ask where we are going, but nothing comes out of my mouth. I'm not ready to talk to him yet. It's taking all the strength in my body to keep from freaking out.

Besides, it's pretty clear that we're heading toward Seattle. There are only three possibilities: we're heading for the Seattle-Tacoma international airport, heading north for the Canadian border, or heading somewhere south. However, if the plan was to go north or south, it probably would have been smarter to go east first. Going west will require us to go through big cities in which we're more likely to be discovered. On second thought, he's made it clear that he has friends in high places, and he isn't worried about being caught.

Not that anyone will know for a while that I'm even gone. Aerick probably won't be up until four or five depending on how well he sleeps. Then again, I don't want him coming after me either, which reminds me. Carefully, keeping my movements small, I slip my phone out of my jacket pocket and quickly turn it on airplane mode. I can't have Aerick coming after me and putting himself in danger.

Movement in the corner of my eye makes me freeze. *Did he see me?* I tilt my head slightly to get a better look as I see him take a flask out of his coat pocket, taking a healthy drink. Great, he's drinking and driving. If I'm really lucky, he will just crash the car and end this himself, but I'm not holding my breath. On second thoughts, if I could hold my breath, it might keep the bile down from the sickening stench of alcohol.

We ride in silence for the next hour. Other than the occasional side glances at me and drinks from his flask, he focuses on the road. While I'm grateful for the silence, the tension only grows, becoming more and more thick in the air.

It's still dark when we exit the freeway near the airport. However, instead of continuing to the airport, we pull into a huge hotel that has to be at least fifteen stories tall.

"What are we doing?" I ask, sounding more timid than I intend to, but at least I've finally found my voice.

"Our flight doesn't leave until later and we both need some

sleep; besides, I hate sitting in airports," he grumbles. *Leave where?*

At least we aren't leaving right away, this will give me some time to play out my plan; well, my sort-of plan. I'm not sure what to do and I'm playing this by ear, hoping it will all work out.

We pull up to the valet section and he gets out, giving me a look to follow. Welcoming a break from the claustrophobic confines of the car, I scurry behind him, trying not to draw attention to myself; this is not the time. I keep my head down, letting my hair mostly shield my face.

He struts up to the counter flashing a smile like there isn't something majorly wrong with this situation. In an overly polite voice, he tells her he has a reservation, and she slides a key onto the counter without further questions. It crosses my mind that he had already planned it. *What else does he have planned?*

The only thing that gives this an odd appearance is when she asks if we needed help with our luggage and he tells her that we don't have any. Seeing the confused look on her face, he swiftly follows up stating we're only staying for a few hours, but he doesn't bother saying that we're merely waiting for a flight.

Her eyes dart to me, making me feel extremely uncomfortable. She probably thinks I'm a prostitute. Only I'm wearing the black warm-up pants that I got from the supply cabin and Aerick's sweater oversized sweater; not the typical fashion of a working girl.

After a glaring once over, she remembers herself and resumes her smile, but not before he notices. His mood does a complete one-eighty, making my stomach drop. He snatches the room key card and turns toward the elevator. It leaves me no choice but to hurry after him. This is not good. At least up until now he was in a better mood, but I know what happens when he's drunk and gets pissed.

The heaviness begins to build in my chest as he stands impatiently at the elevator. His anger is palpable in the air surrounding him. Again, I'm wishing I hadn't done this. His anger scares me enough to freeze me in my spot.

The elevator finally dings and opens after what feels like forever. He walks forward, but my feet are frozen in place until he gives me that look. The look that sends ice through my body. This will not end well if I don't behave. I want to get out of here with the least amount of pain as possible.

Finally, my feet move, right as he starts moving his hand to grab me. The thought of what he might do to me is enough to slide forward. Once I'm in, he roughly pulls me by my arm closer to him, staking his claim despite the absence of other people.

The elevator finally stops on the thirteenth floor. We're almost at the top. Considering the expensive interior, these rooms must cost a fortune. Once in the room, my thoughts are confirmed. It's a striking corner suite. A beautiful sitting room overlooks the stunning mountain view. A large bed is centered in the room through the door that flanks a mini bar area. *Great, it probably has more alcohol.*

"Sit down," he snaps, taking his flask out. Doing as I'm told, I sit down on the larger couch. I fumble with my phone in my jacket pocket as he rummages around the mini bar. To my surprise, he comes over, handing me a glass.

"Drink it." I oblige, but only take a small drink. I need a clear head. The taste of soda only makes me want to laugh. For a moment, I thought he was actually giving me alcohol to drink.

He lets out a grunt. "You didn't think I would give you a real drink, did you?" he mocks. "You really don't use your head, do you?" I punch down the urge to roll my eyes.

"I don't know why you always have to disobey me. I think being around all those boys has really screwed you up." As much as I want to tell him to fuck off, there are some other questions that need answers before I lose my chance.

"Where are we going?"

"Back to Chicago, of course. I was recently offered a new position there, working with troubled teens. How apt," he says, walking over to the window.

"Then what do you need me for? I'm sure you'll have your pick of little girls to satisfy you." I keep my voice monotone in an attempt to not sound condescending.

"Yes, I suppose I will. Working in these positions the last several years has given me the pick of the crop. Troubled girls tend to give in much easier. Some of them even came close to being what I wanted, but none of them can compare to you. Your picture made it hard to forget you." *Picture?* I had a feeling he kept those couple he took of me.

"I found myself being drawn to girls who looked similar to you. Young, similar eyes, body, hair. Most of them gave in much easier than you, even. If I hadn't found you, I suppose I would have managed, but why, now that I have you…" A sly grin pulls at his mouth. "I admit, the younger ones are much more compliant. You were definitely a much better listener when you were younger. I don't know, maybe you will disappoint me, and I'll be forced to get my fill somewhere else; or maybe we can grow our little family."

Bile rises in my mouth and the heaviness starts closing in on my chest. "What?" I almost choke at what that could mean.

"It's an option. It could be fun to have two of you. Then again, you have displeased me by disobeying me. You need to learn your lesson." He sets his glass on the table and begins to take off his belt. *NO!*

"Lie down on your back." My head shakes no. This isn't going to happen. "Are you telling me no?"

"You're not going to beat me."

"Beat you? I'm going to teach you a lesson, there is a big difference. You've been a bad girl and bad girls get punished. Now, do what you are told." My body stays motionless and the crack of the belt echoes off my arm. "NOW!"

Scrambling, I jump over the back of the couch, but not before another blow hits the center of my back, causing me to cry out in pain and fall to the ground.

His hand wraps around my arm before I can stumble to my

feet. "Don't be stupid. Get over here and learn your lesson, or you're not going to sit down for a week." He drags me back around the couch, throwing me onto it as another slap lays across my back. His knee comes down on my back, pinning me in place.

"You are mine, dammit, and you are going to learn that one way or another." Tears fall down my cheeks as several slaps hit the back of my thighs, and then another two in quick succession to my back.

The blows pause. "Now, it's time to be a good girl and listen. You know I don't enjoy hurting you, so do as you're told." The pressure on my back lets up a little. "Are you ready to be a good little girl?"

I nod my head 'yes' quickly before he decides to keep hitting me. "Good, now turn over on your back."

With pain shooting through my body, I do as he commands. Relief spreads across his face as he sees my obedience. "Good girl."

He grabs a chair from the desk next to the couch, setting it right in front of me. I wipe the tears from my cheeks and try to control my erratic breathing. Putting down the belt on his lap, he begins to undo his pants. An unwanted and all too familiar feeling settles in the air.

It's now or never!

With all the energy I can muster, I bounce up and leap over the back of the couch again, but this time I keep my footing. It was never my plan to sit here and let him go through with his delusional plan. I make it to the door in a few short seconds, but he has locked it with a chain. My fingers quickly work to undo it, but he slams into me from behind just as I get it off.

"Bad girl!" My head slams against the door and his arms wrap around me. Without another thought, my elbow meets his gut before my fist meets his balls. A whoosh of air feels like a hurricane on my neck and I throw my head back, perfectly connecting with his nose.

His arms release me, but I grab them before they leave my body. I take a few steps back with him stumbling, trying to keep from falling, and with all my might I flip him forward over my shoulder.

"I'm not a little fucking kid anymore, you bastard," I scream in his face as I jump on top of him.

My fingers grasp his thinning hair and I pull up quickly and slam his head back into the ground. "You fucking coward!" Another slam. "You don't own me!" Slam. "I…" slam, "Am…" slam, "Not…" slam, "Yours!"

He moves his head groggily to the side, letting me know he's still conscious. "If you ever come near me again, I'll kill you. If you ever touch anyone I love again, I will kill you. You don't scare me anymore. You're just a pathetic piece of shit, who gets his kicks off off beating and abusing little girls. Not anymore." A grin spreads across my face as I realize I've won.

"You bitch," he murmurs, and I slam his head hard into the ground again. This time, his head goes limp in my hands. He's out. There's blood on the carpet under the back of his head. I check his pulse to make sure he's not dead.

Unfortunately, my plan is not to kill him. Getting to my feet, I quickly leave the hotel suite, sprinting down the fire escape stairs using what adrenaline I have left. As I finally reach the bottom, I take out the phone that's somehow still in my pocket. Turning off the airplane mode, I dial 9-1-1.

"9-1-1, what is your emergency?"

"A man attacked me and tried to rape me." My voice is raspy and unsteady after my thirteen-flight sprint down the stairs.

"Where are you, Miss? Are you alright?" She's instantly in alert mode.

"I'm fine, I fought him off and he's unconscious. He's at the Seatac DoubleTree Hotel in suite 1310. His head was bleeding pretty bad and he probably needs an ambulance."

"What is your name, Miss? Where are you?" she asks, but I hang up before she can ask anything else, or the call can be traced, and I rush across the lobby, keeping my head down.

Once I'm outside, the rush of cool air is refreshing, but I keep on moving, heading south on the sidewalk. I need to get somewhere safe and call Aerick. The police sirens are already filling the air and my feet speed up, needing to get as far away as possible.

Several blocks away, I come to a large park at a lake. This place should be good for now. I move down the hill toward the water to get out of sight of the main road. Out of breath, I plop down on a bench. *I can't believe that just happened!*

My limbs feel like jelly. I can't believe I did it. I'm free of him and if this next part goes right...

Squealing wheels interrupt my thoughts. In a panic, my attention turns toward the parking lot. Relief floods through me as I see four familiar faces pile out of an SUV. Aerick scoops me up in his arms, squeezing me incredibly tight.

"What the fuck..." he shouts, but it's cut off by my cry of pain.

"What? What the fuck did he do?" he says, putting me down as he starts pulling up my shirt and examining me. "Holy shit." I imagine there are some pretty righteous bruises starting to form on my back, and probably on my thighs and arm too. His hands stop on mine, turning them. It's only then I notice I still have blood on my hands.

Luther, Jeff, and Gavin all converge on me with concerned faces. I grab Aerick's face to make sure he listens carefully. "We need to leave now. I'll tell you everything, but let's go home to our condo and I'll explain everything there. We need to get out of here."

"Explain it now," Luther interrupts.

"Luther, please. The condo's not far; let's go and I promise I'll explain, but if we don't the police are going to find me, and with my record, I won't be getting out anytime soon." He stares as a war brews in his head. "Please."

"Fine. Let's go." We get in the SUV quickly and we head to the condo. It's not far, and that's how long I have to explain what I have decided to do. No one is going to be happy, especially

Aerick, but it was for the best; and it worked.

CHAPTER TWENTY-ONE

(Saturday, March 19th)

"HERE, BABE. I think you're going to want to see this," Aerick says, handing me his tablet.

The news app is open, and a woman comes onto the screen:

"We are bringing you an update to a rather disturbing story we first broke Thursday morning when a well-known Chicago philanthropist was arrested in Seattle after being discharged from Harborview Hospital where he was admitted, suffering from a concussion. Initially Seattle police would only say that he had been arrested for suspicion of attempted rape of an unknown victim. While we still have little information regarding the victim, more details have come to light over the last few days regarding Mr. Redding himself.

Following up an anonymous tip, Chicago's FBI office served search warrants at Mr. Redding's place of work and his home yesterday evening. We have now discovered that those warrants uncovered a barrage of child pornography, going back almost twenty years. Even more disturbing was the admission by authorities that Mr. Redding's employment history primarily revolved around jobs where he worked with young children and spanned nine different states. The identities of his victims are currently unknown, but a detective close to the case said this morning, 'Because the victims are minors or were at the time of the crimes, they will not be releasing the identities.' The detective also stated that with the amount of evidence already compiled, Mr. Redding will likely not see the outside of a prison cell for the rest of his life.

Seattle Police and the local FBI are still looking for the female victim that is believed to have fought off Mr. Redding while at a Seatac hotel in the early hours of Wednesday morning. The only other information they have released regarding the attack is that they now believe it was also the female victim who initially called police to report the attack, and that by the time they arrived, she was nowhere to be found. We will continue to keep you updated as we get more information."

A wave of relief washes over me. *It's over.* He's going to jail for the rest of his life. I never thought I'd see this day.

For the longest time, I was just happy enough to forget it. My walls were enough to keep it far in the back of my mind, and as long as it stayed there, I was mostly content living with that outcome.

Then I came here, where it was all brought back to the surface. It left me wondering how long before I could bury it deep again. I'd have never thought in a thousand years that the last few months would play out like this. But it has, and this week has been the most excruciating.

The last few days have been extremely tense. The worst kind of game of 'hurry up and wait' ever. It has been even harder than getting everyone to calm down Wednesday after we finally got to the condo, where I had a lot of explaining to do.

Flashback to Wednesday

I only make it two steps through the door before Aerick starts in. "We're home, now talk!" he says, stepping in front of me. There's so much concern in his face, but I'm not ready yet. My nerves are shot and still on edge. The ghost feeling of his hands on my body sends a shiver through me.

Taking Aerick's face in my hands, I gently pull his face down to me and place a soft kiss on his lips, attempting to calm him a little. "Babe, I will talk, I promise, but after what I just went through, I need a really hot shower and a few minutes to myself."

I place another kiss on his lips and plead with my eyes for him to understand. After a few moments of silence, I take it as his answer. Stepping around him, I head for the master bedroom, allowing the door to close behind me.

Jeff's words come muted through the door telling Aerick it's best to give me some privacy. When I'm sure he isn't going to follow, I head in to do exactly what I said. Sitting down. I remove my boots and socks. Still tucked into each of my socks are throwing knives. Another item I was able to get from the supply cabin, but I made a pact to myself to only use them as a last resort. It was bad enough that I planned a little self-gratification beating but bringing a weapon into it would up the stakes if I end up getting caught. I'm an adult now – assault with a deadly weapon is a serious charge and with my criminal history, likely heavy jail time. It's bad enough if I'm caught; I could be looking at jail time anyway.

As I peel off my clothes, I examine the damage. Thankfully, they're mostly limited to bruises on my arms, back, and thighs. I think the sweater helped soften the blows to my back, but the marks are still clear to see. The ones on my legs are much darker. He didn't hold back as he hit me this time. When I was little, it was always painful, but it's clear now that he never hit me with full force.

A faint bruise decorates my left cheek, and another on my hip from my fall behind the couch. I guess all in all, I got out of there in okay shape. It may be a few days before I can move without pain, but it's been worse; at least there are no cuts.

The scalding shower feels like heaven washing away the grime, including the small amounts of blood that still stain my hands. I can't help but wonder if I went too far. It wasn't my intention to kill him, but there was a lot of blood, and I still don't even know if my plan is going to work. It shouldn't take long to find out.

Once I finally feel somewhat clean, I get out and throw on some yoga pants and a sweater. Carefully, I tuck the knives into my underwear drawer in the bedroom. It's time to do some explaining.

Timidly, I walk out to the living room, trying not to make a sound. All the guys are scattered throughout the condo, each staring at their phones with the exception of Jeff, who's waiting for the teapot to boil. Naturally, Aerick is the first to notice me.

"Better?" he asks with a half sarcastic, half pissed-off tone.

It takes a deep breath to keep me from firing off something equally sarcastic back at him. Instead I plant myself on the small couch, pulling my legs up in front of me as a partial barrier. After a minute or two of silence, the guys all slowly follow me over to the sitting area, joining me on the couches. Aerick sinks into the seat next to me. After a moment of hesitation and a heavy sigh, he carefully pulls me next to him, wrapping his arm around my shoulders. *God, it feels nice to be back in his arms.*

Jeff hands me a cup of tea with a slight smile; it's what I need at the moment. Aerick's forehead presses on my temple.

"Now, can you please tell me what happened?" He's much calmer and his voice is only filled with concern.

Starting from the argument the night before, I explain in detail what happened. None of them seemed pleased with my decision but they remain quiet and let me tell my story all the way through. Surprisingly enough, it isn't as difficult as I thought. I explained the many different scenarios that I'd planned for, and how if nothing else, he would never be able to hurt anyone again.

Remembering how I finally was able to protect myself, to get away myself, without relying on anyone else, it is… gratifying. As I tell them, it's as if a weight is slowly lifting off my shoulders. The weight of the wall that I carried around for so many years, the weight of my shame and regret, of my weakness. Feelings I never have to feel again.

"Am I missing something?" Gavin asks as I finish my story with them finding me at the park. I look at him confused. "How are you going to prove anything he said?" he clarifies.

Carefully I pull my phone out of my pocket. "With this." I go into the gallery app and hit play on the most recent video. Voices spring from my phone and Aerick snatches it out of my hand before I can protest. He turns it up to the loudest setting and they all listen to the conversation I had with Mr. Redding.

When he was getting drinks at the bar, I opened my video app and pressed play. I was a little worried it wouldn't pick up the whole conversation, but our voices come across clear as day.

The whole room gets tense once he asks me to lie down. I don't think one of them is breathing. Aerick's arm, still slung across my shoulders, tenses and tightens around me as it continues and the sounds of his belt hitting me begins echoing through the room. Jeff's face turns ghost white and Luther stands and turns away.

It's a relief when it finally ends, but the air in the room is thick with emotion from all four guys. I try to stand but Aerick is frozen in place. He's speechless; that doesn't happen often. I nudge him, silently pleading for him to let me up. He releases me after a moment of hesitation. I go over to the sliding glass door and open it for some fresh sea air. Closing my eyes, I inhale a deep breath of it; it's refreshing.

Clearing his throat, Luther walks up behind me. Turning to him, his red eyes give away his reason for turning away from me while he listened. "Nadi. We have to take this to the police. You know that, don't you?"

"Actually, I have a different idea. I plan on the police getting a hold of this, but if it's all the same to everyone, I would rather stay out of the circus show that's going to follow."

End Flashback

Originally, I had planned to go to the police when I was ready. It was the part of my plan that was the least appealing, but the confession of his crimes and the pictures he kept from so long ago got me thinking. The drive back to our condo and me asking for a few minutes wasn't only to get my bearings straight, it was to formulate one last plan to keep me out of the investigation that surely would ensue. Thankfully everyone was more than happy to go along with my last-minute plan.

We left back to the camp soon after I explained it all. With Jake's technical genius, he sent the recording with a carefully prepared explanation to the Chicago's FBI office. He used a local library's Wi-Fi, creating a few bounced signals around the world to hide his tracks and keep everything from being tied back to us.

"It's finally over," I whisper, still staring at the tablet.

Aerick pulls me up to my feet and wraps his arms around me. "Fuck, I hope so. We've had enough craziness to last us a lifetime."

It's still early, but the rest of the staff slowly begin to file into the mess hall for our final meeting to close out this session. With Gavin going back to Chicago and taking Ayla and Lauren with him, it's a little more of a show this time around.

Brand and Tia walk in, making my face light up as I see her bundle of joy in her arms. "Tia!" Me and several of the other girls' gush at the same time. We rush to see baby Sam. He's so small still but his beautiful little face makes you melt in your place.

"When did he get released?" Andi asks.

"A few days ago. We wanted it to be a surprise today." She glances at Luther with a knowing smirk. We all thought he had a few more weeks before he was coming home.

"They released him early because he's doing so well. We'll have a few things to deal with for a few more weeks, but they said they don't think there will be any long-term effects from his early birth."

Gavin pulls my attention as he comes through the door with Ayla hot on his heels, but she doesn't look very happy, making my nerves go on high alert. She moves to Luther, whispering something in his ear, and I know it can't be good. My fear is confirmed when Luther discreetly asks Aerick and I to follow him outside.

We allow him to lead us out the door and my hand tightens around Aerick's arm. "Luther? What is going on?" he asks before I have a chance to. Truth be told, I have a golf ball in my throat preventing me from saying anything.

"There's someone from the FBI here to talk to Nadi. For

heaven's sake, both of you please keep your cool," he warns as we enter the office. Keeping it professional, Aerick and I put a little space between us before crossing the doorway. We already discussed this, and I know what to do.

Luther leads us and offers his hand to the agent. "Hello. My name is Luther, I own this camp. This is my Operations Manager Aerick, and as requested, our newest teacher, Nadalynn Reese. How can we help you?"

"Thank you, Luther, and sorry for the unannounced intrusion. My name is Agent Saul Jeremy. I was hoping to get to talk with Ms. Reese, in private if you don't mind."

"Please, call me Nadi…" I say, but Luther quickly cuts me off.

"Actually, if it's all the same to you, we prefer to stay. Nadi is my employee, and she's on the clock. If there is an issue, I believe Aerick and I should be present."

"The thing is, the information I would like to speak to Nadi about is pretty… sensitive… and quite troubling. I think she would appreciate my discretion in this matter."

In an attempt to keep things cool, I interject, "It's okay agent. I would prefer if they stayed."

He looks at me with stitched brows. "You're sure? This has to do with a camp you attended when you were younger." He hints and when I don't say anything, he continues, "I was serious when I said this was sensitive." He says quietly, his eyes imploring me to dismiss them.

"It's okay, agent. Both of them know pretty much everything

about me." While that's fairly accurate, they never really got the gory details, and chances are they may come out right now, but it doesn't bother me as much as it once did. I knew there was a chance that, despite our carefulness to cover our tracks, they still might find out it was me.

He spends several more seconds looking between the three of us. "Alright, I tried to warn you." He sighs and Luther gestures for us all to take a seat at the small round table in the corner. The agent sits down; both Luther and Aerick nudge me to sit directly across from the agent while they sit to each side of me.

He takes a folder out of his briefcase and pulls a photo from it. "I assume you know who this is." He slides the photo in front of me.

I take a deep breath. "It's Mr. Redding. He was a teacher at the camp I attended when I was younger." The agent obviously knows this much.

"And did you know he was arrested here in Washington a few days ago?"

Carefully choosing my words I answer, "I've seen the reports on the news."

"So, you have seen the allegations against him. What we found when we raided his home and workplace?"

"I have." He lets out another sigh and takes two more pictures out of his folder but keeps them face down, getting my attention.

He glances again at Luther and Aerick before continuing. "Nadi, I am sorry, this may be… I need confirmation on this." He looks down at the pictures lying face down on the table. *Fuck!* "Nadi, can you please tell me if this is you?"

He flips the pictures over but partially covers both of them with his hands before I can stop him. The wind is knocked out of me, and in unison Luther and Aerick look away with gasps of shock. The pictures show my nine-year-old self lying naked on the bed, bruises coloring my thighs, and my frightened young face staring at me. He turns them back over, quickly sliding them back into the folder. Gratefully, he at least hid my intimate parts with his hands.

"Nadi, I know this is hard, but I need your confirmation."

Luther stands up. "Agent, this is…" My hand reaches up and my eyes meet his.

"It's okay, Luther." He bites his cheek and sinks back into his seat.

"Yes, that was me. How did you know?" My own curious nature wanting to know how he put this all together. Mr. Redding even said it, but it was in and out of my head. I never thought they would be able to connect them to me. I was merely a face in a picture.

"To identify the many pictures we recovered, we dated each of them, and then compiled files on possible victims based on where he was working at the time. For these ones, we pulled school records, which included school photos of young girls who attended the camp the summer you were there." Of course they were smart enough to figure it out. They are the FBI. I just never figured it would happen; at least not this fast.

"Funnily enough, your file was the first one I picked up. It was much thicker than most of the files, which drew my attention to it, and I was shocked when I opened it and saw a very striking resemblance." Aerick's hand squeezes my leg under the table and I know he's tense but it brings me a bit of comfort.

"As I investigated you further, I came across a very big coincidence. It seemed you were working in Washington, and your home address listed in your juvenile record was only a few miles from where Mr. Redding was arrested." *Crap!* I'd forgotten. When I was released, we had to give them Aerick's address so they could send my final paperwork.

"Yes, that's interesting." I feign a smile, trying to keep from outright admitting to anything.

"You know what else is interesting? The description given by the receptionist at the front desk of the hotel fits your juvenile record pretty accurately." Well, there isn't much point in denying it anymore, but he continues, "Almost as interesting as that bruise you are sporting on your cheek. I have a feeling if I was to examine you more closely, I'd find many more bruises on you." Luther sinks further into his seat next to me, letting out a sigh.

He continues without giving a chance to respond. "What the media didn't say was what the anonymous tip was. See, we got a recorded conversation of Mr. Redding admitting to abusing the female in the recording, along with implicating himself in others, as well as future intentions. The conversation then turned into an attack, which led us to believe it was the attack in the hotel a few days ago. The attack sounded pretty brutal, but you already knew that, didn't you?"

A deafening silence falls over the room. "So, what now agent? And for the record, I don't think my attack on him would be considered brutal, it was self-defense." Aerick's grip on my leg tightens and is almost unbearable. I know I was supposed to keep denying everything, but there's no point in denying it. The agent did his homework and probably knew he had the right person when I walked through the door.

"I wasn't referring to what you did to him," he says quietly, his shoulders relaxing a tad. "May I see?"

Rising to my feet, I give Aerick's shoulder a squeeze to put him at ease and slide around him to stand next to the agent.

Removing my jacket, I turn my back to him and carefully lift up my tank top. "Ouch," he says behind me. The bruises on my back are bad but not the worst.

"There are more on my legs."

"Can I see?"

Thank goodness, I went for a run this morning and still have my running spandex on. I slowly pull down my track pants and carefully roll up my shorts. The bruises deepened over the last few days and turned some pretty nasty colors, but they don't hurt as much today.

"Jesus Christ. Why in the world did you run the other day? Why didn't you stay there?" he asks.

Half laughing, I pull up my pants and face him, no longer being able to contain myself. These last few days have been overly emotional, and I have not had time to fully recover.

"Is that a joke? After everything he put me through – after all these years of fucking suffering and everything he's done these last few weeks. Isn't it obvious, Mister Fucking Agent, or did you not read that thick-ass file of yours? I've been in and out of trouble for assault, because of everything that sick fuck did to me. I have a juvenile recorded as thick as a dictionary making me the least credible person on the planet, and it's his word against mine. Does that sound like something you would want to face? Because I sure in hell didn't want to!"

Familiar arms wrap around me, pulling me back a little. "Nadi, babe. Calm down." Only then do I realize that I have been yelling in the agent's face, as tears are streaming down my mine. Quickly, I dry my face on my shirt.

The agent's eyes shoot between Aerick's arms around me and his face. A moment later his eyebrows shoot up. "Well, that puts another piece of the puzzle into place."

"What the hell does that mean?" Aerick asks.

"Well, out of everything we found, it was all pertaining to young girls. Except for one photo. We had no idea who it was, only that it was recently printed. We thought maybe his taste had changed, but nothing panned out. It was a picture of you, although you were a bit younger in the picture. I knew you looked familiar when you walked in. Something tells me he knew you two were together."

"Yes, he did." I take a deep breath, pulling my wits together and gathering my thoughts to explain. Aerick sits, pulling me into his lap. Cat's out of the bag anyway.

I proceed to give the agent the short version of everything that's happened recently. All the encounters, why I didn't come forward, and more importantly, why I put myself into danger to get proof. I knew no one was going to believe me over him. I had to make sure that he would never have another chance to hurt me, or anyone else. When I finish my story, he remains quiet, deep in thought.

"Agent," Luther finally speaks up. I had almost forgotten he was there. "Nadi has been through enough, both then and now. She spent all these years suffering and trying to cope. Despite all that, she put her life in danger to stop this psychopath and barely made it out alive. She led the FBI to loads of information that you'll use to put him away; hopefully for good. Even got you a recorded confession. Is there any possible way we can keep her name out of this? The last thing she needs is the public exposure and them digging for the gruesome details."

He sits quietly for what seems like an hour until his lips press in a tight line. "I suppose, but only if I can get a statement of everything. What happened as a kid, and the more recent stuff, along with a detailed description of what happened at the hotel. I will agree to put it in my personal file and only use it as a last resort. However, I think you are right. We have a lot of evidence against him. More than likely we will offer him a plea of nothing less than life in prison without the possibility of parole. With what we have against him, he would be an idiot not to accept. No trial means no reason to put your statement in the case. No one else needs to know your story."

"Thank you, agent. Was there anything else you needed?" Luther asks, standing, and we all follow suit.

"No. Here," he hands me a card with his information on it. "Please send me your statement and photos of the injuries you sustained in the attack. I give you my word, I will do everything in my power to keep you out of this," he tells me, and the sincerity in his eyes tells me he means it.

"Thank you."

"Sorry to interrupt your morning. Nadi, I will keep you updated on the case. My apologies for today. You're a very brave woman, and I know many women are going to be grateful you did what you did. Good luck with your new teaching position, and I hope to not see you in any more trouble," he smirks.

"Yeah, I'll work on that," I say, shaking his hand. He turns and leaves, getting into a black SUV and driving off.

I turn around and hug Aerick. His grip on me is impossibly tight, as if he may never let go. It's really done and over. Now I'll never have that worry that the police may show up someday at my doorstep and take me away. It's over and, God willing, no one else will ever have to know my past.

Luther turns to me. "Well, I knew things around here would

be interesting with you here, Nadi, but I never envisioned all this."

"Luther, I'm sorry…"

He holds up his hand. "Nothing to be sorry for. I'm glad you can put your demons behind you. That's it, right? Nothing else is going to come back and bite you, or me, in the ass, right? Because I don't think my old ticker can handle another session of craziness," he jokes.

"Yes Luther, that's it." Smiling, I look at Aerick. "Unless you have any other crazy exes I don't know about?" He gives me a weird look and shakes his head. Luther laughs. At least he thought it was funny. He pats Aerick on the back.

"Good, now let's go. We're late for breakfast."

Following Luther, we head back to the mess hall, but even as we go inside, Aerick's arm is still tight around me. I look up to him to ask him what's wrong, but his expression stops me. He looks as if he's going to be sick. "Aerick?"

"Marry me!" His rushed words spew out with a finality to them. My body instantly chills to ice temperature. My eyes dart around to see if anyone heard him. *Did he really just say that?*

"Aerick?" I choke out. He can't be serious. I'm eighteen, we've only known each other for a few months. "You… We…"

"Dammit Nadi, I just spent the last sixty minutes scared shitless that he was going to take you away from me. Scared that I may never hold you in my arms again. I need you like I need air in my lungs, and I would die a thousand deaths to keep you in my arms. I don't want to live without you, ever."

More damn tears pool in my eyes, but thankfully don't spill over. Who says Hardcore Aerick can't be sweet? "Well," I mumble, thawing out easily at his confession, feeling much lighter and less frightened of the possibility. "That wasn't the most romantic way to ask but..." Suddenly he drops to his knee and the room goes quiet.

"Aerick!" my loud whisper pleads with him as my eyes grow to the size of saucers. Not in front of everyone! *Shit, there are so many people here.*

With that all-knowing smirk on his face, he takes my hand. "You want romantic?" he whispers before raising his voice to allow the room into our conversation. "Nadi, from the moment I met you, you have been a royal pain in my ass." Chuckles fill the room and he grins before turning serious again.

"But you also pulled me out of my own box. You taught me it was okay to feel, to love, to care. You let me into your box, and together we filled an empty space in each other we both thought was never reachable. We have been through so much, yet there are so many things I still want to do in life. But they are all meaningless, unless you agree to be there to do them with me. So, marry me, please, because now that I've found love with you, I don't ever want to live without it." A grin spreads across my face and tears roll down my cheeks and I quickly wipe them away, semi-aware that everyone is watching.

"Of course I'll marry you," I say, covering my embarrassment with my one free hand. "Now get off your knee." I laugh at his over-the-top public confession and pull him up. He scoops me up in a hug, lifting me off the ground, as he rises and spins me around. A deafening roar fills the hall as everyone explodes in cheers around us.

Setting me down he gently, cups my cheeks in his hands. "I love you," he whispers on my lips.

"I love you, too; but that was a little over the top, especially for you. I never thought I'd see the day." I pull him to me, kissing him passionately until we have to break for air.

All breathy, he gives me a real, genuine Aerick smile, melting my heart. "For you, it's worth it!"

EPILOGUE

(5 years later)

THERE IS SOMETHING so peaceful about sitting next to a river on a calm, warm, cloud-free day with an ice-cold drink. Up until a few weeks ago, I thought there was nothing that could make it better. Looking down at the beautiful baby girl lying in my arms, I know now there was one thing that could. She is almost a month old and one of the most cherished people in my life. A life I never dreamed would ever happen five years ago.

After everything I suffered as a child and teenager, I figured having a happy life just wasn't in the stars for me. Even after Aerick came into my life, so many bad things happened to me. It was like a sign from above that my life was destined to be full of never-ending bad luck. It wasn't until I finally faced the man that I feared the most and put the past to rest that things finally began looking up. I have spent the last four years in almost pure bliss.

"Hey babe, I brought you another glass." Aerick sets down another iced tea on the table next to my chair. "And it's time for my baby girl to come see Dadda." Willingly, I hand her over and she doesn't even stir. "Is my darlin' girl in a milk coma?"

"She sure is," I laugh. "I swear, I can't begin to understand how she can eat so much. It's like she is always attached to me."

He gives me a playful smirk. "Do I get any later?"

"Maybe, if you're good and let me take a little nap out here." Grinning, I take in my surroundings and breathe in the fresh outdoor air.

Our house on the river is everything I ever wanted. It isn't grand and immaculate, but it's a three-bedroom, two-story log cabin with a large back yard that sits up against the river. Our bedroom sits in the center of the upstairs, with French doors that open to a small deck overlooking the river. Another one of my favorite spots. It is so nice to wake up early and sit out in the crisp morning air, listening to the river while I lose myself in a good book and drink my coffee. Of course, those mornings don't happen as much since our beautiful daughter, Tessa Elaine, was born.

I glance over at her snuggled into her dad's chest. When we found out we were having a baby, Aerick and I had agreed that if it was a girl, he could name her, and if it was a boy, I would name him. He was over the moon to find out we were having a girl. Before the doctor even finished the ultrasound, he told me her name was going to be Tessa, after his grandmother. I loved that the name was connected to his grandfather, who adored his grandmother for so many years. It made picking her middle name that much easier. We quickly agreed on Elaine after my grandmother. The names just fit so well together, Tessa Elaine Stephens, which turned her initials back into her name. I love it!

"I gotcha, babe. Close your eyes and rest. I'll wake you up when she's ready for another feeding."

"Yeah, if I'm lucky I might get twenty minutes of sleep," I joke. With a smirk, he picks up his book and gets comfortable in his chair, allowing Tessa to snooze away on his bare chest. Him in only his board shorts is a sight I could stare at for hours. In all these years, the man hasn't lost a morsel of his toned figure.

He still works at the camp, which is only a few miles away. I continued to work there as well until I found out I was pregnant and already three months along. It was a very long and drawn-out argument that lasted days. I wasn't ready to stop working, but in the end, he won. He was right, with all the bad luck I'd endured in my early days, there was no point in tempting fate, so with great reluctance, I agreed to resign for the time being. Thankfully Tia and Brand still live in town, and Tia and her adorable sons visit often, keeping me company. Brand, always out to prove a point, is now a Corporal at the Cle Elum Police department, working directly under the chief of police. His position makes the working relationship between the camp and local police even more unified.

Trent wasn't the only one who stuck around. Trent and

Brayden chose to put down roots here and also decided to join the local law enforcement. The two of them make up one third of the town's patrol officers. They haven't changed much, still playing pranks, and often come around to hang out.

Jeff bought a home just down the road recently and has been dating a wonderfully sweet girl for just over a year. While he has had some hit or miss relationships, it seems this girl may stick around for the long haul. It's all I've ever wished for him. He has also worked his way up to lead instructor at the camp, which he could not be prouder of, though Trent has been pressuring him to join the police force. He hasn't given in yet, but the camp is more of a steppingstone than a long-time career. There isn't much room to move up, and the job doesn't support much of a social life.

I was worried once I was no longer able to work that I would never get to see Aerick. However, Aerick had an ace up his sleeve that he must have been preparing for a while. He laid out a little restructuring plan with Luther that allowed him and Luther to unload a little work. Since Luther was helping set up similar camps all across the US, he was too overwhelmed trying to keep up with tasks at the camp. The new plan allows Aerick to come home every night and on weekends. He still works sixteen-hour days and is on call during the weekend, but I will take what I can get. Our daughter decided to arrive during the perfect time as well, coming soon after the summer session ended, allowing him to stay home with us for over a month. It'll be difficult once the new session starts, but I have a great group of friends these days, made of current and old staff members and a few others I've managed to befriend along the way.

While several people have stuck around, others have not. Andi moved back to Seattle and started her own catering company; Jake ended up leaving to work for the FBI's Cyber Division thanks to a special agent who shall not be named. Jake was replaced by another cadet who passed through the camp. While he's not quite on Jake's level, he holds his own, and thanks to the ever-evolving software the camp uses, the job is a bit easier than it used to be.

Paulo and Terrie also decided to move to the suburbs of Seattle when Terrie got pregnant with a little girl of their own. Paulo got a job working for TSA at the airport and Terrie easily locked down a position at a midsize family practice. I miss them often, but they visit whenever they can. Ayla is still in Chicago working at Gavin's camp which is now flourishing, but which unfortunately no longer includes Laura. We've all lost touch with her. Last I heard, like my old friend Patrick, she was hooked on drugs and working miscellaneous jobs around the city to support the habit. It's a sad ending, but as I've come to learn, you can't save them all. What you can do is help when they are ready to be helped, but until then it's up to them.

I'm continually grateful Evan never met that fate. He did exactly what he said he was going to do. As it turned out, he didn't need all the money he saved up to go to college. He landed a full-ride scholarship to a smaller university playing football. With little hope of making the NFL, he played football to his fullest, but spent the four years in college focused on getting his degree. The day he graduated, he had a great job waiting for him in Bellevue, just east of Seattle. Not only is he closer to me, he's finally settled down a little and is engaged to a perky dark-haired girl he met in college. It's the life he deserves.

There have been a few others that have passed through the camp and gone on to have a life away from here. Many tend to come back and visit, while a small few fall back into their old lawless ways, but overall the camp has maintained a great reputation. Luther's vision has been fully realized.

Aerick's mumblings bring me back out of my head for a moment. "And when you grow up, Dadda is going to teach you how to do everything. We're going to go fishing and hunting and fix up old cars." I try to hold my laughter. The way he talks to her sleeping form is so sweet. Even as hard as Aerick can be, he is mush wrapped around her little finger. I have no doubt she is going to be one spoiled little girl, getting anything with just a small pouty face to her daddy. "And don't worry. When your little brother is born, you will still be my favorite baby girl."

With a huff I question, "Another kid?"

"Well, not just yet, but maybe in six months or so we can start working on another one."

"Christ, Aerick. Give me a little break, will you? We can't even have sex yet and you're already talking about another one." I'm not quite healed down there, and I've only slept three hours at a time for an entire month.

"Aren't you supposed to be taking a nap? Sleep babe, we can talk about it later."

Yeah sure, change the subject – but I'm not giving in that easy. I've spent the last several years working toward my PhD and had finally finished shortly before I got pregnant. My goal is to be able to work at a University as an Online Professor. Aerick and I spoke at length about it, and it makes the most sense. Once my degree was finalized, I stopped taking my birth control in hopes we could have a child before I switched careers. It only took three months for me to get pregnant, but now, instead of me looking for a job at a university, he is thinking about having more kids. Men: give them one baby and they want a whole football team to follow.

No matter what happens in the future, I'm determined to be, and stay, a happy person. I'm now convinced that because I had such a hard first eighteen years, the second eighteen years or possibly longer are destined to be in my favor. Aerick continues to look at me the same way today as he did on our wedding day, six months after he proposed. We had a small wedding in the backyard of Casey's cottage with our close friends and family. It was small, intimate, and perfect for us. Like our home, we didn't need a big, grand wedding, we just needed the people closest to us. When I walked down the aisle on my father's arm, Aerick looked at me like I was an angel there to take him away to heaven. His eyes didn't leave mine once during the entire ceremony. Of everything that happened that day, a small part of what he said in his vows, which we chose to write ourselves, will stick with me and guide me for the rest of our lives.

"Even a heart that was once broken, torn piece by piece and then torn again, can be mended and healed. You've shown it is possible, and I will spend every day until my very last day ensuring yours is never hurt again. Your healed heart is a testament that even something once shattered into a thousand pieces can be unbroken."

THE END

**Samoan Translation: Ou te alofa ia te oe – I love you

Coming 2021...

A new standalone romance novel

About the Author

Danielle Leneah is a person with limitless aspirations. Whether she is working full time to help support her family, designing web sites for fun, or writing books to calm her mind, she always puts her heart and soul into her work.

Her reading and writing ambitions started at a young age. By sixth grade, she was reading full Stephen King novels and writing short stories. Her first publication came when she was in high school. Her work was accepted to be published in a well known poetry book. Even though her dreams of writing were temporarily halted as she began to build a family, it eventually drew her back.

As she began writing, she remembered the peace and joy it use to bring her. In astonishing 50 days, she had the rough draft of the first two books in a her new series completed.

In her mind, if she can make just one person happy with her stories, it would have been worth it.

Danielle was born and raised in the suburbs of Seattle, Washington where she still lives with her husband and children.

To get the latest news and stay up to date, visit her website at:
www.DanielleLeneah.com

Made in the USA
Coppell, TX
28 May 2021